THE PARADISE STAIN

NICK GLADE-WRIGHT

JoJo PUBLISHING

The Paradise Stain
Nick Glade-Wright

Published by Classic Author and Publishing Services Pty Ltd
First published 2015

'Yarra's Edge'
2203/80 Lorimer Street
Docklands VIC 3008
Australia

Email: admin@classic-jojo.com or visit www.classic-jojo.com

JoJo Publishing Imprint

Editor: Ormé Harris

Designer / typesetter: Working Type Studio (www.workingtype.com.au)

National Library of Australia Cataloguing-in-Publication entry

Author:	Glade-Wright, Nick, author.
Title:	Paradise stain / Nick Glade-Wright ; designer, Luke Harris.
ISBN:	9780987609663 (paperback)
Subjects:	Reality television programs--Fiction.
	Australian fiction.
Other Authors/Contributors:	
	Harris, Luke, book designer.
Dewey Number:	823.4

Nick Glade-Wright was born in England in 1950 and emigrated to Tasmania, Australia, with his parents and four brothers in 1965. He completed his education with Fine Arts and Education degrees. He taught painting, ceramics and photography for twenty-six years in Hobart schools and colleges. He has exhibited his paintings in galleries since 1972 around Australia and the UK. He is represented by Handmark Gallery in Hobart and BMG in Adelaide. He has played in various World Music bands since the early '80s, the latest being the medieval band Harlequin, playing festivals around Australia. He published his first novel *Growing Sideways* in 2010. He has travelled extensively; most recently, last year he travelled overland from Sierra Leone to Senegal.

A father of two adult daughters, he now lives with his partner Jacqueline, a creative designer, in Hobart.

The Paradise Stain is Nick Glade-Wright's second novel.

ACKNOWLEDGEMENTS

iv

Rosie Dubb and Danielle Wood, for their insightful manuscript assessments. Gaye Glade-Wright for sharing her knowledge of autism from her teaching. Yeshe, for allowing me to use the words to his song 'Eye for an Eye'. Enormous gratitude and respect to John (anonymous) for trusting me to share his story of abuse, in the hope that there can be more awareness and understanding of these crimes that keep happening throughout our world. Loro Mogga, for his friendship and music. Jacqueline Firth, for her love and sorting out the pronouns. Ormé Harris for her highly professional, perceptive and invaluable editing. Luke Harris of Working Type Studio for his creative work on the layout and cover design. And to JoJo Publishing for believing what I had written was worth putting out there.

For Jacqueline

Chapter One

The young woman had barely moved during the interview. The swollen, pulsing vein on the side of her neck a mere hint at the depth of her trauma as the details of her ordeal lay carrion raw for viewers to pick over. Studio lights glared fiercely. Clasping bony, bloodless fingers, Abrar Abdullah waited, rigid, for the next question. Barry Kant sipped water from his glass, presented a benevolent smile to his latest guest – this asylum seeker, this boat person, this refugee, this Afghan, this human being.

Kant touched his earpiece. The director had just given him two minutes to wrap things up before the audience were let loose with their customary questioning, prying and tactless.

'Abrar, I believe your Muslim name means *a devotion to God.* I'm wondering whether you've been wrestling with your faith since your terrible loss.'

Abrar frowned. 'Rezling? What is…?' But she became momentarily distracted by the sound of titters, unkind ones, emanating from several mouths in the studio audience.

'Well, let me put it this way, Abrar, so these people have time to run through your story in their minds once more.' Kant's encouraging tone belied the knot in his stomach. 'So, you escaped the terrors of war-torn Afghanistan with your husband Khaled and baby boy four years ago. You did this by surviving a perilous sea journey none of *us* would dream of undertaking, halfway round the world, completely at the mercy of unscrupulous people-smugglers. You then endured two arduous years in detention, and finally ... finally finding sanctuary in this beautiful island of Tasmania, safe at last and gaining Australian citizenship, your son Ali who ... ' Kant paused whilst Abrar dabbed at her erupting tears, tears that had so easily welled at the mention of her son's name.

While she struggled for composure Kant turned to Camera Two. 'You are watching BKS nationwide, the show that probes the depths of people's lives, and tonight I am in conversation with Abrar Abdullah, originally from Kabul, Afghanistan, who now lives in Launceston.'

'Please, I am sorry,' she whispered, as if the expression of her grief had been discourteous.

'No need, Abrar.' Kant smiled, paused for a skilful camera moment. 'Ali would be four years old now. But he died senselessly due to an idiotic fireworks prank by drunken footballers outside your new home. So, can you tell the audience, Abrar, and the people at home watching this, whether all of this has affected your devotion to God?'

Abrar lowered her brimming eyes before looking up to face the audience directly. Taut, proud, and with unambiguous conviction she stated, 'It is God's will.'

Kant briefly looked towards Camera One, his mouth pinching minutely before returning to his guest. He had felt a flash of embarrassment but could now not help scrutinising her. *Her hair would have been glossy black not so long ago. And those eyes! Kant knew great loss. But this!*

'And do you think it was God's *will* that your husband Khaled should hang himself shortly afterwards?'

Absurdly ironic, he thought, knowing that suicide and attempted suicide, even euthanasia, were prohibited in Islam. Abrar remained upright, dignified as she turned again towards the audience, who were open-mouthed like fanatical supporters before the kicking of a deciding goal.

'I will pray for his soul.'

Kant sighed, not for any camera this time. 'It's tough, Abrar, *really tough.* So I want to thank you for being so courageous in sharing your story tonight on BKS.' And to Camera Two, 'Abrar Abdullah is the final contestant on this third series of the Barry Kant Show.' And to the audience, 'So, now we've reached the part of the show where it's your turn to ask Abrar your questions.'

Kant faced Camera Two poised to zoom in for a close-up. 'Then it's up to you at home to SMS your all-important votes. Remember fifty thousand dollars is in the balance here. Which one of the ten contestants do *you* think deserves the money?'

In the split second before he spoke again, Kant felt a tremor blaze through his chest. *How on earth can any of this possibly help her? And why the hell am I still doing this?*

A bevy of impatient hands had already shot up.

*

Kant stood naked in front of his bathroom mirror.

Outside, the lights at the ferry terminal across the road flickered feebly through a stinging downpour, which had stabbed at him just now as he'd scurried in. Now his feet were warming on heated slate tiles. He began inspecting his thickly-grey hairline, making a stand like a defiant old-growth forest on the brink of clear-felling. He sipped at his whisky. The melancholy was still there.

Heaving in a deep breath he held his lungs to capacity and then strained to cram in a final sharp in-breath, to stretch their lining a fraction more. His blood began to surge.

'What's the point of this?' he muttered, but continued to repeat the same action until he was eventually overcome by a wave of dizziness. Gripping the bench, he looked at the floor and frowned, saying, 'Huh, who else?'

His old friend Vashna had broached the sensitive subject of Kant's approaching sixtieth last week, and being two weeks younger there was a small window for Vashna to take advantage.

'Your lungs are a bubble, my friend, and at your age you need to keep them to capacity so you don't sink,' he'd added with an ambiguous grin, not believing Barry would actually try it out.

Vashna was full of *dubious wisdoms*, to Kant a fine line between astute and extremely annoying. But Vashna had brought Saki. Besides, Kant had made the phone call, was having withdrawal symptoms from his self-imposed curfew and needed a diversion. The problem was Kant's celebrity. It had brought with it a need to escape his adoring but suffocating public. There always seemed to be someone in his face, complete strangers wanting to prove to their companions what intimacy they shared with the great man. Kant had never anticipated this at the beginning.

'Hey Bas, nailed the show this week. Keep it up buddy', followed by the usual ingratiating pat on the shoulder and, *'Okay, see you round.'* A checkered green cardigan had toadied up only yesterday as Kant was absorbed in cheese selection at the deli. Of course, the rather nerdish young man had loped away before Kant could even look up.

A sharp gust of wind found his bathroom window and delivered a personalised splatter of rainwater, startling Kant. Even in the shielded confines of Waterman's Dock below, boats lurched in the frenzied squalls, their mooring ropes creaking as they resisted breaking points. And through the growl of the wind he could just make out the chorus of wailing halyard wires.

A midsummer's evening in Hobart.

Kant huffed sibilantly, generating his own mist on the mirror glass. 'If only they could see me now.' Stripped bare and alone like this, ordinary, not Photoshopped as when so many magazines had 'played' with his face, he was confident the public would not see a single physical characteristic that could be described as extraordinary.

Not so his enviably stylish harbourside apartment.

Behind the stolid sandstone façade, several split levels had been exquisitely tailored within the space of the top two floors of the building, which had variously housed, in early Settlement times, warehouse and maritime offices. The building's fabric reeked of the island's nautical history, and who knows what else during the more desperate times of convict infamy. Contemporary materials and chic décor coexisted symbiotically with ancient Tasmanian Oak beams, colonial Baltic pine floors, and convict-chipped blocks of sandstone. Dense rock-wool insulation and double-glazing incorporated in the refurbishment maintained a womblike thermal constancy of twenty-two degrees, and the muted stillness of a recording studio, the fury of the evening's storm being a mere suggestion.

A vivacious melody played by a clarinet and string quartet danced lightness around the spacious living area. Obstinate splinters from his heaviness were beginning to dislodge. The spinning LP, Poco Adagio in E flat major by Crusell the Swedish composer, had been one of Sarah's favourites. She had bought the record long before CD technology had asserted its digital ascendancy on the world.

Kant had made the apartment his home for the past two years, and for two years he'd been on his own, ensconced, he knew, in the voluptuaries of his own despair since Sarah, his beloved wife, had succumbed to the ravages of cervical cancer.

How could he forget those final weeks of her illness? Stoical to the last, Sarah had likened their marriage to the bond of clear river water flowing over its bed of rock. 'The water being in constant transformation, reshaping its volume to match the forms of the riverbed as it turns rock into smooth boulders.

And you *must* flow on when I am gone,' she had found the strength to insist to her husband.

But then, over the agonising months of chemotherapy, supplementary drugs, and more drugs to combat the side effects from previous drugs, Sarah seemed to become serenely at peace with what was to come, hovering in a space of tranquility, contrary to Kant's strangled state of being. For him, an infinite darkness had simply swallowed him whole.

And so, Barry Kant, small-time country journalist, husband, father and grandfather, began to wear the jewel of agony around his neck, a talisman for his soul, keeping it polished to remind him that *he* still possessed life, even though in Sarah's river he felt like a fragment of tumbling grit.

Beyond the docks a serrated jag of white lightning abruptly lashed through charcoaled clouds, releasing Kant from the clamp of his memories.

He put on his pyjama bottoms and his old dressing gown and went to the living space, poured two thin fingers of whisky, sat in an armchair, a sleek-lined, black leather number, and allowed his gaze to submit to the darkness beyond the glassed balcony doors. He still wasn't completely at ease with this up-market style of city living, although, he found playing Sarah's record collection a settling reminiscence of their life in the Huon Valley, affording him the solace to endure another solitary night.

But listening to the music was more than that.

Kant's childhood had been bland in blue-collar Lutana, just north of the city, and devoid of any religious nurture, his frugal-minded parents believing it to be an inveigling uncertain force that might upset the balance of their unsurprising lives. But through Sarah's music and particularly her passion for the Scandinavian classical and jazz composers who she thought expressed their geographic remoteness, like Tasmania's, so eloquently, Kant discovered a small niche in his solitude where he felt at least some form of spiritual tranquility.

He found himself thinking about the interview with the Afghan woman at the end of the last series. Over the last week Abrar Abdullah and her fathomless sadness had visited him in his dreams whilst he'd been on holiday, buoying him with her faith and grit. *Does she really find consolation in her belief?* That sort of trust in what he believed to be an abstract was elusive to his way of thinking. At times, as he sometimes lay awake at night he wished it wasn't.

Outside, the thirteen degrees of night air continued to descend on glistening bitumen. Kant could just make out a huddle of hunched figures tilting against the wind. He wondered what Abrar would be doing at this moment in her empty rental, while these friends below were making their way to the warmth of a wine bar for an evening of congenial cheer.

The thought made him fidgety. He went back to the bathroom to turn out the light. As he pressed the small, touch-sensitive, designer-shaped, stainless-steel square Kant watched as the mirror light faded gently over three seconds to dark. He timed it again. It was four really. He shook his head, it got him every time. Gaye Salmon, his interior designer, a newly arrived

Master's graduate from the RMIT Interior Design Faculty, now heading the hip Hobart firm Space Works with her Gen-Y self-belief, had recommended these fixtures for the interior. 'Soothing on the temperament,' she'd assured her client. As if there was an indispensable necessity for someone of Kant's vintage to require such obscenely expensive and by all accounts superfluous devices so that he could feel comforted by their 'theatrically ambient dissolution'.

'She actually used those words!' Kant had snorted to Vashna back then. 'Could have bought a cellarful of vino with the cost of one of those. It's a light switch, for God's sake!'

'That's true, my friend. It's also the key to unlock the freedom caught between darkness and light,' Vashna had replied, albeit incomprehensibly at the time to his grieving friend.

Kant padded to the mezzanine bedroom space and his queen-size bed, still not christened with the press of feminine flesh. He reached for the book *Shantaram* that he was halfway through — the author had also started out as a journo — but unlike in the unfolding saga in the Indian sub-continent, Kant had no beguiling woman in his background, let alone lying next to him, let alone enticing him, let alone caressing him. *Let alone.* Plumping his pillows did allow him a certain amount of calming satisfaction.

As he opened the heavy tome at the bookmarked page, his eyes were drawn again towards the blinking allure of the lights and shadowed machinations of the harbour with which he was becoming inextricably attached. There was a lull in the storm.

He had sometimes imagined his life resembling the unceasing movement of the waters, which hinted at something in their depths, secrets waiting to be dredged like sunken cargo, discoveries that would allow his existence to feel fulfilled once again.

But like an amputee, while cossetted by darkness, Kant could still feel Sarah's soft contours next to him in bed. Once or twice around the city he could have sworn he heard the velvety cadence of her voice. Of course they were just random women. Sometimes, sleepless at four in the morning, he'd stumble from his bed onto the plush, richly patterned Afghan rug he'd bought as a conduit to happiness, open the balcony doors to breathe in the salted air and pulsations of the harbour, welcoming *their* embrace. He longed for an estuarine smoothness, to be set down somewhere peaceful, on a sandy spit or maybe a wild ocean beach, where the salted waves could heal his wounds.

Kant's thoughts floated back to the crèche that Sarah had set up in the Huon Valley. He wondered whether it would still be functioning. *No reason why not, just because she's dead,* he thought bitterly.

He remembered the endless energy she'd poured into nurturing their property when Melinda was little, ' ... so we can all benefit from healthy organic produce,' she'd say, meaning, as well as the wisdoms gained from a rural lifestyle. They had lived simply. Sarah's acre of usable land was home to straight rows of mixed vegetables, an orchard of fruit varieties, thirty fowls and geese, even a troublesome pig and litter one year, and a goat and a cow. They all contributed to a way of life that not only complemented her occasional articles on composting, small farming practices and preserving but enabled her husband to work as a reporter, which for several years was poorly paid with irregular hours.

Kant couldn't concentrate. He snatched up the bookmark, last year's birthday present from Rosie, his two-year-old granddaughter. *Thank God for her.* The rectangle of pink paper, festooned with colourful scrawls, stuck-on gold stars and red hearts had survived the year because it had been laminated by her mother Melinda, a teacher at the Polytechnic in the northern suburbs. The riot of lines in Texta, blunt and fluffy after much scribbling and stabbing, looked so out of place in Kant's minimalist magazine interior, but to him the most precious possession there.

Kant turned off his bedside light to allow the tree lights decorating Salamanca Place's tree-lined avenue to cast their magical shadow play. He listened to the tone arm lift off the record, jerk backwards and click to silence. Tomorrow he would visit Melinda because *apparently* Rosie had made something special for his 60th birthday.

Chapter Two

In the weeks following Sarah's death two things induced Kant's decision to move away from the sanctuary of his home in the country.

Melinda had never before witnessed her father weep, so at the sight and sound of him distraught and defenseless, and grieving her own mother's death to the Cruel C, as she called the disease, she ached with sorrow.

'Please come up town, Dad, so we can all be near each other.' And knowing her father's softness for his granddaughter, 'You know how much Rosie loves her grandpa.'

He did. He felt supremely grateful. Amongst the rips of his emotions, barely keeping his head above water, this little girl, without an inkling of her influence, had buoyed her grandfather up in the bleakest of storms.

The second *thing* happened a week later.

Vashna and Barry's other longtime friend Maxwell Dartford drove down from the city to stay the night at the cottage. *A boys' night's what the maudlin old bugger needs*, they'd plotted. *Get him out of himself and back on track*, they had decided before they phoned, refused to hear any excuses, turning up an hour later with a couple of Johnny Walkers.

'Jesus, Barry, you've got more dirty dishes lying around than a Bangkok brothel,' Max had started as soon as he entered the kitchen where the warm and welcoming aromas of home cooking had been replaced by a rancid and stifled coldness.

Max was a rare breed of human being, knowing nothing of emotional pain in his untroubled existence as capitalist, inheriting a bulging portfolio of investments, giving him the means to live more than comfortably, almost without having to lift a single digit. Financial advisers, brokers and a creative accountant took care of everything. All he had to do was find appealing ways to spend the profits while fostering his small-city mystique and flashy front, which had the side effect of giving Barry's life of solid plodding some pizzazz, like confetti sprinkled over a grazing bull's back.

To give old Max his due, he did help propel the ailing economy when he became an art buyer, an activity that granted him specious social credibility. Healthy rumours that he was bound to be into some kind of unethical practice, and a brief scandal about an exploratory gay liaison, were to his manicured persona like healthy dividends at the end of the financial year.

'Sensitive as ever, Maxi,' Vashna had said. 'Besides, it's not about the dishes but the sustenance that's been offered on them.'

But as Vashna's mystical wisdom flowed, Barry had been distracted by a buzzing black ball of blowfly on one of the plates, spinning upside-down between knife and fork frantic in its attempt to get airborne.

'There I am,' Barry muttered to himself.

Maxwell banged the bottles down on the table with

significance, and began rummaging around for something hygienic from which to drink.

Startled by the noise, then pointing like a foot-weary traffic warden, Barry snapped, 'Fellas, go and find a seat in the sitting room and I'll rinse a couple of glasses.'

An hour later all their banter was witty, to them, and it was in this climate of intoxicated fellowship that Vashna, the group's self-appointed sage, started illuminating his philosophic counsel, 'Mate, mate, come up town and start a new history…'

Vashna's unshaven patches of gorse, on a bony outcrop, never quite cohesive enough to be called a beard, reflected his loose approach to self-grooming. Downy white hair curtained un-styled to his shoulders. Clothes, loose-fitting colourful aberrations, hung from his beanpole frame. Real name, Spencer, but only used in conjunction with his *Broadhurst's Collectables* dealership, giving *his* business public credence, habitually a debatable trade with dubious earnings. He just happened to spend a hedonistic year or so drifting around India in his twenties, before running aground in a pot-infused ashram in Goa on the West Coast, and for the last few decades Vashna had been a self-proclaimed custodian of a number of esoterically wise and mystical one-liners, invariably not backed up with any substantial research *or* reasoning.

'Sarah's had *her* story, shortened but beautiful. Now it's time for *his* story, a new one,' smiling at his old buddy, mind-roaming in some whisky-infused celestial no-man's land while Barry's eyes remained morosely fixed on the dry glass at the bottom of his fourth whisky.

'Clever, Vash, very clever.'

'Haven't finished yet. That's when *my* story starts!' And, in case his old friend had missed the subtlety of his convoluted insight, which he had, and trying not to look too smug at the same time, 'You know … the *Mystery*.'

Maxwell stirred, feeling it an appropriate time to add weight to the profundity of the moment, 'Baz doesn't need bloody mystery. He needs to come up town and get a mistress with a nice pair o' pups.'

Barry wasn't sure if Vashna's wordplay was taking the piss, but it really didn't matter, his good-hearted intentions combined with Max's simple vulgarity had worked their magic on him once again and he found that he hadn't forgotten how to laugh. So when Barry woke the next morning the words *come up town*, first from Melinda, and now these slumped and snoring reprobates, had settled themselves in his head like a mantra. Within the month he'd sold the cottage and bought the rundown apartment on Hobart's harbourside.

No more visceral reminders, etched like a calling card into his memory of his marriage: the familiar growling squabbles of the ringtail possums in the white peppermints and on the cottage roof after dusk; the honking of the geese and swans on the pond; or the rooster sentinel at dawn. And, at last there was an end to the incessant scratching by the Long-Overdue-For-A-Prune-Wisteria on the bedroom window on breezy nights.

And now, two years later, they were fading like the echoes of laughter in a forest gully, the peacefully swaying yacht masts around the harbour replacing the tall creaking eucalypts of the countryside, and the hypnotic inky waters of the ferryman's dock, the reflecting mooring lights and infinite flickering patterns becoming his backyard.

Then a third thing happened.

*

It hadn't taken long for Kant to be wearied by the social rituals of city life, particularly an encroaching nightlife, only minutes from his apartment beckoning like a gaudy, illusory temptress. Initially, heading for the fleshy strip of Salamanca Place clubs, galleries and bars seemed the easiest way to fill the yawning crevasse that stretched across his heart. But to Kant, these glitzy dens of desire seemed only to spawn a young breed of over-dressed, over-cologned office workers who congested the fuggy air with their stealthy glances and overly dull inventories of LOL gossip.

Nevertheless it was in one such *lair of lascivious grazing*, one of Max's little classics, that Kant met James Mackelroy one evening. Or rather, the twenty-years-younger, ex-Sydney television director recently based in Hobart, introduced *himself* to Kant, shouting him a beer, before offering him 'the job of a lifetime with a gold-crested salary'.

'Not sure it's me you're after, pal,' Kant had replied morosely, sipping his beer and wondering if he'd manage to get another expensive stubby of the Belgium Leffe beer out of the conceited out-of-towner before traipsing back to his apartment for another early night.

Mackelroy had laughed. '*That's it*! That very unassuming manner of yours I was drawn to in the first place. It's a *rare* quality these days. So many talentless hacks out there craving recognition.'

'I'm sure you're right,' Kant replied suspiciously. 'And when exactly were you … *drawn* to my manner?'

'Oh, I've been watching your news reporting on the box. It's serious business finding the right persona. And you have a *look* attached to that manner, and in the TV show I want *you* to front, that counts for a lot more than you'd realise. Of course, as director I'll have to do a little chiselling but you're almost there,' Mackelroy said with a devious pat on Kant's shoulder.

Kant shook his head and smirked. The only *look* he thought he displayed these days was jaded. 'Look … James, isn't it? I'll be sixty in a couple of years. I'm an old journo milker whose udder's drying up. To be honest I feel like shit most days, I can hardly get myself to work since my wife died recently, and my greatest pleasure in life is talking to my daughter's baby. Now, why don't you look along the bar here and pick out one of these fine young men?' And momentarily finding amusement in a thought, he added, 'What about spotted bow tie over there? Pretty sure it's not me you're after.'

'We'll just have to see, won't we, Barry Kant? … God, even your name!' Mackelroy replied, gripping Kant's shoulder as if the proposal was already a done deal.

Kant did get a second Belgium, and after a third the conversation had ignited something dormant deep inside him. Sarah was gone and only once before in his life had he felt so alone, and in some primal cell in the core of his body he knew this offer could be the antidote he needed to anaesthetise his grief.

Getting more than he bargained for, Kant, in just two years, became a national household name. His life never seemed to be far away from the newspapers, and dominated women's magazines for months. No more trudging Apple Isle reporting for Barry Kant. The TV icon's unique television show had smashed all the previous ratings records for National television. The now-famous BK-Smile, disarming so many early skeptics, had secured him the position as host of the most watched TV reality talk-show in the country. The unlikely hit had tantalised the voyeur in society with an alternative keyhole to ogle through, which, according to the ratings was just about everyone.

The tiny island state of Tasmania began to parade its engorged pride relentlessly, Kant's celebrated image appearing in tourist promotions and a plethora of local product advertising from clip-lock fencing to men's aftershave to Flinders Island goat's cheese.

The program's format resembled a chat show, but sounded like an hour-long confessional of emotional and psychological collapse with the benevolent host, and depended on a public vote for a winner. The twist came with the cash prize. Not for the best performer with a voice as pure as a lark, or the most inventive mind, certainly not the one with superior survival instincts, or the one capable of devising a delectable, culinary experience. And it didn't even go to some head-bursting brain who could answer inordinately obscure questions about ex-prime ministers, fatuous sporting obscura, or agrarian farming practices in the Middle Ages. No, it would be for a wholly unique superlative, the prize of fifty thousand dollars going to the person whose ghastly life story and misfortune was voted to be the *worst* case. The wretched souls not only agreed to put themselves through the indignity of public exposure but subjected themselves to a final, humiliating question time by a gloating, and in the director's mind, non-too-bright studio audience, a cordon-bleu recipe for excellent TV devouring.

The show was gladiatorial in its intensity, thumbs up or thumbs down. Nonetheless there was an endless queue of hopefuls happy to divulge their bad luck for some easy money. For some, the mere sharing of their traumas became a purging, Barry Kant becoming their saviour, the compassionate oracle who guided them through their perils of the past with his probing but kind persona that the public warmed to and most ended up adoring. At the end of the first series viewers bombarded the station with texts and phone-calls, even the odd proposal of marriage.

There were also the inevitable expressions of outrage. The show was callous and exploited suffering. Simply unfair! One retired Liberal MP had even described it as un-Australian. One mainland newspaper commented that 'The Barry Kant Show is a blatant manipulation of the already down-trodden, particularly the poor souls who put themselves through the wringer to come out at the end, flattened and with nothing'.

Of course, the poor souls who found themselves in the public spotlight were often from a luckless under-class who the rest of society had previously not wanted to admit existed in such great numbers in charming Hobart town, and further afield in the broader Tasmanian tourist haven of outstanding beauty. And so it gathered momentum, the ratings soaring higher and higher with the thud of every outrage and the splash of each tear.

Chapter Three

4.30 am Sunday

Kant woke to the clattering of his alarm clock.

The night's storm had run out of spite. No excuse now not to have that jog he'd promised himself before visiting Melinda and Rosie. It would be an invigorating start to his birthday and the last day of his holiday. Tomorrow, BKS would encircle him once again. He raised himself onto an elbow.

His glasses had fallen into the creases of the doona overnight and become twisted. He tried to straighten and match one arm to the other side. *Damn.* Inspecting the line of the burgundy-toned stainless steel, a shade lighter than his new car, he began to wonder why he'd needed to buy the latest model Audi. 'Wretched thing spends most of its life parked,' he mumbled out loud as he changed into his jogging gear.

And when was the last time I wore shorts, with no shirt, and wandered carefree along a beach, bare-footed on cool sands?

Apart from visiting Melinda and Rosie during his break Kant had dithered around, never quite organising to do anything substantial. He hadn't been able to clear his head of the Afghan woman, lugging her pain around with him like a sea-anchor, and now it was almost time to go back to work. Abrar Abdullah hadn't won, and the least Kant thought he could do was drive her back to her home, a three-hour trip back to her empty flat. She'd sat silently, insisting she'd sit in the back seat of the car, and on arrival had told Kant he was a good man. As he drove back to Hobart his tears had been acidic with guilt.

The Domain was quiet when he arrived on foot half an hour later.

'Where the hell did it go?' he yelled at a row of whispering poplars. 'No, not the holiday; the last sixty bloody years!'

Kant jogged up towards the tennis centre and back down through the wooded hillside, crowded with pines, spruces and cypresses, like an industrial walkout from the Botanical Gardens on the other side of the hill. Fingertips tingling he caught his breath by the rusty bicycle racks near the Cenotaph before heading down towards the docks, emitting pasty puffs like an aged dragon unsure of what to do with any fire that might still be in his belly.

The apartment felt oven-hot. Kant threw open the balcony doors to a cool sea breeze that barged past him and into the interior's cloying warmth as he watched three sleek cyclists below glide by effortlessly. He glanced down at what was the miniscule beginning of a paunch and huffed, 'You're thirty years younger!' to the swishing blur of colourful body lycra.

Kant showered and changed.

In the kitchen he made coffee, tutting at the granite bench, like his mother used to whenever anyone spent money extravagantly. A pang of something flicked him as he ran his hand over the highly polished surface, a lump of coarse rock once, in a Bulgarian quarry, its rudimentary origins now forgotten. *Is that me?* he wondered, his thoughts pressing into the stark back streets of Lutana where he was brought up. He smiled, impressed with his analogy.

It wasn't so much the soulless rows of cheap government housing where his father Desmond still lived after a lifetime that got to him, but that the old man's scope of desire was embedded in a way of life that neither allowed the *new* in or the *old* to be reinvigorated. Many applauded this as being happy with one's lot. But, inside, Kant cringed at the utter waste of potential for his father's lifetime. Kant's fabulous new home, not fifteen minutes' drive through the city, might as well be situated on the pinnacle of Frenchman's Cap on the wild West Coast for all the times he'd had a visit from his father.

Desmond had visited only once, coerced into coming for drinks when the show started two years ago. One of Kant's cameramen had gone to pick him up.

'You done all right for yourself,' his spindly old dad had said, intimidated by the marvellous world his son now inhabited. He had gingerly caressed carefully positioned 'objets', palmed the warm floor tiles in the bathroom, counted the number of colour-coordinated pillows on his son's bed, and inspected the kitchen work surfaces, with disbelief at the unmitigated extravagance.

Life was a procedure for Kant senior, like the smelting of aluminium, a malodorous process he knew all too well from his forty-eight years' labour at the Electrolytic Zinc Company, just a short walk from his home. Sarah's death was 'spilt milk cobber'. Not as an insensitive summation but fathomable like an inconvenient factory mishap. Almost Buddhist in its simplicity Barry had tried to rationalise positively at the time. After the young Barry had graduated with honours at the university in journalism and political science, his father's wisdoms, which had been the family's mainstay, carved from a myopic existence, seemed to become obsolete as academia shoved a wedge between father and son's capacity to converse at any great depth. Any paternal offerings became safely wrapped, clichéd ingots, excusing him from any uncomfortable intimacy that might arise between them, something Desmond had never experienced with his own father. Besides, it was *unmanly*.

Three *Message-Received*s had come up on Kant's iPhone display while he was in the shower. The first was from Vashna, who sang in a high-pitched southern accent the first line of a Neil Young song, 'Old man look at yourself', omitting to sing the second line, pointedly distancing himself further from his friend's age. The next was a voice message from Rosie, who giggled whilst Melinda endeavoured to coach her as to what she could say. In the end she managed, 'Gampa's birthday …' before the rest of the message became swamped in chortling.

The third text read, '*woch your back fagot*'. Kant instinctively deleted the message.

Misspelled or 'text' spelling? he pondered, intrigued by this deterioration of language. Negative calls and anonymous malicious pranks were usually the method of choice for denigration of BKS. He put it down to an inevitable consequence of success, never quite bad enough for the police to get involved. But these messages felt personal and always left a scratchy residue at the back of his mind.

After the success of the first series, the rapid adoption and *hip* use of the BKS acronym by the public was 'a gift from a greater power', Mackelroy had elucidated, as if he'd had a direct line to the Creator. It wouldn't have surprised Kant if his self-possessed director had.

James Mackelroy's head wasn't shaved as a reaction to a receding bald patch. No way. *His* cranium was a faultlessly sculpted classical manifestation, tanned and polished like his self-opinion, positioned elegantly on a lithe body that would have mingled effortlessly in an Olympian athletics squad of marathon runners. Quick-witted and shrewd, qualities he'd sharpened in Sydney's cut-throat TV industry. Mackelroy was wholly ambitious as far as BKS was concerned. Kant's considered reserve was a crucial counterbalance for his director's impulsiveness.

Over the two years the two men had become accommodating friends, almost by default, spending more time in consultation about the show than was probably healthy, drinking gallons of perilously strong coffee together at the station whilst debriefing after each new contestant had run the gauntlet. It was an alliance constructed primarily on Mackelroy's steely belief in the show's controversial format, and his absolute confidence that Kant played a huge part in its success.

One reviewer had compared Kant to Michael Parkinson, whose smooth interviews *"were undemanding because his guests are all celebrities"*. But Barry Kant *"has the uncanny ability to make distraught individuals feel at ease about articulating their worst nightmares, degrading abuses and horrific losses to an anonymous studio audience and hundreds of thousands of home viewers. Or is that millions now? On the small screen Barry Kant's kind face, altruistic brown eyes and luxuriant mane of silky grey, somehow seem to make broken souls feel worthy and at ease in his presence, as if they are alone in private consultation with a judicious oracle"*.

Life for James Mackelroy, single but never short of nocturnal female company, was *all* about BKS, *his* baby, and basing it in Hobart rather than Sydney with exclusively Tasmanian contestants kept a perverse edge on the show. It seemed to reflect the dark passages of the island's history. Mackelroy liked to crow about discovering Kant and grooming him for the position. BKS had injected the success serum into Mackelroy's veins, transforming people's misfortunes into dollars, lots of them.

'BKS! You can't buy *this* sort of marketing. It's pure adulation. We've created a popularity avalanche in the suburbs with your smile and Rex Harrison good looks. Well, your *own* good looks really. You really are The Man BK! Don't get me wrong, you prick, but this is the height of…it's a *fucking triumph*! We're up *there* now,' Mackelroy, exuberantly drunk, had rambled, while pointing to some mythical nirvana in the ceiling, his zeal exploding like firecrackers at the celebration drinks after the second series had finished.

BKS's first two seasons had made a devastating impact on the TV ratings of the conventional current affairs programs with their banal, repetitive social docos. And after the third ten-week season, several reality shows, with their puerile, mind-numbing activities, were sent scuttling back to their drawing boards. Nobody had expected it, least of all Kant, who never forgot his humble beginnings reporting for the Mercury newspaper at sheepdog trials, country fairs, traffic accidents and the court of petty sessions. That life was now an impossible solar system away.

'It's just like CNN, FBI and NYC; the letters are planetary institutions!' Mackelroy had rambled on absurdly, foaming bottle of champagne in hand.

'Don't forget KFC,' Kant had thrown in as an aside, exhausted and slumped on a couch underneath a parched and yellowing rubber plant.

The studio set was awash with the entire Nerve Two workforce. Everyone, including the cleaners, who had also been invited to the party, laughed convincingly at Kant's comment.

'Not so BK!' Mackelroy lurched on jubilantly. 'Some of the dishes might be a bit *unpalatable* but it's *silver service!*'

Kant hadn't meant for such a cynical tone to wash his words. He couldn't argue with the show's popularity, or that he had made a significant, if not the lion's share of the input into the style. So it was with some apprehension that he had begun to have concerns about the ethical nature of the show. Indeed, he even wondered whether he was in fact making a difference at all to the contestants' lives. He knew *that* wasn't Mackelroy's motivation. Was he merely exacerbating their sorrows with false hope?

Then the third series broke all the records again.

Before BKS, the television station Nerve Two, a small set-up in Moonah, just north of the city, had been a fidgety table tennis player frantically struggling for primacy amongst a melee of muscled VFL ruckmen, skipping around, dodging the stamp of giants, wanting to be taken more seriously in a highly competitive arena. The tables finally turned after the success-ful marketing of the Barry Kant Show to several mainland networks, resulted in it connecting up to all other mainland states.

*

Kant's iPhone rang. He picked it up from the kitchen bench. The highland lilt was music to his ears. 'Vinny! Now there's a voice I've missed hearing.'

'Och. Sorry to bust in on your last day of holiday, Barry, but I've just stumbled on a young laddie, almost literally. A big story and he has a fine way with him too.'

It had been a shrewd move by Mackelroy, after meeting Vince MacLean in Sydney, to offer him a crucial role on the show's team in the beginning.

MacLean's reputation as a foreign correspondent, reporting on the Rwandan massacres, and the genocide in Bosnia and Herzegovina, had preceded him. But MacLean was exhausted, burnt out from the years in the field and needed a place to recoup, and maybe never go back to another front line again. The relentless reporting of so much horror had taken its toll in the form of chronic insomnia, his dark nights filled with demons and blood, the screams of innocents and the piercing silence of mass graves.

A haven was what he had longed for. His cousin Hamish told him about the quaint city of Hobart, a peaceful paradise, picturesque and safe from the bad world. So MacLean signed up as crew on a yacht skippered by James Mackelroy, competing in the Sydney to Hobart white water sailing classic. He liked the idea of arriving by sea as the early settlers did. All that salty water and fresh air would surely commence the purge that his soul so desperately needed.

Apart from MacLean's observational expertise and zeal for uncovering the truth, Mackelroy had been instantly smitten by the lyrical sway of his Scottish accent, one thing the highlander would never lose. MacLean's immediate answer was a firm *no*, but the journo in him was a restless spirit and by the time the yacht rounded the Iron Pot light in the mouth of Hobart's Derwent River he had agreed to Mackelroy's proposition. His brief, after a well-earned respite, would be to locate *broken shells,* as he'd later refer to them, and encourage them to become contestants in a new reality show.

Finding the right combination of people was time consuming. To begin with MacLean compiled a list of the hearing times at the Family Law courts. He strolled in the parks at dusk and dawn, he hung about at the soup kitchens, hospital waiting rooms, and bus malls in the city, then further out in the grimier suburbs. MacLean engaged with down-and-outs rummaging for fast-food scraps in garbage bins, aimlessly wandering druggies, and eccentric loners who reeked of stale grog and urine and who slept in impossibly windless and murky crannies of the city.

MacLean soon realised it wasn't only the subjugated underclasses that had the rights to dreadful misfortune. The well-heeled and the comfortable could also share the fact that 'shit can happen, any time, to anyone, anywhere'. And no matter how good their intentions to conceal their suffering from the rest of the world, out of dread or disgrace, it would be that hollow, disengaged look in their eyes that would give them away.

Kant took his coffee and sat near the window, sighing loudly for MacLean's benefit at the proximity of going back to work. 'Can't swing a few more days off for me, can you? I was just starting to get the hang of doing nothing.'

'If I wasn't just a wee cog in the wheel I'd let you have another year.'

'Well, I appreciate the thought. So, who've you got?'

'Young African dude, and when I say *dude* I mean ... DUDE! He's cool as. But when I found him he was slumped like an unwanted parcel on the steps of the GPO in Elizabeth Street. Saturday morning, round four.'

'Don't you ever go to bed?'

'Och, only in my dreams.'

Kant laughed. 'You could've shared a warm milk with me.'

The pause was long enough for Kant to realise that MacLean hadn't a clue what he was suggesting.

'Anyway, thought the laddie was drunk at first but he'd been beaten up something terrible. Said he'd been abducted. Sounded like rednecks to me. Took him up the bush somewhere out the back of beyond and dumped him there to find his own way back to Hobart. Or not.'

'That it?' Kant said, thinking this could have waited till he was back at work. 'Unpleasant as it sounds, it's just another mugging really. Don't you think?'

'Aye, but his big story is what happened to him in Africa. It's huge. Reaches Tasmania, safe at last, *then* he gets the locals' welcome.'

'Okay, Vinnie. Look, I'm off to see my granddaughter in half an hour so … '

But MacLean was clearly wound up with the story and needed to finish.

'He'd escaped a far worse enemy in his homeland. The rebels there, took me back to Rwanda, would make these Tassie rednecks look like a bunch of fairies. Cold-blooded killers, child soldiers too, sometimes even friends from the same village. Four weeks fugitive-travelling with his siblings at night, hiding in caves during the sweltering days, saw them reach the so-called safety of a Ugandan refugee camp. Fifteen he was then.'

'Fifteen! What's his nationality?'

'Sudanese.' Vince chuckled warmly. 'Head like coffee bean, and despite what he's been through he's got one hell of a smile.'

'Okay, sounds good. Well … you know what I mean. Book him in, maybe tomorrow arvo. First cab off the rank.' Kant sighed again audibly, this time for real. 'Oh, has he got a name?'

'Has he ever. Ishmael Abraham Liri Mogamba.'

'Impressive. Thank God for the bible.'

Another of those pauses.

'How's the holiday?'

'Like magic … it just disappeared.'

There was no pause then. MacLean snorted a sympathetic laugh down the phone. 'Oh, by the way, happy birthday BK!'

Chapter Four

Prone in the well-worn armchair in his daughter's living room, Barry Kant, grandfather and family man, held the newspaper between index fingers and thumbs, arms stretched to their limit, eyes straining to focus.

'Left my wretched specs behind. Still can't get used to keeping them with me.'

Melinda replied with a preoccupied 'Mm.'

Barry was waiting for Rosie to finish her morning nap. Melinda was in the adjoining kitchen juggling bread baking, dish washing and surface clearing before Rosie awoke; she was always amused at how far her daughter's little sticky fingers could spread themselves. Barry adjusted his weight onto his left buttock and with a searching hand located one of Rosie's plastic horses, beneath the other, lost in the folds of the cushion.

'Just love the smell of home cooking.'

'Mum taught me everything I know,' Melinda replied wistfully. She was eight years old when she'd baked her first loaf of bread. Now, with memories of her mother, the practice for Melinda was more than just making loaves.

Barry stretched his legs out on the well-heeled patchwork ottoman, complementing the blue family suite, more a bleached grey now. He and Sarah had given the ensemble to

Melinda when she'd partnered-up with Mungo four years ago. The sofa, having borne the weight of the family at the cottage since she was a youngster, was permeated with rich memories from her country upbringing, so it didn't matter to Melinda that it wasn't really *their* style. Not that they could afford one yet. Mungo's musical pursuits were still being developed and they had agreed to give it a couple more years with her earning sufficient bread-winning money as a teacher as long as he put aside two days a week to be with Rosie.

Each time Barry drove past the green-belted Domain and into the shabby surrounds of Lutana to visit his daughter he felt disappointed in their decision to live there. The sixties' government housing was still cheap when they paid the deposit in 2007 on the wholly unremarkable hip-roofed, grey Besser-block box, saved only from total blandness by a stubborn walnut tree in the otherwise bare backyard. Creativity was loose but money was tight, end of story. It was close to the city by Tasmanian standards, and Mungo's DIY skills were definitely improving, the brass number four screwed to the fence out the front was testament to that. He had even managed to put the screws in without drilling first into the gate post. Skilled with an assortment of tools, a hammer proved useful for the final fastening.

Melinda had found stubborn feet to dig in against her father's resolve for them to move *south* of the city, to 'a more reputable suburb where the word culture has some meaning'.

It didn't help that Mungo loved the sport of 'taunting the father-in-law'. Six months after they'd moved in, and the battle of wills was at its peak, he gleefully mentioned that Lutana alongside the infamous Chigwell had found itself in the list of top ten bogan suburbs in Australia, alongside Albion Park in New South Wales and Dandenong in the smog-soaked sprawling outer reaches of Melbourne.

'Don't tell me there's actually somebody who sits at a desk and compiles those statistics as *a job*?' Barry had countered.

'Must be. And, until recently, Frankston, that other Victorian piece-of-work, was up there too. But then Franga embarked on a marketing push to show the city was *perking up*. I LOVE FRANKSTON stubby holders and T-shirts made those die-hard bogans *real proud* for a while, until of course they realised there were a few too many lattes being served up in cafés around the joint. It's amazing how prejudice can be formed by a simple cup of coffee.'

'I don't know how you can be so proud to be part of it with your musical sensibilities,' Barry had answered, appealing with another tack. But he knew he was clutching at straws, besides, and this was the crux of his dilemma, his own father still lived not three minutes' walk away.

'Does it really matter which side of the tracks you live?' Mungo pursued. 'The chiggas, and virtually anyone who lives in the northern suburbs, that you seem to want to disassociate with, albeit with their moccasins, mullets, and flannies, aren't so much removed from your average 4x4 driver for steep driveways to nouveau-riche brick monstrosities in 'poash' Sandy Bay. And you can be sure they'll all be rubbing shoulders at the footy screaming the same obscenities at the umpire.'

An article on page four of the paper about the homeless eighteen-year-old girl, Minnie Donovan, had caught Barry's eye. Editorials recently had given much ink-time to homelessness in Hobart, describing the phenomenon as a *complex issue*, more than not having a job to support renting, owning or indeed feeling part of a family unit.

Mackelroy had intended to get the girl on BKS but before they could make her an offer she had drugged herself silly before cutting her wrists with a serrated bread knife, concluding her short life in a tepid, crimson bath.

The constant line-up of wretched people itching to get on the show had started to weigh on Barry's stamina. This latest holiday break hadn't come too soon. But now, Vince already on the phone with the next contestant and his holiday almost over, it was all starting again. He had become uncertain about whether he still wanted to keep hosting, feeling dismay at society's insatiable need to bask in other people's misery.

Rosie was stirring. Barry could hear Melinda in her bedroom, talking gently to her. 'Yes, Grandpa's here. No, he's not going. Yes, you can have some raisins. I know you do, sweetheart. I love Grandpa too.'

Barry rubbed at his eyes. *Do I really want to keep breaching old wounds? Am I really making a difference, or am I just caught up in an endless cycle of popularising human suffering as if it's a damn commodity?* It was people's casual apathy that really troubled him. He had seen it so often in the responses by the studio audience. He lay awake with it at night. *Am I just as guilty?*

Barry narrowed his eyes to focus on the article again, unable to put it down.

From the hillbilly back-sticks of New Norfolk, " … Ms Donovan had won a massive sum of money in a lottery … " But it seemed that over a frenzied three years of buying, gambling, drug use and a naive generosity towards an endless stream of new 'friends', sprouting around her like malignant mushrooms, she had squandered the lot, leaving herself drowning in debt, homeless, and still illiterate.

She'd hooked up with her first cousin, Shaun Donovan, become pregnant and chosen to abort the pregnancy when she was told the baby had Down syndrome. Her second pregnancy to Shaun produced another Down syndrome child, which she insisted on keeping. It being too much for her cousin, he took his own life shortly after the birth. Shaun's drinking binge had put him five times over the alcohol limit but he'd still managed to drive his Cortina to the top of a quarry cliff halfway up Mount Dromedary, the place of his daughter's conception, stop twenty metres from the edge before speeding off into oblivion.

Minnie had been dossing at a friend's squat and had caught hepatitis through sharing needles and sex with anyone whom she happened to find lying next to her.

'Jesus. Who needs enemies with friends like that?' Kant murmured, eying one of Rosie's soft toys on the floor, and looking up to see if she was in the room.

"The baby girl, who had not been given a name by her mother, had been placed into State care. Her mother, after an incident with a group of drug users and subsequent violent altercation with police, had been placed under State psychiatric supervision where she had committed suicide a week later, the details of her death have not been released yet", the article stated.

Barry felt little hands tugging at his trousers.

'Gampa, Gampa, move the paper, I can't do cuggling. Gampa!'

Barry looked down. 'Hello little one. There, how's that?'

He dropped the paper, a dark omen, onto the floor and rearranged himself, opening his arms to receive his granddaughter, still sleepy and warm from her nap. She had a piece of peeled apple gripped tightly between chubby fingers. Rosie clambered up onto her grandfather's expansive chest and began fidgeting as a cat does, nestling for perfect comfort. She was proudly two years old, 'and a three corters', as she reminded anyone who enquired. She lay her head down under her grandfather's chin, her wispy fair hair so delicate next to his holiday stubble.

Barry breathed with contentment. To him, Rosie, still untainted by a grimy humanity, counterbalanced the maelstrom of anguish in a world that seemed hell-bent on destroying itself. But he feared for her, and prayed that her spirit would never become corrupted.

He kissed her cheek.

'Gampa.'

'Mm.'

Rosie began to giggle and wriggle.

'What are you chuckling at young lady?' he asked, tickling her on the back of her neck.

Rosie reached up and took hold of her grandfather's nose, which filled the child's hand.

'Gampa, why have you got a big nose with lots of hairs in it?' She giggled again coyly burying her head deeper under his chin. Then she lifted her head out to peek at her grandfather, her eyes sparkling with impishness.

Barry opened his eyes wide at her. 'Hmm, let me see.'

Rosie wriggled with delight.

'I know,' he said slowly, deeply. 'It has to be big so all the spiders can sleep there!'

'You being silly, Gampa. There's no spiders.'

'Oh yes, there are.' And in an even slower and lowered whisper, 'They are big ones too. You can see their legs sticking out.' He wiggled his nose. 'See?'

This emergence of spiky, itching hairs protruding from his nostrils, observed since he had been on his break, was yet another irritation that fed Barry's nagging unease about the progression of his age. He knew he should have snipped them back last night instead of defiantly refusing to accept their presence. Again.

Rosie began to fidget, tucking her head in and closing her eyes so she couldn't be seen. Her grandfather wrapped his sturdy arms around her and stood up, shaking her gently. 'And this giant spider's going to take you to his web where he's going to eat you all up!'

Rosie wriggled to get free as he lowered her to the ground. She scampered towards her mother who was drying the last of the pans and slotted herself between her mother's legs for safety. The aroma of freshly baked bread wafted heavily in the air.

'Mummy, Mummy, Mummy. The spider's going to eat me ... what's for dinner, Mummy?'

'What's Grandpa scaring you with now? He's such a Silly-Billy.'

'Yes, Gampa's a Silly-Billy.'

Barry picked up the pink plastic scissors Rosie had been cutting coloured paper with earlier from the floor and cut out the article about Minnie Donovan, folded it and placed it in his shirt pocket. Back at the coalface tomorrow, where Rosie, with her child's virtues would disappear completely from his mind. He settled himself on a red painted stool at the kitchen counter, breathing in the yeasty fragrance. Melinda was wiping her hands at the sink. Rosie was now ensconced in her high chair picking raisins, one at a time out of a packet and making patterns with them on the tray.

Melinda whispered something in Rosie's ear. She stopped fiddling with her raisins and clapped her hands. 'Happy birthday Gampa. You're very old now and here is your book that I made with Mummy. It's a surpise!'

Kant held the stapled stack of coloured papers, covered in scribbles and stick-ons. Of course, for Kant, the manuscript displayed the secret ingredients of eternal youth and happiness.

'What a clever girl you are. Did you do this all by yourself?'

'Yes. Mummy helped me.'

She returned to her raisins which had become scattered on the tray.

Melinda handed her father a bottle of Johnny Walker. 'Happy birthday, Dad.'

'Ooh, thanks sweetheart. I've run out of this particular medicine!' He kissed his daughter on her cheek. 'Very kind of you to spoil me.'

'Gampa, Gampa, look at your book.'

Kant filed through the pages, commenting astutely on each and every mark, blob of colour, and scribble. On the front page was a self-portrait of his granddaughter, a red Texta circle for the head with a single curved line smile that cut through the edges on both sides. There was no body but two long lines came out from the head, the ends of which contained two small circles. From these circles there were at least a dozen smaller lines, little fingers radiating enthusiastically outwards. She'd run out of room for legs, a mere detail.

'This picture has to be the most optimistic statement of embracing life to its fullest I've ever seen,' Barry enthused, kissing Rosie on the cheek.

'Don't be silly, Gampa, it's Rosie!'

Melinda beamed as she lifted the last two tins of bread from the oven.

'Smells nice, Mummy.'

'Thank you, Poppet. It's a new sour dough recipe I'm trying,' she told her daughter informatively.

Rosie tilted her head in the way her mother did. 'Mm.'

'I can see a master chef in the making,' Barry said.

Melinda looked at her father. 'So, who have you got in your sights this season?'

'Not sure I like your analogy. Vince just phoned in with an African refugee who has…' He lowered his voice a little, as if Rosie might understand, and continued, '…a price on his head in Sudan. I'm seeing him tomorrow. There are others according to Vince. Other than that I hope I can ease into it gently. How's that boyfriend of yours, what's his name?'

'You mean Mungo, Dad, you know… my *partner!*' Melinda kissed her daughter on the top of her head. 'I told you Grandpa's a Silly-Billy.' Then poking her father lightly in the tummy she said, 'You gave me away to him five years ago, if you remember, in that little ceremony with Mum on Shelly Beach.'

'Really? Oh yes, that's right… M u n g o.' Barry spoke the word slowly with a pinch of friendly scorn, wishing Mungo was present to hear his retaliation. 'How *is* the musical guru you support?'

Melinda smiled, again not reacting to her father's taunt.

Actually, David Smith was Mungo's real name. He had adopted the nickname whilst he was a student at the conservatorium of music. Obscurely, it was to do with his penchant for riding a bicycle back then, a few too many rough reds one evening with friends, some chatter about bands from the seventies, in particular Mungo Jerry who sang the Pushbike Song, apparently. David latched onto it, liking the exotic musicality of the word – thought it sounded like a Caribbean dance – and also that it went hand in hand with the experimental nature of his endeavours.

'For your information, Mister Skeptic, Mungo and the others have finished setting up the studio in town. The grant they got from the Arts Council helped pay for specialised digital recording equipment,' Melinda said. 'Then it was only a few hundred dollars to buy the computer software.'

'I suppose a normal job teaching music or even playing jazz in a pub would be out of the question, you know, so he can contribute to my granddaughter's wellbeing.'

'He's happy. And Rosie's just fine.'

'Yes, Gampa, Rosie's *just fine*,' Rosie chirped.

'I don't get it really. Why does he…'

'Dad, don't start! There's nothing *to* get. And anyway, since when did you become so narrow minded? You can sound so… *out of touch* sometimes!'

Several seconds of awkward silence stood between father and daughter.

'Sorry Dad, I…'

'It's okay. I know I'm just… Look, tell me about the music.'

Melinda took a breath. 'He calls them sound sculptures. It's cutting edge. Mungy couldn't do it if he had to do a nine-to-five. I'm sure Mrs da Vinci didn't nag Leonardo to get a real job selling pizzas instead of painting.'

'You got me there.' Barry smiled. 'Maybe *that's* why Mona Lisa has that supercilious grin.'

Melinda wiped another surface, allowing her discomfort to disperse. 'Good one, Dad.'

'Good one, Dad,' Rosie echoed.

'Mungy played me a demo the other day. It's really fascinating stuff and it's amazing how many dissonant sounds there are around us that we just take for granted. But if you don't push the boundaries you'll never achieve anything really great or worthwhile. You'll just be floating with all the other debris in the current.'

'Is that what he tells you?'

'No, Dad, it's what *you* used to tell me when I was younger. Remember?'

'Mm, maybe I should heed my own advice then.'

'I'm happy for Mungy to be doing that. We don't *need* tons of money at the moment anyway.'

'I suppose I'm a bit old-fashioned about responsibility for family.'

'Oh, don't be such a fuddy-duddy, Dad.'

'Fuddy faddy, fuddy faddy,' the little sponge in the high chair chortled to herself.

Melinda turned the last bread tin out onto a metal cooling tray.

'For someone who heads a cutting-edge show on the box you can sound so ... *yesterday*. Mungy puts in his share.'

'Okay, I'm hearing you.'

Barry tickled Rosie under the chin, but she pulled away, sensing her mother's annoyance. Besides she was concentrating on placing eyes into a circle of raisins.

'Well, young Rosie Posie, Grandpa has to go now and get ready for work tomorrow. You got a kiss for me?'

'Mummy, Gampa's got spiders in his nose ... and they're very big!'

Melinda smiled warmly at her father, giving him a hug. 'I know. And I'm glad I didn't inherit that conk! Go on, you silly old thing, off you go. Go and give some money to some poor down-trodden wretch. We're fine here.'

Barry leaned over and blew a raspberry into Rosie's neck. 'Old spiders love dark places,' he whispered.

'Gampa!'

'Here, Dad, take a loaf, and these rolls. But eat them soon while they're fresh.'

'Thanks. You look after me too well.'

'Gampa, I like apicot jam.'

'Me too.'

Barry put his nose inside the packet and breathed in. 'Mmm. I'll see you in a week or so; it's going to be hectic for a while.'

As Melinda walked her father to the front door, three hood-ied teenagers on skateboards rattled by on the pavement bouncing affable expletives between each other.

'Don't let the show get you down, Dad,' Melinda said.

'I'm fine, really. Remember, I'm just the Front Man. It seems it's what ninety-five percent of the population needs to see and hear.'

'Maybe it puts their own lives into perspective.'

'Who knows? I've always hoped the show might be able to

turn some of their lives around. You know, give some hope. But I'm really not sure how long I can keep on doing it. I wouldn't mind doing something a little less stressful. You know, like baby-sitting Rosie. I could even join Mungo's band and play the triangle! How stressful could that be?'

'I'd love to see that.'

Melinda had watched the last series. Her father was highly skilled at interviewing vulnerable people revealing their internal scars and bruises, not gratuitously but enough to expose the crucial aspects of their hapless lives, the bottom line being to give them all an equal chance to come away with a hefty wad of money. Melinda recognised it was the stuff of commercial television viewing. Tabloid trash Mungo called it. She even found herself being sucked into the vortex of intrigue. Her students seemed to talk about nothing else these days. And she knew that money alone wouldn't solve the problems. On the contrary, she believed it even exacerbated them, Minnie Donovan being a testament to that.

Barry kissed his daughter.

'Oh, I forgot to ask, how's school?'

'Started back last week. Pretty good generally. Some of the same old. I lost my mobile on Tuesday only to find it entombed in a slab of wet clay on Wednesday. Didn't lose anything inside luckily. Hey ho!'

Barry settled in his car. The Audi's engine fired up, the electric window came down.

'When are you going to move back south of the city?' he called out.

'When you stop asking!'

Melinda came to the car window.

Kant took hold of his daughter's hand. 'I don't like the idea of my granddaughter being brought up in this godforsaken suburb forever. And that's not a question.'

'When we can afford it we probably will move to the *southern gardens of Eden*, but believe it or not we are very happy here, Dad.'

Rosie had wandered out chewing at a bread roll, and wiping at a blob of apricot jam on her front that was seeping southwards. She waved, licked the back of her hand and blew her sticky sentiments towards the car.

The house Melinda and Mungo bought, originally built by the Zinc factory for their workers, was at the end of a nondescript cul-de-sac. The plan was to do it up gradually over a few years, double their money in five to seven and move nearer to the sea. Melinda even had thoughts of returning to her birthplace in the Huon Valley.

She and Mungo were oddities in their street. They were the only family who owned a piano, novels filling the bookshelves and artwork on the walls, albeit dominated by Rosie's colourful masterpieces. They knew this because over time they had visited all the other houses, making a point of attending as many street parties as they could. There was the Grand Final day sausage sizzle at number ten – imperative to find out for whom the hosts barracked. And the infamous Boxing Day fully-padded cricket friendly, played on the road, which ended with several broken windows, drunken threats and a punch up between Merv from Number One and Dirk, his enormous Dutch mate. A keg was shared sometime during Easter. Australia Day barbecues were held across the road for some of the Harley Club members, where Southern Cross flags flew proudly and were draped around anyone who could remain standing. The Queen's birthday barbecue at the covertly royalist Sanderson's place three doors up was an easy excuse to crack a slab.

Cranky old Todd Mullins from number six, an ex-workmate of Melinda's grandfather and retired boiler-maker from the smelter, who had lived in the area all his working life, had advised them to keep up this practice if they could, so that their house would be taken off the unspoken *list* for burglaries. On the whole it worked perfectly well, except they did lose a large garden gnome playing a banjo that Ziggy, one of Mungo's muso friends, had given him for his twenty-sixth last year. It was sort of fair enough because the kiddies from number sixteen really needed something for air-rifle target practice. Small shards of the happy chappy were found at the base of a fence post near the rivulet where Mel and Mungo would sometimes walk in the evenings.

Later that afternoon Melinda fetched some logs for the wood stove to heat the evening's water.

'So much for summer. Come on, sweetheart, come and help mummy get some food ready for dinner. Daddy will be home soon.'

'Is Gampa coming for dinner?'

'No, he has to go back to work tomorrow and needs to prepare, and then go to bed early.'

'Gampas don't go to bed early!'

*

On the day of the house purchase Mungo had said, 'We've got to be patient, do it up, bit at a time, gradually,' wondering when they would find it. Not the time, the inclination. Music was his world and the thought of scraping, sanding, painting and hammering sent shivers through his body.

'A lick of colour will transform it. That's all it needs in the short term.' Melinda had inherited her mother's patience in lean times. 'And we can dig a pond, surround it with nestling ground covers, plant some pockets of bird-attracting natives, you know, grevilleas and callistemons. It can't be that difficult.'

The place had been vacant for some time so the real estate agent had given them the keys before final settlement. Vandalism was minimal: a couple of broken windows only, a car's skidruts on the front lawn, nothing they couldn't fill or repair.

'Natives'll cope better than exotics with the soil here,' Melinda said, anxious about what might be released as they dug into their patch.

It had been the contamination of the soil in the area from decades of dusty, noxious fallout from the zinc works that had contributed to the affordability of the place. Of course for the young couple, content in the confines of their own love-bubble, it was nothing short of *their* patch of paradise on earth.

'We'll get a truckload of nourishing manure. We can put in raised beds for the veggies, broad beans first. They'll put some nitrogen back into the soil. And we can start a worm farm too,' Melinda had enthused, even though inside she knew the task of giving life to soil that had suffered a slow death by poison would be a painstaking one. But she wasn't going to let a little thing like the sickness of the planet discourage her. Besides she had the dog-eared copy of her mother's self-published 'Love that Dirt' booklet, all about *re-establishing and nurturing damaged soils,* and the benefit of her mother's gardening passion falling about her all her life like soft rain in a herb garden.

'Our example of what's possible will catch on around the suburb; we'll take our prize-winning pumpkins to the Royal Hobart Show, and eventually property prices will soar,' she had quipped, half-serious.

Mungo hugged her. 'And the neighbourhood will be enveloped in social harmony, spreading far and wide, infecting the State, then the rest of the country and finally the world, with so much love and peace and a desire to make love and grow nutritious pumpkins that ... '

'Even the Obamas will want to come and live next door,' Melinda laughed. 'Then we can start making babies.'

But they didn't wait. They chortled like naughty kids, scampering into the house to have unprotected sex on the most comfortable patch of flooring they could find.

Chapter Five

A gleaming, sizzling sun bathed the morning city in radiant warmth. Local radio stations sent out panicky alarms about melanomas and Tasmania's depleted ozone layer, forewarning listeners that it would most likely hit the high twenties by midday.

Porridge and sliced banana breakfast was being prepared, eaten, and put away at Four Luck Avenue in Lutana. Rosie was skittish with anticipation because it was the homecare-lady Yetta Gorski's day to look after her, a workday for both Melinda and Mungo.

Harbourside on the other side of town, Kant had already showered. He was anticipating his first day back at work with a modicum of joy and a second coffee.

Breakfast had been guava juice and a croissant with leatherwood honey. He'd stopped buying newspapers, getting most of his news from canteen griping at the station. It had been too much to expect that the reporting in the local rag might contain something close to intellectual rigour. Besides, every other page was bloated with advertisements from prime sausages to pimple cream, and he'd stopped buying the weighty *Age* because his new home had no garden to be weed-suppressed.

The Audi purred like an adoring feline as it sashayed out

into the Monday-morning traffic, his car a bubble of calm reflection, floating through the torrent of busyness and self-obsessed humanity as he made his way north through the city centre and out the other side. The Frank Sinatra Greatest Hits CD was up loud enough to hold at bay the rest of the world's clamour until he arrived at Nerve Two.

After many consultations over the years with Vince MacLean about the walking wounded he'd observed around the city in his searches for contestants, Kant began to imagine that he too could detect subtle behavioural disparities amongst the congestion in the streets.

'It's a particular unhurried, aimless step you notice after a while, eyes fixed on a vague middle-distance, no apparent objective other than the next tread on an endless pavement. Eye contact with the rest of humanity almost non-existent, protected within the confines of their own debilitating solitude,' MacLean had told Kant after his first year of scouring the city.

As the car left the city centre behind, Kant gave Sinatra's song more volume. " *... As free as the wind blows ...* "

'Unlike the damn traffic,' he complained to Frank. 'Flowing like tepid trea ... cle,' he sang.

Kant was feeling lightheaded when he arrived and parked at Nerve Two, allowing Old Blue Eyes to crescendo the final words of his rousing anthem, " *... And I did it ... myyyyyy way* " before stepping tentatively out into the car park.

Kant passed through the automatic doors into reception,

gave a nod to the new face at the front desk, a Kiwi, Vince had informed him yesterday.

'Good morning. Janine, I believe?'

'Yeah, that's right,' the young, tightly clothed receptionist replied.

Janine twisted in her seat to check out the new arrival, her blatant cleavage a revelation to anybody who approached her for assistance. Kant nodded awkwardly, trying to keep his eyes on her face. The girl swivelled back to her task of buffing her nails to a shiny opaline finish. Her auburn hair was firmly pulled back into a ponytail, leaving just enough short strands for a spray-stiff cockatoo fringe at the front.

The formal reception area of Nerve Two, with its sound-muting carpet, burnt-orange with blue squiggly pattern-repeat prints of the docks and Mount Wellington by local waterco-lourists dotting the wall spaces, was more a *de*-ception area. Once through the swing doors that led to the studios, sound booths and offices, the buzz of anarchy prevailed. It appeared to be partially a warehouse for innumerable boxes of *stuff*, which were everywhere. Kant had often wondered if there was anyone who actually knew what was in them. Lounge suites seemed to have been randomly air-dropped around. There was seldom relief from hectic schedules so no-one ever reclined in them. They were habitually congested with discarded bits-and-pieces anyway. Struggling big-leafed pot plants, mulched with paper scraps, rubber bands, screwed up gaffer tape and anything that needed a quick 'filing' seemed to be more in the way than giving any aesthetic relief. The high walls containing this plangent momentum had never *quite* received their final top coat. Every deadline was overlapped by the next. Nothing had changed in the week Kant had been away.

'Morning Damon.'

One of the cameramen scurried towards Kant, a coil of heavy, black cable slung over his shoulder. He could have been going rock climbing.

'G'day Barry. Bet *you're* glad to be back,' he snorted through a sardonic smirk.

'I didn't realise I'd been away.'

'Huh, you tell that to bloody Mackerel.'

Kant began to feel assailed by the hyperactivity and pervasive urgency. It was like everyone was on speed.

Not so when he entered his own office. Even the size of his name on the door became calmly diminished to BK. Kant's office was one area of the station that *had* been completed, the final coat of paint being a warm, light tone of sun-soaked Tuscan orange. Barry had personalised the space. It could have been one of the rooms in the old cottage. Objects collected with Sarah on various adventures abroad, discouraged by Gaye Salmon from congesting the rigorous minimalism of his apartment, were casually cluttered around. Ms Design-Fascist-Salmon had no authority here.

In fact, clogging up the spatial clarity was *exactly* the theme Kant had aimed for in his office. Books on fishing and travel, magazines and journals were intentionally sprawled on a bench.

Two wicker baskets housing collections of shells, seed pods and other random items collected on walks with Sarah were strategically placed so he could feel the memories at a glance, and a series of small woven tapestries of the Kimberley in Western Australia hung in a row above his desk. And on the opposite wall a large traditional dot painting he had been given by an Aboriginal friend in Alice Springs, and two cherished Cretan embroideries he'd bought with Sarah in Knossos over thirty years ago, were transfusions of joy each time he rested his eyes on them.

Indoor plants, well-fertilised and watered, softened one corner of the room where a circle of four old armchairs were set up for interviewing prospective contestants for the show. A claret-coloured Afghan rug on the floor, faded Balinese throws draped over the chairs all added to the ethnic ambience. And with resplendent disrespect, on a Queen Anne English oak side-table sat the most important item in the room, the coffee machine, which, for some reason, was not working. Kant suspected overuse by the caffeine-addicted camera crew in his absence. No wonder his interviewees felt comfortable with him; it was a comfy refuge away from home.

James Mackelroy burst in with his director's urgency.

'Ah, BK, you're back,' and without taking breath, 'African lad, coming in at two. Vince is bringing him in. Okay?'

Kant smiled at his director. 'Coffee?' but omitted to say what he was thinking: that Vince was highly organised and the arrangements had already been firmly set in place the day before.

'What a week! I'm glad your damn holiday's over.' Then slipping smoothly into well-crafted and charming clumsiness he added, 'You know what I mean, Baz, my man. I'm delighted you've had your well-earned breather and all that, and are now back amongst the fold. Right, where was I?'

Barry was still smiling. 'Was that a *yes*, James?'

'Yes? Oh yes, of course, only way to start the day. And you'll be impressed – I've dropped my caffeine intake to five a day.'

'Mm, noteworthy.'

Kant pressed two numbers on the in-house intercom to the front desk.

'Yis?'

'Hello Janine, Mister Kant here. Could you possibly bring Mister Mackelroy and me a couple of strong blacks? And Janine, that's coffee, not rugby players.'

The girl giggled. 'You wanna coupla buscuts too, Muster Kant?'

Kant looked at Mackelroy, who smiled back and put both his hands in the air, palms up like an Italian chef maintaining tight lips about a secret ingredient.

'That would be lovely. We'll be in my office.'

Kant looked back at Mackelroy, shaking his head as a father might when told by his fourteen-year-old daughter that she is in love, wants to go on the pill and is moving out of home to marry the local butcher's apprentice on Bruny Island.

'Yes, I know what you're thinking,' Mackelroy said.

'No, you don't.'

'She turned up when *you* were lounging around sipping camparis and nibbling nuts in the noonday sun, while the rest of us beavers were busting our balls trying to restore some decorum around here so the bloody dam didn't burst.'

'I did notice that the floors are still dry, so you must have done something right. Anyway, young Janine comes across as a bit … inexperienced.'

'Let's just call her a work in progress. Her old man was a cleaner here but had a bad stroke. Poor sod was only fifty and now he sits around at her flat most days struggling to even open cans of beer with his one good hand. The other half of him went all paralysed or something. I put in a good word for her, that's all.'

'Never known anyone with such a big heart, James,' Kant replied.

'Look, I know she seems a pixel short in the computer room but … '

'I'm sure she's not, I'm just thinking it might be a good idea to get Dorothy to have a quiet word in her ear about dress codes for receptionists. Kid looks as if her … *attributes* could burst through her shirt at any time. I'm sure she's got a heart of gold, but … you know … first impressions.'

Dorothy West was the technical wizard at Nerve Two with anything to do with digital equipment. Her placement had initially got up the noses of a few of the younger breed of male techies, more than likely because she was old enough to be their mother, and *old* people, female at that, weren't supposed to be clued-up about all that technical stuff, let alone your mum.

Kant was quietly pleased for another reason that Dorothy was still on the staff. It was because she was two years older than he. But her main attribute, amongst her multi-tasking abilities, as far as he and Mackelroy were concerned, was the *monthly management* of the younger female staff, pacifying them when fractious and mothering them when they became emotional.

'So, how *was* your break?'

Kant puffed air. 'Oh, I could have done more with my time. Seeing my granddaughter was what I enjoyed most. It restores my faith in the future of this crumbling planet knowing she'll be in charge one day. And by the way she rules the roost at home it won't be that far away.' Kant paused, lifted an eyebrow. 'Did I just have a holiday?'

But Mackelroy's perfunctory curiosity had been satisfied after Kant's first sentence and his thoughts were already speeding down the programming fast lane. He rushed back to his own office to fetch a file he'd forgotten.

As Kant settled in his chair, a wave of melancholy washed over him as he looked around at the accumulated belongings in his office, all overflowing with nostalgia.

'Muster Kant... Muster Kant.'

Kant looked up. 'Oh thanks, Janine.'

'Couldn't find any buscuts though. I'll get some in.'

'Thanks.'

The girl pirouetted self-importantly and left.

'Okay, moving on,' Mackelroy said as he scurried back in,

settling himself next to Kant in an armchair. 'Format the same as before. Except now I want to present to you my little piece of resistance, namely…' he paused theatrically, 'the prize money has doubled to one-hundred-thou.'

Mackelroy waited with a self-gratulatory smirk, knowing Kant would be surprised, shocked even. So now he would linger patiently for Kant's reaction so that he could revel in the triumphant coup that he had pulled off whilst Kant was off having a good time. Mackelroy watched his main man even as he sipped at his coffee, eyes peering out of the top of the rim of his mug. He didn't want to miss a second. Kant sipped too, looked up and held Mackelroy's gaze.

Mackelroy could restrain himself no more. 'Well?' he burst out.

'Oh, you want me to comment on the deal you made with that pommy Network to broadcast BKS up over? Sorry, Vince filled me in on Sunday morning. We really need to get him a desk job; poor fellow never seems to sleep.'

Inside, Kant chided himself for not pretending ignorance and giving Mackelroy his moment of glory. He suspected he sometimes used his feelings of grief over his wife's death as an excuse to be ungracious to others.

Mackelroy began to hiss. 'You're a canny bastard.'

Kant shrugged, looked down at the floor, imitating a forlorn spaniel.

'What's up? Am I detecting a little reticence about being back?'

Kant looked at his director, unable to shift the hang dog expression. 'Probably. No, it's not that. And sorry, I didn't mean to be rude. Let's just get on. It's nothing.'

'No, go on. We can easily postpone interviews for a day if you like. Ease back in.'

'It's nothing, *really*.'

Mackelroy waited.

'Okay, well, it's just that when I came in just now I felt all the old ... *heartache,* around Sarah, just bubble up again. It'll go. I just have to get stuck into these other people's lives again. They've got far more to complain about than me.'

His colleague's use of the word *heartache* had come out as if it was a profanity. Mackelroy grinned, but to Kant's surprise not reassuringly; it was more a lascivious leer.

'Jesus, mate, I know what's wrong with you,' Mackelroy laughed, tapping his forehead with the palm of his hand as if he'd just had a Dr Julius Sumner Miller moment of scientific breakthrough.

'I didn't say there was anything *wrong* with me,' Kant replied defensively.

'You didn't have to. I can see the signs.'

'Signs? Look, let's just get on with it. I shouldn't have mentioned it. Tell me about who we've got on the list.'

'No, BK, you're not going to get out of it that easily. Jesus, I'm good, I can read you like a book. Tolstoy's *War and Peace* no less.'

'What the hell are you talking about?'

'A woman! That's what you need. Put it this way, you've been at *war* with yourself too long, now you need a *peace*! A *piece* of the action.'

'Is *that* what you think?'

'Don't get all innocent on me. You've just had two weeks to dust off your ... your heat-seeking missile and put it to good use but you're still faffing around in no man's land.'

'And that's from someone who bombs a different erogenous zone every night.'

'Malicious rumour,' Mackelroy replied smugly. 'Anyway, if you don't put your scud to good use soon it's going to fall off its launching pad. From boredom! So I'm going to arrange a little something to ... turbocharge things a bit. I'm going to see what I can dig up for you. How's that?'

'Hell, James, I'm not a bloody dog.'

Mackelroy chuckled. 'Oh, come on, I'm sure you've got a bit of *the old dog* left in you. You're not *that* old!'

Kant felt a flutter in his stomach. *Is that excited anticipation?* 'I never thought I was *that* old.' Kant retorted. He thought for a moment. 'I suppose it couldn't do any harm, but I don't want one of your ... you know, leftovers.'

'What do you take me for?'

'I don't want to answer that without my lawyer present.'

'Besides, I can't have my main man moping around like a frustrated adolescent. Leave it with me, Monsieur Kant,' Mackelroy replied in a surprisingly chirpy French imitation. 'I'm certain we can *unearth* somesing testy vith ze dirt screpped off.'

'No cadavers! I want the flesh *on*, and lots of it.' Kant shook his head. 'I don't believe I'm actually engaging in this conversation.'

But the two men began to snicker like a couple of pre-pubescent choir boys at the broken window to the girls' changing room. The front desk intercom buzzed.

'What is it, Janine?' Kant snapped, embarrassed by his silliness, as if she'd heard them.

'Sorry, Muster Kant, but there's a man here at the disk to see you. John Sturges. He says he was told to come here by V'nce. He has a tin o'clock appointment to see you.'

'You should have informed me earlier. Get him a coffee. Tell him I'll see him in ten minutes. I'm in an important meeting with the director at the moment, so no more interruptions please.'

Kant didn't wait for her reply. He turned back to Mackelroy. 'And you can lose the smirk.'

Mackelroy didn't.

'And this is between you and me, right? Right!'

'Sure. I'll arrange a little soirée soon, a get-together with a couple of friends. Not too soon though. We need to be *on top* of things here before the start of filming next week!'

Kant suddenly felt the grip of anxiety in his stomach that was normally reserved for the dentist's waiting room. 'I don't know about this, James.'

'Oh, don't start. Look, relax, I promise I won't let you come to any harm. Now can we get on with the minor situation of the fourth BK fucking S series?'

Kant suddenly felt the reality of his life hit him like a medicine ball to the solar-plexus. He breathed out heavily. He'd been holding his breath again.

*

While Kant was on his holiday Vince MacLean had come across John Sturges, a prospective contestant for the show, booking him in for a preliminary interview. He had observed the grey-haired, unkempt man wearing an old greatcoat a size too big for him, with his right hand fixed deeply in the pocket, as if his fingers were gripped around the neck of a bottle of cheap sherry. There was nothing too remarkable about that, except that the man was attending an exhibition opening of contemporary furniture and large abstract oil paintings in an exclusive gallery in Salamanca Place.

From his high octane existence as a foreign correspondent MacLean had found solace in the quiet of art galleries, and surprisingly to him, an admiration of abstract paintings in particular.

The scruffy man was clearly out of place amongst the loudly effervescent company, fashionable outfits and glistening jewellery. And yet he sustained an intense scrutiny of the exhibits, oblivious to the cerebral and artsy persiflage and sequin-crackle of wealth around him, avoiding all eye contact as he moved about the exhibits. MacLean waded through the stifling, perfumed air towards the man, whose concentration had fixed on four square metres of wildly intertwining streaks of mauves and blues. MacLean sipped his Pinot and reflected on the painting for a moment.

'You like abstract painting?' MacLean spoke cautiously, still studying the work as he stood side-on to the man, who nodded.

'Me friend's over there,' the man, in a low, gentle voice replied obliquely, his friend's company apparently of far greater significance than the $25,000 painting 'Flight of the Dryads' on the wall before him.

MacLean looked in the direction of the man's gaze. The friend was younger, more dishevelled, intellectually impaired, standing alone in camouflage by a pillar, and self-contained in a naïve sensibility. His fingers on one hand were playing with the tips of the fingers and on the other as if he was working out the answer to a complex mathematical problem, or checking that all his appendages were intact.

'We come to galleries sometimes. Do you know Sebastian?'

MacLean peered over again. 'No, pretty sure I don't, pal.'

'What's your job?'

MacLean was momentarily thrown by the sudden change in tack and openness of the question. 'Oh, er... I've been a journalist but I'm...'

'You wanna write about my story?'

'Your story? Oh, er... well...'

'I bin in and out of State *care* ... you know, real bad 'n' that... 'n prison too...'

The man's stress of the word *care* sent a shiver down Vince's spine; he sensed deep trauma. He'd seen it, felt it too many times. Images of obliterated villages, orphaned children and the smell of charred human flesh had impressed themselves into his psyche.

'I'm not reporting at the moment. But, you know there is something else you might be interested in.' But this wasn't the right time or place. 'Look, I'd like to listen to you; how about we make a time and have a yarn?'

'I'm not queer or nothin'.'

'Sir, I'm sure you're not. Not that I'd give a toss if you were.'

'I better get Sebastian; like 'e gets a bit jumpy if I leaves 'im on 'is own for too long.'

'Sure. Do you have a phone number?'

MacLean wrote the mobile number and address on the back of his catalogue.

'I'm Vince, by the way. What shall I call you?'

'Oh … er … John. Yeah, John.' He repeated it, as if, prior to the asking, having a name had been of no great importance for him.

As John turned and began meandering through the crowd, Sebastian lifted his hand surreptitiously and wiggled his fingers towards his friend, smiling brightly. The guileless face completely happy, waiting for his friend to reach him before following him to the entrance.

Later in the week MacLean drove into the heart of Bridgewater, to his journalist's eye a disregarded suburb, *except possibly by the police* Vince thought, as he drove through its streets.

It felt even more isolated than the grimy northern disintegration of light industry and unremarkable suburban sprawl. The district, a collection of so-called broad-acre housing estates, had been dumped on treeless wastelands away from prying eyes decades ago, without a heart and totally inadequate infrastructure. Bridgewater's only claim to fame, apart from the notorious tribes of Bogans, entrenched crime, high rates of teenage pregnancy, record levels of family breakdown, physical, mental and sexual abuse and homelessness was that the High School had been opened by one of the world's wealthiest and most famous women, Queen Elizabeth the Second.

Regrettably Her Royal Highness missed out on her opportunity to return to see how the school was going because on the approximate thirty-year anniversary of its opening the place was burned to the ground by arsonists-unknown, more than likely disgruntled students with nothing better to do on that particular night.

As MacLean drove slowly, looking around for John's house, teenage girls in obscenely tight track pants pushing prams wandered aimlessly along the barren streets with suspicious stares, puffing cigarettes. Bleak cul-de-sacs were decorated with skid marks and burnouts, furtive ten-year-old boys with shaved heads and scraggy mullets played truant in dusty gardens, smoking and chucking rocks at cans and road signs. Rows of young trees along the sides of the road, planted, no doubt, by an exasperated council to supposedly beautify, stood bare of branches, vandalised down to single dead stalks.

John Sturges' fenceless house was at the end of one such cul-de-sac. The burnt-out shell of a car sat outside the house next door like a well-parked meteorite visiting from a remote astral galaxy. A dog was asleep where the driver's seat had been in more sober days. Weeds grew in the gathered dust around clomps of molten vinyl and tyre rubber, and a rusting shopping trolley, one wheel missing, lay on its side gathering leaf litter and empty soft drink cans.

After he had been in Hobart for only a few months MacLean was staggered by how many staring, standing, lying, and wandering wounded there seemed to be around the city – not so different from the broken souls he had written about in the aftermath of civil war. The sobering difference was, Tasmania was a free and beautiful island and yet it was as if these people had become invisible to the rest of the population in the more profligate suburbs.

MacLean squinted in the harsh light as he emerged from the house after an hour. He could hardly wait to report back to Kant. In the curtained depths of this man's miserable life he'd stumbled upon gold.

Chapter Six

Rosie's days, with Mrs Gorski the home-care lady, were lots of fun. Yetta had become surrogate grandmother to Rosie since Sarah had passed away. Even though she didn't understand some of the old lady's words, she loved to hear Yetta talk about a magical place called Poland a long way away on the other side of the world. Sometimes she fell asleep whilst Yetta described little anecdotes about her childhood there.

Mrs Gorski, whose white hair was usually tightly braided like a fancy loaf of bread, had even said that Rosie was grown up enough to put her hands out to hold the skeins of knitting wool while she rolled them into balls. Once they made a pompom together, by winding colourful lengths of wool around two hollow cardboard sandwiched discs, lots of times, until it was tight and then cut around in between the discs very carefully. The fluffy ball appeared like magic.

'Yetta, can you sew it on my beanie, pease?' Rosie had asked. Yetta did, and Rosie told her Mummy later that afternoon it felt funny wobbling on top of her head.

Mungo kissed his family goodbye and left first, his little statement that, although he was only a *self-actuating musician*, it was indeed a real job that required discipline and a regular starting time. And with some assiduous application mixed with fearless creativity, he would one day bring home more than just a few dollars he earned from the weekly gig at Night Owl – the nightclub for experimental music. There were also the 'mate's rates' piano lessons he gave to a couple of his friends' kids at home, on his days with Rosie while she was sleeping.

'Eeni maru, goodbye to you, crochets and quavers, tickle your tum, have a nice day and be good to your mum,' he sang with a marching beat to a giggling Rosie as he lowered her to the ground and headed out to the Red Devil, a twenty-plus-year-old Volvo station wagon. As he drove towards North Hobart, where he and his muso accomplices were renting a first floor warren of gloomy rooms, ideal for their experimentation and recording, clear blue exhaust smoke puffed up into a clear blue sky.

Melinda gave Rosie a bath in a large plastic tub she placed on the kitchen table, more for fun than the wash. The old claw-foot bath they'd picked up at a salvage place looked as if it might need a few more goes with some strong bleach and scourer before use. Mrs Gorski, punctual to a tee, was due to arrive in ten minutes.

Melinda was wrapping Rosie in a towel when she became aware of someone approaching the front door. She'd left the door open so the house could breathe the morning's fresh warm air. She recognised the visitor's looming form as their neighbour who had moved next door a week before, an AC/DC fan, as they'd found out the first night she'd moved in, a raspy nicotine-voiced single mother of three young boys.

Standing in the open front door, the woman's silhouette sucked the light out of the day. After a quick rap, and before Melinda could reply, she stepped into the passage. Her eyes wandering around as if she was a prospective house buyer and she had come to inspect the premises.

'Can I help you?' Melinda said guardedly.

But then, seeing that the woman was carrying a three or four year old on her hips quickly dispelled any fear of threat. The woman looked as if she wasn't quite ready for the day. Her lank black hair was dishevelled and her blotchy mascara had been trying to remove itself for some time. She took a last drag from her cigarette and flicked it expertly backwards along the corridor and accurately through the front door into the garden. Faded black jeans hung from bony hips, and her bra-less flaccid breasts were squashed shapelessly beneath a blue sleeveless truckie's wife-beater.

Melinda thought that in a gust of wind her ears would surely jangle with the lineup of piercings. One protruded from the side of her lower lip, and another in her eyebrow looked inflamed. Her shoulders and upper arms were a battlefield of clumsy, smudged tattoos.

Her child, already with crudely shaved head, tufted mullet-in-the-making and shifty eyes, was attempting to reach a comfort breast through the side of her shirt with a grubby hand. Wearing spent Ugg boots the woman scuffed casually towards Melinda as if they were old friends meeting up for a morning joint.

'From next door, darl. Lippy, to me friends.'

'Yes, we saw you move in a while back. Hi, I'm Melinda. And this is Rosie. How are you settling in?'

'Yeah, all right for shit 'ousing.' Lippy peered into the kitchenette giving it the once over, 'Looks noice 'ere.'

'Thanks. We had to do a bit of renovating. My husband's just gone to work, I'm afraid.'

Mungo and Melinda had agreed that referring to each other as *husband* and *wife* sounded too much like ownership.

'It's the dissolution of self,' Mungo had argued, more protectively of himself when they'd first decided to live together. It was as much to do with the idea of Melinda earning money as a teacher whilst he struggled with his musical creativity, and knowing how her father thought of him as not contributing financially. It used to bother him each time he drove off to the studio.

Melinda and Mungo had devised their own union ritual, inviting family and close friends, and had made promises to try harder to understand the other person when things inevitably got bogged down. In the meantime they wanted to show the people they cared about how much they loved each other at this particular point in time. How long it would last was not the issue but getting pleasure from the moment. To begin with, Barry had thought the whole thing nebulous and hippy, but to his surprise it seemed to be working.

This morning Melinda thought the concept of having a husband gave her a bit more clout. *This woman looks as if she could hold her own in any bar fight*, she thought as her neighbour approached. For now the term *husband* would be adopted as a protective mechanism.

'Yeah, I seen 'im. Is 'e a poof or summit? Never seen a bloke wearing red trousers neither. Talks funny too.'

It was impossible to take offence at Lippy's manner. She was unpretentious and authentic, Melinda observed, like so many of her students at the Polytechnic who'd also been scraped from the same mold. Melinda relaxed a little and smiled.

'My husband's just one of these arty types, a muso,' Melinda replied lightheartedly, lifting her eyebrows to give the impression she was siding with Lippy. Better to deal with an ally than an assailant was her rule number one when dealing with difficult students.

A turbulent existence had clearly stunted this woman's formal schooling and her remark was simply about a man she had observed being unlike anyone she had experienced before. That's all. Melinda's grandfather had advised against any form of *backchat* if they were to *get on in this jungle*. He should know. He had been as much a fixture in the area as the street signs, most of which were unreadable because of graffiti. *A bit like the old man himself,* she'd often thought.

As Lippy entered the living area and began looking around with wide, inquisitive eyes, Melinda speculated about whether the woman's frown was ingrained or whether she was concentrating on the objects to judge if there was anything of value worth stealing at some later date.

Lippy suddenly snorted with bewilderment. 'Jeez, you got a pianna!'

'Mungo gives lessons to some young children on Thursdays.' She smiled outwardly. 'They can go on a bit. You know, a bit hard on the ears. Might be a good day for you to do your shopping!' she added slightly apologetically but trying to be conversational.

'Thas if fuckin' Cenna Link giz us what's owin'. Tryna get money outa three fuckin' fathers is...' Lippy stopped, puffed air, clearly sick and tired of banging on about them. 'Better go, eh? Cute kid. My other two are probably tryna burn the fuckin' house down, little bastards. Nice to meetcha, Mel. See yas round. Bring pianna man round for a drink sometime, eh?'

'I'll let him know. Bye then.'

She could quite understand why Lippy had such a nickname. Rosie had fallen asleep in Melinda's arms, snug in the thick white bath towel. Melinda kissed her daughter's forehead. She looked so content, so serene, so... *not* wanting to meet the neighbour. 'I know your trick, you little poppet. If only we adults had that sort of audacity.'

Rosie, too young to go to crèche quite yet, adored these Mondays with Mrs Gorski, as much a loved member of the family now. And Melinda, unlike most of the staff at the Polytechnic, also loved Mondays because first up she had a free line, giving herself time to prepare the pottery studio for her *Licorice* class at ten, filled with *Allsorts* of odd-bods.

Yetta Gorski, stocky, smooth leathery face with a strong jaw line, a mother of five, now grown-up men, exuded warmth and a selflessness that had been fashioned out of privation. Her late husband Leszek, once a miner on the West Coast, who departed his dusty world with an incurable lung infection, left her early to raise their brood on her own. She never remarried, she never complained. Now that her *boys* had flown the coup her ingrained need to nurture was even stronger.

Melinda would fantasise about getting Yetta together with her father whenever he became maudlin. Complete opposites she knew, but it was the pampering he could have done with. And Rosie, well, she became the sweetest granddaughter Yetta Gorski still didn't have from her boys.

Yetta, dead on time, came bustling into the house carrying a cane basket containing her knitting, a dog-eared Romance novel and two bottles of home-brewed beer for Mungo. She hadn't been able to give up the practice of brewing even though her lads had disappeared interstate to the WA mines. She always had a few bottles in the fridge for their returns. When Rosie had her naps, Yetta found peaceful escape in books whilst knitting at the same time, an action that had become a wholly automatic function of her anatomy.

'Hi Yetta. Rosie's gone back to sleep. Don't think she was too impressed with the woman next door.' She chuckled. 'Just sauntered right in to introduce herself to us. I'm sure she's not a danger but just for a while I'd keep the front door closed.'

'Yes, I will keep my eyes wide.'

But there *was* something about the woman, an inclination for violence maybe? Exacerbated by the brazen way she talked about her own children, and even Mungo? *Or am I just preju-diced?* Melinda wondered. *She's pretty scary with those tattoos round her neck and arms, and that voice.*

'I'd better get these breakfast things cleaned up before our young lady is demanding my full attention. Now you get your-self off to those little terrors at school,' Yetta said firmly.

'Little! If only. Most of the boys tower over me. I've got the class of regular kids mixed with the *special needs* today. It really is like a mad house sometimes.'

'But you couldn't do without it; is that right?'

Melinda just smiled.

Attending the School of Art had been an exasperating time for Melinda. Whenever she opened the kiln door after a firing, and the magic of metamorphosis was revealed, her highly anticipated creations never seemed to come out as she'd wished.

She had dreamed of having a career as a ceramicist, exhib-iting her highly acclaimed textural slab-built constructions in swish galleries. But ceramics was a competitive field and the cost of setting up kilns and workshop at home was prohibi-tive, so teaching became a realistic alternative. Not completely letting go of her dream she kept her hand in by demonstrating techniques to her students.

One day, she kept reminding herself.

It wasn't always simple at college, now a polytechnic, some-thing *else* later no doubt. In the last couple of years classroom teaching had become more complex and arduous with the addition of *special needs* students to the mainstream classes.

And on top of that there were more qualified art teachers than available positions, so Melinda found herself in front of Home Economics classes for half her time. *Cook'n* to the students.

She took pleasure from the fact that both her subjects were about mixing ingredients, ovens and metamorphosis. Melinda told Mungo she was an alchemist where basic elements, like mud or flour, could be transformed into astounding creations. She hoped her students would transform similarly, emerging from their grey and sticky capsules triumphantly as brightly coloured winged creatures. Another dream she endeavoured to keep alive.

'They've all got character, Yetta, and most are shameless when *expressing* themselves. A bit like our Lippy next door! One lad's in a wheel chair as he has cerebral palsy. Mason – he works the chair with one withered claw of a hand controlling the steering knob. I kid you not but the other day I was setting the kiln temperatures, the rest of the class had gone to a break, and bold as brass he wheeled alongside the drying bench and with his other hand managed to swipe two or three drying pieces of work belonging to other students onto the floor.'

'Mm, that seems shameless enough. How do you discipline that?'

Melinda shrugged. 'No idea really. Most people treat him as if he's invisible because they don't want to feel uncomfortable communicating with him.' She smiled naughtily. 'He can sound a bit like a mating whale. So the other kids make empty platitudes, then move away. It's not easy, and can be very frustrating, but he's had a lifetime of being alienated simply because of other people's social embarrassment. It doesn't seem fair to be born with that sort of life sentence.'

'Possibly *his* special need is to get the rage out of his system, hence the pot smashing.'

'For sure. The depressing thing is that it's hard to tell who's neediest sometimes. Autism, Asperger's, Down syndrome, they all require specific ways of interaction, but it's the so-called *normal* mainstream ones, real deadshits some of them, excuse my French, who have no physical or mental disability that cause the most trouble and are hardest to deal with. And we teachers are the jugglers trying to keep all their different needs airborne at the same time.'

'For you I should sew one of those pointy hats with bells on!' Yetta laughed. 'But maybe all they need is an old-fashioned firm hand and some motherly bosoms to be cuddled in.'

'You're not far off the mark. The mother of one of my students is in Risdon Prison, but unfortunately for the lad his father's *firm hand* is a lot more than just that.'

Melinda suddenly shuddered at the thought of Tony Macey cuddling up to Yetta. A six-foot lump of a boy, volcanic acne, and self-esteem lower than his pitiful IQ, who thinks that wiping wet clay into girls' hair is hilarious, even a possible career option.

'Yetta, I'll be back around four-thirty. Stay safe.'

'Off you go now. You have no need for worry.'

Of course I have no need to worry. Melinda picked up her keys and left the room.

Chapter Seven

Kiwi-Janine, who was wearing a smart shirt with jacket and slacks, knocked and entered Kant's office. Kant looked up from a share prospectus Maxwell had advised him to study. *Phew, Dorothy's had a word in her ear,* Kant thought as she ushered John Sturges in.

'Here's Muster Sturges, Muster Kant.'

'Ah, welcome John. Please sit down. Can I offer you a coffee?' Kant said, standing up and shaking his hand.

'I'm pretty right, thanks. The lass 'ere just made us one.'

Janine lingered at the door. Kant suspected the girl had aspirations to be more involved with the proceedings at the station. Television stations often brought out romantic notions of fame with some of the younger employees.

Kant nodded at her. 'Thanks, Janine.'

She swivelled and disappeared.

'Nice lass,' John Sturges said warmly.

'Yes, very pleasant.'

'Told me she come from Christchurch. Real bad about that earthquake.'

'Yes, it was terrible. Please John, have a seat.'

Kant sat in the other armchair, crossed his legs and leaned a little towards his guest, who had perched himself near to falling on the edge of the chair holding his knees.

'So. Vince has had a preliminary chat with you at home.'

'Well yes, he did. He come round, brought some little cakes too. Nice fella.'

Kant smiled. 'That's why we employ him. And I have to say, John, he must have really liked you.'

'Oh? How's that?'

'Well he's never brought *me* any cake before.'

John grinned with pride. 'Sorry about that.'

'It's okay really. Now...'

'I don't know what 'e told you but it's hard to just remember everything off the top of me 'ead. Dunno why I agreed really. But he made me feel kinda easy, you know, to tell stuff.'

'Sure. All right, well how about you start at the beginning, and if we decide that your story is suitable then we'll go through how the interview will be carried out on air – so there are no surprises for you. The program is not live so we always have plenty of time in which to edit things that don't work well for you, or indeed us. Think of this as just a chat between two mates ... in a pub, very relaxed. How does that sound?'

'Righteo then, sounds fine.'

John Sturges looked about seventy years of age but he had told Vince he was sixty-four. It had not been a compassionate life that had embraced him. The gritty lines, parallel furrows in arid soil, had long been ploughed across his forehead, signs of life's brutal grip. His wiry unkempt grey hair was in need of basic grooming and his clothes were op-shop specials. But it wasn't so much his appearance that gave the man a washed-up look but the way he carried himself. This was not an assertive man with straight back, looking assuredly into a bright future, no. This man's whole demeanour was weighted down as if merely keeping his body together, his arms, his shoulders, his head, was an effort.

But to get on the show there would have to be more than just feeling sorry for yet another down-trodden old fella fallen on hard times.

'I told the other bloke about how I was treated real bad when I were in State care. Like, you know, Wyborough Hall up Mangalore, 'n' Ashley Boys' Home, 'n' that.'

'Ashley Boys' Home?'

'Yeah. I also spent some time earlier with the Salvos too. That was real bad too. Then when I was at Brighton Area School this kid died of a brain tumour; they reckoned it were me what killed him. I's called *murderer* 'n' stuff. The psychiatrist, he said there was nothin' wrong with me. The kids and even summa the teachers said I bashed 'is 'ead on the concrete. I never did. Even in Ashley they bashed the guts outa ya.'

'The boys' home?'

'That's right.'

Kant was already losing the continuity of the man's nervous ramble. Things that had happened to John Sturges forty or fifty years ago had fused together into a cluttered medley.

'John, you mentioned the Salvation Army. Surely they would have provided a safe haven for you?'

'You'd think so, wouldn't you? There was Major Finlay and

Captain Sullivan; keep y'in a dark empty room with nothin' to keep warm, no bed all night.'

'How old were you when this was happening?'

'Five, thereabouts.'

'Five!' Kant repeated. 'Surely you could have told someone. What were your parents doing then?'

'Dunno. They sent me there 'cos I were a tearaway really; runnin' away, stealin' stuff.' John smiled at this description of himself. 'I were a bit of an 'anful, see. They just took off, I s'pose. I think someone said they went to Queensland, or me father did anyway. I dunno.'

Although John had clearly endured a hard time growing up in the fifties in Tasmania, there were lots of other people who did it tough. Social support networks were not so much in place then, and so many were left to their own devices, to either sink or swim. There would have to be more to John's story for him to be a viable contestant.

'Your dad, what was he like?'

'Dunno really. Used to bash ya when 'e was drunk. Never touched me sister though. I s'pose I couldn't fight back being a bit younger 'n' that. Back then, as I said, I was a bit of an 'anful, you see, a bit wilful like.' Again, the sheepish grin.

'So how old *were* you back then? When your father ... hit you, John?'

'Two.'

'Two!'

'I think so. Oh, maybe two 'n' a 'alf,' he added, as if the extra six months made a difference. To Kant it sounded like an apology for being such a handful, excusing his father's violence because that was all he had possibly ever known.

'Jesus,' Kant whispered. He hadn't meant to lose his composure but all he could think of was Rosie, proud to be two and a half, steeped in so much love and nurture.

'See, I reckon it was me being a tearaway. That's why they sent me to the Salvos. Later, after I left the Brighton school I was sent to Ashley in Deloraine. I was twelve by then but they still kept it on the books like. You know, me being a murderer an all.'

'You mean the misguided *suspicion* that you had hurt the boy?'

'I dunno. I think they always thought it were me, like they wanted someone to blame for stuff. Summa them guards, like I don't reckon they were very happy themselves.'

'Yes, I can certainly understand that.'

John scratched at the stubble on his chin. 'Them kids there, and even the staff, still used to bash ya. I run away, I did. Just took off. They told me eventually that it wasn't me. Not for a coupla years though. Like, you begin to wonder whether you really *did* do it. I stole a few things, nothin' real big, when I took off to the city, you know … like a bicycle off of a verandah to get round and stuff.'

'How do you feel about that part of your life now, John? It was a *long* time ago.'

'Yeah I know but … '

Kant waited. He suspected there was more to the story. There must be. How could anyone remember such details after half a century? Just then a text came through on Kant's iPhone. Ignoring it, he looked at John with a reassuring smile.

'It's hard, isn't it? So much from our past can get lost, or hidden,' Kant said, not realising how prophetic his statement would become.

'It's not that; it's hard 'cos *some* things just don't go away and … ' John heaved a sigh.

'It's okay, mate, your story's safe with me. And if you don't want to go ahead, everything you've told me will remain completely confidential.'

John looked around the walls at the artworks, his eyes remaining for several seconds on each piece before moving to the next.

'You have some nice things 'ere, Mr Kant.'

'Thanks, but call me Barry, please. I collected them all over a lifetime really. They're like a chart of my travels with my wife.'

'I like that.'

John breathed in and filled his lungs. He allowed the air to smooth out a clench that seemed to have constricted his chest. 'See … like … like there was this *other time* … I spent in Dominic; you know, the Catholic school.'

'Here in Hobart?'

'Yeah. I spent some time there, only a few months. Me older sister Elsie, who lived down Primrose Sands, said it would be a good safe place to go and … like … get better, be cared for, but … '

A fearful realisation began to churn in the pit of Kant's stomach. *Oh God, here it comes, I should have guessed.*

After a few minutes Kant wound up the interview and booked John Sturges into the show. He had to remind himself this was not a counselling session as he watched the old man trudge heavily from the room. His was a big story, even for BKS, and Kant, already feeling the enormity of the responsibility, needed time to assimilate the dreadful nature of a crime that had been perpetrated on this gentle old man so many years ago and was still poisoning him like a rusty spike driven deep into his soul.

Already, Kant's first day back had given him more than he was ready for, so he postponed the afternoon interview with the African lad for a later date, to be confirmed, and fixed a strong coffee for himself. While the coffee machine was doing its thing he opened up the message on his iPhone. It read: *your fulla shit fagot.*

Kant stared at the message for several seconds. It was his turn to sigh. 'Is that a fact?' he said, pressing the delete button. Boiling brown liquid began to splutter into his cup.

*

At the top of the wooden stairs, rising directly from the street to the first-floor landing, Mungo flicked a light switch that activated several low wattage globes in the dim passageway and in the largest room to the left, which had become the main studio. There was no light switch *in* the room. Random, dodgy modifications over the years had presented such anomalies to the workings of this *character* space but suited the nature of their experimental work. The three men had all made various forays into the Art School as well as completing degrees at the Conservatorium of Music. A solid grounding in formal techniques was essential before the true creativity of bending all the rules could take place.

Below on the street frontage was a Moroccan rug shop next to a milk bar. To the lads, Moroccan *food* in a *Kasbah* would have been preferable.

Elizabeth Street was the main artery connecting the city's heart, several blocks down the road, with the fashionable North Hobart nucleus of cosmopolitan activity a few blocks up, with its restaurants and trendy cafés, wine sales, pubs, alternative cinema, art galleries and music venues. Not with a Lygon Street sort of Melbourne ethnicity or with a Kings Cross Sydney exuberance, but in a *'there's-no-one-around-after-ten-in-Hobart'* sort of graveyard way, as Sammy, the band's twenty-four-year-old percussionist often complained about it.

At night, Hobart's CBD, several blocks down the street, was a desolate and windy place where the homeless hunkered down and the crime-intent scuttled around *'like underfed crocodiles in a caravan park'*, another of Sammy's little lyrical triumphs, particularly when he was on the weed.

The band, Global Synthesis Trio, a purposely pretentious mouthful, (and sick of the tax the genuinely penniless still had to cough up), had set up the studio with the banks of second-hand keyboards in two rows facing each other, giving easy access to all the wires, cables and connections in the middle. To one side the drum kit and associated percussion instruments had been set up on a higher plinth, giving Paul elevation to see Sammy and Mungo at their respective keyboards.

Paul Leonard, solid build, head insulated with black curly hair had been brought up in Cairo in his early years. He was often mistaken for being Greek but his parents, archeologists, were actually English. Much of their research was based on hieroglyphics, deciphering the secrets of the past. Paul had met Lena, a Tasmanian who had been visiting the pyramids. Not long after their meeting under the Sphinx *she* had tempted him with her beauty and the lifestyle of Hobart. To his parents' disappointment, Paul flew back to Australia with Lena, but they went their own ways a year later. Paul's brief emotional vacuum became occupied again after teaming up with Mungo and Sammy, drinking buddies only at first until they all realised they shared the same passion for eccentric music.

Whenever another musician ventured into the space a jam session would ensue, injecting a different sound into their music, twisting it even further. Electronic sampling was an important aspect to the finished product, as Mungo explained to Melinda when they first started. 'You start with something that is basic, unadulterated like a baby at the beginning of life. You take its pure nature and manipulate it through recording it and redesigning it electronically, the denaturing of innocence.

In our case we end up with a multi-facetted soundscape. An amalgam, representative of all the urban sounds we take for granted and have stopped hearing, but are at the very core of our lives,' Mungo continued earnestly.

'I love it when you talk dirty,' she'd replied.

Littered around the remaining spaces were extraneous objects, junk retrieved from a disused machine factory that tantalised their uninhibited musical impulses, to strike, shake or rotate. PVC plumbing pipes of various dimensions hung from the rafters; the longer they were the lower the note that emanated from them when hit with a rubber thong. Two dismembered piano frames were suspended too, to be plucked, hammered or ruffled. As well, there were sheets of steel, hub caps, even an old vacuum cleaner with the pipe connected to the outflow opening and the other end inserted into a large plastic drum filled with table tennis balls. It was within the process of unconstrained *play* where the magic was found, recorded then merged with conventional percussion beats and scale structures.

Sammy arrived eating a cold slab of what looked like two layers of last night's pizza. Paul, the same age as Sammy, breezed in seconds behind, coke in hand, grin on face. The smug expression, cultivated to a fine degree, needed no explanation. Apart from being a reliably accurate barometer for some recent carnal interaction with the opposite sex, he was hopeful it conveyed an alpha male image, suiting his reputation for being unattached and therefore, in his mind, irresistible to all women.

Mungo, who was several years older than the others, had taken on the role of Godfather in the band, ostensibly because he had a kid and lived with a regular partner. This seemed to allow him the unique status of *responsible adult* which the others were not yet ready to accept for themselves. Sammy and Paul liked to play the single, *we-have-lustful-sex-every-night-you-poor-married-bastard* game with Mungo, who played along with it because he knew it patently wasn't true. The lads spent most days and evenings playing music until their bodies were so tired they couldn't raise the flag even if they'd wanted to.

Mungo looked up. 'Morning.'

The others replied in unison, 'Morning.'

Mungo, who had already activated his Korg effects system, microphone hanging in the middle of the room, record button red, played the greeting back to them: Morning … morning …

Then on a loop: Morning … morning … morning … morning … morning …

He sped it up to about twice the speed, inserted a chorus effect, then added an octave below. Paul picked up his drum sticks and began to play along. Kick bass in time with the words, high hat on the offbeat, sticks playing counter beats with the snare and toms and cowbell. Sammy shoved the last two mouthfuls of pizza into his mouth and began hitting two large metal pipes with a lump of wood, the doleful ecclesiastical tones befitting an elegy in some country churchyard.

Mungo adjusted the key to suit the pipes and began

improvising a melody with his other keyboard, on top of what was happening. They seemed to play as if their lives depended on it, for a while not even looking at each other, simply imbibing the sounds, the rhythm, feeling and reacting to each other. After about ten minutes they began to give each other knowing glances, their actions getting more radical and the melodies more complex. It was the point where the synthesis of the sounds found a groove, fusing as one. They were all appendages of the same musical body, their minds tuned into hearing and predicting the others' moves.

Mungo suddenly flicked his keys off, Paul ceased drumming and Sammy burst into laughter.

'John Cage, eat your heart out!'

And so the young musical revolutionaries' day had begun.

Chapter Eight

At the same time that John Sturges had entered the Nerve Two reception area, hesitantly making his way to the young girl at the desk to check in for his interview with Kant, Melinda was leaving home to the sound of Yetta singing in the kitchen as she went about preparing the ingredients for her famous spiced biscuits.

'Kosi kosi łapci … pojedziem do babci … Babcia da nam mleczka … a dziadzius pierniczka.'

Melinda had heard Yetta sing the Polish nursery rhyme many times to Rosie, who loved to clap, clap little hands like the young girl in the song, when heading off to grandma's house to be fed on milk and gingerbread cookies.

Half an hour later, when Melinda opened the kiln room door, she was instantly wrapped in its womb-like heat. The kiln had reached temperature overnight, an 1100-degree glaze firing turning silica into glass. It still wasn't quite ready to open up. If she opened the door too early because of impatient student demands most of the pots would crack with the inrush of cold air onto hot clay bodies. She switched the buzzing extractor fan off and came back into the studio to prepare for the students' arrival.

From the damp cupboards, lined with tin sheeting to extend the drying time of clay, she lifted out several works and began placing them around the room for the students when they arrived. Melinda felt it was important to have the works in place, particularly for the special needs students who were creatures of habit, always sitting in the same spot at the same table.

Mason's *piece* was essentially a lump of clay on a craft-wood board into which he would prod with his withered fingers, grunting and forcing subterranean sounds from his mouth. His head, neck and shoulders, twisting and contorting as his tongue moved in and out of a mouth that had minimal muscle control, writhed like an ancient creature from the depths of a sea cave. His cerebral palsy movements were involuntary and his noisy expulsions spasmodic and alarming, but his interaction with clay, in this room, with these other human beings, made his eyes shine with joy.

As it turned out Mason was away sick today. The merest cough would require regular massage and gentle thumping on his chest and back to break up the congestion. A lack of this constant attention could result in something far more serious or even death.

Pammy trundled in. Big lady, thirtyish; records of her birth had gone astray. She was intellectually impaired, and irrepressibly cheerful due to a complete lack of comprehension about negativity, an attribute Melinda wished would rub off onto some of the sixteen-year-old hoodied *rabbits* that had just burst in, in a flurry of chatter, ribbing and punching, girls and boys alike. And these were the so-called *normal* ones.

Here's my pack of primitives, Melinda mused as they jostled for a position around the same table. The smell of sour smoke infused in their hair and clothes made it almost as difficult to teach them close up as it was with the impoverished Jeremy Sedgebrook, whose trousers invariably ponged of week-old, slow-dribble urine.

'Hello Miss Kant,' Pammy said, with the muted voice of someone who didn't want to be noticed this morning, but she adored Melinda so she often gambled with her safety. She sat in her place and waited for Melinda to say, 'All right Pammy, we going to do some work now?'

'Yes, Miss Kant. I'm going to do some …'

'Melinda!' one of the shabby boys interrupted. 'We git our fings from the kiln now?'

'It's not quite cool enough yet, Phillip. If I were to open it up now, the cold air would rush in and all your hard work would explode.'

'Cool.'

'If you get going with something new it'll be okay in about half an hour. Maybe you could try something a little taller this time. What about a vase for your mum to put flowers in?'

'Oaw,' he tutted. 'I ain't a poof. I want me ash tray so I can 'ave a smoke arfter.'

'You're going to have to wait till you get home anyway. You know there's a no smoking policy on campus.'

'Oaw.'

Pammy giggled and whispered inaudibly to her table top, 'Smoking's not healthy for you.' Almost inaudibly …

'Fuck off Pammy, ya spaz.' A runt of a rabbit sneered without looking up from his own table top.

Pammy giggled again.

'Ya der-brain.'

Pammy smiled, puffed with pride at her audacity in engaging a hostile enemy. Unlike the College campus, there would be no physical retaliation in the classroom with the teacher present – an insignificant skirmish by all accounts but for Pammy a major military triumph.

'Right, come on everyone, let's get started. And for once let's try to keep the language *clean*. There are new bags of stoneware clay, and I've mixed up a new cobalt under-glaze in that bucket there, which will give you a strong blue for your designs. I've made up *new* white slip, since someone decided to mix the last lot with some iron oxide. The clean slip, and let's *keep* it clean too, is now in this bucket here.'

Like constant radar Melinda scanned the room with her peripheral vision. 'You two, Jenny, Maureen, stop your nattering. Your boxes need the galleries scraped a little more so the lids fit. Here Pammy, try this *wooden* tool; it won't cut so deeply.'

Melinda was never on her own teaching these composite classes. There was a ratio determined by the Education Department of the number of support aides per disabled students, like Mason, who needed to be wheeled to the toilets and '*sorted out*', and Kevin Saunders, an autistic lad of twenty-two, who had just arrived with his father, Jackson Saunders, an accountant with the Hobart City Council.

The two regular carers, David Wenderby and Carol Symmons, were both endlessly patient. Of course, it was easy for them to remain calm because the sole responsibility for discipline was Melinda's. They were there to assist with technical problems like carrying heavy pots for their students, wheeling some of them to the toilet, wiping dribbles from faces and keeping a vigilant eye out for safety. Carol, who was studying autism as part of her Master's degree, had applied for the job because of the inclusive programs that had been set up for special needs students at the Polytechnic.

'Kevin doesn't see the forest, only individual trees', had been how Carol had explained Kevin's condition to Melinda when she first joined the class. Her studies had equipped her with an armoury of theoretical descriptions encased neatly in nutshells, most of which seemed irrelevant once she found herself in the middle of the classroom theatre.

Kevin had been diagnosed as having a higher functioning autism. Research had shown similarities between this and Asperger's Syndrome, where behavioural patterns could oscillate between 'normal' behaviour and severe autistic behaviour. It had been shown that high functioning autistic adults can meet the criteria for a diagnosis of autism yet show no cognitive delays, and can speak, read and write with an average to above-average IQ.

With Kevin there were difficulties in communication, language and social interaction. His repetitive behaviour and narrow field of interest were usually deterrents for relationships with other students to develop, positive ones anyway. Abstract language concepts like irony, and even humour were often beyond his comprehension. Kevin could not 'read' people and was incapable of seeing or understanding manipulation, something the antagonistic rabbits quickly picked up on. In short, to them Kevin was fair game.

Kevin found it difficult to maintain eye contact when people spoke to him so the other students assumed he was always disinterested in them. So a cycle of indifference commenced, except when he was displaying his obsessiveness with cleanliness. The rabbits would wait with pent-up anticipation whenever Kevin arrived. His first task was to go straight to the dirty, clay-smeared sinks and taps to clean them. Then he would wipe clean the light switches, and state, without humour or joy, to no-one in particular, 'Spotless.' Of course, being a pottery workshop the sinks and light switches provided Kevin with endless occupational activity.

The class caught on to his routine, and by the end of first semester they would watch the cleaning process and just as he finished they would all call out, 'What do you call that, Kevin?'

He would look around and in a flat, matter-of-fact voice repeat, 'Spotless.' After a while something must have touched him deep inside because this 'sport' often resulted in the faintest smile.

Since Kevin had been attending these classes, his confidence and ability to engage in minimal conversation had improved out of sight as he developed an off-beat fascination in numbers, quantities, percentages, and dates. His endlessly patient parents and Melinda were bemused by this fact, particularly as they were usually in relation to disasters, natural and man-made. Kevin's parents did not discourage Kevin from watching the news on the television; on the contrary they thought he should go through life like everyone else. His father had managed to teach Kevin how to use the internet by keying in salient words, only to become perplexed at his interest in words like Cyclone, War, and Catastrophe.

'I suppose that's the reality for all of us. Isn't it?' Jackson had tried to justify to Melinda several weeks ago after she'd told him Kevin had been entertaining the class that morning with the disturbing numbers of people that had been killed in various conflicts in the history of the world.

And this morning too, Melinda noticed Kevin seemed troubled again, too unsettled to play with his clay or even clean taps. Several times he'd got up from his stool, sat down, got up, walked around, and sat down again.

'You okay, Kevin?' Melinda asked.

'Yes Melinda, I'm okay,' he replied without the slightest inkling that anything about his behaviour was different. Then he began to speak, quite out of the blue, monotonously, 'On May the eighteenth 1980 at 8.32 am, 52 people died because the Mt St Helen's volcano erupted.'

'Wow. I didn't know that, Kevin. But I remember it was a huge eruption.' 'The summit was reduced by 1312 metres afterwards.' And then, as if the two incidences were related, 'In 2009 in the Victorian bushfires 208 people died.'

'It was a terrible disaster, Kevin,' Melinda replied as she scraped a lump of soggy clay up from the floor under his feet. She, unlike Kevin, whose comprehension was only fixed on the unemotive facts, understood the consequences of destructive bushfires, and had been moved by the suffering caused at the time.

As Melinda stood up, Kevin, who had sat on the stool next to her, began to ramble into his hands. His words, like a dooms-day monologue, were not directed at anyone in particular, and had no correlation to the previous conversation. Melinda held back and allowed the words to flow – a torrent.

'Eight million died in World War One. Nineteen million, five hundred and thirty-six thousand wounded. In World War Two twenty million, eight hundred and fifty-eight thousand, eight hundred soldiers died, and twenty-seven million, three hundred and seventy-two thousand, nine hundred civilians died. Three thousand, nine hundred and twelve kamikaze suicide pilots in the Japanese Air Force died in the Pacific region between 1944 and 1945 ... '

'I wish you'd go an' bloody join 'em,' one of the rabbits grum-bled, aggrieved by Kevin commanding so much attention.

Kevin continued as if he was sitting by himself in the room.

'Eleven hundred people died in the floods in Pakistan, eighteen died in the Queensland floods this year, one died in Cyclone Yasi, seventy-one died in Cyclone Tracy in 1974, four hundred died in 1899 in Cyclone Mahina in Cape York, one hundred were Aborigines.'

'Okay, thanks, Kevin. That was most informative. But I think that's probably enough facts for now.'

'Yeah, why don't you go and clean the bloody sinks, ya dick head?' a greasy-haired female rabbit finally sneered through a lip-load of piercings.

'All right, all right, thanks, Tracy. How about we take a break? Ten minutes. When you come back I'll open the kiln and you can collect your masterpieces.'

''Ooray!' The rabbit mob chanted, scuffing their stools back, having already forgotten Kevin's recital.

''Bout bloody time,' one mumbled as he barged past Pammy, rudely knocking her.

The cheers were a hollow expression of delight for Melinda, for she knew the practices of some these hooded, sneaky-eyed delinquents and their real motivation. Behind a service area, on the southern end of the campus there was a tall brick wall, on the way to the rabbits' backstreet warrens. Over the past few years there had accumulated a large pile of broken clay shards at the base of it. Brightly glazed bowls, quirky animals and masks, the occasional teapot, albeit with dribbly spouts, platters, carved boxes and sculptural forms constructed with fine white stoneware clay, and delicate crackle-glazed Raku-fired pots had been hurled at the brick wall with idiotic cheers. No ashtrays though. Red target rings had been sprayed about two metres off the ground. In the centre was a crudely painted penis and testicles with the words *smash all poofs* sprayed underneath.

Melinda could understand the desire to create an explosion. And the sort-after adrenalin rush that followed. By all accounts, while they were under the teacher's watchful eye, they had professed a primitive pride in something they had created themselves. Melinda could see it in their eyes as they took hold of their glazed works, still warm from the belly of the fire. So it was beyond her why these boys, and girls, would want to destroy their *own* work that they had given so much attention to, given birth to.

That was until a young student at the end of last year, David Such, a sensitive and unusually creative lad from a background almost completely devoid of nurture, made the most delicately carved figurine of a mother holding a child in her arms. It was a simple but profound representation of family love. It had been on display in the cabinet by the principal's office for several weeks, admired and talked about by teachers, visiting parents and students alike. Knowing the boy's home-life Melinda was fascinated. It was so realistic and so evocative of a mother's devotion to her child, it belied reason.

But a fortnight later, Charlene Peters, the only girl in Melinda's pottery class then who was quite at ease working at the same tables as the *spazes*, had told Melinda that David had removed the figurine from the cabinet, and had taken it to The Wall. Charlene had retrieved the mother's decapitated head amongst the rubble and handed it dolefully to Melinda.

'Why David?' she'd asked him later, her eyes beginning to glaze like the lustre on the little figurine's face.

David had mumbled to the ground, 'Me Dad reckons I'm gay if I do stuff like that.' Then raising his heavy, sad puppy eyes to look at Melinda, the one person in his life who had given him a sense of his own worth, his potential, he'd added forlornly, 'I'm not, ya know.'

Melinda had smiled sympathetically at the boy, but felt utterly defeated. *Why the hell do I put myself through this?* she screamed inside.

This year she would contact parents to try to encourage them to support their children's creative efforts in pottery, but Melinda knew that the task of getting through to parents was often more daunting than classroom management. Home was usually the battleground where neglect and dissent festered.

The kiln firing was a success. By the time the students had returned to the studio Melinda had taken their work from the kiln and placed it on their tables. She'd let them fetch their own work directly from the kiln once. It had been a disaster. After the lower shelf props were dislodged in a shoving match the whole six layers came tumbling down.

A quiet pride existed over the next fifteen minutes as everyone admired their own finished work placed carefully beside them.

'Good job everyone. Now let's spend the next ten minutes cleaning up before recess,' Melinda called out to the chattering class.

She began replacing the lids on the glaze buckets. Tables were wiped. Unfinished works shelved in damp cupboards. Students and carers filed out.

As Melinda closed the studio door she noticed that Kevin had made a good job of the light switch.

Chapter Nine

A deceitful Time had taken Kant by surprise, two months pocketed unseen. Preparations for the fourth series had been finalised, timetables drawn up, contingency plans set in place, and five episodes had successfully gone to air. BKS, an electric prod to a dozing populace, had once again activated fevered gossip and speculation around the country. And now Mackelroy was standing over Kant in his office with a slice-of-watermelon grin that he'd marched in with without knocking.

'I've been in contact with this extremely handsome woman. Well, actually, *she* introduced herself to me some time ago.'

'Aren't you the lucky one?' Kant replied.

'No, Sieve-Brain, remember our little chat a while ago? She was interested in meeting *you*. God knows why, ya prick, but there you go. She's clean … you know … I haven't … been *involved*.' He smirked. 'Some women prefer elderly men anyway.'

'So you've finally rounded up a *blind date* for me.'

'Well, don't sound so ungrateful. There's been a lot going on lately, if you hadn't noticed. And no, she can *see* perfectly well. Mind you, when she sees what a maudlin old bastard you can be she'll probably wish she *was* blind. And deaf.'

'Sorry, I didn't mean to be ungracious. I didn't think it

would happen that's all.' Kant took a deep breath. 'Okay, start again. That's wonderful news, James; who *is* she?' he asked with affected enthusiasm.

'As I say, she actually contacted me a while back, phoned the station. She phoned again this morning, assured me she wasn't a fanatical admirer but would be interested in having a drink and a chat with you. Popodopodopolis or some such Greek name.'

'How come you didn't tell me about her before?'

'You were on holidays. No doubt doing what most cantankerous old monks do in their spare time in the shadowed seclusion of their cloisters. Besides, if I told you about every female devotee who wanted a slice of you or was trying to get through yet another midlife crisis by ingratiating themselves into your personal life I wouldn't have time to scratch myself.'

'Thanks ... I think.'

Mackelroy smiled. 'And you'd better be careful; she's got style. You're going to have to smarten up your act, BK. Anyway, enough of this. I've invited her and some others to dinner next Thursday. Keep an eye on you that way,' he said, raising an eyebrow irreverently.

Kant remained fixed behind his desk, then began shuffling papers, trying not to look apprehensive. 'Thursday, you say? Isn't that a bit soon? Um ... clothes?'

'Yes, I'd suggest you wear some!'

'Ha ha.'

'Just come as *you*. Do you know who that is?'

Kant twitched his mouth sideways.

'Seven sharp, bring a bottle, and the rest will unfold.'

'Look, are you sure this is the way to go? I mean ... '

'Don't get all coy on me now. You've just put your spikes on the blocks. Now, get set ... and bang, *go* for the sprint.'

'Maybe I'm more the marathon type.'

'You've been trotting round in bloody circles for two years; you should be fully warmed up. Now just relax. It'll just be my unique home cooking, some fine wine, sweet dessert, some liqueur, brandy and maybe ... who knows?'

The prospect of an intellectual, maybe even a physical liaison, and more than just shaking hands with a new woman, activated a bevy of surface frissons around Kant's chest and belly, and then even lower.

'I feel like I'm sixteen again.'

'And your point is?' Mackelroy laughed. 'In that department most men *never* get past that age.'

*

Although Kant and Mackelroy hadn't socialised a great deal outside work Kant felt confident in Mackelroy's experience with women. But not only females – the first time he'd visited his house he'd presumed it would be ostentatious, showy, in keeping with his director's public manner. But on arrival he had been surprised at the thoughtfully managed sloping native garden which nestled naturally around the small but distinctive timber, hillside dwelling, giving, for some reason, the illusive Mackelroy greater substance and credibility in his eyes.

The house had been built out of celery-top pine some thirty years before, several split levels with open areas cleverly flowing in and around the more utilitarian spaces, the kitchen adjoined to one end of the living space. The ground floor walls were mainly ceiling to floor windows, the interior of the house cohabiting with the garden. Sliding doors opened up to a flagstone patio and the warmth of northerly light. From the side you could see up through the spindly foliage of casuarinas towards the Nelson lookout.

Kant remembered the distant hum of the city and harbour below, tugs and tankers, white yacht triangles in constant motion painting streaks across the Derwent River canvas. In the distance Mount Direction created a brooding, silhouetted hump on the horizon, and on a wall above a stone ingle an oil painting by the artist Lloyd Rees reflected this exact view. Mackelroy had told Kant he felt the exercise pointless when he'd brought it home from the gallery.

'If I want to have an image of that view I can just look out the bloody window!' he'd huffed.

In the end he justified his purchase by calling it an investment. The beautifully created Monet-like asset hung amongst an assortment of other artworks and artifacts collected from his personal overseas travels, and not, as he had adamantly assured Kant, conveniently picked up from the Importers' Emporium down the road.

Being single with a usefully disposable income Mackelroy, like Kant's friend Max, had spent a considerable amount of money buying paintings, prints, ceramics, and craft objects. But not always with a sound knowledge of what was good quality. Then gradually as the works began to crowd the spaces in his house he became more selective, reading and researching and reselling the works that did not move him in some way, or reflect his own empathies with life.

*

When Kant left the station it was drizzling. On his way home he diverted towards the Hill Street deli in West Hobart to buy some groceries. Sixteen-year-old guesswork about blind dates was still creeping around in his head. As he slowed to enter yet another new roundabout, inserted by obsessive town planners, *probably sent down from Canberra to upset the status quo*, he became aware of the squeak of rubber on the windscreen. The rain had stopped. He flicked off the wipers and turned the radio on to the ABC. Retired gardening guru Peter Cundall happened to be talking about his retirement and the fact that the word *retirement* was a misnomer.

Sarah had devoured his TV shows on gardening and used to joke that with his broad dialectal Northern English accent the show could have done with sub-titles. Now he was remonstrating that his life would only be retired when he was dead.

'I'll make grand compost, that's for sure. Think of all that nitrogen, right, from my unique brand of blood and bone,' he chuckled.

He couldn't imagine sitting around *waiting* for the inevitable to take him, 'like a withering cabbage that no one wants to pick, let alone eat. I don't smoke a pipe, I haven't got time to read the papers and I don't even possess a pair of slippers, right? But if you build up your compost in the autumn, right, then you can ... '

Kant's drifting thoughts into becoming a withering cabbage himself were suddenly terminated by his iPhone ringing. Pulling the car into the side of the road, he picked up his phone from the passenger seat.

'Kant here.'

'That Barry Kant?'

'That's me.'

The voice, a young man, sounded tense. 'From that telly show?'

'If you're referring to BKS then I am he, but cut to the chase, son. I'm on my way home to a warm cup of cocoa.'

The voice on the line seemed to find confidence at the sound of Kant's irritation.

'Hey, I don't like your fuckin' attitude, Mr Kant.'

Kant found himself replying to what was obviously an immature young man with something to get off his chest. There had been other calls to the station, not to mention the narky text messages. Usually young men who'd had a skinful and were showing off to their mates with Dutch courage. The fact he was being addressed as *Mister* confirmed this.

'Sorry to hear that. Now go and annoy someone else, okay?'

'Yer gunna be sorry. Yer think yer so fuckin' good on the telly. What's so fuckin' special about your show, faggot? You just wai ...'

Kant *didn't* wait for the rest of the tirade. He hung up, surprised he'd let the conversation go on as long as it did.

'Damn kids.' *Maybe I should change my Sim card. But ...*

His phone rang again. But before Kant could muster his thoughts the voice said, 'Eighteen dead. An' who's next?'

'Who is this?'

'Fourteen still missin'.'

'What are you on about? What's your point, son?'

'Up in them Queensland floods.'

Kant wasn't sure why he called this very annoying little shit *son*. There was something not quite authentic about the way he was speaking. There was definitely a threat amongst the confusing babble. He even felt slightly intrigued.

'No, I didn't know that. Do you want to tell me what this is about?'

'No, I fuckin' don't,' the voice yelled belligerently. 'People die all the time, just when they don't expect it. Like forty-two thousand people went missing after that Boxing Day tidal wave. And ...' Kant's heart rate had sped up, 'it makes you wonder when *youse* are gunna die ... Mister *Kunt.*'

Okay, enough's enough.

'Listen, sonny.' Kant fired back, jolts of adrenalin hammering at his chest. 'I haven't got time for this. Go and have a beer, smoke something settling, and if you want to get on my show, ring my producer at the station in the morning and tell *him* what a sorry little shit you are.'

Kant instantly regretted losing his cool, but before he could open his mouth to say something more insightful, conciliatory even, the voice cut him short.

'Or maybe Rosie who loves 'er faggot granddaddy so much.'

White noise filled Kant's head like the head-bursting bewilderment one might feel after a devastating tsunami. Chaos scrambled to make sense of what had happened in the last thirty seconds. Was he really being threatened? Was he about to be blackmailed? Sure, his show was hard-hitting emotionally for some people, but it was never a gratuitous probing of people's misery. They *wanted* to be on the show. They had the opportunity to earn some real money, turn their lives around even. *Or could they?* He wasn't sure anymore. And to exacerbate his rising anxiety, the ethical nature of BKS was something that had been scratching at the sides of Kant's conscience recently. He felt disturbed by this intrusion. *Is Rosie really in danger?*

'Yeah, that shut you up, didn't it? ... You still there, faggot?'

Kant hung up without replying. He thought of switching his iPhone off but some part of him didn't want to miss anything that might be crucial. He'd always made his mobile number accessible to the public so he didn't feel he was locked away in some celeb's ivory tower. But now, all he could hear ringing in his mind was the sweet voice of his granddaughter saying, 'Rosie loves Gampa', over and over.

He placed the iPhone in the breast pocket of his suit and opened the glove box. He flicked on his gold lighter, the one he'd bought on a brief sojourn with Sarah five years ago from a blind hawker on a beach in Bali, who swore on his mother's life it was solid gold. He jammed a cigarette into his mouth, lit it and inhaled deeply. He was sure the guy had been faking his limp too. Kant had morbidly given up the smokes after Sarah's death but he hadn't *quite* got round to throwing that last packet away. He got out of the car and leaned against the side. The smell of damp bitumen piqued his nostrils. The smoke provoked a spasm of coughing.

Kids play pranks all the time. Melinda had amused him with a few anecdotes from school, he tried reassuring himself, but he felt troubled by a niggling question.

How does he know about Rosie?

A tight fist had clamped on his stomach. He'd felt a similar grip on his being as he'd watched helplessly the pale vestiges of Sarah's life gradually fade.

Kant knew all about oddballs under the radar, sideways-looking loners and angry victims of a cruel world; the show thrived on their company. BKS beamed the heart-wrenching intimacies of family destruction and loss, incest and suicide to an insatiably gloating and anorexic public that surely must despise itself so much it was prepared to habitually feast on the sorrows of others, confident it would make them sick to the stomach, if not the heart.

As a presenter, rule number one had been – don't get

personally involved, he wasn't their therapist. The contestants consented to have their personal humiliations, their anger, their grief broadcast to half the country, then to be perversely voted by the public to be the most humiliated or powerless, the most down-trodden and wretched so they could pack their pockets with cash at the end of the series. It would be easy money, a quick cure for all their woes. They'd be able to squeeze through the railings surrounding paradise with their tarnished souls, stuffed with enough dollars to save them.

On some nights, still haunted by Sarah's death, Kant fantasised with bitter delight about applying to be a contestant himself. He knew the studio boom-man would put his hand up to interview him. He also knew only too well that a recklessly extravagant car, a desirable waterfront apartment, fame and ample money to spend had not worked as an antidote for his sorrow. They had merely emphasised his inability to find true happiness within himself.

Kant breathed in deeply. This phone exchange had become too personal with the mention of Rosie's name. The intruder had violated the sanctity of his family's domain.

The iPhone rang again. The vibration in Kant's chest added to the trembling sensation he was already experiencing, and reminded him of the fright he'd had just before that *minor* stroke last year. His doctor had tilted his head and said, 'Which bit of *slow down* don't you understand, Barry?'

So Kant *did,* had to. He changed his diet, took to the gym, started jogging, and he'd been feeling much healthier as a result.

He put the phone to his ear. The young man's voice had taken on a more vicious tone, but ludicrously, and like a bad dream, as if he was channelling a Capone-like wise-guy.

'Hang up on me again and she's a gonna.'

'Okay, take it easy,' Kant replied with exigent self-control. 'What is it exactly that you want?' Nothing had been demanded so far, just a rant.

'I'll ask the questions, tough guy. Next time I phone, youse had better be ready to do as I tell ya. Or the little girl gets it,' he finished with a sneer. 'And don't worry, faggot, I'll find her.'

The phone went dead.

Rosie was the only person in Kant's life whom he could describe as untainted by the darker forces of humanity that had become the backbone of his show. This, of course, made her utterly vulnerable. He didn't want to imagine how he would feel, or Melinda and Mungo for that matter, should something unimaginable happen to her. He suddenly felt the horror of him being the one responsible. Rosie reminded him of those hallowed days at the cottage where he and Sarah had conceived Melinda, the blush of apple blossoms carpeting the Huon Valley as they lay in the grass by the pond, the warm spring sunlight tantalising their nakedness. And years later, after Melinda had given birth to Rosie, she reminded her father that 'love is the most powerful force on the planet'.

'Not weapons of mass destruction, military muscle, or under-cover terrorist cells. *They* don't make the earth spin smoothly. It's the influence of love, Dad. So simple I don't know why they don't bottle it for all the heads of state, company CEOs and politicians. And it's just a human feeling. Imagine if everyone drank from that bottle, Dad,' she had said, filled with a young mother's rapt love for her child. 'One drop and we'd all breathe the fresh air of peace.'

Now what? Should I tell Mel and Mungo? I don't even know what he wants. Oh look, it's just a prank and he'll be happy now he's got it off his chest. But what exactly did he get off his chest? I bet he sent those texts.

'If I get hold of you I'll wring your damn neck,' Kant muttered to the ground, deciding the best course of action was to talk to Melinda tomorrow evening, see where it went tonight. Better to be forewarned should there be a more sinister connivance at work.

The sun had well and truly sunk behind the mountain now: a bloodshot hue sharpening the silhouetted ridgeline, a jagged demarcation between here and an uncertain tomorrow.

Kant felt chilled.

A short-haired, short-legged dog trotted up, cocked a leg against the front car wheel and loped off, oblivious to the owner's inner turmoil.

Kant began reflecting on the people who'd been distraught on his show. It was pretty much everyone. But they made sure people were informed in pre-show interviews of the potentially harrowing nature of the show. Of course, some were stronger, more resilient; some were even grateful for the opportunity to finally have someone listen to them.

More likely the caller would be a friend or family member of one of the contestants, at home in front of the telly, angry at what the show had flaunted on National TV. Maybe he'd been reminded of some dark deeds in his own past, spurred on by guilt or hostility. *Maybe. But who?*

Kant was the Presenter, the Front Man, the Host with the face and manner that put people at ease, put their trust in. He was perfect for the job. People felt safe in his company. But once, earlier on, he had misjudged a personality, missed something vital about their background, not out of vindictiveness though, or trying to milk their emotions. But *this* threat, if that's what it was, weighed on him.

Towards the end of the first series he had quipped to Carol Macey, the troubled grandmother, that she could suck her thumb as a substitute for smoking eighty cigs a day. It was a soft liner, meant to be a lighthearted alternative to inhaling gallons of tar and toxic chemicals into her decaying lungs. Carol had been brought onto the show primarily because of her age. She had been almost fifteen when she'd given birth to her daughter Janis, who'd been fourteen when she'd given birth to *her* daughter Missy. Carol had been looking after her granddaughter since Janis had abandoned 'the little one' on her mother's doorstep before shooting through to Western Australia to start all over again.

But Kant's remark had backfired. He had regretted his comment for weeks after. Of course, Mackelroy had congratulated him on his ratings winner.

'Can't script that sort of direction; it's tough but we're not in it for the soft touch,' he'd said in Kant's office after the show. It was true but Kant struggled inside with what must have appeared to the viewers around the country as gratuitous insensitivity.

'It's 'ard to quit,' Carol had replied through crackling sobs, 'since Janis' fella 'anged 'iself in the garden. See, he'd untied the rope from the tyre jus' after he'd ... *tampered* with little Missy. The smoke makes me 'ead fuzzy 'n' that, so's I can't feel nothin'.'

Kant remembered himself being in that space of not wanting to feel. Never would he forget the scraping anxiety he'd experienced as he'd looked down at his wife's lifeless face, the creeping agony usurping control of his own body, his mind and his heart. And here, on his show, they weren't in the business of putting people down. *Life* had already done that. Underneath the rawness of betrayals and so much neglect was the hope that people could find resolution, closure, even forgiveness within themselves, and hope. And Kant would be their guide. That had always been his motivation.

Why hadn't he been informed about this 'aspect' of Carol Macey's life, this rape of her grandchild? Seething inside to be put in such a position where he didn't have complete knowledge, Kant had almost lost control of the interview, jeopardising, he thought, any hope that the show might somehow encourage self-reflection out there in the burbs-TV-land.

The poor woman had been accepted for the show, hoping to

win some sympathy cash for being unemployable and habitually depressed, but not just that, a simpleton. Mackelroy loved her kind: the hapless kind who didn't know that others were laughing *at* them instead of *with* them. When Carol had been born her umbilical cord had all but strangled her, then she was abandoned in a supermarket car park two days later by *her* acid-infused mother, now herself part of a miserable cycle of neglect.

A bevy of abusive phone calls self-righteously demanded Kant's resignation. His callousness was un-Australian. But Mackelroy reassured him these people would be tuned in next week, eyes glued, feverish with anticipation and complacent about the bleakness of their own lives. From then on, the vetting and interview process had tightened so there would be no more similar repeats. Of course, the show's ratings had soared that week.

Kant twisted his head sideways till several vertebrae in his neck cracked. He got back into his car. Heavy drops of rain began to plop onto the windscreen before dispersing in an even flow, like the glass frontage of Victoria's biggest Fish 'n' Chip Shop – he couldn't help remembering Mungo's description of the frontage of the National Gallery in St Kilda Road.

Mist hovered amongst the grevilleas and small eucalypts in the park across the road. Kant had brought Rosie there only last weekend. She had often scampered in and out of the large concrete pipes and, with her grandfather's help, clambered around on the brightly painted train; times of such joy for both of them.

Kant rubbed the back of his neck, vacillating whether he should phone Melinda immediately about the call, but decided it was better to leave it for the time being in case the lad had more to get off his chest. Pushing the gear lever from park to drive, he eased the car back onto the road, and home.

The garage door closed behind him and the sensor lights automatically flicked on. He switched the engine off and slumped in his seat, trying to settle his thoughts. The apartment was on three levels including the garage. Stairs led up to the living space where another curved, open myrtle flight took you up to the bedroom and viewing area. Once inside, Kant looked out towards the water but couldn't take in what was there. His mind was humming like the extractor fan in the café below.

He poured himself a Scotch, a Tasmanian single-malt he'd been given last Christmas, extravagantly, he'd thought, by Dorothy at the station. He'd even speculated about whether she was secretly in love with him but soon realised it was just his vanity playing tricks on him. Hectically married with three kids, she was simply in love with what she perceived to be his freedom.

The flow of the golden liquid washed a soothing sensation through his mouth and throat. Opening the freezer he reached in for a frozen container of something Melinda had cooked for him last week, and put it in the microwave. He missed Sarah's cooking.

Kant moved back to open the balcony door and let his eyes

roam around the docks. A hunched elderly couple arm in arm wandered unhurriedly. A seagull perched atop a yacht mast. The microwave bell tinged. Emptying the contents into a bowl he began to eat, not knowing, or caring really, what it was. The chunky bits in the middle hadn't quite heated through. He mashed the food with his fork and continued eating.

His iPhone rang.

A spiky pang flicked through Kant's chest again before blossoming into a cherry-coloured anger.

'Listen, you little shit. I've had enough of this nonsense. If you …'

'BK, James here.'

Barry tried to laugh off his faux-pas. It only partially worked.

'Apologies, mate, I thought you were …' Kant grunted awkwardly. 'What can I do for you, James?'

'I meant to tell you before you left earlier. That Sudanese fellow you interviewed last week, I really do think we've got a champ. Boy, he comes across like some American rapper, cocksure attitude and he's got one hell of a story to boot. The public are going to love him. But I just wanted to let you know I booked him for tomorrow. I know it's late notice but.'

Mackelroy's 'buts' translated precisely to fait-accompli. A wizard with a manipulative tongue. Kant took a mouthful from the plastic container, still unsure what the solid bits were.

A light breeze had sprung up from across the water. Kant gave Mackelroy the answer he wanted, closed the balcony doors and pulled down the blind. He topped up his glass and sat at the kitchen counter with a folder he'd kept for press releases and articles cut from newspapers since the start of the show. The menacing phone call had inserted a sharp splinter deep under the fingernail of his family's soft touch. This was not what he'd signed up for.

'What the hell have we done?' he whispered as he opened the folder.

Had the whole thing got out of hand? He thought of the queues of prospective applicants, all swaddling their heart-wrenching stories, who had been turned away because diversity was an essential element of the programming, left to evaporate again, nameless and formless.

Maybe the caller is one of these, Kant speculated, pointlessly.

He could still remember what Mackelroy had said when they'd first met at the bar all that time ago.

'Success will come down to product variability. It's the first law of economics – supply and demand. Even all that gorgeous bad news is boring if it's repetitive.'

A jaundiced and unquenchable public had made sure of that.

Kant picked up a yellowing newspaper clipping. Jonathon de Saville, the Melbourne newspaper commentator, known for his eloquent diatribes, had accounted in *The Age* after the ratings of the second series had gone ballistic: 'The Island Variety Show of social collapse and humiliation, BKS, has moved away from the endless, predictable suburban sob stories that the shabby current affairs programs regurgitate. People still flock to be on the show after the first series has ended even though many of the previous contestants looked as if they had been mauled by tigers in the Coliseum by the end of filming. (A Mackelroy-fed press release analogy.) There are many people who don't just want to watch other people being mauled but want to experience the clawing themselves. We have to ask ourselves, is self-harm at epidemic proportions in our lucky country? Or is this yet another avant-garde form of social therapy? What exactly is going on over there?'

The mainland papers had had a field day, titillated by the antics down in the odd little island State.

'And once again in the history of Australia the name Tasmania has become synonymous with the phrase *'agony in paradise'*, it had been reported in an editorial in *The Australian* about social decline.

The *Sydney Morning Herald* editor had written: 'Australia's convict cul-de-sac of despair once again raises its ugly head. Just when the convict stain of degradation and ancestral shame appears to have been wiped clean by making convict lineage fashionable, there has been a dire revelation. Apparently, within the Tasmanian community, which, by all accounts exists in an ocean-washed Eden, there exists a frightening percentage of the populace who are victims of horrendous deeds in what appears to be a disintegrating society. These are the undetectables, damaged human beings that the rest of society wishes to ignore.

'Of course, these people exist in all cities of the nation, but somehow the revelation of this crawling underclass in the beautiful, compact island State, swarming with tourists, has been heightened by the parading of these sorry characters in the popular Barry Kant Show, broadcasting from inside the Tourist State. What marks this show as being unique in style is the large amount of money to be won, not by merit, or cleverness in any way, but by being judged by a studio audience and postal voters nationally to be a worst case scenario.'

Kant closed the folder.

Only a month of work and already he was feeling the tug of fatigue. Since the interview with John Sturges, the man's resigned pain still echoed. There was something about his dignity that seemed to conceal the real torment in his life. Kant had signed John Sturges on for the last time-slot of the season. To put someone after him might somehow demean his senior standing; his story had moved Kant in a way that he hadn't felt before with other contestants. *The inevitable poisoned crown of thorns,* he winced. *Sleep now.*

Chapter Ten

A jumpy little goateed guy in jeans and red Mambo tee-shirt, the one with a dog farting out a single black crochet, was earning his wage by revving up the ductile studio audience into frenzied applause. He waved his arms excitedly, cracking undergraduate jokes, running up and down in front of the tiered seating, then calming and hushing with slow downward hand movements before repeating the performance. He could have been conducting Wagner's Tannhauser Overture. He'd never had such power in his life before.

'Okay, thrill seekers, when the music starts you go ape-shit. But when it starts to go quiet, so do you. Even you lot can handle that,' he said, his tone just missing the subtlety between humour and scorn.

Mackelroy scanned this procedure closely from his director's glassed-in viewing room. Some thoughts he kept to himself. Each cameraman, and even Kant, had a tiny earpiece fitted, into which Mackelroy could direct proceedings at will. Although with Kant he rarely used it, allowing his Main Man control of the rudder during the interviews.

The BKS theme music began to play, and a hundred and twenty Pavlovian audience dogs started to applaud, drooling with expectation. Mambo-Dogman was in his element. The lights shifted through a sequence of changing colours before settling on a warm orange glow, oscillating through the program, to give added drama to the unfolding story. Barry Kant's voice, resonant and alluring, floated above the music as the volume faded.

'Evening vampires, looking good tonight. And tonight, a real treat on … ' small predicted pause for the dogs to catch up, 'BKS!' The crowd erupted with self-conscious cheers, applauding at the mere mention of the famous acronym. A now-beaming Dogman fantasised they were cheering for him.

'We have as our guest a man with an extraordinary tale to tell. Nothing unusual about this guy when you look at him … well, maybe a little darkness of the skin shows him up a bit in this pasty-faced city of southern blasts. Am I starting to rave?'

The audience yelled back impatiently, 'Yes!'

'Imbeciles think they're at a bloody pantomime,' Mackelroy muttered to his smirking technician, who dined on his boss's cynicism. He'd become really quite overweight.

'Please welcome Mister Liri Mogamba.'

Since Vince MacLean had plucked Liri off the steps of the GPO in the depths of a frozen morning, the Sudanese man, barely twenty, seemed to have developed a theatrical and self-confident manner. Or maybe, as Kant speculated after he had interviewed him it was simply his nature. The lad had openly enthused about the possibility of a hundred grand in his pocket.

'Mind you, he would have been pleased with a hundred

bucks,' Kant had confided to Dorothy in the canteen after the initial interview.

From the side of the stage, and with the cocky attitude of the streetwise, Liri loped towards Kant with an ivory grin. His slim, tall body was home to oversized, unlaced basketball shoes, baggy trousers, the legs of which were covered in fashionably superfluous pockets with numerous zips and buttons. On top he wore a baseball cap backwards and sloppy tee-shirt containing the monogram NYC. He flopped into the easy chair opposite Kant, his shiny mahogany head bobbing gently as if music was pulsing in his ears. Surely he'd just arrived from downtown Bronx to promote his latest world tour – Cool on the Street.

Kant welcomed Liri and his beaming smile, a smile that belied the horrifying events that had forged themselves into the psyche of this newly arrived refugee. Rows of faintly raised scars, the result of a tribal coming-of-age ritual, lined his forehead and cheeks.

Backstage, ten minutes before, Kant had prepped Liri on the general form of his interview.

'Wait for my questions, relax, look at the audience occasionally, no need to be nervous. They will be fascinated by your story. I will guide you through it so don't worry if you think you might forget something. You're in safe hands now.'

'Okay, man, cool.'

On stage, between the audience and the interview chairs, three cameras on wheeled tripods, gliding sharks just beyond the surf break, positioned themselves for every eventuality, panning and zooming in at a moment's notice. Several omni-directional microphones hung from wires above the audience and one hung above and between Kant and Liri: highly sensitive apparatus, the country would not miss a heartbeat.

One of Kant's fortes was pre-visualisation. Through the first three series he'd become highly attuned to fluctuating displays of human reactions, predicting these as each cathartic point in the interview was reached. Kant and Mackelroy had discussed the importance of the body's symptoms of stress as an integral part of the final TV presentation. Close-ups of rigidly raised shoulders, fidgeting fingers, flitting eyes, facial tics, and of course the tears, would be filmed exclusively by one camera, this intimacy being edited into the mix for maximum impact on the small television screens in the suburban homes of ratings land.

Kant lingered, increasing expectancy, before leaning amiably towards his guest.

'How ya doin', Liri?' he began. *Keep it light, street vernacular, to put the young man at ease*, he'd decided. Not that he needed to.

'Yeah, good, man.'

Liri's voice was resonant for someone with such fine body structure. He fiddled with his cap as he tried to remember what Kant had said to him backstage earlier.

The audience had become pin-drop silent.

'He won't bite, you know,' Kant quipped, allowing the

voyeuristic, bloodless faces a chance to relieve their own tension with a snort or a titter.

One of the side cameras spun around panning and zooming in on the eager faces. Liri was the first dark-skinned man to appear on the program. Africans were still a novelty around Hobart, so many of the single young men had headed off to Melbourne or Sydney looking for work. Liri leaned back in his chair and folded his hands behind his head.

'Now, Liri, this audience ... they don't get out much, so would you tell them a few things about your life in Sudan first?'

'Okay. Er ... you mean about my home?'

'Yes, how about you start with that.'

'Okay. My village was small and we were all friendly to each other.' Liri smiled. 'Well, you know what brothers can be like. My father was a hunter. He was gone for days sometimes because the animals were far away from the village. I had lots of friends and we played a lot in the water holes. It was very hot and the water was cool.'

'What was village life like?'

'Yeah, it was good. Everybody helped each other. We didn't have television like here in Australia. Sometimes we made things, like toy cars made out of wire we could push along the ground, with a steering wheel and turning wheels. That stuff was just normal. My mother was a good cook and my father always brought healthy animals to eat. I went with him when I was old enough. We grew pumpkins and corn.' He shrugged.

'Of course, we had to go to school. It was a simpler life but … like, we were happy.'

'Sounds idyllic. But things changed because of the war. Then you were sent to a government military camp. Is that right?' Kant looked out to the audience … paused. He opened his mouth to speak but closed it again.

Liri looked hesitant, then nodded.

'Liri, a long time ago in Australia we had conscription into the army to fight in the Vietnam War. You had to be twenty-one years old, and you were trained for a year, in a military school, before you were sent into action. Would you tell the audience what process you went through?'

'I was thirteen, well nearly. I was tall for my age. My brothers were too little.'

'Are you saying that you were thirteen, twelve really, when you decided to train to become a soldier? Boy, when I was twelve I was still in short pants wondering where my next ice-cream was coming from.'

Liri smiled. 'I didn't decide, man. The soldiers came to my father's hut in the night and I was grabbed and put into the back of a truck.'

'In the dark?'

Liri laughed. 'Yeah, man. It was the middle of the night! We were all asleep.'

'Of course, silly me.'

And as if he was describing an outing to the local park, Liri continued. 'The truck was full with other boys from my village and we were taken to the training camp in the desert.'

'You told me earlier it was two weeks away. That's a long way from home.'

'No, that was how long it took me and my friends to walk home after we ran away. We had to hide a lot.'

'I see. Liri, may I say, your English is very good.'

'Thank you. I learned in the Christian school where we were taught lots of stuff.'

'Yes, you did tell me that you also have a Christian name, Ishmael.'

Liri nodded.

'I researched the name and to my surprise I learned that Ishmael was the son of Abraham, your other Christian name. But it also means *outcast*. After what's happened to you, being exiled from your homeland, do you still have faith ... you know, in God?'

Liri looked uneasy. 'I still have a bible ... somewhere.' Several people in the audience began a half-hearted clap, which died out; no doubt they were unsure why they felt the need to applaud. 'I do think of Him sometimes.'

'What do you think, when you think of Him, Liri?'

Liri twisted his head around, stretched his neck, uncomfortable with the question – it wasn't one he had talked about previously in the preliminary interview with Kant. For Kant it was always important to keep one or two unrehearsed questions up his sleeve so the interviews maintained an edge. Kant suspected that deep inside this young man there must be a burning heart, having been abandoned by this supposed, all-powerful Being, who he had sung praise to in church in Sudan and later in the refugee camp in Uganda, plucking at the strings of his adungu. Kant had heard so many previous contestants talk of God just standing by, looking heartlessly at the devastation around them. He'd ignored the plight of Liri's parents and millions like them, and had since done nothing to help his siblings to escape the hellish camp in Uganda, making it impossible for the family to reunite.

'I'm wondering if God might have sacrificed his authority in Africa,' Kant said.

'Sometimes I…I think he's looking somewhere else,' Liri said nervously as if God might be watching this one time, taking notes. 'It's a big world and He's probably been busy,' he added, giving the benefit of the doubt to his God for His apparent ruthless indifference.

Audience titters reflected his uncertainty.

'Why did you run away? And tell us what happened after you got home?'

Liri smirked as if he was about to tease Kant, twisted his head sideways and asked, 'Have you ever killed anybody, Mr Kant?'

'No.'

'Nor have I, but I have seen many many dead people.' Liri looked at the floor. 'So many. The rebels use machetes as well as guns. Everywhere was like a butcher's shop. But I just couldn't use a rifle to kill another person no matter what they had done. It's one of God's commandments. Me and my friend Joshua, we ran away a few days after we arrived. The soldiers there, they had no hearts. Some of the young kids thought the war was just a game. Joshua got weak and became ill. We couldn't find food. A week later he died of a fever. The heart can become fragile with so much death. I found him in the morning when I woke up. He looked peaceful. We'd slept in a cave. I covered his body with stones and I prayed.'

'What did you feel then?'

'What could I feel? But I was still alive and I wanted to stay living,' Liri continued, not wanting to dwell on yet another pointless death that had become so much part of his existence. 'When I got back to the village my mother and father hid me, up in a hill behind, and when the soldiers came later to the village my parents refused to say where I was. They said they hadn't seen me.'

'So they left?'

'They took my parents to prison to question them.'

Kant waited.

'They were tortured and they died there.'

Liri's words did not result in an anguished crumple at the memory, which would have earned him valuable sympathy from viewers glued to their TV screens. His articulation of such unimaginable horror for a young man was expressed with matter-of-fact simplicity, seemingly devoid of agitation. Or maybe so much violent disregard for human life had become so subsumed into his way of life that it was no more significant than another rainy day. But Liri's stoicism and apparent ambivalence weren't what the Barry Kant Show was about. Where, after all, was his visible public ventilation of tortured suffering? Plain and simple, it was the fulfilment of the vampires' craving for spilled blood that would put Liri one step closer to winning the prize.

Kant paused to give the studio audience time to embellish their individual pictures of potential torture scenarios. One of the cameras zoomed in on Liri's face. After one particular inebriated late night discussion with Vince, Kant's eyes had been opened to the cruelty one human being is capable of perpetrating on another.

'Do you miss them, your parents?'

Liri frowned, raised his shoulders, incredulous of the question. 'Yeah man, of course.'

'Sure. I know I would if my parents were taken to Risdon prison here in Hobart and tortured to death.'

'Even if my parents had told the soldiers where I was they still would have been killed.'

'Never to taste your mother's cooking again, or see them smile again. How does that make you feel, Liri? Did you want to take revenge?' Kant knew he was sailing close to the wind, but he was well aware of the rules of play. It didn't stop him feeling uncomfortable though.

Liri lowered his head.

When he finally looked up, his eyes were smoldering, protective and defiant.

'There was no time for that!' His voice had sharpened. 'We have a custom in Africa, and I am the eldest son. When my father died I had to look after the family. There is no time for revenge. What would be the point?'

'How did you know they were dead? Did you get a letter from the government saying they were sorry, that regrettably your parents passed away whilst incarcerated?'

Liri scratched at an itch under in his armpit. Kant knew his tone sounded too facetious for such an extreme situation, but over the course of the program varying his questioning techniques so that the flow of discussion and answers didn't become predictable had become second nature.

'What is incarcer ... ay ... ?'

'To be put in prison.'

'Oh.' Liri twitched his head to one side, locked his fingers together, stretched his lithe ebony arms towards Kant and cracked his knuckles. He looked around at the audience. 'My English ... you know ... there is much I have to learn.'

'Your English is excellent.'

Kant took a sip of water from a glass.

'My young brothers and sisters came to get me from the caves, about a kilometre from the village, where I was hiding. They did not talk to me, but I knew. They just brought me to our parents' hut. They refused to come in. My sister Mary was crying a lot. I knew something terrible had happened. The soldiers had cut off my mother's head and had put it in her big cooking pot in the fireplace. My father's head was on the table. He was looking at her. Is *that* what you want to hear?'

A bespectacled young woman in the front row let out a strangled gasp, then becoming instantly horrified that the cameras were upon her like hyenas spotting a corpse, she endeavoured to stifle her sobbing with her arm. Now Kant needed to maintain the momentum. Liri's last comment showed strength, it was not the behaviour of someone crushed by his experience. If the prize money was to be within *his* grasp there would need to be more to show that his experience had somehow devastated him, because society had become numb, immune to the nightly TV tally of death around the world.

Kant knew that despite the horror of having one's parents' severed heads slung into the heart of one's home, the audience would not want to hold onto that thought for too long. Besides, it was just the sort of thing those savages did over there in Africa, that fearful, dark continent so far away from the safe tree-lined streets of picturesque Hobart. The audience wasn't there to give pity either. They were addicted to the thrill they received from experiencing someone else's agony, and like junkies they habitually craved an increase in the variety and potency of their fix.

Kant asked Liri about his adungu, the harp he had made himself when he'd arrived in Hobart, its base hand-carved from a solid block of timber. He talked of the joy he got from entertaining in a Hobart restaurant. But then Liri's head began to bob slightly as he looked around the studio audience and back to Kant, who was sipping water from his glass. While Liri leaned forward and reached for his own glass he whispered to Kant, 'These people think I'm a freak because I show I can be happy.'

This young man had been born into war. His life had been infused with an acceptability of death as a solution to life's problems – religion against religion, family against family and fear against fear.

Kant steered the conversation to the trek Liri had undertaken for several weeks, travelling only at night, leading his younger siblings, three boys and two girls, towards Uganda, to the prospect of safety in a refugee camp. He spoke of how they had constructed a small hut out of sticks and mud and had grown vegetables because after six months the free rations of rice that had been given to them would dry up. Liri told them of the random rebel cross-border skirmishes into the camp at night, targeting the slow for amusement.

'Liri, your brothers and sisters are still in Uganda, in that same refugee camp. Are they going to meet up with you soon? And can you explain why you are here and they are still there?'

'It was too dangerous for me to be staying. They will kill me because I ran away ... '

'So you were a marked man?'

'Yes. That is how I received permission to come to Australia.'

'But you told us about your custom of being the eldest son and looking after your siblings after your father dies. Your sisters, I believe, are still quite young. How can you protect them if you are here?'

Liri looked down and began rocking. Kant hadn't expected this; his heartbeat quickened.

The boy's raw, vulnerable wound, the real damage, had revealed itself.

It wasn't the blood and gore, the terrors of war or even the murder of his parents that stabbed cruelly at Liri's heart now, it was that he was now powerless to be 'father', protector and guide to his younger siblings. Whilst he was here in Hobart, out of harm's way, ensconced in one of the safest places on earth, his siblings were still cooped up in a foul and claustrophobic refugee camp, cut off from everything that was precious to them. So, how could he now look after them, as was his responsibility? How could he justify his own freedom?

'They *are* coming out to Australia too, aren't they? Soon, I would have thought,' Kant said, but remembering what Liri had told him in his first interview with him. But it was necessary to probe like this to give him, like all the other contestants, an equal opportunity to win.

There was anger, frustration in Liri's reply when he looked up, wiping glassy eyes. 'I had no choice! I would have been killed. The Australian Government said my family would soon follow if I came here. They *told* me! But when I got here they said I had to have $10,000 to pay for my family to follow. I had no job, I couldn't find work and…'

'Are you saying that the government expects *you* to pay this sum if you want to be reunited with your family?'

Liri's jaw began to clench in little pulses of anxiety.

'That was four years ago, but Mary, who's only thirteen, developed juvenile glaucoma but has now gone blind and I have been told by the government that it would cost too much to look after her here, so *none* of my family can come now. They were all put on the same immigration papers. My brother Samuel took Mary to see a ... ' Liri paused, 'a witch doctor, a few days' walk away from the camp. The doctor told her she must eat some herbs he gave her. But she got worse. I am told in Australia the doctors can cure glaucoma if it's treated soon. In the camp the toilets are very far from their hut and it is difficult for her to go there at night. It is very dangerous.'

Tears welled up in Liri's eyes again.

'When I arrived in Hobart I tried to get a job to raise the money. They sent me to a chicken factory first. I had to cut the throats of chickens all day! Was that a joke? It made me sick so I had to stop. They told me I was ungrateful for turning down a job. Now I try to earn money by playing my music. It's all I have left. I send my brother money sometimes so he can buy rice for them. But it costs me fifty dollars every time I use Western Union.'

'So are you saying that your family has been refused entry into Australia because of your sister's blindness?'

'Yes. Maybe I can talk to an immigration lawyer. Someone must be able to help. I have to find a way.' But there was defeat in voice.

Much as Kant felt the boy's agony, his frustration, his desperation, BKS was not a support service, and neither was it equipped legally to ask for donations. It was, after all, just another commercial television reality show vying for ratings.

'Liri, you are a remarkable young man and we wish you all the best with that. Maybe there's someone out there watching who can help you. But now we've come to the part of the show where the audience has a chance to ask you some questions. Hopefully straighten out some things that might be confusing to them. What do you think; are you up for it now?'

Recomposed, and as if he was a contestant on 'Who Wants to be a Millionaire', he said brightly, 'Yeah man, I'm ready.'

Farting-Dog-One-Note scurried up and down in front of the audience again as the program's theme music began to play. The lights went through a series of colourful changes before settling on a softer yellow hue. While the music played, the cameramen repositioned themselves, and Dorothy trotted out quickly from the wings to dab the two men's faces with tissues. Both had worked up quite a sheen. Kant leaned in towards Liri and asked if he was good to go. Liri nodded. He had replaced his cap and had sunk back at an angle in his chair, his legs outstretched.

The music faded.

'Righteo, let's go. You all know the drill. Introduce yourselves first. Make your questions clear and don't ramble on,' Kant instructed like a sergeant major.

A flurry of hands shot up. They waved and fluttered, frenzied faces squawking like an over-crowded nest of hungry chicks at the arrival of a fat worm. Dean Shorter, a skinny man with overly indulged sideburns, and who secretly fantasised about having what it takes to be the host of the show, held a boom rod with a microphone attached to the end. He had been given the authority to place the microphone in front of people of *his* choice. Swinging into action he was patently in a blissful state of self-importance.

The microphone hovered before the face of a gargantuan woman in her early forties. Dean unkindly envisaged seventeen cream donuts and coke for every meal. Sitting in the front row, pink track pants and white cotton top that was indecently tight, her strident, nicotine-infused voice snarled like a hostile pound dog.

'Yeah roight, me name's Joyce and I wanna know what Larry thinks 'bout...'

'Hi there, Joyce.' Kant cut in. 'It's good to have you on the show. But it's *Liri*, Joyce. Our guest is called Liri. Okay?'

'Yeah, oroight. Leary. What do youse think, *Leary*...' she repeated emphatically, 'bout 'obart, bein' black an' all?'

Kant groaned inside. Mackelroy rubbed his hands together. Liri smiled.

'It's a beautiful city, Kurramajong. But I am sorry to say it is a very cold place. Sudan is a very hot country. And as you say, I am black. But I'm sure you heard, black is beautiful.'

Applause from the audience. An uncomfortable head twitch from Joyce.

'It's cool too 'cos everyone thinks I'm an American basketballer.' Liri laughed. 'And as you know ... girls love basketballers, particularly black ones.'

Dog-Man didn't need to encourage laughter.

Joyce's blush was two shades darker than her track pants.

'Anyway,' Liri added as an aside, 'didn't there used to be black Tasmanians living here first?'

Joyce went silent, pretended invisibility. She wasn't sure. The question was beyond her.

'Liri's quite right, of course,' Kant spoke out into the audience, 'and maybe we've all been in utopian denial, but like so many barbaric acts in the history of the world we've perpetrated our own genocide on those very people, the black Tasmanians, as Liri calls them.'

For the next ten minutes the quality of the questioning didn't alter.

Kant was making movements to wrap it up when a hefty man in his late twenties stood up and yelled narkily from the back row. A three-day growth shadowed his pinched and pallid face and cavernous chin dimple. His complexion looked as if it would benefit from some sunshine, and a hearty meal with greens.

'Youse ought'a be bloody grateful. How come you come 'ere and start complaining…'

'What's your name, buddy?' Kant called out over him. 'But please, just wait till we can get the microphone to you.'

Boom-Man-Dean, momentarily flustered by not being already there, stepped closer, arms outstretched. Some heads, 'family' no doubt, around the man at the back were nodding, working up some of their own hostility.

'Yeah, g'day Barry, Moik's the name.'

Mike was clearly agitated, kept looking sideways at his friends, needing their approval for his bigotry.

'If you're gunna whinge, cobber, ya know where youse can go? We got people 'ere who you're taking jobs from, so if ya don't like it, ya know what you can do. And if you ain't got no job how come ya wanna bring all ya fu…, ya brothers and sisters out 'ere? What are they gunna do, eh? Take more jobs? My old man worked thirty years in a poultry farm an' 'e never complained about nothin'. Never. If ya don't like it 'ere, mate, ya know where youse can go.'

Unfriendly-Mike sat down, twitching with awkwardness. It was his debut on National television. But his hostile, repetitive tirade had lost impetus amongst the rising buzz of audience impatience.

Something inside Liri's chest buzzed like a chainsaw. He'd seen this man before, a few weeks ago. And how could he forget that voice, that cruel sneer.

Nasty Moik had been in the gang of shaven-headed men who had been encouraging Liri to keep drinking at the pub.

Drink up buddy, mate, they'd cajoled.

Some friends at last, Liri had thought. But he'd passed out in the back of the dirty 4x4 after they had tossed him in. The journey to the hills had been a blank. There'd been a hut with animal pelts nailed to the wall, smoky. The dirt floor reminded him of home, back in Sudan. After a kicking they'd dragged him down into a gully, dumped him under the dense canopy of man-ferns by the creek and urinated on him, in the country where he thought he'd found a refuge from hatred.

'If I could just say something first, Liri – sorry to interrupt again,' Kant smiled at the African and looked out into the audience. 'Mike, a statement of fact about feeling the cold I don't believe is a *criticism* of our pleasant city of Hobart. You know, I've known locals bang on about the weather till they're blue in the face. Good Lord, there wouldn't be anybody living here if we shipped off everyone who complained about the cold. I, for one, think the weather's appalling, so there goes me!'

Kant gestured to his guest with raised eyebrows. Liri, who remained unfazed and amused by Kant's rant, chuckled loudly.

'This is more like it,' Mackelroy said to his technician, eyes fixed on the game.

'Hobart's a good place to be, man,' Liri replied, dipping one shoulder and splaying the fingers of both hands like a dance pose. 'And refugees have no choice about where they are sent. I could have been sent to Norway, so I'm pretty lucky. And *most* people are very welcoming here,' Liri added, shifting his cap slightly and smiling boldly at his accuser.

Good note to finish on, Kant thought.

'Well, our time's up. Thanks, Liri, for coming on the show. Thanks also to the studio audience, the stage crew and of course, all of you at home.'

Dog-Farting-Man jogged up and down waving his arms.

'Don't forget to SMS your votes; the numbers are on the bottom of the screen. See you next week with another extraordinary tale. And remember, it's your considered choice that could help one of the contestants over the next few weeks to *cash up,* one hundred grand it is now, and hopefully turn something important around in their lives. This is Barry Kant saying good night to you all.'

The lights dimmed. The theme music swelled. The audience filed out. Off stage as Dorothy handed Liri a coffee, four sugars, Mackelroy swooped in patting Liri on the back.

'Well done, son. You did well.'

'Thanks, man. Maybe you'll come hear me sing one night at Afritas where I play on the weekends.' He smirked cheekily. 'I'll tell the man on the door to let you in for free.'

'Now *there's* an offer I can't refuse,' Mackelroy said.

'Tell me, Liri,' Kant said. 'You called that woman, Joyce, the first questioner, something. Kurra something or other. What did you mean?'

Liri chuckled to himself. 'At home, out in the wild country, the desert, there is a tribe of nomads; they just wander around. They are ignorant of modern life and uncultivated like cavemen. We use their name, Kurramajong, like you use the word *old bastard* in Australia. It can be a friendly name, like *g'day you old bastard*, but it can also be a true description of someone. You can choose.'

Kant and Mackelroy nodded to each other, keeping their mouths shut. True professionals. For the moment.

Liri disappeared into the warm evening air, clutching a fifty-dollar note that Kant had given him from his own pocket to buy some groceries. Liri's bouncy gait showed no symptoms of the malaise he found himself in, cut off from his life in Africa, powerless to support his siblings, and stuck in a strange culture where his experience of genuine acceptance was a thin veneer.

Chapter Eleven

Message received popped up on the screen of Kant's iPhone as he was tapping in Melinda's number so he could talk to her about the menacing call. With an index finger swipe of the glass he saw it was his father on voice mail, urgent, fretful, just like all the other annoying times. 'Barry… Barry… Barry, are you there? Barry? Can you come over? Barry, are you there? I need you to come over.'

Barry pressed speed-dial to his father's landline number.

These days Desmond Kant had no sense of time, phoning his son at any hour of the day or night with the most absurd news or demands. The last was only a week ago, at four in the morning, when he couldn't sleep, wanting his son to pick up some new washers for the bathroom taps for God's sake!

'Yes it's me, Dad. You phoned earlier.'

'Barry? That you, Barry?'

'Yes, Dad, of course it's me. But I've only just got home. It's been full on at work. Now I need to relax. How 'bout I bring lunch round tomorrow? We can have a chat then, eh?'

'I'm going to die soon – reckon it could be tonight, son.'

Not this again. Kant cricked his neck. *What's the old buzzard up to?*

The canny old bugger had still managed to go swimming at

the Glenorchy pool once a week during the summer, and still had plenty of zest for ogling bikini-clad adolescents.

'What's got into you, Dad? You said that *last* week. You're as fit as a bloody mallee bull, and knowing *you*, you'll probably outlive me.'

'I got a feeling, that's all.'

'Yes, I get that feeling at the end of every week. Cameramen who think they're Fellini, egos bigger than Ben Hur's dick, and now I think I'm having threatening phone calls from some brazen little shit. Probably one of your neighbours,' Kant spewed out crossly.

'How d'you know?'

'What, that I'm being threatened or that they're one of your neighbours?'

'I suppose we could talk about it over the phone, son, but it'd be good to see you. I might not have much longer.' He stuttered a pert little cough for extra effect.

'Oh, for heaven's sake, Des!'

'I suppose if you're too tired then I'll just have to ... ' another cough, 'I just hope that ... '

'I *can't* tonight. Okay? I have to see Mel. I have to deal with something that really *is* important. I'll drop round tomorrow.'

'What's happened? She been robbed?' he asked, his curiosity momentarily overruling his impending demise.

'No. Where d'you get that from anyway?'

'Oh well,' the old man managed to utter, an expert in performing self-absorbed disappointment, finding it inconceivable that there might be something that could take precedence over his immediate need for attention. 'I'll just have to be on my own then.'

'All right, all right. You can stop the act. If it's not too late, I'll come round after I've seen Mel. There's nothing I'd rather do. And God dammit, you'd better bloody well be dying this time!' Kant voiced with frustration. He shook his head with disbelief then breathed deeply.

Kant looked at his new stretch-out easy-chair, flown over from Melbourne's fashionable Prestigios, the consummate Italian furniture design centre in Prahan: laminated timbers, steam-curved for the ultimate postural comfort, lined with the most body-friendly foam composite and secondary layering of down wadding. The velveteen upholstery fabric, with its warm-hued geometric shapes, could caress his weary body into deep slumber in minutes. But not this evening.

'You're a good boy, Barry.'

'And you're a pain in the arse, Des.'

Kant called his father by his first name whenever he thought he was being unreasonable, which seemed to be most of the time these days. Of course, Desmond thought his son was being pally and felt warmed by this alternate familiarity. Desmond had called his son Jeffrey on a couple of occasions earlier in the year. Kant hadn't been too concerned. The doctor had said his father was fit enough for someone in their eighties, no onset of dementia or Alzheimer's, 'just a bit absentminded' he'd said in that casual-doctory-sort-of-way. But then, the exasperating old man wasn't the doctor's own father, was he?

Turned out that there *was* a bloke called Jeffrey, a pest exterminator who'd come round to spray the place a while back.

'You got ya'self a regular zoo 'ere, Mr Kant,' he'd said, whistling his surprise, 'what with the silver fish, moths and cockroaches. Some pretty 'ealthy-lookin' rodents too. But I'll kill 'em, too easy. After today, your 'ouse'll be as still as a nun's naughty.'

Desmond Kant lived only a couple of blocks away from Melinda and Mungo in Lutana. You could just about run the distance on one breath. He had moved there with his wife Patricia back in nineteen-fifty when the bouncing boy Barry was born. Kant senior secured the empty block next door soon after and filled it with veggies, berries and fruit trees, a veritable garden 'like that one in the bible', his wife'd say. But when Patricia died the whole yard was concreted over. A sickly, yellow-leafed lemon tree was the only sign of life now, trying vainly to make an existence for itself, by itself, in rock-hard dirt held together by a pile of tread-bare car tyres.

A creek used to trickle past the garden at the back. Its weedy banks too had been concreted back in the sixties. These days, under-age motor bikers and BMXers gathered there at weekends for tricks and turns. Bit of drinking, dope too.

'Dopey bastards,' Kant's father used to call them. For his own amusement.

Further up under a large derelict culvert, needles, perishing rubber straps, tarnished spoons and other druggy detritus were mindlessly scattered around.

'They found a kid there couple a years back. Dead she was

from some overdose of whatever it was they took then. Lying on the edge with her head flopped over into the drain she was, just as if she was having a drink. Mind you the stuff that comes down that rivulet was probably enough to kill 'er anyway,' Des had said chattily when Barry had visited once with Rosie.

Barry had reprimanded him. 'Your great-granddaughter doesn't need to hear all this.'

'Council needs to fence it off or something. Dunno what the world's coming to.'

'It's bad enough she lives amongst it. She certainly doesn't need to hear *your* running commentaries, Dad.'

'She's going to find out about the world soon enough – may as well be now.'

Kant had changed his clothes, subconsciously dressing down to go to Lutana. Tapping his daughter's quick-dial number he waited. It only rang once before Melinda answered. Once Rosie was down for the night the cordless phone in the bedroom was usually kept within arm's reach.

'Hello.'

'Mel, it's Dad.'

Melinda gushed, full of concern. 'Oh Dad, I've just heard. Are you all right? What's happened? You aren't hurt are you?'

'Whoa, slow down, darling. Nothing's happened to me and I'm fine. That stupid old grandfather of yours been on the phone to you, has he? I could wring his damned neck sometimes.'

'So you're okay? The way he spoke it sounded serious.'

'Always does. Old fool's just angry because I wouldn't go round to see him at the drop of his hat. He makes it up as he goes along. But look, there is something I need to talk to you and Mungo about. Can I come round now?'

'Sure, Mungo should be here by the time you arrive.' There was a pause. Barry waited. He knew what was coming. 'Dad, are you sure there's nothing wrong? Granddad said you'd been threatened. Have you?'

'It was just a strange call, that's all. I think it was just a practical joke from a kid. I've had them before, but it's best to be aware.'

Melinda relaxed. 'Same. I have to constantly be on the ball with what my rabbits are getting up to.'

'Rabbits?'

'Tell you later. I'll put the kettle on.'

The litany of brainless practices her students got up to on a regular basis flashed through Melinda's mind, but there was never anything she couldn't handle. Mostly they were just bored, and a good telling-off was all the attention they needed.

Fifteen minutes later Kant was locking his car just as Mungo turned up, a large plume of silvery exhaust billowing behind as he glided in towards the kerb. Kant watched the fumes disperse noiselessly into the cul-de-sac like a light-footed burglar.

'Evening squire. To what do we owe this unexpected pleasure at our hovel?'

'You know me. I like to keep up with current affairs in the badlands. See how the peasants are faring.'

'So you haven't come round to look after Rosie so Mel and I can have a night out sans enfant?' Mungo grinned. 'That means without her highness.'

'Definitely on the cards, but not tonight, I'm afraid. There's something I wanted to pass by you and Mel.'

'Sounds intriguing. If it's about a wheelbarrow load of cash you've just found, then the answer's yes, we'd love it. Even half would be fine!'

'Sorry, you're still going to have to work for it. Now, come and fetch me a glass of your hardest liquor.'

Barry's lighthearted barb wasn't lost on Mungo. He pretended ignorance, and deafness. Inside he longed for the time he would earn more money as a musician, and fought down his frustrations at Barry's attitude that he was a useless bread winner.

The house was warm. Music played: an African woman singing in rich, dark tones imbued with the struggles within a harsh landscape, accompanied by a Kora, the gourd harp. The melody fell soothingly from two speakers hooked high up on one wall in the living room, two things Mungo *didn't* want Rosie to fiddle with. She'd already poked holes in the paper cones of one set with her inquisitive fingers.

The singer's voice, uplifting and proud despite the starkness of life, seeped into Barry's body. It didn't take much to impel him back to the mountains in Crete these days. The soulful Cretico songs he and Sarah had listened to during those ouzo evenings at the kaffeneon in Piskochefalon all those years ago had recently been making a nostalgic revival. One evening during his holiday, Barry even managed to unearth an old mono cassette player from the pile of boxes in his garage and got it going, dancing around the apartment with his arms up and shouting *oopah* and *yassou*. The next morning he had nursed a thumping headache, a tedious guest who refused to leave him alone.

Mungo went to the fridge and took out a beer stubby and handed it to Barry.

'Hope this is hard enough for you.'

Barry considered for a moment with a frown. 'Actually, I think I'll pass. Might go that cup of tea Mel's doing instead. You go ahead though.'

'I'm having a dandelion. I have to keep my head straight. Got a musical score to jiggle with later.' Mungo kissed Melinda. 'Hi hun, good day?'

'Just the usual death-defying acts at the school of the damned. Dad's got something to tell us.'

'Yeah, so I hear. Although he's already said there's still no money coming our way.'

'Mungo!'

Barry sipped at the steaming mug and sat down on the old sofa.

'I had this call from what sounded like an angry delinquent. It's nothing to worry about. I get them sometimes. I don't even know what he wanted. He didn't make any demands, like *do such and such or I'll whatever*. He just ranted really.'

'So how come, Dad, if you don't mind me asking, if it's nothing to worry about you needed to come round and talk to us about it?'

'Probably some moron that doesn't like BKS,' Mungo said, evening the score. Barry didn't rise to the bait.

'Could be, I couldn't gauge it. He seemed to be ... I don't know, all over the place. Almost as if he was play acting, if that makes any sense.'

'What did he say exactly?' Melinda said, sensing her father was building up to something that would affect *them* personally.

'Well, stuff like *you think you're so great* sort of thing. I have to admit I got a bit cantankerous with him.'

'Rightly so. Did you phone the cops?' Mungo added.

'No, not yet. I thought I'd talk to you two first.' Barry hesitated. 'I've had crank calls in the past. They're nothing new. But, there was ... '

Melinda began to feel nervous at her father's hesitancy. She felt a tightening in her stomach. 'Okay, Dad, *out* with it. What did he say?' Her voice had jumped a few decibels. 'Look, stop beating around the bush and tell us! You're starting to scare me.'

'Look, I'm sorry, I don't mean to. It's just that he mentioned ... Rosie.'

'Rosie! What?' Melinda's voice filled with anger. 'What do you mean *mentioned*? What *did* he say about her?'

'It wasn't really a threat to her. I think he just wanted me to know that he knew her name, *who* she was, and that ... '

'What? Dad!' Panic filled Melinda's face. She put the boiled kettle down and folded her arms as if to give herself some strength and security, fighting off the horror she would experience if anything was to happen to her child.

'He didn't actually say he was going to hurt her. He just wanted me to know that he knew who she was and that…'

Melinda banged her hand on the bench top and reached for the phone and started to press in the numbers. 'I'm going to call the police.'

But then, catching her by surprise, Mungo moved towards her and calmly took the phone from her and switched it off.

'What are you doing?' she yelled, tears welling in her eyes. 'Give it to me! *Give* it to me!'

Mungo put his arm around her and held her. 'Let's just get a few more details before we go off half-cocked. Rosie's safe now, she's asleep in her room. We're all here, so nothing is going to happen to her right now.'

Mungo felt Melinda's body loosen slightly. He knew that she would do absolutely anything to protect her daughter from harm, he would too, but for the moment it was necessary to stay unruffled.

'You're right, I'm sorry, I just couldn't bear it if…'

'I know. But we're all together here. And you know your dad's a secret kung fu specialist.'

Melinda attempted to giggle, then buried her head into Mungo's chest to sob. He led her to the sofa and sat her down next to her father. Mungo grabbed the nearest piece of fabric for her now-dribbling nose, a clean tea towel decorated with souvenir pictures of the mines of the West Coast as it happened, a present from her grandfather the Christmas before last. Melinda could only laugh when she saw it, and blew her nose in it anyway.

Barry held his daughter's hand. 'Look, I haven't handled this very well. I really don't think it's anything serious. Honestly. I'm just being over cautious because Rosie's name was mentioned. I really don't think she's in any harm. The guy sounded like he could have been drunk and was just showing off to a mate. I've had this sort of thing before.'

'How would he *know* about Rosie?' Mungo asked.

'Well, that's the weird thing. I don't really know. But he just seemed to be angry at *me*.'

'Is that all he said?' Mungo had replaced his dandelion with a beer.

'Pretty much. It didn't sound as if he'd thought it through.'

'Sounds like just another nutter, high on something, low on himself,' Mungo added.

'Oh, I don't know. He even wanted to tell me about the Queensland floods. It was all just a bit weird.'

'Maybe he knew someone who'd drowned and wants to take his angst out on somebody else,' Mungo suggested. 'I mean, that is sort of what your show does to people. All that exposing of the dark side seems to have shifted something in the suburban psyche.'

Barry tried to guard himself against the punch of Mungo's

words, but for a moment he felt the thrust of a sharp pin immobilising him like a collected butterfly.

'People are motivated by money. I don't *prise* it out of them,' he finally said defensively.

'Mungo wasn't suggesting that,' Melinda said, putting her hand out protectively towards her husband. She often found her loyalties a bit wobbly when Mungo and her father where acting out their verbal jousts.

'It's okay, it's just me. The whole shebang's been getting to me lately.' And to Mungo, 'I'm sure you're right. I've been thinking it's probably time to leave it all behind.'

'I actually think you're doing a pretty amazing thing,' Mungo said, backpedalling frantically.

Barry raised a knowing eyebrow.

'Actually I'm just keeping you sweet in case that wheelbarrow does materialise,' Mungo replied, backpedalling from his backpedal.

'Mungy!' Melinda squawked. Her father was smiling.

Barry patted his daughter's knee, stood up and gave his quasi-son-in-law a friendly poke in the stomach. 'Anyway, I think we should leave the mystery caller for the time being. I'll let you know if there's more. I don't think the police need to be involved yet. I just wanted to keep you both up to speed.'

'I think you're right, Dad.'

'Yeah.'

'Okay, good. Now I've got to go and sort Dad out. Apparently he's going to die tonight, again, wants an audience.' Barry sighed, the tension of one potential disaster being replaced by another.

After her father had left, in the half-light of Rosie's bedroom, Melinda held onto Mungo, neither of them speaking, just feeling each other's warmth, grateful, the womb-like stillness punctuated only by the gentle rise and fall of their daughter's contented breathing.

*

Kant drove into his father's driveway, as close to the house as possible. The first time he'd driven his Audi, when it was new, to visit his father he left it in the street. Six days it was off the road waiting for a re-spray. *I WOZ ERE* – a single word per panel, each letter twenty centimetres tall scratched into the duco by something sharp and spiteful. And it wasn't even as if the words had some originality.

The evenings were getting shorter. Eight o'clock and a dull film had already been painted over the sky.

Barry opened the front door, rarely locked, and called out, 'I'm here.'

'Down the bedroom, son.'

'What's all this *son* business?' he mumbled to himself as he wandered down the threadbare passage.

Barry's thoughts were a clutter. Not just from his nagging discontent with the show, but the phone call had unsettled him. Even Mungo's comment had unsettled him. Were these signs for him to give it all away? And now his dippy old dad in the middle of everything saying nonchalantly that he thinks he's going to die.

Barry pushed the bedroom door open halfway and peered round. 'You still alive?'

He forced a smile and walked over to the bed and sat on the end, out of reach so neither of them would have the discomfort of physical contact. He'd learned at an early age it wasn't his father's thing, never had been since.

'Don't need to be touching and stuff just 'cos we're family,' Desmond had said once to a confused six-year-old Barry.

'So what's going on with you, old timer? You look all right to me.'

'Saw this thing on telly the other night, 'bout them Aborigines. Like they just walk off and die. Or was it Africans? You know, some of them dark fellas know when it's their time. I guess they don't want to trouble no one.'

'Unlike you. So, you're turning Afro-Aboriginal and you're about to wander off into… where… the park, and lie down? How about the median strip along the Brooker Highway? And you've decided tonight's the night. Well, at least you won't need to pack a bag.'

Unmoved by his son's sarcasm, Desmond made a submissive scrunch with his mouth. 'Feels that way, son.'

Barry looked at his watch. Sighed.

'Melinda catch that burglar?'

'She wasn't robbed! I *told* you before, there's nothing wrong. And I wish you wouldn't call her and … '

'She ought'a get deadlocks on her doors. Can't trust no-one these days.'

'I told you she … oh never mind. Look, I'm not staying long. I haven't even eaten yet. D'you want me to make you a cup of tea before I go?'

'Yes, son, that would be very nice. No sugar. Did I tell you I've stopped taking sugar? I think I've been losing a bit of weight.'

'Hardly matters now, eh? Besides you never know what crap they'll serve in heaven. That's if they'll take such an irritating bugger like you. And what's with all this *son* stuff? You haven't called me that since I was a kid.'

Desmond shrugged. 'You know.'

'Do I? You're a mystery, Dad. I suppose if you've lost weight your coffin won't be so heavy to lift. At least that'll be a bonus.'

'You can cut that out. And I don't want no fancy box, you hear? Chipboard, that's all. All that nice timber 'n' handles 'n' fittings going up in smoke, it's a waste.'

'Fine.'

In the kitchen Barry filled the old yellow porcelain jug and plugged it into the wall socket by the sink. *Wouldn't pass building regulations these days,* he thought. The palaver he went through when he was having his apartment renovated. *No electrical points near the sinks, blahdy-blahdy-blah.*

'Are you sure you don't want me to put a bloody fence around the sink so I don't fall in,' he remembered ranting to the unsuspecting building assessor when he came to sign off on the job. Of course, the council man had no *blahdy* sense of humour.

As the jug rumbled on the faded green Formica, Barry began to absentmindedly lift lids off jars to sniff and diagnose the contents. He pulled out drawers to determine mouse populations by the number of little black pellets scattered around. Stuff still there from when he was a kid. The flour bin smelt rancid, even the weevils had gone to look for something fresher. He pulled open the oven and peered in. Some foul, malodorous beast, desperate to escape its greasy tomb, lashed out at his nose. The light had blown too. *Back in 1960.* Barry smiled. There *was* a funny side. What else was there to do? The archeology of his father's kitchen was commensurate with how much priority the old bugger put on maintaining the house to the degree Patricia had been resolute about it.

Dotted around the room were pale yellow post-its that Desmond had scrawled messages on decades ago, now only faded reminders of a family once under the same roof. One on the wall behind the hot tap exclaimed not to turn it off so hard. (*It takes a few seconds for the nozzle to drain!!*) He had written in brackets. That one had been when Barry was a boisterous teenager. One on the dresser said *Don't forget to glue the knob on.* The knob was nowhere to be seen, and the words on the paper, embossed and inkless. The outside of the fridge door was a montage of birthday reminders, ancient faded postcards and paid bills curling behind an assortment of greasy plastic fridge magnets, furry with dust.

One of the washed-out postcards was from Knossos, the ancient Minoan capital just outside Crete's capital city Iraklion.

A muscular man was acrobatically dancing over the horns of a large bull. The exact day he and Sarah had posted it was still clear in Barry's mind, even the fragrance of the air and the land's heartbeat cicada chorus. They had come across an abandoned two-storey Venetian house in the midst of an olive grove. Venetian architecture, obstinate stone blocks like their empire. At some stage in the house's history it would have exuded wealth and privilege, taunting the simpler Cretan dwellings further up the rocky escarpment with its luxuriant terraced gardens of fruit trees and ornamental orange bushes.

Sarah and Barry had taken a picnic of crusty bread, feta, olives, marinated octopus, tomatoes and cucumber to its flat roof and had drunk red wine from the bottle until they'd felt heady in the shimmering afternoon heat. Later they had dozed in the shade of an olive tree, the clatter of three-wheeled monkey-trucks and cicadas, braying donkeys and the bustle of the countryside beyond their zone of contentment. Barry's memories of the architecture and art of the temples of the extraordinary Minoan civilisation, 'which even had *in-house* flush toilets three and a half thousand years ago', he'd written on the card, had become insignificant in relation to his fostered memories of love-making and desire he and Sarah had shared, another lifetime ago.

Barry's mother Patricia would have had a fit if she'd seen the state of the kitchen now. Seventeen years it had been since she died. A mastectomy for starters, the malignant disease deciding to ravage her bones afterwards, the family surviving in various compressions of trauma. Desmond welded up his emotions in a metal box and continued his factory work as though Patricia just had a bad cold. It had been Barry who had driven up from the country to organise the visits to the hospital for chemotherapy, radiotherapy and whatever else was needed. Patricia struggled on for a couple of years, going in and out of remission before the cursed demon finally spewed its venom into the rest of her body, poisoning her bone marrow and finally her brain.

Her personality transformation had been the most frightening part for the young, earnest Barry. His mother had always been a modest, home-loving woman with uncomplicated desires, nourishing her family's happiness with her own unwilting sense of duty towards maintaining a predictable and orderly home, nutritious cooking and plenty of home-grown parsley, which accompanied almost every meal she cooked. There was hardly an interest outside this noble cause.

Eventually, the pain, fashioned by the relentless absorption of toxic compounds into a softhearted body, shattered Patricia's sensibilities, reducing her exchanges to the foulest of verbal outbursts and frightening acrimony. To this day Barry still felt baffled by the rancor that randomly spat from his mother's mouth in those last fearful weeks. *Maybe there's a sleeping demon curled up in all of us, waiting,* he'd wondered. One moment she was calm and demure, the next she'd let loose with a stream of vile expletives and crazed accusations. Melinda was in primary school then. Barry and Sarah had tried to shelter her from her grandmother's outbursts, but one day he had had to leave her with Nan in the house while he helped his father lop some branches from a tree in the back yard. Melinda had nightmares for weeks after.

Barry closed the oven door.

He placed a teaspoonful of powdered milk into a floral cup, wildflowers from the red centre, poured the water over a teabag, and unclenched his teeth. He took the unopened anachronistic packet of English breakfast leaf tea he had brought round several months ago from the sideboard and put it on the kitchen table to take when he left. Barry opened the door under the sink to put the teabag into the waste container. The cupboard was empty. Annoyed, he dumped the bag in the sink.

Patricia's best blue willow-pattern teapot sat dusty and resigned on the sideboard.

'Here you go, this should chirp you up for a few more minutes,' Barry said, attempting cheeriness as he returned to his father's bedside.

Eyes closed, his father made no response.

'Dad, here's your tea,' he said more forcefully, flat, irritated.

Barry put the cup on the unvarnished and cup-ringed pine bedside chest of drawers.

'Dad, here you go! Drink it while it's ... Dad?'

Barry gingerly touched his father's shoulder. There was no movement. A knife-sharp pang cut through his chest and into his heart. He heaved in air. *Jesus Christ, I could have been here listening to him instead of rummaging through the damned kitchen like an obsessive health inspector. What the hell's wrong with you!*

Barry subsided lightly on the edge of the bed, utterly deflated. After a while he leaned over and felt his father's wrist with his index and middle fingers. Patricia's doctor had mentioned that the thumb has a pulse of its own. He knew that. But now he was at a loss, didn't really know what he was doing, or feeling for.

Can't feel a damn thing!

Barry stared at his father; he couldn't remember the last time he'd been so close. He could not think what to do. His head was silently imploding. It wasn't the same as when Sarah had died. She had been his world. His body knew what to do then, it was as if they'd shared the same anatomy.

I'll kiss him on the forehead. A small thing, Barry thought, *but symbolic ... before he ... goes cold,* an action so intimate for Barry that, as he got up and neared his mouth to his father's head, he began to shake. Leaning closer he placed his lips on the dry speckled skin of the old man's forehead, a numbing tiredness now spiking the flurry of jangled explosions charging up from his stomach to his chest.

In a whisper he said, 'I'm so sorry, Dad, I should have ... '

But he was stopped short by a grunt that suddenly surfaced from deep in his father's scrawny throat, then, 'Jesus boy, what are you doing!'

Barry sprang backwards, his heart palpitating electrically as if he'd been caught in the act of tampering with a corpse. He found himself tittering childishly with nervous release. He was six years old again, in the kitchen, his father seated, eating thick toast, nearly ready for work. Little Barry had come in and put his arms around his father's neck and kissed him on the cheek. *That was the last time,* Barry suddenly remembered. His father had pulled back instinctively and had held out a callused workman's hand towards the boy. 'Here you go, son – you take hold of the hand and shake it firm like this, up and down, looking the other man in the face. That's how we men do it.'

The young Barry had looked at his mother for a clue as to what had just happened, but she'd simply smiled and winked at him, as if to say, 'From this moment on you will receive what you need in that department from me. Now eat your breakfast'.

Barry coughed to regain his composure. 'Sorry Dad, I really thought you were ... Great doctor I'd make.'

And why the hell am I apologising to my own father for showing some affection? Even his thoughts felt strangled.

Desmond forced a little equalising cough in return. 'Musta nodded off. You made that tea yet?'

'Yes. Oh yes, here.'

Barry breathed out, handed him the cup after placing a couple of extra pillows from Patricia's side of the bed behind his father, fussing, distracting his ineptness. Two single beds had been pushed together. His mother's side, preserved like a mummy, was still embalmed by the same linen from when she was sick. For years after Patricia had died, Desmond used to say he could hear her breathing at night sometimes, in the interminable sleepless hours. One of the few things his father spoke of that Barry could truly empathise with.

Resettling himself on the end of the bed again he looked at his father.

'What else did you want to talk to me about? I really can't stay long. It looks as if you might survive another night after all. Not sure about me though.'

Desmond sipped noisily from the cup. 'In my study. In the safe, key's on a hook behind the curtain on the left. Bring the box.'

Study? Safe?

'Look, can't this wait till tomorrow?' Barry snapped, relieved that the only emotion he was experiencing now was surging irritation.

Desmond pretended not to hear and slurped at his tea.

Barry plodded down the corridor. On a door a faded plaque read 'The Home Office' in Barry's uneven teenage lettering. Inside the small room, the faded and perished curtains were drawn. They were always drawn now. If they were touched the material would certainly disintegrate. Dark speckled grey-green mildew had resurfaced the ceiling like boulder lichen in the Lost World. It was well on its way down two of the walls. The airflow vents near the ceiling had been papered over by Patricia, probably in the seventies when wallpaper was still all the rage.

A conglomeration of second-hand computer parts, spare outdated monitors and keyboards were scattered amongst the home-made extension benches held up by empty cardboard boxes and milk crates, shelves held up by odd bits of three-ply and dried-out masking tape. A frenzy of wires, adaptors, and extension cables hooked over pictures before disappearing amongst the jumble. Desmond had had an idea to write his memoirs once, just after Barry had graduated thirty-five years ago.

The space had diminished to such an extent that Barry found it a squeeze just getting down to a Chickenfeed facsimile safe, in reality a thin tin. Safe, one thing the contents would never be. He inserted the key only to find its door was unlocked. Inside were a Four Roses chocolates tin, and strangely, a bundle of Christmas cards and postcards tied up in a red ribbon, left-overs from a long-gone family life.

'Here you go, Dad.' He placed the contents of the safe on his father's lap.

'There's some of your mother's jewellery in here. I got no use for it no more. Reckon its time to take the pearl necklace and sell the damn thing. You get it valued properly before you do though. It'll be worth a bloody fortune now.'

'Didn't know Mum had any jewellery. I never saw her wear any. What do you mean *now*, anyway?'

'Got it when I was courting your mother. No, that's right; it was in Hong Kong where we went later for our honeymoon.' A mnemonic smile slipped out. 'Bloody long time now. Pearls have gone up a real lot. Harry down the RSL told me. Your mum used to say she felt like a movie star when she wore them. I reckon you could pay your mortgage off with it.'

'I don't have a mortgage,' Barry fibbed petulantly. 'How come you didn't sell it before? If it's worth so much you could have bought a new washing machine when the Simpson bust, fifteen years ago, wasn't it?'

'Laundromat's easy.'

'And you've been driving around in that clapped-out old wreck when you could have ... '

'Hey, if I want a bloody preacher I can go and see Father what's-his-name.'

Barry breathed deeply. Vashna was right about the floating.

'Huh. Well, pull it out then. Let's have a look at it.'

The necklace did look impressive even to Barry, who had never bought a single piece of jewellery for Sarah in all their times together. The hundreds of strung, iridescent, opalesque beads could have been wound loosely around a neck several times.

Barry, even in those passionate carefree days when he and Sarah were blissfully ensconced in Crete, had never seen the need to express his love by giving her bits of stuff to hang round her neck. They were half naked most of the time anyway. When they did eventually get married he kept his own wedding ring in a small bronze box on the chest of drawers in their bedroom. It had been Sarah who had actually bought their small bands of gold. Barry suddenly felt mean. Even his father, stingy old bugger, had made the effort to show his appreciation for his wife by lashing out and giving her this lavish piece of adornment.

'Might get twigs caught in it when I'm pruning the trees,'

Barry had once remonstrated to his be-ringed married friends, in his defence. And they all knew how much pruning *he* did.

And around the same dinner-party table he'd rationalised, 'Did Michelangelo feel the need to bedeck David's fingers with rings? Of course not. The hand is the most intriguing part of the human body with its own delicate sense of touch, its capacity for reshaping itself into a million expressive meanings, like classical Indian dancing, and it possesses the secrets of our future inscribed like hieroglyphics within its palm. So why would you defile it with trappings?'

His guests had applauded warmly after this little outpouring. And Sarah's smile had been filled with pride.

'What are we talking about here, Dad?' Barry asked, holding the necklace out like a flamboyant lasso from the Sydney Mardi Gras.

'I'm no expert, but I reckon thirty, maybe even fifty grand, could be a lot more. I been watching that pommy antiques show, you know, the one where people bring their old junk and get it valued. Some posh biddy recently had inherited a pearl necklace from her grandmother when she was young and it was worth a bloody fortune.'

'That program's on the same time as my show. Traitor!'

'Whoops,' Desmond replied with twinkling eyes, once more forgetting about his impending death. 'Some real surprises there.'

'*You're* a real surprise. Look, I really do have to go now, early start tomorrow. I've got a huge pre-production thing to get through tomorrow and if I don't get some shut-eye, James isn't going to be too pleased.'

'You let him push you around too much.'

'He's the director – that's what he's paid to do! Thanks for showing me this. I'll come round tomorrow and pick it up when I take you out for a walk. Climb the mountain if you're still alive! We can go round to see your great-granddaughter too.' Barry's voice softened. 'She is such a beautiful little creature.'

'She's got you round her little finger. Anyway, I haven't finished yet.'

'Too bad, it'll have to wait. You'll just have to put your death on hold for another day. They tell me there's a very long queue waiting to get into heaven anyway. So there's no hurry. Now get some sleep.'

Barry placed the Christmas cards and the tin on his mother's side of the bed.

'I'll come round tomorrow, yeah? Bring something nourishing for you to eat. Think you can postpone getting your angel wings?'

'Get outa here, ya cheeky bugger. An' bring us some sugar when you come. I think I'll take it up again.'

'Well that's got to be a good sign. If you get much thinner the mayor'll be using you for a flag pole at the council chambers.'

It was times like this, heavy with fatigue, driving slowly home through the night city, stopping at pointless red lights in deserted streets, feeling the oppressive weight of his workload and its recent consequences, and sensing the press of loneliness again, that Kant could understand the benefits of having a chauffeur. Not to mention a valet, a cordon bleu cook, and a masseuse who specialised in happy endings.

'*Where to tonight, sir? To the weekender with your old pals?*'

'*No, Bartholomew, I think I'll have a quiet one with the wife this evening. Tomorrow we'll be taking the yacht down the coast to catch a spot of breeze. Fresh nor-easterly forecast.*'

'*I'll have a picnic prepared, sir. Will that be all, sir?*'

'*Thank you, Bartholomew, and make sure you put in some hefty slices of that Cajun salmon the wife and I adore so much.*'

'*Very good, sir.*'

'*Oh, and have a good weekend yourself, Bartholomew.*'

'*Yes sir, thank you, sir.*'

The sound of a blaring horn made Kant jump. He'd sat through a green light. He hadn't wanted to leave his reverie – Ingrid the masseuse had just walked in.

Chapter Twelve

Mungo turned off the computer and the effects console.

It had been a successful day adding to his collection of extraneous sounds recorded around the city, like the hum of an air-conditioning unit in C sharp and a generator that growled F minor, rattling in its cage at the back of the multistoried car park in Argyle Street. The beeping at a pedestrian crossing for the sight impaired, in particular, resonated with one of his short melodic compositions he'd called 'Speechless', pure language without words.

But the unexpected sounds that Mungo really got a kick out of he discovered whilst thumbing through the Yellow Pages in the telephone directory to find the number of a PVC pipe company. As he was searching the pages he'd absently tapped them with his pencil, the sort with a rubber fixed at the end, and found that as the book differed in thickness the pages produced varying notes, resonant, as if a sound box was attached to the layers of paper. Being a byproduct of timber this tattered and floppy lexicon of information, asserted itself to Mungo's ears. As a musical instrument, it was now inextricably bonded with every wooden musical relative in history, standing tall amongst its Stradivarius cousins, its Steinway grandfathers, and of course its ancestral log-drum fathers wildly articulating rituals of life, death, and communication throughout the hinterlands of the African continent.

Opening the book at different pages Mungo began to test the notes with his electronic tuner. Glass Merchants and Glaziers gave a C sharp, Nannies and Naturopaths was in E major, Security Systems was in G natural. Then he methodically went through the book locating a full scale of notes with which to work, and noting the names of the different businesses and companies for conceptual reference. They could be woven into other tones achieved from tapping the ends of various lengths of PVC piping with a rubber thong. When he amplified the *Directory Notes*, as they were now called, he recorded them into the computer program.

The sound alphabet that he'd been collecting for a year now would be morphed digitally into a multiplicity of musical *words* when he came to compose. The more he could discover and record, the more diverse his soundscape narratives could become.

Before Mungo left the studio he phoned Melinda.

Rosie answered.

'Hello, Rosie speaking.' The child's voice was clear and deliberate. Melinda had taught her well. 'Can you tell me who you are, pease?'

'It's Daddy.'

'Daddy! We are having sketty for dinner.'

'Yum yum, I'm hungry. Can I speak to mummy now, sweetie?'

Rosie dropped the phone in her excitement. It clacked onto

the floor as she trotted to the bathroom where Melinda was putting folded bed sheets into the airing cupboard.

'Mummy, Daddy is on the telepone and wants to talk to you.'

Melinda kissed her on the head and went to the phone.

'Hi, you going to be late?'

'No. I just had this feeling to phone you and see if everything was okay. Rosie obviously hasn't been kidnapped. Sounds silly now I'm talking to you.'

'No, it's not. But I've had a most wonderful day with her. I haven't let her out of my sight though, and any terrorists that might have been skulking around here have gone on holiday.'

'I'll buy some red for that spag. We got parmesan?'

'Yep.'

'Need anything else?'

'Just you.'

'See you soon.'

'Oh, Yetta dropped off some of her home-made cheese cake.'

'I'll see you sooner!'

Melinda felt such relief the day had passed without incident. At breakfast that morning, while she was preparing a batch of home-made toasted muesli, Mungo and Rosie had been teasing each other by putting their hands over their ears each time the other spoke. Watching them, so close and happy, chortling together, had made her quake with terror as she pondered how she would feel if this was taken away from her. As the day had progressed, her father's phone call had vanished from her mind. Four Luck Avenue would remain a prophecy for their little patch of paradise.

Melinda put the spaghetti into the boiling water with a dash of olive oil. Rosie was lining up her furry and plastic animals along the couch, telling them about the food she had cooked today. She was mid-sentence when she jumped up and ran to the front door. 'Daddy, Daddy, you're home. Hello Daddy.'

'Hello my little rosebud. What sort of mischief have you been up to today?'

She giggled. 'Lots of mishiff, Daddy.'

'Aah, that's my girl.'

Mungo came into the kitchen carrying an upside-down giggling Rosie by the ankles and gave Melinda a kiss before lowering his daughter onto the sofa amongst her family of toys.

*

On the other side of the city Kant parked his car at the kerb in the street outside James Mackelroy's house, just down from bend five, on the zigzagging road up to Mount Nelson, a lofty, tree-lined neighbourhood. Seven-thirty. He was bemused by why he always seemed to be on time these days. It was only since Sarah had died, but blamed his father's genes, who probably blamed the clocking-in machine at the Zinc Works.

As he opened his car window his nostrils were brushed with a minty fragrance wafting from a patch of native shrubs speckled with small mauve flowers. Sarah would have known its botanical name.

Kant had showered, shaved, then again in case he'd missed

those persistent long hairs just under his ears, put on his black sports jacket, not a suit, and grey flannel trousers. James had suggested casual so the new rusty-orange hemp shirt would do. He had brought two bottles of wine with him: a chilled sauvignon blanc and a shiraz. Earlier at the Battery Point Nine/Eleven he had mulled over the choice cautiously by regarding the label designs and the relative reductions in price, not too cheap but not unnecessarily precious. The shiraz had numbers on the label, Seppelts, *looks formal, serious business. And a little conceited!* Taking pleasure in his naïveté.

The white, he thought, *Isn't that what women like to drink these days? Oh, I don't know.* On the back label there were comparisons between all sorts of fruit, bananas, strawberries, even chocolate, but the word *grape* was nowhere to be seen. The front label had an uncomplicated design, stylised rows of vines on a slope, not too folksy, nice gold lettering on a pale green background.

It even has a cork instead of a screw top. Must *be quality.*

He twisted his neck around; something sinewy creaked. His hands were clammy and already he could feel a light tickle of sweat just below his right armpit.

Must keep my jacket on.

Kant couldn't remember the last time he'd been invited to someone's *home* formally for dinner. Socialising with his diminishing corral of friends in wine bars was about it these days. Well, Vashna and Max really.

Looking around – no other cars there yet. It would be light

for another hour or so. These things were always easier after dark. Mackelroy had suggested he come early so he could be comfortable, drink in hand, when the others arrived. He felt like a panicky neophyte on his first appointment with the bishop, not the celebrated TV host who had the whole country hanging onto his every word.

'It's not a blind date for the high school dance, you prick,' Mackelroy had said encouragingly that afternoon as they'd got into their respective cars in the Nerve Two car park. 'It's a simple get-together with some friends. It's what people do, male and female, who probably even watch BKS. They might even think you're some sort of TV icon, God or whatever, and they'll all want a piece of you.'

'Shit, James, I dunno about this.'

Mackelroy had laughed mischievously. 'Jesus, I can't believe I'm seeing the famous man all jittery like some panicky teenage debutante.'

'Yes, very amusing.'

'I've invited Vince too. Still eating in the most dubious food haunts even though he doesn't do much 'hunting' these days. He seems to enjoy mixing with the strangest of company. Mind you he told me that after all his time in war zones the average backstreet soup kitchens feel like cosy homes.'

There was no front door bell. Kant knocked and the door swung inwards a little. Mackelroy's voice summoned from within. The house was nonchalantly unguarded. Soft aromas of Asian cooking drifted in the air, and as he stepped into the spacious, timbered entrance hall there was something else Kant could smell but not quite discern. There were no shoes placed around the parquetry floor so he assumed it was a *shoes-on* house. That was a relief. His feet seemed to get cold more easily these days. He couldn't imagine Mackelroy being the type to worry about all that hippy-shit anyway.

Sarah had insisted guests put on special house slippers she supplied. In his new pristine apartment Kant had chided himself once or twice for flopping onto his bed without even removing his street shoes after an exhausting session at Nerve. She'd bought the silk slip-ons on a trip to Thailand about ten years ago. And only now Kant remembered how it used to annoy him that she could be so controlling, with what he thought then, silently to himself, to be a ridiculous charade.

Kant placed his car keys on a wooden box in the entrance. *That's it!* The other smell. The carved, antique Cantonese trunk was constructed out of camphor wood. He and Sarah had almost bought one themselves, not from any exotic foreign lands but from 'Wing and Co' in Sandy Bay, about a kilometre from here.

Mackelroy was uncorking a red in the tastefully furnished living room. The tracked glass doors to the outside deck were open. They had been granted a still, warm evening.

'Can't go on meeting like this,' Kant opened with.

Mackelroy simply smiled. He seemed different.

'Here, think you might appreciate this one,' he said, handing

Kant an all-the-rage stemless wine goblet. 'Found it in the Hunter at the tiniest boutique winery. Last summer.'

Kant took the glass as if he had just been handed the Holy Grail. The wine looked dense, was the colour of spilled blood on white marble. He held up his glass, imitating a thoughtful gaze, put it to his mouth, sniffed and, pleasantly surprised, he felt some inexplicably intricate essence arouse his taste buds as it danced around his sensibilities.

'Impertinent little bastard,' he managed. The sort of thing he might have said forty years ago as an undergraduate, having sloshed a chipped cupful of acidic claret from a cask gathering dust on top of the fridge. He felt annoyed with himself for trying to disguise his discomfort by sounding like…well…what he wasn't anymore.

Mackelroy moved on amiably. 'Some of these smaller wineries don't even use their own grapes, you know. This place, Home Row Winery…' he continued, holding up the bottle like a trophy he'd won for discovering the place, 'buys ninety percent of their grapes from our very own Tasmanian cool-climate vineyards and the rest from the Clare Valley. Nothing's as it seems these days. The terraces of vines at Home Row were just a stage set.'

'So there *is* somebody who appreciates our abominable weather.'

'Can't complain tonight though.'

They walked outside onto the spacious cantilevered timber deck that extended out from the patio and sat at a large rectangular cast-iron table, topped with a fitted sheet of clear glass. Several colourfully glazed pots with Mexican designs contained an assortment of cacti. A dark glazed bowl was home to a bonsaied Tasmanian myrtle, a five year old looking like a septuagenarian. Cushion covers were brightly Matissian patterned.

'Some superior smells coming from the kitchen,' Kant offered knowingly.

'Slaving over a hot Chinese Takeaway since we parted at the car park. As long as the rice is cooked while the guests are here I don't think it's cheating.'

After a while sounds of chatter and laughter drifted through from inside the house. A male voice called out, 'Anyone home? Burglars here … robbing you!'

Mackelroy chuckled. 'That'll be Donald. Bit of a prat but we go way back. Anyway, I invited him so I can feast my eyes on his delectable new woman.'

Kant felt a pang in his stomach.

He took a quick swig of his wine and stood up motioning his director to go back into the house to direct his guests. He then spent a few moments constructing a casual pose leaning against the stainless steel railing and began studying the view, the harbour, and the houses on the eastern shore, a rash of spots lining the river's edge. The casino's cylindrical tower looked small from up here, foreshortened from this angle. Soon the dark would allow the city to flaunt its twinkling light-show, a giant glittery beast crawling along the coastline with tentacles slithering up into the hills.

He had dined with Sarah at the Casino's revolving restaurant about three years ago. The middle of winter it had been. She'd loved the new woollen scarf he'd bought for her birthday. It had been an extravagant night, with garlic prawns, Crayfish Thermidor with walnut, pear and rocket salad, crème brulee. They had opened a second bottle of Moet when they'd arrived back at the cottage. It had tasted even better in the comfort of their snug home. They had fetched the mattress from the bedroom and put it on the floor of the sitting room and fell into languorous lovemaking in front of the warm, orange glow of the wood fire.

Kant was suddenly ambushed by a recollection that hurled him back thirty-five years to the summer heat in the Mediterranean when he first set eyes on Sarah. She, twenty, becoming utterly besotted by him, and he, twenty-four, oblivious to anything that wasn't superlatively wonderful about any aspect of this young sexy woman's being – two souls sinking into the unfathomable depths of love.

*

Young Barry had arrived from London, passing through France and Italy, hitching rides in trucks travelling through the night along motorways, auto routes, autobahns and autostrades. Milan cathedral had bedazzled the young Tasmanian but still it was the-small-village-in-Greece scenario that he was heading for. That was what had captured his imagination when he was looking at brochures in the travel agency in Hobart five weeks before.

Flying to London first was the cheapest way to go, of course, then two weeks doing the pubs, Madame Tussauds, the Tower, a Led Zeppelin concert at Wembley Stadium and a couple of irritating nights in Earl's Court flicking off other first-time Aussies, in his face like enthusiastic mosquitoes.

Travelling through the continent was exhilarating. With an insatiable appetite for the *other*, Barry devoured exchanges with the drivers, signing and stumbling his way through schoolboy French when English went awry. He unloaded three tons of yoghurt in Salzburg with Hermann in exchange for sleeping in the spare bunk behind the driver's seat, saving on a night's accommodation. An overcrowded train took the wide-eyed Barry down through Italy's leg, the musical chatter of the locals and engorged rural landscape, the grape-red blood in its veins, captivating him in ways that he'd never thought possible back home in the bleak streets of Lutana.

Aboard the Brindisi ferry, which took him to Corfu, Barry, filled with the romantic traveller's zeal, avoided anyone whose first language was English, particularly brashly enthusiastic Americans. Overseas travel could only be authentic when you couldn't understand the language. Such simple tasks like buying a beer or the circuitous challenge of asking how long the crossing would take became quests in themselves, pitting against alien rivals in the adventure of communication.

On disembarkation he began wandering in and around the

Neo Limani, mesmerised by the way the silent Venetian, French and Sicilian architecture, despite the historic battles for possession and generations of bloodshed, managed to show no signs of animosity now. Lush olive groves, pink and red hibiscus flowers, rough stone walls, meditative donkeys and unhurried people, cypress trees and brightly painted stucco on Byzantine church walls, coexisted harmoniously in this Hellenic heaven under a tranquil, infinite blue sky.

This must be the Garden of Eden; Barry's head had reeled as he'd breathed in the scented fragrance of the orange blossoms. *And the waters, the sky, so blue, like sapphire, azure, and cerulean. It's so translucent it feels as if this whole isle, this fecund garden of earthly delight, is floating in infinity,* he wrote with lyrical intensity in his pocket-sized diary in the shade of an ancient wall.

'I should become a poet, not a hick bloody journo,' he'd said to the tethered, ashen donkey, which had been observing the newcomer with a reluctance to commit to any form of conversation.

But still, Barry's destination had been Crete. Vashna, who had been there the year before, said his mate wouldn't regret it; he'd mentioned something about the quaint villages coexisting in a brutal terrain. Two more days of hitching rides through the Aegean peninsula, a rickety rooftop bed, sleeping a star-speckled night under the Acropolis, made adequately comfortable by an overdose of Retsina, but which induced a nausea-filled ferry trip the next day from Piraeus to Iraklion.

He survived the infamously terrifying ride in a crammed, jarring bus, sharing it with several barnyard passengers, along the tortuous Cretan coastal road, which finally deposited him sweaty and fatigued on Sitia's serene harbourside. Wispy, pink-flowered tamarisks haphazardly lounged around the waterfront squares. Frenetic Greek songs, accompanied by bouzoukis and guitar, jangling from worn-out speakers in every café and shop, competed in the scorching air, emitting the joyfully brash essence of the place, soon to embed itself into Barry's consciousness.

A brawny, mustachioed second-hand book seller, with passable English, from whom Barry had just bought a dog-eared Alistair MacLean paperback, *The Guns of Navarone*, pointed out the hostel at the other end of the quay, a rambling three-storey Venetian building with faded yellow stucco walls and bright blue shutters. The book seller also told Barry an Australian was the manager there.

'Blonde lady is boss, like Swedish film star. Maybe you get ficky ficky tonight!'

Barry felt a fleeting spasm flip in his stomach.

As he made his way around the curved harbour's edge, peering at what people were eating in cafés, observing the oleanders and ancient trees whose trunks, for some reason, had been painted white. Barry felt triumphant as the smells and noises of this new destination began to seep into the pores of his skin. He had saved assiduously before leaving Hobart. He didn't know, or even want to know when he would return. For now, with the excitement of an indefinite future he would make this place his home.

A young bearded German lad, Claus, at the front desk booked him in for a week to start with. He was shown up a flight of timber stairs to a dormitory of four beds on the first floor. For the first time Barry noticed how heavy his haversack felt as he hefted it from his sweat-damp shoulders, dumping it on his bed by an open window. Metal springs stretched and creaked.

That evening he ordered a *carafachi* of ouzo from a grubby soft-edged menu and sat outside. Vashna had prepped him that any word with *achi* on the end meant a small one. Barry had written a list of potentially useful hints in his notebook at the back. At a small round table underneath a sprawling grape vine he sat munching peanuts, artichoke, feta and olives. There was still a bite in the sun as it hung languidly, a huge glowing mandarin above a watery horizon. Stout, brightly painted fishing boats roped up to the stone jetty were abuzz with activity. Barry was intrigued by the men who held up octopuses to inspect them before dipping them into large buckets of water, agitating them furiously. A strange practice that he was sure would become clear with time. A pile of sea sponges was being sorted further up on the jetty, and at several tables along the water's edge, seriously combative men were playing backgammon, the clack clack of the pieces like duelling tap-dancers.

'Hello there.' A young woman's voice came from behind. She

sat down at his table, carefree and welcoming; sun-bleached sandy hair, sun-tanned skin. 'Welcome to paradise.'

Barry smiled. 'G'day.'

'I'm Sarah. I manage this little haven.'

'Great spot. I was told there was an Aussie here by a guy selling books,' Barry said, pointing to the stall, and then trying not to give too much of his attention to her firm curves that seemed to be beckoning him from beneath her thin, faded blue tee-shirt.

Look at those blue eyes, and that blonde hair, that dimple, oh Jesus, what a figure and...

'That's Stavros, the old crook. If you bought a book from him he's probably already sold it a hundred times before. Mind you, when *you've* finished reading it he will buy it back from you, and then resell it again. And again and again, until the paper disintegrates. His annual profits are astronomical. But that's the Greek way.'

Barry laughed. *Just arrived and I've fallen in love with the first chick I've met. That's got to be a good sign.*

'Where are you from?' he said, wishing now he'd opened with something less prosaic to demonstrate his newly acquired worldliness.

'I'm from here. When I'm here I'm nowhere else.'

'So beautiful!'

She grinned at him. The dimple in her cheek depressed and Barry melted a little more.

'The harbour's pretty nice too!' he said, trying out some old

Tassie charm, throwing caution to the breeze and pointing towards a small red boat that was tying up to its mooring.

Sarah's eyes continued to search the newcomer's face. 'This really *is* paradise. But you know paradise is just a concept that is merely enhanced by a backdrop. Can I get you something more substantial to eat, on the house of course? Jeorgo at 'Klimateria' does the *best* moussaka in the town.'

'What's kleemer … tera?'

'Klimateria – it means climbing vine. It's that café over there,' she smiled.

In the space of four and a half minutes young Barry had already become completely smitten by Sarah, if a smidge confused about her enigmatic summation of paradise. Already he wanted to live here with her for the rest of his life. Already he had forgotten utterly his past, his family and where he had come from. Even what planet he inhabited. They would probably have four kids too. All blond.

Sarah smiled as she watched the newcomer with what she had termed 'the look' when travellers experienced the enchantment of this lethargic once-Venetian port for the first time. She got up and wandered, unhurried like he'd witnessed in Corfu, over to the neighbouring café. There was no rush for things to begin and end in this place. Barry heard her waffle on in Greek before sauntering back to the table.

'He'll bring it over.'

'Your Greek's good.'

'I get by. It's a bit different to mainland Greek. They have a dialect here and there are lots of words that are actually different. Guess what *yes* is here.'

Barry shrugged. 'Yah?'

'Nai!' She laughed. 'You won't forget that in a hurry! But there are lots of contradictions here. I think that's why I love it so much.'

Within a week Sarah had fallen with Barry into the timeless space of devoted affection. Barry had ensconced himself on the third floor in the manager's room where they made love with the verve of first encounter, glowing with sumptuous delight, as their crimson juices surged through their veins and arteries.

It wasn't long before Sarah resigned her position as manager and they found a place to rent a few kilometres inland up the grape-growing valley where there were seldom other *touristas*, where they could become absorbed in the unadulterated village life of Piskochefalon, feasting on its and each other's alluvial fertility.

But six months later their paradise was suddenly and utterly shattered (and indeed lost), damaged irreparably by a single horrific act of violence, bludgeoned in a nightmare. And during the many distraught weeks that followed, try as he did, there was nothing the young Barry could do or say to help alleviate Sarah's pain. Prophetically, their paradise had become a concept, a contradiction, and now, even this earthly sanctuary they had lost themselves in, wasn't enough to keep them together.

Sarah, who could not be cajoled into revealing to Barry

exactly what had happened to her, packed up her bags and flew to London. At least that's where Barry thought she had gone. No amount of his love and eventual pleading could change her mind. She didn't even want him to come with her in the taxi back to Sitia where she would catch a bus to Iraklion, from there flying back to…where? Athens? London? Melbourne, where her parents lived? Parents whom he'd never met.

Although they had been in the throes of mutual adoration they didn't *really* know each other, an unnecessary detail in youthful love. It had been unambiguously clear they would, they had agreed, spend the rest of their besotted lives together.

*

'Barry. Oi, Barry.'

It seemed an eternity before Kant found release from his thoughts of that terrible time in Crete. As he straightened himself he turned to see a cluster of faces all viewing him with cheerful curiosity. *Mackelroy's place, that's right.*

'Barry, meet Donald and his partner Maritia Sherbourne. Great fans of you know what. But that's off limits tonight,' he added sternly to his guests.

They shook hands, smiled, and nodded while Maritia expertly took in what Kant was wearing: the shirt, the shoes, the jacket, no ring, that smile. Kant couldn't help but observe Maritia's jewellery that seemed to bedeck every digit on both hands. He'd seen less dangerous-looking knuckle-dusters in gangster movies. And perched amid a shapely cleavage sat an impressive baroque-like silver pendant, containing all but an avalanche of tiny turquoise stones and cast silver forms, all in the grip of gravity, in a place where Barry assumed Mackelroy had a hankering to be perched.

Donald's handshake, Kant thought, was overly assertive. So was the smile.

'And this is Gillian Papadakis, and you know Vince, of course.'

Switching his gaze back to the dark-haired woman who had just stepped around Maritia, Mackelroy added, 'Gillian, whom I have to admit I've only met once before, says that her daughter, whom I've *not* met, is going to be a little late, plane delayed in Melbourne. But if she's as charming as you, m'dear, then she'll be very welcome.'

'You'd better watch this man, Gillian,' Donald trumpeted. 'He has something of a reputation.'

Kant was enjoying watching his conniving director play the charming host.

'I'm sure I'm in good hands. But we mustn't wait, James,' Gillian said. 'I didn't think you'd mind me bringing my daughter along; she doesn't know anyone in Hobart. Not yet anyway,' she said tentatively.

'More the merrier,' was Mackelroy's ebullient reply.

So, this is my 'seeing-date'. How does he do it? Gillian's short, almost black hair blended with strands of grey which, to Kant's eyes, could be the result of three hours in a salon. But he'd never paid much attention to female subterfuge before. She was strik-ing, at ease with herself, and her patterned clothes reflected a love of colour. *But she doesn't look a bit Greek,* Kant puzzled.

'Enough of the formalities. Come and grab a glass everyone and find yourself a drink. I'm not going to be your waiter all night. This is a laissez-faire domain,' Mackelroy boomed over his shoulder as he made his way to the kitchen with Vince.

Kant was amused to see Mackelroy so relaxed, so unlike his usual hyperactive antics at the station. These people, even Vince, were completely comfortable socially with him. Since *they'd* met just over two years ago Kant had only ever visited Mackelroy on matters of the program.

'It's lovely to meet you in person *at last*, Barry,' Maritia Sher-bourne gushed, moving towards him and handing a glass of red to her partner at the same time without looking. There was a sense of deprivation in her voice.

'Likewise,' Kant replied, even though it was the first time he'd set eyes on the woman. He always felt aggravated by this form of hunger, especially with someone who was so obviously well educated, existed in a privileged bubble and who probably lacked for nothing.

You've just met someone who is being friendly, that's all. You sound like your cranky old Dad, he reminded himself.

'We've been thoroughly enjoying the latest... and I know it's supposed to be a no no tonight...' Maritia made a twitchy, theatrically coy movement with her head while lifting her eyebrows and shoulders, 'BKS,' she whispered.

Before Kant could reply, Donald butted in with gusto. 'We think it's marvellous what you do. Very tricky all that stuff, you know, handling *those* people.'

Some of those *people are actually wealthy knobs like you,* Kant thought as he endeavoured to squeeze out a smile. He grimaced and gave Donald a pert little nod, then making a strategic side-step, said, 'James was telling me just now that this wine, it's … um … it's from the Hunter Valley in New South Wales, is actually made from Tasmanian grapes. Can you believe that?'

Donald and Maritia looked at each other quizzically.

'Wadda you know!' Donald puffed.

'So, are you *into* wines too, Barry?' Maritia responded, clearly unhappy at Barry's evasive answer, but happy to top herself up with another aspect of the 'great man's' life. 'Is that an interest of yours, as well as your show?'

'*Our* show,' eaves-dropping Mackelroy called out whilst midsentence with Vince in the kitchen. 'Rice'll be ready in five.'

'To be honest I'm not sure what my interests are these days. The show, well … it's a job, I like it and who knows, maybe I'll become an airline pilot next year. Life can be so unpredictable, if you *allow it in*.' Barry smiled inside and thanked his old buddy Vashna.

Donald and Maritia chortled politely.

'Couldn't agree more,' Donald replied with ingratiating pleasantness.

'What are *your* interests?' Kant asked perversely, not wanting career or job to be the defining attribute of someone he'd just met. But before Donald could answer, Kant shifted his gaze towards Maritia.

Addressing the dominant male first, on matters of profession, is so old school, Barry thought, feeling bolshie towards the man already.

Maritia made a fleeting glance at her partner as if to apologise that she had usurped his dominance. She began twisting her wine goblet in her hand. 'Oh me? I just love catering. I … er … '

Donald butted in again as if he was his wife's publicity agent. 'Maritia's a highly sort-after *functions* planner, but she's hopeless at blowing her own trumpet. Very up-market stuff. Her last gig was at the Governor's pad. You know, Government House.'

Kant wondered about this garrulous, coiffure-haired poseur, but even though Donald had enough of his own wind to blow a whole big-band brass section by himself, his natural cockiness was quite endearing. But then he spoiled the illusion.

'Maritia and I first met at one of her dos at a State Liberal Party convention, where we were lucky enough to meet John Howard and … '

Maritia playfully placed her hand over her partner's mouth. 'Go and fill my drink my lovey, the tide's gone out.'

An obedient dog trotted off.

Then turning back to Kant she said, 'He's very … supportive. It was a hobby for years. Ever since I can remember I've loved cooking. I suppose I'm lucky my pastime and passion could become my job. I never seem to tire of it.'

'My daughter teaches cooking and ceramics at the Polytechnic. Calls herself an alchemist.'

'What a lovely way of looking at it.'

Gillian, who had been listening, sipping at her glass of white, looked relieved to see Donald totter off. She smiled at Kant, who suspected that Donald's proud but potentially tiresome account of his wife's business was building up to a long-winded rendition to pamper his own shaky ego.

'Nice sav blank. From your cellar, Barry?' Gillian said as her eyes fixed on his face. Kant looked down for a moment, feeling a little uncomfortable with what felt like scrutiny.

'Oh, er, quite right, from my legendary cellar, third rack down, tenth aisle across, a very good year that *particular* one. Eastern slope, picked by four generations of left-handed Italian migrant workers with viticulture in their blood,' he found himself replying, surprised at how light he suddenly felt in the company of this woman, who seemed unconcerned about joining Maritia in the BKS fan club.

'Do you live locally, Gillian?' he asked, realising he didn't mind if she was checking him out; her gaze was hypnotic. Neither of them noticed Maritia wander off towards the kitchen.

'I have a tiny terraced house in Hawthorn, in Melbourne, which I have just bought, but for the moment I'm also on an eastern slope here in Hobart,' Gillian replied, taking a sip but not taking her eyes off Kant, 'of Mount Wellington that is. Not a grape to be seen up there though. Except the ones I buy from the supermarket, and, of course, the pictures on the side of wine casks!'

'I think at this point I need to confess.'

'Oh, I wouldn't. I like the sound of your cellar. So many old-fashioned ideals are disappearing these days.' Gillian tapped her glass against Barry's.

'Your daughter – where's she coming from?'

'Oh, Agalia, yes.' With the mention of her daughter's name Kant noticed a twist of tone in Gillian's voice. She began to talk more quickly. 'BJ's coming from my place in Hawthorn. But she's lived her life in Greece. I was married once to a Greek, in Athens. My husband died several years ago, car accident, and I decided to return to Australia to reconnect with my roots. I used to live in Melbourne as a child, but I'd visited Hobart once with my parents when I was a teenager.' She paused and took a breath. 'One of the few things I actually enjoyed doing with them then. I remembered how beautiful the city was, and friends of mine have gone on a sabbatical in Canada, Toronto, and asked me if I'd like to house-sit for the year. So here I am, being questioned by the famous Barry Kant! You're a household name in Melbourne too.'

Kant was lost for a direct response. And there was more to this woman than met his eye. He drank slowly from his glass to gather his thoughts.

'I've only moved to Hobart fairly recently too, from the Huon Valley. Well, a couple of years ago actually. Not nearly as magical as Athens though.'

'There's more to Athens than the Acropolis. It can get very over-heated and can also be a seething hotbed of corruption and malpractice, and, if you're middle-aged and widowed, daily life can become quite … well … oppressive.'

'Your husband … '

'Cons was a diplomat. We spent time moving from place to place. It was fine while his job was more stationary but as he began to have different postings I began to feel like the diplomat's attaché case. It became difficult to have a sense of myself. He had a stint in Baghdad, which for me was like being in a prison. We couldn't go anywhere freely and then one day he was killed by a terrorist car-bomb explosion just outside the green zone. I tell people it was a car accident because it sounds … I don't know, easier to understand somehow.'

'I'm sorry to hear that. It must have been a ghastly time for you.'

'It was but … life's a funny thing, Barry. And I'm not sure why I'm telling you this, but the morning it happened I'd told my husband of twenty years I wanted out. His highly tuned diplomacy skills had begun to blur the edges of our relationship. And so had a long line of bored and pretty, young consulate personnel.'

'That's tough,' Barry said, feeling uncomfortable with the intimacy of Gillian's admission. He drank some of his wine and made a quick peripheral glance towards the kitchen to see what Mackelroy was up to. Steam from the rice cooker was fogging the window.

'It was tough for Agalia too. Truth sits on a precariously fine line when it's suspended over temptation,' Gillian said. 'All that seems a long time ago now. I have, as they say, moved on.'

And so too did the conversation.

'Are your parents in Australia, Gillian?'

'Sadly, my father died last year and my mother has fulltime care in a hospice. She has advanced dementia. But their house in Moonee Ponds has not been sold, and my older brother, who's somewhat of a recluse, lives there.'

Kant laughed. 'Do you remember Edna Everage giving Moonee Ponds a hard time in the seventies?'

'Don't mention it. As a kid growing up there it was embarrassing. But like so many things, you can only make fun of a place for so long before it wears thin, then you look for somewhere new.'

'A healthy Australian pastime. It's probably quite a fashionable place to live these days. Tell me … BJ?'

Gillian smiled. 'It's funny how we Australians like to alter and shorten perfectly beautiful names with silly nicknames. Agalia's a Greek name; it means *bright joy*,' she shrugged. 'Hence … '

'I've heard worse. So you haven't seen her, your daughter, for a while then?'

A rush of laughter came out of the kitchen. Donald was looking very pleased with himself, having just cracked a boysy lewd joke.

'Not for a year or so but we've been on the phone a bit lately.' Gillian's voice seemed to tense up a little. 'She's coming here on a … a bit of a mission. I have a son too, twenty-six. He's a *real* stay-at-home, runs a restaurant in Athens and has never travelled further than Italy. And that was to check out a new coffee machine. Flew back in the same day.'

'I have a daughter. She's a teacher, thirty-one, or is it two?' Barry laughed. 'I hardly remember my *own* age these days,' he lied. 'The years seem to scoot by.'

'BJ's just had her thirty-fifth. Maybe we can all get together sometime.'

'Mm. I'm sure Mel would love to.'

Barry also sensed this would be a good time to move the emphasis of the conversation. He didn't want the friendliness of this interaction to deteriorate into over-familiarity quite yet. This was foreign territory. But he needn't have worried. Mackelroy's voice boomed, a benevolent admiral's orders from the quarterdeck.

'Attention everyone, tuck in! Sit anywhere, there's no hierarchy of seating positions in this establishment. Help yourself to rice first, on the stove, plates here, and we have four different dishes on the table. That greenish-looking one is vego, so *you* don't starve, Maritia sweetheart. Some of you might though if you can't get a handle on the chopsticks. I refuse to put out forks for Chinese.'

'Smells gorgeous,' Maritia said.

Everyone present was titillated by Mackelroy's methods of procuring such culinary delights for a full table of guests at a moment's notice, the different dishes being surreptitiously transferred from the plastic takeaway containers into large, heated, square white bowls embossed with Chinese calligraphic characters. Once done, the food, like magic, transformed into cordon-bleu sophistication. The chopsticks sat in a pile in the middle of the table like spillikins at the beginning of a game.

Kant began to feel pleasantly insouciant amongst this friendly informality. He sat across from Gillian at the long Blackwood table so he didn't have to crane his neck sideways to look at her.

Two hours of chatter passed with good-humoured jostling and joking, rude banter about James' 'cooking' abilities. Finally there was a more subdued mood, due mainly to the consumption of several more bottles of wine from James' 'cellar' and the complete demolition of the profligate piles of sweet and sour chicken, Beijing prawn, and although not strictly Eastern, beef Mandalay. These had been followed unceremoniously by a large, irresistibly lascivious, irreverent Black Forest chocolate gateau, covered with fresh cherries and a treacherous glacier of whipped cream, which of course had nothing about it that complemented Asian cuisine. It just happened to be Mackelroy's most recent *discovery* from a German delicatessen in a Newtown back street, impetuously bought on his way home.

The outside temperature had dropped. The glass doors had slid closed. The electric fire with a stainless steel back-plate and perfectly realistic flames was turned up. With port in three hands, Cointreau in two, lounging bodies in low leather sofas and armchairs, the conversation had melted to one person at a time. Madeleine Peyroux, a contemporary-sounding Billy Holiday, sang soulfully in the background, of lost love.

Vince MacLean had become reflective, having a gnawing irritation with Donald's boorishness. The more he drank the more garrulous he became. Maritia who was the designated driver, remained sober, but to Donald's perceptible annoyance, was able to hold others' interest with her witticisms.

'So tell us, Vinnie, old man,' he said with inflated bonhomie, 'or should that be young man,' he roared with laughter, interrupting his wife's amusing account of the Governor's butler's loose-fitting toupee slipping sideways whilst serving a dignitary, 'how is the old daark continent? They still in need of mish ... missionaries and wish doctors?'

Donald's drunken remark finally goaded MacLean to his limit. He detached himself from the music and before he eyeballed Donald he glanced sympathetically at Maritia, who returned a longsuffering and apologetic shrug.

'Well, I've not been in Africa for a while, Donald, but in one occurrence eight hundred thousand human beings were massacred in Rwanda in just four months in 1994. Not so long ago Tasmania was celebrating their population reaching five hundred thousand.'

Donald looked towards his wife for backup, but she was otherwise occupied, fiddling with her rings.

'As you would probably know,' MacLean continued, 'it hurts when you nick yourself with the bread knife. Over there they use the machete to *hack* people they don't like. Knee caps and

Achilles tendons were anatomical favourites. The poor bastards who did survive will need more than missionaries ... Donald, old man.'

Donald fell silent. MacLean's words were a sobering punch.

'Come on. Let's talk about something nice now, shall we?' Maritia said.

'Yes, that would be nice, but isn't that the problem? The West, that's us, we turn our eyes away expediently from genocide, particularly when it's committed in third world countries where there's no political gain, and certainly no reserves of oil. Let me ask you, Maritia, do you think that particular genocide was any worse than the eight thousand men and boys who were murdered only one year later in Srebrenica?'

The question and answer were too colossal for Maritia. They'd been too colossal for the world. She simply stared back helplessly, her lower lip trembling. Donald sought invisibility by slowly pouring himself another drink, while Madeleine Peyroux sang "This is heaven to me" in the background. MacLean knew he'd stepped over the line but continued, unfazed about whether anybody was listening or not, he'd held his silence for too long. Was there ever a right time to talk about such things?

'I was embedded there for five months. I was in my thirties. I'll never comprehend how ordinary human beings are willing to carry out such barbaric acts on other ordinary human beings. And you know, a lot of those boys were under fifteen and the men over sixty-five. Their crime? Their religious belief.' MacLean's jaw clenched.

These barbarous acts had been pushed into history's shadows now by other more recent atrocities, but the reporting of that time still haunted MacLean at night.

'It was the largest mass murder since the end of World War Two,' he murmured to himself.

'That's so ghastly,' Maritia said, furtively dabbing at her eyes and staring accusingly at her husband as if *he* had been the perpetrator.

MacLean looked around contritely. 'And we shouldn't have to abandon the truth by sanitising it. It's bad enough these things happen; it's worse when the rest of humanity turns its back.' MacLean sipped at his port and then said, 'The indifference of silence, now *there's* a crime!'

Kant, who was glad not to be in the hot seat for once, had been feeling himself sinking further and further into the comfort of the leather sofa that he'd been sharing with Gillian, enjoying the warmth of her left thigh against his right.

'It's a shame BJ couldn't make it,' he whispered to her, not sure if MacLean had more to get off his chest.

But it was Donald who responded, loudly, clearly not wanting any more to do with MacLean's truth, sanitised or not. 'First the bloody airlines take away our meals and then they take away their punctuality.'

The mass of MacLean's words had been successfully fractured into tiny forgettable pieces.

'Tawny for anyone? We may as well finish the bottle,' Mackelroy asked, not looking at anyone in particular. He had surreptitiously been clearing the table while MacLean was taking the spotlight.

He might just as well have said, 'Okay you lot, party's over, go home, I'm off to bed,' because Maritia and Donald jumped to their feet feigning overacted yawns, and the rest of the company followed suit. After MacLean's rant all other conversation seemed trivial and pointless.

At the car Kant noticed Gillian had held back after the others had driven off and was in fact standing next to her car a little way up the road. He wandered up towards her.

'Everything okay?'

'I think the fresh air has just made me realise I might have drunk too much,' she giggled.

'Would you like me to drive you home? I can pick you up in the morning to take you to get your car if you like.'

'That would be very kind of you, Barry. I really don't think it would be safe for me to get behind a wheel.'

'It's no trouble.'

'I feel a little foolish. I usually have a good sense of when to pull back.'

Gillian pushed herself away from her car, pressed the lock remote and held on to his arm. Kant hoped that *he'd* pulled back enough.

The timber and stone house was tucked into the side of a spur in the shadow of Mount Wellington, much higher up than Mackelroy's place on the more diminutive Mount Nelson. Her friends had gone to a lot of trouble with the garden, making sure the exotic plants coexisted happily amongst the native vegetation.

Gillian had told Kant at the dinner party that she loved the quiet in their house. 'Living in my little terraced cottage in Hawthorn, I sometimes forget about nature. I reside on the banks of the ever-flowing delta of the River Traffic.'

The home in Fern Tree was surrounded by impressively huge eucalypts and thick stands of rhododendrons that, even in the dark, Kant could see were covered with clusters of crimson flowers. The zigzagging sandstone path down to the front door was lined with solar lights, some weakly shining from behind ferns and other ground covers that had overgrown, giving the garden a mystical ambience. Kant put his arm around Gillian's waist, held her elbow with his left hand, and navigated a steady course down towards the house.

At the front door he felt his anxiety level rise like effervescing soda intensifying in his chest.

Now what? It's been two years. You have a new life now, and here's an opportunity. Yes, but... Gillian stumbled slightly.

'Steady,' Kant said.

'Barry, it was so kind of you to escort me home. You're a life saver. I feel I should make you a coffee before you ... oops, what do you think?' Gillian's foot skidded again on some loose gravel. Kant managed to steer them both in one piece to the front door. He was beginning to wonder about his own intoxication.

Concentrate now, she's concerned about the amount you've drunk. A coffee, and the time it takes to make it, will sober you up enough to drive yourself back down to the city without kill-ing yourself. She's probably got a nice tin of chocolate diges-tives in the cupboard too, you poor old bugger. You could even ask her for one of those nice milk and honey drinks you love so much.

Kant looked down and realised Gillian had been gazing up at him, anticipating an actual verbal response. *I'm really not very good at this.*

'I'll take your considered evaluation of my question as a *yes* then.' As Gillian fumbled with the front door key she said, 'Come on mister, you don't have to be scared of me. I haven't had sex for some time either and who knows we both might even remember how to do it.'

Kant put his other arm around Gillian's waist, thrust caution to the wind and kissed her on her lips. *If only the girls I fancied when I was a teenager were …*

'Whoops'.

Clinging to each other as if they might fall off a ledge if they loosened their grip, they successfully made it inside and shut the door without incident, all notions of coffee instantly evapo-rating.

Gillian guided them both through to her bedroom like courting crabs scuttling towards a hole in the moist low-tide sand. There were no curtains or blinds in the room, the windows leading one's eyes east away from the mountain across the sweeping green-greys of the bush. Ghostly eucalypts, the lifeless remnants of bushfires, stood tall and ashen above the shadows. Kant felt exhilarated, as if he were a young boy who had just climbed into a tree house in the canopy of a mysterious jungle. *Me Tarzan, you Jane,* he almost said.

Gillian fell backwards onto her bed still clinging to Kant, until their bodies hit the softness of the doona. Kant immediately felt giddy from the scent emanating from the intimacy of this new female space as flickers of thrill punctuated his body. They lay motionless for several minutes in the cocoon-like safety of each other's presence before each undressed the other, fumbling bashfully whilst remaining horizontal on the bed.

Naked beneath the doona, Kant allowed the vibrations of this woman's body to gradually envelope his senses. Gillian closed her eyes, her hands surveying unhurriedly the contours of this man's realm, feeling the pulse of his heart and the potency of his masculinity.

The dormancy of Kant's yearning was about to be uncorked like a wine, cellared for years to complete maturation for its unique character to unravel, releasing its complexity. As he began to stroke her cheek he noticed that she had fallen into a deep sleep. He was quite content to feel the proximity and warmth of her body, aligning his breathing with hers until, within minutes he was asleep himself. Through the night he drifted in and out of slumber, and it wasn't until the early hours of the morning, when the eastern sky, beyond the shadowed city below, radiating with brilliant oranges and pinks, that Gillian and Kant were fully consumed by each other's desires.

Chapter Thirteen

As Kant stepped out into the car park just after six he sucked at the fresh evening air to restore himself from the weight of yet another traumatic interview. His body was still buzzing from the previous night spent at Gillian's place, primarily from the last hour when they'd made love before she'd shunted him off to work. *Or was that sex?* There had only been the touch of one female body in his life before and now he felt so inexperienced in such matters. *I wish it had been this simple when I was a randy teenager,* he mused again as he strapped his seat belt on. On arrival at the station that morning he had thanked Mackelroy for a nice evening and had gone straight to his office in need of a strong coffee, glad Mackelroy hadn't asked for a post-mortem. It was all so matter-of-fact to him.

'Whisky o'clock,' Kant had said to Mackelroy just before he'd packed up to go at the end of the day. The two men knew it wasn't an invitation. Too much of each other's company would end in tears.

'Another time. *I* have a date myself this evening. My formidable mother's in town, and she's informed me she'll have my favourite waiting for me when I get home.'

'I didn't realise she solicited for you.'

'Oh, *she's* good. Boiled fish with limp beans, soggy cauliflower cheese and mashed potato with murdered carrot through it.'

'A mother's love!'

'All you need ... See you at the coal face tomorrow.'

Kant found a parking space next to the Parliament House lawns and walked beneath the dense shadowed canopy of elms and oaks towards The Quarry wine bar where he had organised to meet Vashna and Max. A bowl of potato wedges with the usual glob of sour cream and sweet chili sauce would be waiting for him. He'd phoned ahead. There was still the faintest tingle in his groin, but the rumblings in his stomach were now a priority. His mother had always said that you could cope with life better on a full stomach.

Max, of course, had just swished into a parking space immediately outside the wine bar.

'How do you do it?' Kant called out as he trotted across the road to catch up.

Max welcomed Kant with an enthusiastic pat on the shoulder. 'A connection with higher powers, mate.'

'In that case, I can see you can get your higher power to have my whisky ready. Oh, and it's a double.'

Vashna was already halfway through a stubby of beer, chatting to the bar attendant, a young Irish lass seeking the world in her gap year. As Max and Kant approached he waved them straight to a cubicle at the back of the room where lounge suites created a more intimate space. They obeyed, hunching in like conspirators before a coup. Within seconds two whiskies and a fresh stubby appeared.

Vashna thanked the girl and gave her a five-dollar tip to support her travels.

'Tanks very much, Spencer.'

Max and Kant looked at each other.

'Spencer!'

'Your granddaughter?' Max mocked.

Vashna beamed innocently, and said, with a convincing Emerald Isle accent, 'She was telling me about the little old granny of her friend, who just happens to harve some interesting knick-knacks she moit warnt to arfload to a reputable antiques dealer for a pleasant price; lives in Battery Point would you believe, not a stone's throw from here?'

Kant smirked. 'And you of course, Mister Broadhurst, said you didn't know any antique dealers with that particular quality.'

'It's a fine line we tread. Anyway, enough of my nefarious activities. Tell us more about that African guy you had on last week. Interesting fellow. I wouldn't mind hearing him play sometime.'

Kant took a sip of whisky. 'We'll have a meal at the African restaurant soon. Anyway, Vince found him. He'd been beaten up by some of Tassie's finest. The lad seemed to take it all in his stride though. For someone who has experienced such a shit life none of *us* could possibly comprehend, he was buoyant, optimistic and even a little cocky. Game-wise I don't think he did himself any favours though – the audience wants the full descent into hell; they don't get high on survivors I'm sorry to say.'

'I wonder if any really survive. The small numbers of refugees we see here just represent the countless millions from so many third world countries, suffering because of the old man's inhumanity-to-man thing. But you take them out of their place of suffering bring them to a safe place like Australia and it isn't long before our memories are short circuited and all we see is a black dude bopping around the streets like a street-wise brother from Harlem,' Vashna said.

'That's true, and they've escaped one form of prejudice to be confronted by another, which I reckon's a lot more insidious because our country is supposed to have open arms for them, excuse the pun. So many refugees are confronted by a sort of silent hostility that's almost as deadly. It's beginning to make what I do seem so pointless.'

'You had enough?' Vashna asked.

'I guess I'm feeling I can't reconcile with what the show does anymore. It's gnawed my belief system down to the bone.' Kant hadn't expected this escalation of emotion.

'Sometimes you've just gotta sell up if your stocks aren't performing, to use a fiscal metaphor,' Max added, draining the last of his drink and signing to the waitress for another round of the same.

'Anyway, I'm not talking shop tonight because I have just…' Kant swiped his fingers through his hair, but suddenly found himself going all coy. He was saved by the waitress.

'Your drinks, gentlemen,' she said, placing the glasses and fresh stubby on the table.

'Gentlemen. I like that,' Vashna quipped.

'Here you go, love.' Max said brightly, offering her a twenty. 'And keep the change.'

Without batting an eye the girl looked at him and replied, 'Dat'll be twenty-two dollars, tank you, sir.'

'Well *there's* inflation for you.' And to show his magnanimity, and not wanting to be out-done by Vashna, he added, 'Here's another ten, and you really can keep the change this time.'

It was the diversion Kant needed, deciding it was too early to spill the beans about Gillian, knowing his friends' comments would be anything but helpful. He nudged Max in the ribs and said, 'So, how's the art world?'

'In Sydney last week, visiting an old dealer friend. Put me onto this painter called Malcolm Staines. Good name for an artist, eh? Ex-pat Tasmanian. Jeremy took me round to his place in Potts Point, *huge* warehouse for a studio. Always good to meet the artist.'

'I hope you bought something from him. Support a local bohemian and all that,' Vashna said.

'Huh, he doesn't need *my* support, he's raking it in. He had about ten enormous landscapes on the go at the same time. All sold before they're even finished ... New York, Hong Kong, even Cape Town, I think he said. Twenty grand a pop.'

'So you bought a couple then?'

'What do you think?'

'You're supposed to be the fine art guru.'

Max sighed contritely. 'Well, yes, but just a little one. The big ones were a bit exy even for me; I have to trade the Beemer in soon.' He held his hands out about two feet apart. Big isn't always better. 'It's called 'Nostalgia'. An abstract image supposedly inspired by the paddocks along the North West Coast, near Burnie, where he was born apparently. I have a soft spot for that area.' Maxwell's voice had softened in one of his rare moments of vulnerability. 'I used to stay with my grandmother, who lived in Penguin when I was little. There was something about it that ... '

Vashna chuckled. 'Spoke to you, did it?'

'Yes, actually, it did,' Max retorted defensively. 'So you can wipe that smirk off your face, you philistine.'

'What did it say to you?' Kant asked, unsuccessfully suppressing *his* smirk.

'It said,' he began, and then continued in a squeaky voice, 'watch the company you're keeping, they seem to be taking the piss.'

When each man had bought a round, Kant downed the last of his drink, stood up and patted his friends on the shoulder and said, 'Just a quick nip tonight, but as ever, good to catch up, boys.'

As Kant strolled back towards the apartment through the park and around the edge of the docks, he became aware that the name of the painting had flushed up a silent stream of memories of random times spent with Sarah. There had been apple picking at the end of a hot summer. Ribald sex in a haystack on the East Coast that time after eating some hash cookies had been followed by sneezing violently with hay fever for hours after. And there was that time when they had kneaded the dough with their hands together, giggling as the mixture slimed through their fingers, a precursor to another afternoon of capricious love-making. He remembered watching Melinda slither into the world as a newborn, but then his mood darkened as he thought of feeling helpless during the times when Sarah had been violently sick after the chemotherapy, and of the utter relief as she slowly regained her strength for another month.

My life's just filled with nostalgia, Kant pondered. But now that I've met Gillian it feels it's putting the brakes on having a future. God, I wish I hadn't allowed Sarah to manage everything. She was so good at running our lives. I didn't have to think after a while; I just did whatever she planned. They call that control these days. Vashna's always going on about it. I seem to have lost sight of who the hell I am. Did she erode who I was by being too caring, or did I just get lazy and give it away? Kant stopped walking to let a jogger pass and took a deep breath. *She couldn't even let me decide for myself what I should do after she died.*

'Flow on,' he mimicked sarcastically. Then, 'I'm sorry, my love, I didn't mean that. I'm just...'

As Kant came out of the Parliament gardens he noticed Melinda sitting in her pale green VW beetle parked across the road. When she spotted her father she got out and crossed the road to meet him.

'Hi Dad,' she sighed, 'I thought you'd be coming from that direction. You know, I'm still worried about Rosie. I got the feeling you were playing it down the other night and I can't seem to get it out of my head.'

Kant gave his daughter a quick hug. 'Come up. We can talk there.'

As they ascended the stairs to the living space Melinda asked, 'Tell me again how he sounded. Did he sound like an adolescent or could he have been more…I don't know…an adult? You hear about so many cases of kids being abducted around the world these days. Why *shouldn't* it happen here?'

Melinda went straight to the balcony window and stared out onto the quayside. Barry made coffee. 'Here you go.' But as she turned round he could see his daughter was unsuccessfully trying to suppress tears. Barry placed the cups on the side table and held her.

'I couldn't cope if she was harmed, Dad. Mungy's with her now,' she stammered through her rising emotion. 'I didn't want to go to school this morning. I don't know what I'd do without Yetta. She was adamant I should. She is so good with Rosie.' Melinda sniffed and wiped at her cheeks with the back of her hand. 'God, I'm a baby. You'd never think I was a capable teacher of the hordes.'

'Heavens, Mel, don't be so hard on yourself. I'm to blame. I brought this on you. It's my wretched show. I don't know why I got involved in the first place. I do, but it didn't work.'

Melinda blew her nose hard. 'Okay, Dad, let's just take stock.' She seemed to have found her grit again. 'I mean, what can he do, really? Rosie's never left alone. And this isn't the Middle East.'

'Absolutely. I'm pretty sure he *is* a young kid. He was sort of all over the place, and he hasn't phoned back either. Probably got bored and has gone on to his next practical joke somewhere else. Here, come and sit down. You haven't seen my new chairs.'

'You're getting pretty fancy these days, Dad. I wonder what Mum would have thought about all this.'

'About what?' he asked, suddenly aware that, after his thoughts in the park, he felt guilty. And he wasn't ready to tell his daughter about Gillian either. He wasn't even sure if there was anything *to* tell.

'It's all right, Dad, I'm sure Mum wouldn't mind you splashing out on some exorbitantly luxurious furniture.'

'It was *you* that told me I needed the sea change!' he protested.

But Melinda was grinning. 'Got ya! Only joking. Dad, you're sixty years old. You're entitled to do whatever you darn well please!'

'Well, that's a relief.'

They finished their coffees in the comfort of familial silence. Melinda had dispelled her fears for the moment and was feeling calm again. She smiled at her father, who she thought seemed to be embracing his new life rather well these days. She loved it when he looked so relaxed. Barry glanced out towards the darkening docks; the inside of his head was an aviary filled with querulous, flapping wings.

Chapter Fourteen

The graceful arc of the Tasman Bridge was all but empty of cars, just the sporadic damp swish of weary returnees. A week had passed and there had been no more phone calls, threatening or otherwise. Mungo, who had just left from the fortnightly gathering at Paul's place in Rose Bay, a sheltered suburb that hugged the eastern shore, was about to drive onto the eastern approach to the bridge. Paul had managed to secure the use of a boatshed where the G S T would go once a week to talk and drink and be musically still for an evening, the lapping water being the only accompanying background sound. There hadn't been enough air movement to even flicker the candle flames.

The grey lanes were shiny from recent drizzle. Mungo was driving cautiously when the Volvo got onto the bridge. Hobart was the State's capital city but here he was, at only 2am, and it was as if a curfew had been slapped on the city. He had been talking about the film 'On the Beach' with Sammy and Paul, and how spooky the emptied Melbourne city streets looked: the end of the world; the end of humanity.

'It would have been easier to film it here. The streets are like that after nine here,' Sammy had complained.

On the other side of the bridge, before Mungo had set off from Paul's place, a figure, that of a solitary man, had set off, eyes fixed on the top where the bitumen disappears abruptly in a sharp horizon, the white lane markers leading to an unseen other side.

The man had been smoking joint after joint through the evening. His lungs rasped weakly with complaint. The man wasn't a smoker but he had been offered a packet of the stuff earlier on. A pathetic weasel had approached him near Franklin Square, emerging from the stench and gloom of the public toilets' netherworld. The man had been taken aback by the emptiness in the weasel's eyes. He'd had severe pock marks on his face his only dividends from a miserable adolescence, a shaved head and a tattoo of something ghoulish on his neck. The weasel, barely into his twenties, had snatched the fifty-dollar note and disappeared like a wisp of exhaust fumes, leaving behind the odour of sour cigarette smoke and a sour, peaty smell of unwashed skin. The man had pondered mirthlessly about whether it could be classed as a donation to a charity, tax deductable. He'd grimaced with bitter humour.

As Mungo neared the top of the bridge he noticed a person climbing up onto the railings at the highest point.

'Oh shit. What have we got here?' he whispered to himself.

It had been the third night this week the man had made the journey, from the privileged, tree-lined heart of Sandy Bay. On Monday he hadn't reckoned on the southerly being so strong, ironically it was off-putting. When he'd reached the top of the Tasman Bridge the chill had inserted an illogical doubt in his mind. He would come back when the low had passed. He knew the Tasmanian weather patterns well. In the past months he had spent much of his time sleeping rough. He couldn't bear the feeling of comfort his home had once provided.

A Woolworths Frigidaire truck hissed by, startling Mungo, who had subconsciously slowed down, setting off a spasm of fear that reverberated in his stomach. But as the truck passed, the man on the railing showed no reaction, as if he was disconnected to the world outside his immediate zone.

Mungo came to a stop about twenty metres away. He didn't want to scare the bloke. It was a man, he could see that now. He was sitting on the rail with his legs over the outside. It looked as if he was just admiring the view. Not about to jump to his death.

Mungo didn't know it but the man was thinking of the day a ship had rammed the bridge back in seventy-four. He had been quite little, three or four. His parents had delayed a trip to visit his grandmother in Rokeby. He and his sister and brother had been running around the kitchen chasing each other and his father had turned to tell them to go and play upstairs till it was time to go. The bread knife had slipped accidentally cutting a slice off the end of his father's index finger, not too serious but quite a flow of blood. The children had giggled because their father had used one of the pristine white slices of bread as a bandage. His father did things like that, putting his family's protection first, making light of what could have been an apprehensive experience for his children. They would visit Gran the next day.

But they didn't, couldn't, because like so many other people in Hobart that night, who all had similar lucky-escape stories to tell, they heard the news on the radio around nine or so later that evening.

'How can a giant ship just ram our bridge and bring it tumbling down into the water?' his mother had kept repeating.

'It's unthinkable,' his father had said.

It was an absurd idea, a practical joke by the radio station. But the reports filled the airways with alarm and astonishment. And, apparently there were some cars suspended over the edge with their front wheels spinning above the massive drop to the water. The drivers had to climb over into the back seat to get out. Speculation was rife about the damage done to the human body after falling that distance, trapped in a car.

Next morning their father drove them all round to Cornelian Bay. It seemed as if half of Hobart was there too, enticed by the sheer danger, the disbelief and thrill of disaster.

'Look Daddy, you can see the big gap,' little Gabby had said.

'Those poor people,' his mother kept repeating. But then, as a little boy Gabriel'd had no concept of the height of the bridge, let alone the consequences if you were to drive over. All he could see was the gap, as he was protected by his youth and innocence.

Now he was over forty and blindly protected by grief.

Mungo inched the car forward slowly. Only ten metres now.

The man had perversely worked out that here on this spot he

would be one hundred and ninety-seven feet, or sixty point five metres above the cold ink waters of the Derwent River. His preference had been the southern side. The blackness of the river was straddled by twinkling lights, the casino's tower of hope and disappearing dreams taunting him. In the far distance he could just make out the silhouette of Betsy Island cutting an ominous horizon. Everywhere he looked there seemed to be another edge to an alternative infinity.

His family had flown over to Melbourne, just after he had been born, to stay with his mother's sister, a nurse who lived near the Zoo.

Two cities, two bridges and I was there on both occasions. If this was the Westgate Bridge you'd hear the rumble of life, the man began to think. *But here … this damned city. It's like a fucking morgue.*

The man's mind was racing now, flitting – *thirty-two feet per second per second* – he'd never given it another moment of his time after he failed high school physics. He never knew what it really meant, but you didn't have to be Einstein to realise that the soft weight of a human body, after falling nearly two hundred feet, gathering speed, would not be the enveloping sluice of a dive from the side of a pool, degree of difficulty 6.9, in the pike position. It, unable to control its aerodynamic best, would gain momentum, tumbling, twisting – turning water into concrete. *Another of God's little miracles,* he thought bitterly.

He and a couple of his classmates had speculated with

teenage bloodthirstiness that the impact would rupture every organ in the body: blood squirting like fountains from every orifice of the body, scrambling the brain into a jelly, and dislocating limbs. Immediate and total severance from life.

What did it matter now? And yet, the man's distraught mind floated in a bizarre, comforting fog. Every now and then it cleared before sinking again into the horror of that fateful night a year and a half ago and then becoming swaddled in the mist again.

Mungo had managed to bring the car to just under where the man was perched.

There had once been grace in the man's life. It had been a life filled with beauty and elegance. But that had been taken away, taken by chance, one in a trillion possibilities, completely obliterating every vestige of happiness, passion, family.

'You right there, mate?' Mungo said gently.

A muffled sound suddenly entered the man's consciousness, nudging him. He refocused on the black void ahead of him. He wanted to hold onto the beautiful memories one last time, but there was something there, interrupting the moment like an audience cough in the opening bars of the sonata.

There was muted talking, cotton-wool voice, sucked from incongruity like a hopeless warning in a nightmare, relentless and futile.

'Hey mate, why don't you come down and talk to me?' Mungo persisted, maintaining a steady tone.

The man felt confused. It was as if the words had been sewn

together at random and spoken backwards. Individual words were recognisable but their formulation made no sense. Just noise. It could have been dialogue, speech, but there was no structure, like the Tasmanian Symphony Orchestra he played with for fifteen years, tuning up at the beginning of a performance. Until of course they all found the same note on which to alight, sounding the way for perfect orchestral interaction.

Pitch perfect, he could hear a single droning note now – the low hum in F sharp of an idling engine.

Maybe it's a boat below. Surely not, it's too dark, another ship about to ram? That's irony for you, or is that coincidence?

Mungo, struggling to get the man's attention, began to feel the pressure build in his chest. 'It's never as bad as it seems after a chat, mate. Hey, look, I'm down here. Yeah, here I am. Why don't you come down and we can have a chat?'

The man began to feel dizzy. The garbled noise was starting to break up into separate parts, words, words that were attached to another human being. He lowered his head slightly until he could make out the figure of someone standing about a metre below him, holding his hand up towards him.

'Yeah, that's right, here I am. Take my hand,' Mungo said.

In a sudden movement the man swung himself round, flipping his legs over to face the person looking up at him.

Mungo's heart flipped. 'Whoa, Jesus! Careful, mate.'

'What are you doing here?' the man asked flatly, annoyed by the intrusion.

'Thought you might like to talk about it.'

'It?'

'Well, you know, why don't you come down and … look, I'm sure we can work something out.'

You fucking crazy bastard! Mungo's thoughts screamed.

A change began to wash over the man, like ice gushing over his chest, as if he was not the same person that had just sauntered up to the top of the Tasman Bridge to commit suicide. Mungo could see his grip on the railing suddenly becoming more critical.

'Tell me what thirty-two feet per second per second means and I'll come down.'

'What? What do you mean?'

Crazy Man huffed out a squeaky, crazy man's laugh. 'It's just high school physics.'

He knew it wasn't fair because this guy was being kind to him. But nothing seemed fair to him at that moment.

'I couldn't get my head round any of the sciences,' Mungo replied as if encased in his own bizarre nightmare. 'I was into music. I think it might have something to do with velocity, when er …'

'Getting warm.'

'Oh look, come on, come down, *please*. I'm sure we can work something out. Then you can tell me what it means. I'd really like that.'

'Would you?' Crazy coughed words. 'Would you really? I couldn't give a shit.'

'Surely you don't want to do anything stupid … no I don't

mean that, I'm sorry. I mean … come on, mate, this really isn't the way to solve anything. I don't know what's happened but you look like a sensible bloke. Come on, I'll buy you a coffee and we can talk.'

The man blinked his eyes to maintain focus on Mungo, who, he began to comprehend, was offering him a hand, and real kindness. This much younger man could have driven off, left the old loser on the bridge and got on with his life.

Then, impassively, Crazy Man, who didn't seem so crazy now, said, 'It was all because of Barry Kant.'

For several moments Mungo was stunned. Reality had just become far stranger than fiction.

'What! What was that?'

'B … K … S. Haven't you heard of it.'

The all too familiar letters were coated with loathing.

Mungo remained immobile, frozen, frightened at what he was about to say.

'He's my father-in-law. Well, he's my partner's dad anyway,' he said quietly, desperate to extract himself from the nightmare.

'I don't believe this! This is so bloody Hobart. I can't even take myself out in the middle of the fucking night, on top of the fucking bridge, without bumping into some fucking considerate guy whose father-in-law just happens to be Barry fucking Kant, the bastard who put the final shit straw on my sorry fucking life.'

'So you've been on his show?' Mungo asked incredulously.

'What do *you* think?'

'Shit.' Then more assertively, which surprised Crazy Bridge Jumper. 'You *really* need to come down and talk to me.'

The conversation had taken a subtle turn and had become conversational, chatty, intimate even. It was as if they had been buddies passing the time of day in banter. It had become evident to both the men that this was neither the time nor place to continue this discussion, or in fact, jump to one's death.

'My name's Mungo. I live with Barry Kant's daughter, Melinda. Jesus. Look, come on, mate, give us your hand. Fuck coffee, let's get a whisky, Night Owl is still open. We can have a quiet chat. I'm in no hurry to get anywhere. Come on, yeah, that's right.'

'My name's Gabriel,' the man replied as he fell to the footpath.

As his feet touched the concrete his legs buckled under him and he toppled forwards. Mungo grabbed him under his arms and lowered him to the ground. Gabriel's body began to tremble. Within seconds he was violently shivering as if he'd just been plucked from the waters below. Mungo took off his jacket and wrapped it around the stranger's shoulders and squatted down by his side.

There was still the inner guard rail to get Gabriel across. Mungo swung himself over and managed to manoeuvre Gabriel, who was shuddering wildly now, under and through the lower rung onto the road.

'You'll be right, mate, it's just shock.' Mungo reached for the car door. 'Here, get in the back seat. I'll turn the heater up and you'll be warm in a minute.'

Mungo struggled as he hauled Gabriel up, guiding him onto the back seat where the stranger crumpled as if his skeleton had dissolved. Mungo shut the door and trotted round to the driver's side. He was shivering himself now. He turned the heater on high and drove slowly towards the city.

After a couple of minutes Mungo spoke. 'Maybe we should get you checked out at the hospital.'

'There's only one thing wrong with me. I'm a fool.'

'You're still here. So you're not a fool.'

'Shit… Fuck, I'm sorry for… I think…'

'Don't start beating yourself up, mate. But I do think a little top shelf is in order now.'

Mungo turned into a lane off Elizabeth Street in North Hobart, a block up from his studio, and parked. The lane was poorly lit but halfway down, a single low wattage light shone at the top of some wooden steps that went up to the first floor of a decrepit stone building. A sign on the ground floor said, 'Adam's Antiques and Collectables'.

'Reckon you can make it up there?'

Gabriel peered out of the window. 'Yes. I think my blood's flowing again. What is this place?'

'Night Owl. It's a hangout for musos who want to have a bit of a jam, meet other musos… and drink. It's about the only nightclub in Hobart that stays open all night. The owners live here; dunno what they're on but they never seem to sleep.'

'I used to play oboe with the TSO,' Gabriel said quietly, almost as if he was simply reminding himself. 'But after… Anyway, my daughter was starting to learn the piano.'

'My kid's a bit young. Want to get her onto the keys in a few years. I teach a bit at home. Mainly get paid in veggies though!'

Mungo came round to the back door and opened it for Gabriel. The warmth of the car and the few minutes of rest on the back seat seemed to have given him back some strength, and colour was brushing his face. He looked to be ten years older than Mungo, the smooth skin around his eyes and mouth had been creased by pain, his fair hair greying at the temples.

'Here, you'd better take this back,' Gabriel said, giving Mungo his jacket. 'Suits you better.'

'Vinnies.'

'I didn't mean…'

'Don't worry about it. Barry tells me I ought to *up* my game a bit.'

The loft space was warm and humming with pockets of conversation. Two young women were playing acoustic guitars in one dim, candle-lit corner, humming through a melody together, trying alternate harmonies. A tall gangly man in his mid-twenties was wiping the top of the bar. He was talking to another young, bearded man who was showing him his newly purchased oud, a strange-looking instrument with a bulbous back like a lute.

'Bought it in Sydney last week. From this bloke in a Leb café. Farouk or something.'

They both chuckled.

The barman looked up when the two men approached, saying, 'Mungo. Thought you'd be curled up with that woman of yours by now.'

'Just living outside the square. Meet Gabriel. Eddy. Can we have two Haigs? Stick it on my tab, can you?' He winked.

'Where you sitting? I'll bring them over.'

'We'll take the chesterfield suite.'

'Okay.'

Mungo led Gabriel to a darkened space with a very battered old sofa and a couple of armchairs. Tea candles flickered in saucers on a low table. Both men subsided heavily, Gabriel in an armchair, Mungo sprawled across the chesterfield.

'Welcome to my *other* lounge room.'

'You obviously spend a lot of time here,' Gabriel said. Although he went down at the end of the sentence it felt like a question.

'Yeah, much to my wife's chagrin. Shit, can't believe I actually used that word! Anyway, I'm sort of trying to get together some avant-garde music. I experiment with keyboard and effects, sampling real instruments from different cultures. I have a studio down the road a bit, in another building with dilapidated character. That oud, fretless, nice bendy notes on Arabic scales, is a Middle Eastern instrument and would be perfect for what we're doing at the moment.'

'We?'

'There are three of us. We call ourselves … don't laugh … Global Synthesis Trio.'

Gabriel didn't laugh. His mind seemed to be only partially present. 'You sound as if you've got a pretty good life happening for yourself. Creative work, teaching, wife, child … '

There was deep sadness in Gabriel's voice, but Mungo decided he'd wait till the whiskies came before he'd broach the subject of the bridge, if at all. *It could be a long night,* he thought.

'Just need to take a slash, back in a sec.'

As he passed the bar he said to the barman, 'Keep an eye on him, yeah?'

'Sure. And by the way Mungo … '

'What?'

'You don't *have* a tab!'

'Yeah I know but … big story.'

'Usually is.'

Mungo leaned over and whispered, 'Just found him on the bridge, you know … a jumper.'

'Fuck,'

'I *will* pay you but … bit short at present.'

'Don't worry, mate. I know you will, but no worries for the moment, eh?'

'Ta.'

In the toilet Mungo made a quick phone call to Melinda on his mobile. He knew she would be asleep already but he didn't know how long he would be with this guy. He didn't want to leave him alone yet. She was used to his late hours on the nights he went to Paul's, but this might take till the morning.

Her voice was sleepy but reassuring, trusting. 'S'all right, darling, I've got Rosie keeping me warm. Do what you need to do. And Mungy…'

'Yeah?'

'You're a good man.'

'Thanks.'

'And Mungy…'

'What?'

'I love you.' The phone went dead.

When Mungo returned Gabriel was sitting exactly as he had been left. He was staring at nothing in particular.

'That's better. Now, drink up. Here's to…'

Gabriel looked up and reached for his glass and lifted it in the air. 'How about life?'

'Good one. To life!'

They sat for several minutes sipping at their drinks until their glasses were empty.

'I'd buy the next round except I didn't bring any money with me.' Gabriel looked around the room and grinned coyly. 'Didn't need it where I was going.'

Mungo puffed out some air, relieved by the other man's humour. 'Jesus, you gave me a scare.'

'You think *you* were scared!'

The release from both men gushed out. Mungo's eyes

watered up and Gabriel began to sob into his hands. The barman looked over towards them.

Mungo returned a look. 'It's okay, Eddy, he's a musician! Can we have two more please?'

Eddy had seen it all before. Arguments over composition, or over whose instrument would play the solo and whose would harmonise, passionate outbursts of joy, of anger, of just about every emotion that a temperamental maestro-in-the-making could let fly with. Eddy couldn't believe how many intensely earnest musical masterminds there were at any given time in Night Owl. All searching for something unique that would set them apart from the rest. Mungo was no different.

Mungo fetched the drinks.

'Here ya go.'

'Sorry about that. It's just been ... to be quite honest, a living hell this last two years. And I'm sorry about what I called your wife's father back there. It wasn't anything to do with him really. I just needed someone to blame.'

'Barry's got his heart in the right place. He's a compassionate man. What happened on the show? I must have missed your night. I would have remembered.'

'It was a year or so ago. The second series.' He shook his head. 'Jeez, I don't know why I went on it. Maybe I thought it would be cathartic, and something might change in me and I wouldn't feel the pain anymore.'

'How come you managed to get on? They don't just take

anyone with landlord problems or dodgy dealings with used car salesmen.'

Gabriel smiled.

'I can't stand all those current affairs programs. They're so full of the same old shit. I thought going on your ... on the Barry Kant Show would be a distraction for me. I got sucked into the magic of it. I can't believe he's your father-in-law!'

Mungo waited. He didn't want to push this guy. He'd talk when he was ready.

'You must be the only person in the country who doesn't know about my story. I was married once too, had two children, Sara and John. God, they sound such boring names now,' He sighed and waited for a tremor to pass through his body.

Mungo held back from telling him what *his* real name was. And then the question just fell from his mouth. 'Where are they now?'

'Now?'

Gabriel turned his head as if he'd been expecting his children and wife to be patiently waiting at their father's side, ready to be taken home after he'd finished his drink with this stranger.

'All dead.'

His voice was impassive as if he had spoken the words a thousand times. Just two words to explain so much, and yet clarified nothing. But his unfocused eyes spoke the real pain behind the words: that he still could not comprehend it, and would never be the same again.

'I used to believe in some sort of Almighty Being who gave me a life that was so rich and full of love. I felt privileged that my children were so healthy and wonderful.' He looked up at Mungo. 'I should have chosen a less greedy God because he takes more than he gives.'

Mungo held onto his impulse to express sympathy. Nothing he could say would change anything. Gabriel's torment was absolute.

'The bible tells us He killed His own kid for world peace. How do you work that one out? What a prick. I didn't want my family to die, not so young, not before they could at least have a good go at life.'

Mungo remained attentive and silent.

'Some therapist I saw, bloody Catholic probably, even had the nerve to tell me they were all in God's loving hands now. Loving hands don't kill their own child. Well fuck that, and fuck God. The bastard even had the gall to bring His own son back to life again: the cruellest trick in the bible if you ask me. With so much death in the world, I ask, if he's such a loving God, why did He only bring *His* son back? Eh? That's some awful example if you ask me. It's coldhearted and selfish.'

'I'm really sorry, mate, I didn't...'

'It's okay.' Gabriel brought himself back and drank from his glass, then scoffed into the emptiness between them. 'What am I saying? Okay. That's one thing it'll never be.'

All Mungo could visualise was Melinda and Rosie tucked up

in their bed, cosy and utterly safe. His parallel thoughts sent a tremor of terror through his body.

Gabriel downed the rest of his whisky and continued as if he felt better for shifting another fragment of his burden.

'We were out in the country. Went up to the Russell Falls for a picnic. You been there?'

'Couple of times.'

Mungo didn't tell Gabriel he had asked Melinda if she'd like to live with him as they frolicked amongst the spray from the falls, tantalising each other with wet tee-shirts. And six months later they had skied at Mount Field where Rosie had been conceived, their precious little Rosie, born out of love in the warmth of a ski hut.

'On our way back, there must have been black ice on the road; it was early spring. The weather can turn on its heels up there. We skidded a bit and I got freaked out because the kids, they weren't very old, started crying in the back. My wife told me to pull over so she could settle them. So I pulled off the road and parked in a siding. While she was leaning over into the back seat sorting them out, I went for a slash. I crossed the road to where there were some bushes. While I was there this truck, loaded with ten tons of rock, came down the road, hit the same ice patch, skidded and rolled onto our car.'

Mungo couldn't speak. A claw of glass was gripping his stomach and a weight, ten tons, sat resolutely on his chest.

'You know what the worse thing was?'

Mungo could only look at the guy with pained eyes, as his

mind raced back to 4 Luck Avenue again, the thought that maybe he shouldn't have persuaded Gabriel off the bridge crossing his mind. Mungo knew he couldn't bear a similar fate.

'I had just been irritable with the kids too. You know what it's like when they're little. They were still damp from the waterfall mist and were grizzling. I was telling them to be patient. The car would heat up soon. They had such fun at the falls. The skid put the wind up me and I was a bit snappy with my wife as well. So the last moments of my life with my family were ... '

'You'd all had fun at the falls. That's what's important here, mate. It's not about the last minute; it's about the *whole* life. Sounds as if you were a good dad.'

'Thanks. But really, they're just words, kind, but still just words. I have to accept what's happened, and just ... I don't know ... just get on with it, whatever *it* is.'

'Hey, listen, why don't you come back to my place tonight? We've got a spare room. There's just a foam mattress on the floor but you'll be, you know, have company, hang out a while and see how you go.'

'I couldn't impose.'

Mungo was tempted to say Rosie would love to meet him, but was prevented by an uncomfortable guilt that his own family was still alive. Doubt began to needle him. Maybe it wasn't such a good idea bringing him into the home, reminding Gabriel of what he'd had once. It could trigger something unexpected. He could be putting his own family in danger. After all he'd only just met the guy. Gabriel could have some mental disorder for all he knew that could suddenly go off. The whole thing might even be a subterfuge. Backpackers were being murdered all around the joint because they were too trusting.

Jesus, what am I thinking? No wonder society has become so suspicious and self-centred!

'No, mate, I insist. You'd be more than welcome.'

*

Just before Rosie crept out of her bed at her usual time at six o'clock for snuggling in between her mother and father, Mungo had explained to Melinda his night's activity with Gabriel, who was now sleeping in the spare room.

'Hope you don't mind,' he said, still only half awake from only twenty-five minutes of actual sleep.

'Of course not. The whole thing is so shocking, the poor man.'

Mungo felt cold hands on his bare back. He rolled over and pulled Rosie over him and hugged her into him. A surge of intense relief washed through his body as his tears brimmed.

Melinda shuffled over and held on to her family. They lay in silence, their breathing never before had sounded so precious.

After several minutes the bedside alarm buzzed thoughtlessly, reminding them of the reality of the day ahead. Planetary rotation makes no compensation for lost sleep. Jobs needed to be done and incomes needed to be earned. And so the morning's flurry of activity at No 4 began in preparation for a new day.

Twenty minutes later Rosie was in her high chair spooning strawberry yogurt, or most of it, into her mouth when Gabriel entered the kitchen.

'What's your name?' she asked, scrutinising the new arrival's dark fungal bags protruding under his eyes. He was rubbing them.

'Gabriel,' he managed with parched throat. 'You must be Rosie. Your Daddy told me about you last night.'

'Oh,' she replied, proceeding to tip Rice Crispies from a miniature packet onto her yogurt, as if the sudden appearance of a stranger at breakfast time was the most normal thing in the world.

Melinda entered the kitchen carrying a cane washing basket and dumped it in a corner. 'I hate washing. Oh hi. You must be Gabriel. I'm Mel. Hope the foam mattress was okay for you; it's a bit basic in that room at the moment I afraid.'

'That's its *style*,' Mungo quipped.

'It was fine, thanks. I'm indebted to you guys for putting up with me.'

Melinda smiled. 'Mungo tells me you're a musician.'

Gabriel looked momentarily surprised as if he'd forgotten that particular detail about himself. 'Oh yes. I used to ... I play with the Tasmanian Symphony Orchestra.'

Melinda sensed he didn't want to go further with any musical exchange so simply nodded her understanding. But then, unpredictably, Gabriel, whose attention had been taken by Rosie in her highchair, concentrating on each mouthful of cereal, said, 'You're a lucky girl, Rosie. You live in a nice house.'

'Yes. And Daddy says we don't have lots of money so he's going to put it in *never-never*,' she giggled as if she understood the precise comic nature of her interpretation.

Gabriel looked at Rosie, *this little girl, so confident with a rich and happy life in front of her.* His heart felt like cold lead. Rosie concentrated on her next mouthful.

'That's where most stuff goes these days,' Mungo said, pouring boiling water into the tea pot. 'Did you get *any* sleep?'

'What time is it?' Gabriel asked.

'Nearly eight.'

'That hour was the longest sleep I've had in weeks.'

'There's bread and cereal over there, just help yourself. It's free-for-all in the mornings here.'

'Yes, Gabbial,' chirped Rosie, 'the house is free.'

Gabriel reached for the Cornflakes packet.

Melinda swiped at Rosie's mouth with a damp flannel. 'Now, my little Rice Crispy, you know who's coming today?'

'Yettaaa,' she sang. 'Mummy I'm not a Rice Crispy. Rosie *eats* Rice Crispies. I don't want to be eaten!' She momentarily collapsed into a fit of giggling before she stopped abruptly and looked at Gabriel, who had sat down next to her, 'Why haven't you got a home to seep in?'

Melinda looked nervously towards Gabriel, who was about

to respond, then at Rosie, 'Come on sweetheart, eat up. Yetta will be here soon and you have to brush your teeth.'

Gabriel smiled at Rosie, who, he could see, hadn't been palmed off. 'When you're a bigger girl you'll stay at your friends' houses sometimes. It's called a sleepover, and you know what?'

'What, Gabbial?'

'Even big people have sleepovers sometimes with their friends.'

'Is Daddy your friend?'

'Yes, he is.'

'Daddy.'

'Yes, honey bunch.'

'Can Gabbial be my friend too?'

'I think he already is.'

Chapter Fifteen

Carol Symmons, the support teacher, had just taken Pammy to the girls' changing rooms so she could change into a clean windcheater. In the staff room she'd found one in the lost property box that would be large enough for Pammy's fulsome body. In a moment of enthusiasm Pammy had wiped her clay-covered hands onto her chest to clean them. Once outside the classroom, now lunch time, she would be fair game for mockery, as it looked as if her breasts had been mauled from behind.

Melinda's class were just leaving the pottery studio when Kevin began another commentary, quietly to himself, on the numbers of people who had drowned, died of starvation, perished from famine, finishing with a repeat of the numbers that had been lost in the Queensland floods. Satisfied he trotted off to clean the sinks again.

After he had finished, and everyone had disappeared into the campus, and trying not to get too bothered about yet another ashtray that Vernon had sloppily put together, Melinda headed to the canteen for a sticky bun and a chocolate milkshake. While she was in line, not wanting to push to the front like some teachers did, a very large penny dropped in the forefront of her thoughts. Without making it to the counter she turned and rushed to her staffroom to fetch her mobile phone. She went back outside.

'Hello, oh hi, it's Melinda Kant here, I don't suppose my father's available to talk to me?' She waited. 'Okay, could you ask him to ring me as soon as he has time please? Thank you.'

She flipped her phone shut and returned to the canteen for that bun.

The final afternoon cooking class, making pizza, passed without a return call. As she was driving along the Brooker Highway to home her phone rang. She pulled into the side of the road where the river bank was shallow and reedy.

Barry's voice was full of concern. 'You okay, Mel?'

'Yeah, Dad. Sorry, I hope I didn't scare you. I think I might have worked it out.' She raced on. 'Can you think carefully about what that guy said to you on the phone? Tell me again what he said exactly.'

Barry described what he could recall. It hadn't changed since the last time he had been quizzed.

'Think Dad! You said he mentioned the Queensland floods. What did he say about them?'

'Oh, I really can't remember exactly, Mel. I worry about my memory sometimes. Well, hang on ... oh yes! He did say something about the *number* of people who were missing in the floods. He might have even said how many people actually died. That's right, he did. Thinking about it now, it was a strange thing to even mention. Why, what's that got to do with anything?'

'I've been going over the possibilities. Kevin, remember the autistic boy I told you about? He was giving another one of his ... ' she sighed, 'soliloquies. I'll explain in a sec. And, well, I smell a skinny little rat.'

'Well, I feel utterly confused, particularly as he hasn't phoned back again with any demands.'

'He's not going to phone back. He doesn't want anything other than the buzz he got from his nasty little prank.'

'Well, I'm relieved ... I think.'

'Dad, my autistic student has some quite odd interests.'

'Like?'

'Okay, look, he has an extremely limited range of things that interest him, no peripheral perceptions. He loves cleaning the taps and light switches in the pottery room at school, but has no forward thinking that can say if he makes certain actions in clay it could end up becoming a pot or whatever. He doesn't even get upset when the other students in the class dirty the taps again on purpose. He just sees dirty taps that he wants to clean.'

'What's all this got to do with the phone call?' Kant sounded impatient. It had been another tiring day.

'His other idiosyncratic fixation is the *number* of people who have died in various disasters in different countries at different times in history. He was telling us the other day how many civilians died in the First World War, then how many soldiers, but not as a comparison. You see he doesn't have the ability to compare, or make logical deductions. It's just a list of facts. His father has taught him how to Google. It's bizarre what he locks in to.'

'Who is he?'

'Kevin Saunders. Believe it or not his father's an accountant with the council.'

'Well, that's good. He'll be able to tell his father how many angry people there are because of the recent ridiculous rise in the rates. I'll give Mr Saunders a ring tomorrow and tell him what his son's been up to and maybe we can sort something out,' Kant said in an outburst, a strong coffee still on his mind.

'It's not him, Dad.'

Kant needed to get out of the office and head for home. 'So why have you told me all that then?' Kant rarely lost his patience with his daughter, but he was still feeling jaded after a particularly difficult interview. A hopeful contestant had to be refused because of an obvious violent propensity, and BKS policy simply did not allow for risky confrontations.

'Sorry, Dad. My head's just full of it. Look, Kevin wouldn't be able to make a phone call like that, let alone have the presence of mind to make veiled threats that may or may not have a consequence. His mind doesn't understand conceptual progressions. It's just not possible with the condition he has. He simply can't manage any form of planning. Besides, his nature is gentle. It's almost as if he doesn't understand negativity because that involves too much mind-work, for want of a different expression. He's incapable of transposing his thoughts into justified forms of aggression; there's too much mental process required.'

Kant tucked the phone under his chin and set the office coffee machine going. 'The world would be a better place if everybody had those tendencies,' Kant added, abandoning the idea of a quick getaway.

'Actually, some pretty exceptional people in history were autistic, probably because they didn't get distracted by a zillion other things like I'm doing now.'

'Talking of distractions, can you get to the point, my lovely daughter?'

'I think someone has mimicked Kevin. Hence the Queensland floods bit. There's no other explanation, Dad. And if you'd spent a few days in my pottery class you'd understand completely. And I've got a good idea who's done this. He would have engaged Kevin, who would have had no idea he was being manipulated, in a friendly conversation. These kids make up their sordid little pranks as they go along. And, trust me, they don't need a reason. I don't talk to the class about my private life, but I *have* talked to Kevin about Rosie once or twice. This boy, Vernon, whom I think it is, is the ring leader. He could have come across Rosie's name by chance while egging Kevin on. He often spouts facts that he's picked up randomly. The rabbits think it's hilarious and lead him on for a laugh but resent the amount of attention the special needs students are given.'

Kant sighed. 'I really should have a silent number on my mobile phone.'

'Not boring you, am I?' Melinda laughed.

Kant returned a laugh. 'You could never bore me. I love to

hear you talk about your students. You *care* so much about them.'

Melinda huffed. 'Vernon Davidson, I'm certain it's him, is a kid who's never had anything go his way. I'm pretty sure he pocketed my mobile a while ago. I found it jabbed into a lump of wet clay. He would have found it, and saw an easy opportunity to cause mischief.'

'What's he after?'

'Just to feel important for a few moments or just noticed. Kudos amongst his friends.'

'It's a peculiar way of going about it.'

'It's a peculiar world he exists in. It's not the same as the rarefied one we live in. Well, *you* anyway, Dad! Vernon's father's been in and out of Risdon Prison since Vernon was a baby, and his mother has a different *live-in* once a month almost. He and his two older brothers live precariously between their mother's constant irritation of their presence at home and drunken vandalism around the suburbs. He is one of hundreds who live like that around Hobart, an underclass no one wants to know about; spurning education, they have low self-esteem and self-confidence, and lack basic resiliency through having almost nonexistent life skills, not to mention poor health. They barely survive in a vicious cycle of poverty, abuse and their own family's collapse. They have poor social skills and become perennially unemployed.'

'Sounds as if you're quoting from a manual. Don't get me wrong, it's still all very interesting but can we talk about this some other time? I *really* do need to get home now.'

Melinda laughed. 'Sorry. I get carried away when I think of what my students have to put up with when they get home each night.'

'It must be a hard roundabout to get off,' Kant said sadly, forgetting the fearful state they had all been in not so long ago.

'For some of them that's where BKS comes in.'

Kant fell silent.

Melinda continued. 'So many teenage girls get pregnant just so they can get a hand-out from the government. And here's me trying to teach these kids the subtleties of making objets d'art in clay that will invariably end up in a smashed pile on the ground.'

'What do we do then, with this Vernon boy?'

'I'll speak with the principal tomorrow and try to sort something out. We won't solve anything by going in with all guns blazing, and certainly not by involving the police. That's water off a duck's back to these kids anyway. I'm pretty sure I know where we stand now.'

'I hope you're right.'

'Me too.'

*

The following afternoon, after the final class for the day, Melinda finished stacking the kiln with dried green-ware. After setting the thermostat for a slow rise to 1000 degrees for a bisque firing she strode down the paved external walkway that ran the length of the campus. Classrooms, student common room and teacher offices lined up on either side. The canteen, with billiard and table tennis tables in an adjoining alcove, was halfway down The Avenue, as it was known. It had a glassed roof, and steel framework that had been painted with bold tertiary colours. Colourful, cold metal seating had been bolted to the ground, in groupings for controlled social placing. The Postmodernism architectural style amused Melinda, with its self-conscious protrusions and cheerfully superfluous geometric facades, *like Noddyville,* she thought as she neared the principal's office.

As Melinda was only part-time at the Polytechnic there never seemed to be enough time to build substantial relationships with many of the staff other than formal. She'd only managed a polite five minutes at the beginning of the year staff meeting with Judith Thompson, but she had a formidable reputation for dealing with tricky situations in innovative ways.

'See ya, Miss Kant,' a soft, timorous voice called out.

'Enjoy those rolls, Sue,' Melinda replied to a petite, unkempt girl carrying a paper plate of spicy spring rolls she'd made in Melinda's midday cooking class. *And your hair could do with its yearly shampoo too,* she smiled kindly back at the girl.

'I gunna eat them *all* before my bothers see 'em! Real guts they are.'

'Good for you, Sue.'

The campus was almost empty. At four o'clock precisely it was as if some invisible force hypnotised the reluctant students and marched them off with spritely steps towards the waiting buses, like UFOs waiting to transport them back to their often inhospitable alien planets, away from the relative shelter of the school campus.

'Sss … seen your old man on the telly last week, Miss Kant.'

A sagging, overweight, thick-necked, dopey lad wearing a Hawthorn football guernsey and tattered black jeans was slumped on a bench plod-tapping at a game on his mobile phone. Melinda had seen more energetic lumps of clay in the pottery.

'Oh, hello Derek,' she replied brightly. 'Not going home tonight?'

'Me mum's ppp … picken me up. Got a sss … sore rankle.'

Melinda had heard Derek had been bullied again at lunch again. It was the fate of so many obese kids to be used as punching bags, both verbal and physical. It didn't matter that they were IT smart, or topped the class in physics. It was their size, a visible human defect in an ever-thinning world of media-driven Barbie doll models, that was fair game to the predatory hoards of rabbits who themselves were ignorant of the flaws in their own self-regard.

'I have to admit, I didn't see that particular episode, Derek. Was it good?'

'Reckon them sss … specials would do good on 'is show. Sss … speshly that ssss … spaz who cleans all the light ss … switches.'

The pecking order, Melinda thought sadly.

'Not sure that's an appropriate way to describe Kevin. You should know better, Derek. Besides, Kevin's a very contented lad who probably only has a hard life in *other* people's minds.'

Derek looked back at his phone and began tapping again, puzzled by her words.

'Bye Derek.'

Melinda knocked on the open door. 'Hi Judith, thanks for seeing me.'

'Nice to see you, Melinda. I get so little time really to get to know my part-timers, what with the time I seem to spend on discipline, disgruntled parents and the constant lineup of *waggers* outside my door ... and that's just the staff!'

Melinda laughed politely at Judith's little teacher joke.

'Please, come and sit down. Would you like a drink – coffee?'

'I'm fine thanks.'

Judith settled herself back into her chair, in her benevolent principal's pose, hands resting on her lap, head turned slightly to the side like an expectant retriever waiting for its master's command.

'So, tell me, what's on your mind?'

Judith sat patiently as Melinda explained. She was an attentive listener. That was a good start.

'And you are certain it is Vernon?'

'He might be a total ratbag but he's smart. The other boys, they just follow him; wouldn't have the nouse to think up something so ... I hate to say ... clever.'

'All right. I have an idea. I had a comparable situation a few years back but what I'm going to suggest you might vehemently disagree with. If so, I'll completely understand and we can consider an alternative method.'

'Sounds intriguing. I think you've got me.'

As Melinda walked back to her car she felt excited by the outcome of the meeting. Judith had indeed *got* her. Yes, they did seriously discuss all possible consequences before she agreed, and trusted her principal's thirty years of experience. She was astute with a strong grasp of adolescent nature with all its idiosyncratic facets. There was a Child Care program at the school for the single mums, so it wouldn't be so unusual to see a three-year-old in the class. So Melinda had agreed that tomorrow Vernon Davidson would be Rosie's personal carer during the morning pottery session.

'Bye the way, I've heard superb reports from senior staff about the inclusion program you run, Melinda,' Judith had concluded. 'You will, of course, have the usual support staff there. I feel this approach will work well for young Davidson. It could be a behavioural management strategy we adopt in other areas. Keep me informed how it goes, will you?'

'I will, and thanks.'

Those frequently circulated rumours about Judith must have come from seriously disturbed and malicious minds, Melinda mused cheekily – that Judith was on the 'other side' of seventy, still single and a virgin, a lesbian who lived with her schizophrenic grandmother in a flea-ridden hovel, and carried out sadomasochist activities with Ms Pringle the sports teacher at weekends in the gymnasium. It was true, every school needed to have one of those on the staff. Such was the mind-activity of almost the entire student population, and even some of the staff. It made school assemblies bearable.

Of course, Melinda was savvy, through staff chitchat, that Judith Thompson, after leaving her beloved institution of learning and skills for life at the end of a day, lived cheerfully in the quietness of Taroona, a leafy river-hugging, middle-class suburb south of the city. She had two children, one of each gender, appropriately three years apart in age, both at university – one completing honours in medicine, the other embarking on a Bachelor of Education, and a husband, George, a paediatrician and Rotarian who never missed golf on Wednesdays and Saturday afternoons at the Kingston Beach Club. She maintained a well-nurtured garden, and tirelessly gave her energies to being a mother, wife, bridge partner and occasional ambassador for the Girl Guides Movement.

But above all she was passionate about the educational enrichment of the thousands of students, many from deprived homes north of the pyjama line, who passed through the portals of her educational establishment.

Chapter Sixteen

Nerve Two was in its usual manic state of preparation. Any number of potential phone calls Kant might have made to Gillian simply got flushed in the rush. But then, *I've not heard from her either,* he noted. What would they say to each other anyway? It had been so long since he'd been in this predicament with a new woman he quite honestly didn't know the protocols anymore. And of course the last and only time it had been with Sarah, before even the dawn of the dinosaurs.

Gillian had taken a taxi to pick up her car after their night together. In the morning she'd told Barry to go to work, knowing his schedule at the station was hectic, the fourth series being in full steam.

'Off you go,' she'd said. 'I'll catch a taxi to get my car after I've made a couple of calls. BJ's arriving on the ten o'clock flight.'

She had seemed distracted. Needing to be alone, too much too soon Kant had thought.

As Kant drove towards the city, his mind had rattled with threatening messages, thoughts about a potentially dying father, priceless jewels, and nagging feelings about John Sturges' story, not to mention being perched on the brink of letting go of everything that had been sacred about his life with Sarah. He had enjoyed the somewhat exploratory night with Gillian, so he was perplexed as to why he felt as if he was wearing a blindfold.

*

Direct sunrays warmed Melinda's cheek as she drove north along the Brooker Highway towards the Polytechnic the following morning. Rosie was humming to herself whilst looking at a picture book.

'You're a clever girl reading all by yourself,' Melinda said into the rear-vision mirror, smiling because Rosie's book of the forest monsters was upside-down and still captivated her curiosity.

A recurring incantation was attempting to wash and condition the tangled doubts in Melinda's head. *It'll work, it'll work,* the affirmation still on a loop as she parked the car.

The pottery studio was warm from the overnight bisque firing, an enviable classroom in the freezing winter months, and it always amused Melinda how many staff visited her 'to look at the students' work' during their free periods. She turned the extractor fan off and showed Rosie where she was going to sit.

'Now here's your bench where you can work, sweetie. I'll just help you put on your pinafore that Yetta made you. So you can keep clean,' Melinda said, knowing that she would be speckled from head to toe with white stoneware creativity before the lesson was over. Melinda felt a tad guilty for using her daughter like this, but from experience, when other mature-age students had brought little ones in because of babysitter problems, they usually had a calming effect on even the roughest rabbits, who probably didn't want to show a *real* child how immature *they* were.

Rosie was sitting proudly at the bench on a high stool as the students began to file in, all making gleeful comments and wanting to touch her and say how cute she was. Pammy grinned and prodded Rosie to convince herself that she wasn't a doll, and then continued to grin for the next hour until the lesson was over, looking up at intervals to shower the little girl with innate maternal pride.

Vernon Davidson, chief rabbit and wily culprit, came scuffing in with two slovenly hoodied mates, shoving and pushing each other before coming to a standstill in front of the new arrival.

'Bit young, ain't she?' Vernon said, then shuffling to his seat before Melinda could answer. He wasn't wanting an answer anyway.

'Who's that?' Kevin asked his father, who had brought him to the door. He approached Rosie warily and sat opposite her in his usual place.

'Everyone, this is my daughter Rosie. She's going to be my assistant today.'

'Make a better teacher than that Miss Kant she would,' a hoodied rabbit mumbled just audibly enough for Melinda to hear. 'Nah, only kiddin', Miss Kant. You're the best. True!'

'Kind of you to say so, Johnno.'

'R o s i e,' Kevin said, articulating the word slowly. 'Rosie is Melinda's daughter. She is called Rosie.'

For the next few minutes Melinda allowed time for the students to run out of things to comment on about Rosie, find work from the cupboards, settle themselves, and in some cases actually commence work. She observed Vernon surreptitiously from a distance. He seemed to be in his usual cocky mood, vulpine features alert whilst working out, no doubt, devious ways in which to be disruptive. The other rabbits were always a little behind him, relying on him for the direction of their misbehaviour.

'Vernon, could I have a word please?'

''Aven't even done nothin'!'

'Yes, I know. I just wondered if you could assist me with something this morning.'

Vernon tutted and slunk over to where Melinda had positioned herself just by the kiln-room door, where she could gain his maximum attention with his back to his reptilian cohorts.

'Yeah?' he said, arms folded with his usual suspicious slouch.

Melinda smiled at him. 'I was wondering if you could help me with Rosie this morning. You see ... '

Vernon tutted, 'Oaw, do I 'ave to?'

'Well no, you don't, but I thought you'd have the right sort of *skill* to look after her.' Melinda lowered her voice and leaned towards him conspiratorially. 'You see, you're stronger than the others and I wanted someone to make sure she doesn't fall off her seat, and sort of protect her.'

'You mean from the spazes?'

Melinda bit her lip. 'Well, anyone really. But if you don't think you're up to it I can ask Johnno and ... '

'No, you don't 'ave to ask that faggot, Miss Kant. I'll thump anyone who comes near 'er for youse.'

'No, I don't want any *thumping*. Just some gentle *looking after*. You know what I mean, Vernon? She's just a little girl. We don't want to scare her, do we?' Melinda said, using the word *we* as the last piece of bait for him to take ownership of his mission.

'S'pose.'

Vernon went back to his table and picked up his tray with the beginnings of yet another ashtray on it and went to sit next to Rosie. At first he acted a little coy, not even bothering to tell Kevin, who was still watching Rosie intently, to piss off to another table. It was as if Rosie's presence, so close to him, and this new position of responsibility, was holding him in check. He couldn't bring himself to look straight at her; just eyed her sideways and prodded at his clay with uncanny precision as if demonstrating to an apprentice the finer points required in the final stages of a masterpiece.

'I like paying with cay,' Rosie said brightly to him. 'Mummy says it goes hard when you put it in the oven. Just like a biscuit.'

Vernon turned slightly to view Rosie, still unable to engage fully. 'Yeah. The oven's called a kiln,' he added informatively.

'I like you. What are you making with your cay?'

'Ashtray.'

Pammy, who had repositioned herself on a table as near as possible without being noticed, whispered. 'Smoking's bad for you.'

Vernon's head pricked up like a weasel sensing an incursion. He was about to let loose with two barrels of demeaning invective when he stopped dead, allowing his prey to breathe another day.

'It's for me dad. 'E smokes,' he explained defensively to his young charge.

Melinda began to unload the bisque-ware and place it on shelving behind Rosie's bench. Eventually, Kevin wandered off to the sinks to inspect their cleanliness, and for the next forty-five minutes Vernon fiddled assiduously with his ashtray, seeking perfection in its form, dents in its side to hold four cigarettes, whilst Rosie chattered away to him, hands and face covered in clay. When one of his mates came over to see what he was doing, like a junkyard mongrel, Vernon barked at him to piss off. Rosie beamed at the theatrics of it all.

In the final minutes of the lesson Melinda came over to their table to see what progress had been made. Vernon was now helping Rosie to shape a small dish which looked remarkably like an ash tray. But in the middle of it he had formed and attached a butterfly.

'Look, Mummy, the man has made a butterfie in my bowl.'

'It's very beautiful. Vernon's very clever. Maybe he can help you another day.'

'Yeah, I reckon that'd be all right if ya brought 'er in some more, Miss Kant,' Vernon replied, not looking at his mates so they couldn't witness his swelling self-esteem.

'I might just do that. My father will be very pleased. You know who my father is, don't you, Vernon?'

There was a moment when it all could have fallen to pieces, but Vernon's culpable awkwardness at the question was overruled by any good feelings he was clearly experiencing from being needed and trusted with responsibility. Not to mention being called clever.

'Your old man's on that telly thing, in't he? I seen it a few times, pretty good.'

'Oh yes. And I know my father will be very happy to hear that his granddaughter has had such a lovely time with you, Vernon. I'll let him know how you've looked after her.'

'Cool.'

'Well, I appreciate your help, Vernon.' Melinda looked up and addressed the class: 'Time to get cleaned up now, everyone. Don't just dump your tools in the sink for someone else to clean either.'

There was a flurry of activity, teacher aides and students wiping, clearing, stacking and trundling off to their next destination of learning.

Vernon hung back and lifted Rosie up off her stool and carried her over to Melinda.

'She got 'erself a bit dirty, Miss Kant.'

'But she's had a great time doing it! Thanks to you. What do you think?'

'I reckon.'

Rosie placed her hand on Vernon's cheek, 'I like cay, Vernon. Can you be my friend?'

For the first time in his life Vernon blushed. He gave Rosie a quick peck on the cheek, lowered her to the ground and scurried out into the Avenue keeping his head down.

*

Mungo had convinced Gabriel to hang out with him at the studio that morning. Gabriel was a professional musician so Mungo hoped music might be the way to find some sort of equilibrium in his life again. He knew that playing music had been the most therapeutic activity for him whenever he had felt down. But he'd never felt so helpless that he'd contemplated suicide.

Today was usually his day with Rosie but now he had the morning off because, as he had teased Melinda earlier, Rosie was being used as bait by his mother in a social experiment to try and tame a Rabid-Bogan-Rottweiler.

'Bye bye Gabbial,' Rosie had said. 'Will you come and have a seepover again?'

Mungo had kissed his daughter and said, 'Yes, Gabriel's going to stay tonight so you can tell him all about what you made with Mummy at the big school.'

Unable to gauge where Gabriel was at, Mungo had held his trepidation close to his chest and prayed that he was doing the right thing. He'd wondered whether Gabriel should make contact with a professional self-harm counsellor; the last thing he wanted was to be involved in an aborted attempt to help the guy. But like all good musicians he'd gone with his instincts and they'd driven off towards North Hobart.

'Sammy and Paul usually come in a bit later.' Then he regretted his next chatty comment, 'Not having kids they have no sense of time.'

Gabriel was silent for a second or two. 'It's weird. I lost my watch last week.'

'Sorry, mate, I didn't…'

'Don't worry about it. And you know what's *really* weird?'

'What?'

'I've developed this peculiar sense of humour in the last week.'

'How's that?'

'Well, I didn't feel any animosity about what you said; I just thought that's like saying to a blind man, "Do you see my point."'

Mungo relaxed; it felt healthy that Gabriel's mind wasn't just stuck on the one track.

'That's the foible of language for you. And talking of blind people, I recently recorded the bipping noise for the sight-impaired at a pedestrian crossing. I want to splice it into the concept piece we're working on.'

'Interesting,' Gabriel replied and then added in a sombre tone, 'sometimes there are no words in our language that can describe how we feel.'

And Mungo found no words for a response.

He parked the car just outside the studio entrance.

At the top of the stairs he unlocked the studio door and they entered. Mungo was relieved when Gabriel's curiosity was ignited as soon as he saw the setup. He had been feeling apprehensive by the responsibility. Mungo flicked a few switches. Neon lighting above his keyboards hummed and flickered on, and then the sound systems blipped to life. He took dustcovers off the keyboards and pressed a few notes to check everything was activated.

'Do you play keys as well?' Mungo asked.

'Actually, I started with piano and sort of drifted to oboe. Too many pianists wanting centre stage. But the oboe is the instrument that soars higher than the rest.'

'That's some drift. There's some cool contemporary jazz that combines oboe in traditional ensembles. Barry burned one of his old recordings for me, from the early seventies, a sort of jazzy folk fusion, 'Icarus' by the Paul Winter Consort. He reckons it's one of those rare 'perfect' recordings, like Sergeant Pepper and Dark Side of the Moon. Anyway, I love the unexpected fusions in it. The oboe is great. I'll burn it for you.'

But Mungo's enthusiasm was lost on Gabriel, whose attention had drifted. 'May I?' he said.

Mungo smiled. 'Knock yourself out,' and regretted that too.

Gabriel sat at the keyboard and tapped a note. A strange guttural gargle popped out of a large speaker to the side. 'Nice. Don't s'pose it does ... piano?'

'You look like a *grand* man. I don't have much use for it at the moment. Most of what I do involves sampling extraneous noises from the city.' He leaned over the equipment and pressed a couple of buttons. 'Try this.'

Gabriel's fingers spread out above the keyboard and then gradually they lowered till the tips of his fingers were just touching, like the blind fellow feeling for the first time something wonderful. Then the notes emerged, slow, separate notes shaping themselves in gentle arpeggio, the simple descending bass octaves, the bed from which a dream can unfold. Within three notes Mungo recognised the familiar melody of Beethoven's Moonlight Sonata as it began to unfurl like a yearning into the room.

Mungo remained still, hesitant to distract in any way. He observed Sammy, who had appeared soundlessly at the door, motioning with Marcel Marceau hand and facial expressions that said, 'Wow. Where the fuck did you find him?'

Gabriel continued playing, eyes closed, oblivious to his company or where he was. Mungo couldn't even begin to imagine what was going on in his head, but while Gabriel's fingers moved, the beauty of the music turned dust into sunshine, tears into hope, and for just a few minutes transcended all feelings of despair. When he had played the last notes Gabriel looked up, self-conscious when he realised what he must have just done.

'Whoops.'

Sammy spoke first. 'Jeez, mate, that was some piano playing. I'm Sammy, by the way.'

Gabriel stood up and walked over to Sammy, holding out a hand. 'Gabriel. Sorry, musos, eh, just love showing off.'

'Anytime, mate. G'day Mung, where'd you find Rachmaninov?'

'Oh, just sittin' around, up to no good. He's actually an oboe player for the TSO; thought we could sting him for a few fills for our big production number.'

'Well, mate, if you play oboe half a good as you do the piano, you're on.'

'We better go and get it then.'

Mungo drove Gabriel to a modest, weatherboard house in Sandy Bay. They didn't linger, but Mungo noticed the place was all but bare of furniture and possessions. No toys scattered around to trip parents up, no childish pictures blue-tacked around the walls, nothing except a wooden kitchen chair which lay on its side in what would have been a sitting room. Gabriel told Mungo he had phoned St Vinnie's and the Salvos a few days before.

'They were very appreciative. Said donations like these would keep some disadvantaged families from going under,' Gabriel said without a trace of ill-will.

When they returned to the studio Paul had arrived, and after a quick introduction the four men lost themselves in five hours of inspired jamming, playing loops, adding layers of sound, recording it backwards, and banging out a mélange of rhythms. And through it all, like an exotic bird singing out amongst the anarchy of a jungle, Gabriel played his oboe, the melancholy notes soaring effortlessly in and around the lofty storm clouds of improvisation.

When it was done and they had finished a stubby of beer each, and a congratulatory post-mortem, Paul and Sammy left Mungo to lock up. Gabriel helped Mungo tidy up what looked like the dismemberment of a music shop by a tornado. They were quiet: Gabriel pensive and Mungo savouring their day's achievement.

'Do you think Rosie would be terribly upset if I didn't come back this evening?' Gabriel suddenly said.

'I'm sure she'll be okay, but don't you reckon you should come back just…'

'Look, you've been really generous, saved my life in fact, and I was just thinking I have to take hold again. You know what I mean?'

'Sure, but… what's the hurry? I mean…'

'There's no hurry. But when we went back to get my oboe I could see how empty my life had become, literally, and like, after playing with you guys today I realised how much joy there was to be had and how I needed to try again to do something about it.'

Mungo sensed Gabriel was talking on the run, but felt helpless to counsel. Trying again was something only Gabriel could do by himself. It would be a tough undertaking, needing immense strength of will, but not impossible, Mungo thought. He didn't even want to envisage what he would do if they were to swap places.

'Well, if you're sure. You've got my number; call if you need to chat. And hey, let's play again, soon, it was great. Your oboe sounded amazing amongst all our carnage.'

'You know, music was so very important to me. I have to confess it felt more important than my family at times when the orchestra was in the middle of some monumental piece by Mozart. Practising, performing and touring took me away from my kids though and I have regretted that ever since ... I just could have spent more time with them. But now, who knows? Maybe I will find something else. And Mungo, you don't need to worry about me, okay?'

'Sure. I'm glad I was driving by. It was rather an unorthodox way of meeting you but ... it's been a pleasure.'

The two men descended the stairs and went out onto the pavement. A cool river breeze had made its way up through the city streets.

As Mungo locked the street door he said, 'Gabriel, let me at least drive you home.'

'No, it's fine really. I like walking. So thanks again, give Rosie a big hug from me, and can you thank your partner for letting a stranger stay over? You've all been very kind.'

Mungo bear-hugged Gabriel firmly and hoped these vestiges of friendship would be enough to sustain this broken man for a while longer. The two men nodded to each other, an unspoken bridge that said more about the fleeting friendship than any amount of spoken words.

And yet, as Gabriel strolled unhurriedly down towards the

city, Mungo felt the enormity of the man's suffering like a clamp on his heart. He felt swamped by a wave of helplessness and began to sob. He had wanted to do more but knew that this man's crossing to a better place could only be a solitary venture. He fought off his own fears about his own precious family if the unthinkable were to happen and looked in the rear-vision mirror. He could just make out Gabriel's diminishing silhouette, trudging along an inflexible pathway towards the impersonal city and beyond, heavy with the weight of eternity pressing down upon him.

Chapter Seventeen

The apartment had cooled. Kant had forgotten to close the balcony doors before he had left that morning, and now the visiting evening sea breeze, which had strengthened, had made itself at home. Autumn leaves from the stretch of trees along Salamanca Place were beginning to fall, clogging the gutters and giving young children something to throw in the air. One or two, large, crisp and brown, had floated up onto Kant's balcony.

He filled a mug with milk; then, after pouring it into a saucepan, he stood watching as a ring of tiny bubbles began to fizz around the edges. He poured the milk back into the cup and added honey and a sprinkling of nutmeg, and stirred.

John Sturges would be on in two weeks. The fourth season had simply evaporated. Kant put on some music and subsided in his easy chair, opened Shantaram, which he'd not picked up for several weeks.

Bliss.

His phone rang.

He dropped the book to the floor. 'Kant here,' he growled irritably at the intrusion.

'Hello Barry, it's Gillian.'

'Gillian! Oh. What a surprise.'

'A good one, I hope.'

'Yes, yes, of course. I do apologise for not getting in touch, been crazy at work and … well. How are you?' The words just tumbled as Kant attempted to work out whether indeed it was a good surprise.

'I'm fine, actually. Although I do have a sort of confession to make.'

'Oh dear, do you think we need to call for a priest?' Kant replied lightly, having decided he was thrilled that she had got in contact with him again.

Gillian laughed her warm, engaging laugh he remembered from the dinner party at Mackelroy's house, a night that seemed to have faded into the accumulation of events.

Until now.

'No, a priest won't be necessary. It's you I need to come clean with.'

'Sounds a bit ominous. Shall I come up to Fern Tree, or would it be easier to come by here? We can chat in comfort. I'd certainly be in favour of seeing you. I already have a Savvy Blank in the fridge.'

'I'll come to you. I'm not far away, in the city actually, but you'd better give me some instructions.'

The apartment's bell rang ten minutes later. Kant greeted Gillian warmly at the street door. He kissed her on the cheek, feeling somewhat restrained by coyness, then led her up the stairs to the living space.

'What a delightful place. I'm sure passers-by wonder who lives in such a sensational location.'

'*I'm* only just getting used to the fact that it's me. Apparently it's the sea change I had to have, from my old life in the country, which seems to be drifting further and further out to sea as the days go by. Glass of wine?'

'First things first.' Gillian reached for Barry's hands and held them softly, leaned forward and kissed him on the cheek. 'I've been thinking of you ... a lot.'

Barry couldn't concentrate to answer; he was breathing in the fine fragrance of her perfume, feeling giddy with delight as his hands reached around to stroke her back. And now, buzzing from the warmth of her body once more against him made him recognise that repeating this sensation he was feeling right now could become a high priority for his life.

Gillian walked to the balcony, which Kant had just reopened after her call.

'Now *that's* what I call an outlook!' she said to herself more than to Kant. She turned. 'Yes, I'd love some wine.'

While he was preparing the drinks Gillian came and sat on a stool at the counter. 'Sorry if I sounded a bit cloak and dagger on the phone. It sort of is really, and I'm not entirely practised at this sort of thing, and I pray that it doesn't create any unnecessary hurt, but ... '

'Gillian.'

She looked up from the bench surface where her eyes seemed to be fixed. 'Yes?'

'Look, I've pretty much heard it all on my show; there's not much that shocks me any more so why don't you, you know, take a deep breath and come straight out with it?'

'I'm sorry if I appeared to *move you along*, you know, after our night but…'

'I hope there'll be more…'

Gillian had that distracted look again, Kant noticed. 'Are you okay?'

'Yes, yes. But our…night was an utterly unanticipated prelude to what I have to tell you now, so I hope you don't think I've been manipulative in any way.'

Barry handed her a glass. 'Here, let's toast to the mystery of the unexpected.'

He wasn't sure exactly what he meant by that; it definitely had a positive connotation. *Maybe that's the mystery Vashna rambled on about in the cottage that drunken evening. It seems so long ago now.*

Even as they chinked glasses Barry felt uneasy about why she now looked apprehensive.

Gillian looked into Barry's eyes as if she was trying to predict his response to what she was about to say to him. Her expression became wan, fearful even. Barry waited, not speaking, anticipating the unexpected.

'My daughter Agalia.'

'Oh yes. BJ, I remember.'

Gillian nodded, appreciative of his recollection.

'She got here all right? I was sorry not to have met her.'

'She did finally get here the day after. She hasn't been too well so she's been laying low. Oh, it's nothing serious. Just needed time to rest up.'

'I'm glad of that.'

'It's the first time she's been to the house at Fern Tree.' Another pause, and then, 'Barry, I'm sorry but there's no easy way for me to say this. My late husband Constantine and I adopted Agalia in 1975 in Athens. She has lived most of her life there. She has returned to Australia to find her birth mother and to make contact with her. I've been helping her. She's thirty-three now and … your late wife … Sarah … gave birth to Agalia.'

Barry gingerly placed his glass on the counter as if the contact might give him an electric shock. She was right – there was no easy way to impart that sort of staggering revelation. He obviously hadn't *heard it all.* His head began to move, throb, eyes searching the objects around the kitchen – the coffee machine, the bowl of fruit, the scraps of paper with scribbled memos, *I'm just like my bloody Dad,* a magazine, as if they had all spoken to him at the same time and he wasn't sure which to answer first. Or maybe they would clarify for him this piece of life-altering news.

'Sarah's her mother?' Kant murmured. 'But … '

'I *know* this must come as a huge surprise to you, particularly now as Sarah has passed away.' Gillian went to him and held his arm, 'Oh Barry I … '

But he moved away from Gillian, drifting slowly as if sleepwalking towards the balcony. 'Sorry, I think … I need to … have a moment … '

Gripping the balcony rail Barry Kant craned his head towards the night sky, to the darkness which had embraced all his fears, his sorrows and solitude over the past two years, and released a dull primal moan from deep inside his being. It was leaden with the very essence of long buried pain, suspicion and uncertainty, going back deep into his past. For several moments Kant stood paralysed, feeling utterly alone with the truth.

Eventually he turned around towards Gillian, not really seeing her through the opaque wall that was his thoughts and inched his way back inside.

'I never knew. She *never* told me. She *never ever* told me. Not even when she was *dying!*' Anger had sharpened his tone. 'Why would she give birth and give her child away without telling me *anything* at all? We were ... '

For so many years he had closeted a fear that suspected in some dreadful moment in his life, a revelation, in some shape or form would divulge itself eventually. Why else would he have been attracted to presenting a show that dredged up other people's past agonies.

In a deluge the sham of his whole beautiful existence with Sarah crashed around him. The one dreadful experience in *her* life she was unable to share with him, or ask for his support. It had now cruelly revealed itself after her death. How mocking his job felt. And for him there would be no answers now.

Barry felt Gillian's hand on his shoulder. His body flinched, then sagged, the life energies that had kept him going through all the dark days were seeping from him like a bleeding animal.

'Here, come and sit down,' she spoke gently.

She led him to the sofa. 'I'll get your glass.'

Forgetting he was actually talking about Agalia, Barry mumbled, 'The baby must have been my child too. 'Seventy-four, we were in Crete, together. We were … Jesus, we were so … '

The whole glass of wine sluiced down Barry's throat. Gillian sat down next to him, leaving space between them.

'Oh Barry.'

But Barry had fixed his stare towards the Afghan rug beneath his feet, unhearing, unseeing and numb. For several minutes they remained motionless, Barry endeavouring to make headway in the maelstrom that was whipping his whole body.

Gillian spoke first. 'There's something else.'

Barry slowly lifted his head, turning towards her. 'Something else? What in Christ's name *more* could there be? Tell me that!' There was a hard edge to Barry's voice – he could feel the astringent rise of rage in his chest.

Gillian dared not hold his hand as she had wanted. 'It's all right. There's something I have here to give you.'

'I'm sorry Gillian. I … I didn't mean to … shoot the messenger.'

She fetched her handbag from the kitchen counter and produced a yellow envelope which she handed to Barry. He looked curiously up at her, his response still lined with truculence. 'What's this?'

'You'll see.'

Barry tore a strip along the top edge of the envelope and reached in, and in a barely audible whisper said, 'Good God, where did you get this from?'

Chapter Eighteen

Piskochefalon was sweltering in the hot, languid summer.

Sarah was chatting in Greek to a gaggle of older women, black head scarves, black dresses and colourfully hand-embroidered aprons, in the narrow lane just outside their house. She had been accepted instantly into the intimacies of their lives because of her understanding of the language. Young Barry loved to hear the Greek words clatter from her mouth. It made her even more adorable. He had tried to remember a few words himself like yassou (hello), kala (good) and endaxi (okay), but he didn't feel the need to have conversations. He was happy to just absorb the village life, to listen, to sense what was going on. He was, for the first time in his life, completely at ease with himself.

'I think I might go for a wander up the mountain today. There're a couple of villages I'd like to have a squizz at. You interested in coming?'

Sarah enveloped her arms around him, and then began rubbing herself sexily against him, kissing him deeply. The women laughed and squawked like crows, nudging each other bashfully, their bygone memories of such play surfacing fleetingly to titillate them.

'You go, my sweet-hearted adventurer. I'll have something

special waiting for you when you return from your expedition. And I'm not just talking about the delectable feast I'll prepare for us.'

Barry kissed Sarah goodbye, gathered some snacks, a bottle of water and marched off down the hill. Once out of the village the path meandered through terraces of grapes, plots of plump tomato plants and crawling cucumber vines, makeshift chicken coops and shady olive groves. Nestled on one of the terraces was an old crypt, shaped like a miniature church, whitewashed walls and darkened, musty interior. Through a thin wall opening Barry noticed a shelf containing organised piles of human skulls. He had been told that some skeletal remains were sometimes put to rest here to make more room for more practical activities like growing food. The cold, dank odour tugged at his nostrils. Feeling suddenly intrusive he headed off again down towards the dry stony river bed. Once there he began his ascent on the other side.

By mid-morning the temperature had risen to the high thirties. It was much harder going now. Sweat trickled, his head thumped and his calf muscles felt like nails had been driven into them. The track was rocky and unyielding. In the second village, Makrigulos, he sat in the shadow of a gnarled olive tree and drank the remains of his water. As he sat there trying to recoup some strength, he observed two men drinking coffee from small glass cups.

Their donkey, looking mangy and weak, was so heavily laden Barry feared its back might snap at any moment. The men, serious in conversation, showed no concern. The harshness of the place suddenly revealed itself to the young Barry Kant. Until this moment he had been blinkered by sentimentality. He had been floating around with Sarah in a tourist brochure. A dog walked up to one of the men, who kicked it hard with his heavy boot. The dog yelped in pain before skulking away to the shadows. Barry wiped the sweat from his eyes, confused by the sudden rise of unease within him. He decided to go back, back to the comfort of Sarah's company. They could do the walk another day, together. It had been the first time since they'd met, just a couple of months ago, that he and Sarah had spent time apart.

Barry got up and began to make his way back down through the village, the gritty and dusty track oven-hot beneath his feet, the dust harsh in his throat. He rested a moment to look down across olive groves and terraces of vines towards Piskochefalon, its pale blue church with faded yellow dome nestled amongst the haphazard maze of buildings, pinks and whites amongst a sea of green. He could just make out the sultana factory further down the valley, nearer Sitia. The smell of the drying grapes laid out on every available flat surface in the village a few weeks ago had become quite overpowering, an aroma that would remain with him for a long time.

'Not bad, eh?' A voice behind him spoke.

Barry turned to face a young Greek man, of similar age to him. He seemed to appear from nowhere.

'Yeah. You live here?'

'Nah mate, Melbourne. Just come back to see my yiayia ... my grandmother, who lives up there. Couldn't live here now though. It's like the bloody Dark Ages. Huh, and no bloody chicks neither.'

'Well, what do you know? I'm from Hobart. Tassie.'

'Yeah? Got a mate who went there once, bit quiet. Tassie that is. Me and him opened a disco in St Kilda last year; lots of chicks in Melbourne, mate. Should come over 'n' visit one day. It's called Travolta's, down behind the Palace Theatre.'

'Oh yeah.'

Barry noticed the man's gold neck-chain, and his fingers which were home to several nuggety gold rings, one with a large red stone poking out with flashy confidence. Disco-Man was wearing black flairs, the bottoms of which had succumbed to the rough Cretan terrain, and a crisp white tee-shirt. His thick black hair was slicked with something shiny.

'Sounds good,' Barry fibbed amiably. 'Hey, what's that blue stuff down there? See, down there in the riverbed.'

The man snorted disdainfully, 'Garbage, mate. Crete looks all beautiful in all those glossy tourist brochures, but when you get here you see they don't really give a shit what they do to the place.'

'What do you mean?'

'Blue plastic shopping bags, mate. That's what I mean. In the summer when the river dries up, the people from the surrounding villages chuck all their crap into it so that when the rain comes in winter it all gets conveniently washed away into our pristine Mediterranean Sea, probably the most polluted waterway in the whole fuckin' world.'

'I wondered what all the blue dots along the coastline were when I arrived.'

'Take my advice, mate, get back to Australia. It's a dump here; they're all backward and don't give a shit about anything that isn't in front of their noses. That's why they chuck their shit upstream from the village. Don't reckon I'll see my yiayia again.'

Barry had heard enough from his cynical tourist guide, bade farewell, and trudged off again feeling decidedly uneasy. When he finally reached Piskochefalon he was feeling irritable and exhausted, blisters were threatening to burst under both big toes. As he strolled along the contouring laneway towards his house several people whom he smiled at, and who would normally return a friendly gesture, turned their heads down as though they had not seen him. Barry shrugged. He still hadn't got used to the local idiosyncrasies.

As he approached his house, really only a ground-floor room with bathroom attached, one of the old women who had been talking to Sarah earlier waved to him to come over to her. She was standing in the shade of her doorway on the other side of the lane.

'Yassou,' Barry said. 'Ti kanis?' he added, it being the longest sentence he'd ever uttered in Greek. He felt quite pleased with himself.

The woman twitched her head up once in acknowledge-ment. 'Kala. You lady, she bad.'

'What? What do you mean?'

It was the woman's turn to shrug. Her understanding of English exhausted, she turned and disappeared into the dark-ness of her house. Barry spun round on his heels and ran into his house where he found Sarah lying on the bed in the dark-ened room.

'Hi sweet thing, I'm back,' he said tentatively. But she did not move. Barry stepped closer and sat on the bed next to her and reached out and stroked her hair. 'Are you not feeling well?'

The shock that Barry received was blinding when she rolled over, revealing a massive blue-black bruise around her right eye, which was so swollen her eye had become a mere black slit in the doughy livid mass which was the side of her face.

'Jesus Christ, Sarah, what's happened?'

Sarah's jaw too was so swollen and inflamed she could not speak. Her other eye was filled with a mixture of tears and clot-ted blood. She winced as she tried to move.

Barry pulled a blanket over her. 'I'm going to phone for a doctor. We'll get you down to the Sitia hospital in a jiff. Oh Jesus, I don't know what's happened but we'll get you better.'

Barry was torn between staying and protecting her and leav-ing her alone again. But his body rushed out into the laneway again and sprinted down to the small square. Wheezing, he fell into the telephone box, which was almost buried beneath the lazy branches of a huge tamarisk tree. There was no telephone book. Not that he could have read it.

'Fuck!' he cried in desperation, banging the phone back on the hook.

Barry ran to the largest café, another Klimateria, and asked the owner, who, he knew, spoke reasonable English, if he could phone the hospital for a doctor for him. He briefly explained Sarah's condition. The man looked serious.

'Is no doctor to come. You take her youself to Sitia.'

'But I don't have a car!' Barry's voice trembled, tears filling his eyes.

'Endaxi, I am calling you a taxi.'

At any other time Barry would have plunged into uproarious laughter at the comedy. But now he was fighting back desperation. 'Oh thank you, please can you be quick.'

The man, grey-haired and walnut-skinned, stepped into the square and bellowed, 'Stavros!' Some very animated instructions followed. Another gnarly man, across the other side of the square, playing backgammon, jumped up from his seat, scuttled down a side alley and within seconds was revving the clamorous engine of an exceedingly battered car in front of Barry, furiously beckoning him to get in, as if he had been waiting there for hours.

How they didn't kill a donkey or run over any playing children on the way was a miracle. Stavros was quite simply a maniac driver. But Barry didn't care. He held Sarah in his arms as she winced and moaned at every pothole until they arrived ten minutes later at the hospital.

Sarah remained confined to bed for several days before she was even able to speak. Barry camped on the floor beside her. On the fifth day she told him she had been robbed of her camera and kicked ferociously by a person unknown. She told Barry that she had been knocked senseless before she could look at the attacker. All she could remember was the rough voice of a man. Even his nationality was unclear. Running the hostel had given her plenty of time to get used to the different European tongues, but after she had been knocked to the ground, sound had become distorted, her vision blurred.

A week after she returned to the village Sarah was still unwilling to talk any more about the attack to Barry. She became more and more insular, disinclined to eat much before throwing up, unable to find joy in anything that Barry attempted to do with or for her, and after another three excruciating weeks she told him she was going, leaving him, and would not say where.

'Please don't follow me. I need to recuperate on my own. I will let you know if I feel able to see you again. I am so sorry for this. It's all I can do.'

'But I can help you!' Barry pleaded, feeling utterly helpless. 'Can't I? Please let me help you!'

'You can't! No-one can,' she had cried desolately.

Every sinew of his body screamed in agony, his thoughts were a mountain of tumbling blue plastic bags in a bruising winter torrent, their putrid contents being disgorged into a polluted sea. As her taxi drove down the road towards Sitia

Barry stood transfixed. Never before had he felt so alone. Then, after an endless eight weeks of waiting and false hope, having heard not a solitary word from Sarah, his money running short, and his enthusiasm for work dehydrated, young Barry Kant flew back to Australia on his own.

*

Kant turned the thin and faded book around in his hand, studying it as if it were a precious, holy manuscript, not the discoloured and frayed paperback of The Guns of Navarone by Alistair MacLean that it was, the first thing he had bought on arrival in Sitia, in Crete all those years ago. He had given it to Sarah to read when he'd finished. She too could have returned it to the crafty book seller to resell for the umpteenth time. But now, here it was again like a menacing omen from the lonely days he had spent in the village of Piskochefalon after Sarah had disappeared from his life ... the first time. 'Cons and I were given it when we adopted Agalia. The agency allowed it as a favour to her mother. Sarah had asked that whoever adopted her child keep it until she was old enough to appreciate having something that belonged to ... '

But Barry took over Gillian's sentence for her, reading the words he had found scrawled across the width of a postcard of Sitia harbour, tucked inside the front cover of the book.

'Barry Kant is the best thing that's happened to me.' He swallowed to free his constricted throat. 'I will never tell him

I was raped; it will only stain the beauty that we have shared in paradise. I am heartbroken. Bright Joy will have <u>two</u> loving parents. I pray she will forgive me.'

'I've been assuming that Agalia is *my* child. Why didn't she ask me to help if she was raped? I don't understand. God, it was so long ago, but it seems like only yesterday now. I was so frightened when I found her. She'd been so badly beaten up. We'd been so much in love that ... God, her torment must have been overwhelming.'

'I think a lot of it was probably about not being able to tell you, to share with you. By the sound of it she wanted to protect you.'

'Protect! It was *me* who could have protected *her. And* the baby! I wouldn't have judged her; she was the *victim*! Jesus Christ, she held the secret inside her all those years. We had such a contented life. How could she keep it a secret all that time?'

Barry's tears flooded the anger and confusion in his eyes, and once again the sorrow he had felt all those years ago surged up again in his body, gripping his heart and mind in a cruel vice. Gillian moved closer and held his hands. Barry was oblivious to her presence.

After several muted staring minutes the sounds of the harbour, the streets, and life outside began to gradually filter back into Barry's consciousness. He heard seagulls shrieking, car engines changing gear, people laughing below, and coffee being ground.

Looking at Gillian now, he said, 'You've been very patient. You know, deep down I always had an inkling something more dreadful had happened. It was a very long time wondering if I'd ever see her again and I think once we did meet up neither of us wanted to return to that time. But I had it all wrong. She did too, but I can't imagine what it did to her, conceiving and bearing a child from such violence.'

'The innocents shouldn't have to bear the cross for the sinners.' Gillian sighed, then looking up and emitting a breathy, shy laugh, she said, 'Oh my, that sounded appallingly biblical.'

Barry returned a strained smile.

'It has biblical proportions. Tell me; did you and your husband give the baby that name?'

'No we didn't. We loved the name Sarah had given her, what could be better than *Bright Joy*? And that's exactly what she brought to *our* lives. But ... Barry, there *is* one more thing, probably *the* most important thing.'

Barry breathed deeply, then emptied his lungs hesitantly in a slow breath. 'Go on.'

Gillian stood up and went to the side table near the balcony and picked up the colour photograph in an antique silver frame. She studied it for a moment, replaced it and returned to the sofa.

'That was taken some years ago,' Barry said, his tone brighter with the memory. 'Sarah used to tease me. Said I liked to display the younger photos of her, particularly after she turned fifty. I think she kind of liked this one anyway; it shows her in her element, grubby and tired from working in the garden.'

'She was a very striking woman.'

'Yes. Yes she was,' Barry repeated wistfully. 'Of course, it was her spirit that totally ensnared me in the beginning. She always seemed to push herself so hard to get the best out of life. I can see why now.'

'BJ's the same.'

'If she only has half of Sarah's genes she's bound to be.'

'Well, it's interesting you should say that because I'm *absolutely convinced* that the other half, of the genes, in fact, belong to *you*.' It was Gillian's turn to sigh. 'That was the other *thing* I wanted to tell you.'

Once more Barry was speechless until his thoughts scrambled to catch up. 'What are you saying? Are you saying that Agalia *is* my daughter too?'

Gillian nodded. 'That's exactly what I'm saying.'

Like a conjuror she reached into her handbag again and presented another photograph to Barry.

'When I saw the photograph of Sarah, I knew I was right. The likeness is unmistakable. Not just with Sarah but with *your* eyes. You're definitely her father. And there's another reason why I'm sure.'

Barry had stopped listening. He stared at the colour photograph of a woman, not much older looking than Melinda, sitting at a table with piles of books on either side of her. She had a pen in her hand as if she was about to write something. Her fair hair was cut short, slightly boyish but chic. She was looking straight at the camera, confident, and yet unpretentious.

She had the clear likeness of Sarah at the time when Barry had reunited with her all those years ago in Melbourne, just after he had received her letter in 1977, wanting to meet up with him again. And yes, Barry could uncannily see himself reflected back at him in those eyes.

'Ever since we brought her home as a baby she exuded contentment, and as she grew up she seemed to have this innate capacity to make other people happy. She even writes children's books. That was taken at one of her book launches in Athens. She's doing well. And Barry, her qualities don't come from hatred and violence – they are borne of deep love. It's in her make-up, it's been hard-wired. We can get a DNA test done but that will only confirm my absolute belief. After all, and don't underestimate this, I have been her mother for thirty years. Believe me, she's *your* daughter.'

Barry stood up and fetched the bottle of wine, refilling their glasses. 'I don't think I can take any more today. She doesn't have a twin sister by any chance?'

Gillian chuckled, glad to release her tension. 'No, but she has a younger sister by the name of Melinda, by the sound of it, an adorable niece called Rosie, and you let slip at James' place, a cantankerous old grandfather called Desmond Kant. And, of course a father called Barry Kant from Hobart Tasmania who is a thoroughly decent man.'

Barry brought Gillian to him and they held each other, both treading water madly in a spuming fountain of joy and confusion.

They sat in silence for some time before they both started to speak at the same time.

'You go,' Gillian said.

'No, you go.'

'No, really.'

'Okay. I think that...'

'I agree.'

'What do you agree?'

'I think we should both go back to our corners and talk to our daughters. BJ doesn't know that her birth mother is dead. She'll need time to absorb the fact she won't ever meet or know her. But then she also doesn't realise her birth father is standing right here in front of me. I think it might be wise if we give ourselves some time before we take the next step. Is that a good plan?'

'Absolutely...' But Barry didn't know what else to say.

'And for Melinda, she suddenly has a sister she's never met. It will be hard for BJ because she has been working up to this point for years to find the person who gave birth to her.'

Barry's thoughts swirled in a vortex of uncertainty. 'My daughter,' he managed to whisper through a constricting throat. He looked up suddenly, 'Oh sorry, Gillian, I didn't mean, I mean I don't...'

'You don't need to fret. I have some idea what you're going through.'

Maybe it's easier for Gillian because she has no blood ties with Agalia, Barry had already tried to analyse, and feeling guilty for even thinking it. *Gillian is indisputably Agalia's mother, blood or no blood she's given a whole life of love to her.*

'We are all going to have to get used to *the new*,' Gillian said. 'And Barry, I hope you don't think I've been scheming … with us. I admit, I *did* help Agalia track you down as a way of finding Sarah, your reputation made it easy to do so, but I had no idea that I would find you quite so … well, you know. I hope it doesn't complicate things.'

In the minutes they had been talking, Barry had begun to feel an overwhelming sadness inch its way into his being, at first stroking his nervous system with a warning. Gillian was indeed only the messenger who, with Constantine had guided Agalia through the most influential decades of her life as their own. Now he wanted to remain dignified, even though every part of his brain wanted to scream out loud. He wanted his words to sound decorous, understanding, even though his heart shrieked at the terrible deception and miscarriage of justice. But for whom?

He felt like grabbing Gillian by the shoulders and yelling, 'She's *my* daughter!' Or was it Sarah he wanted to shake? Brutally. She alone had made the decision to give *his* child, *their* child, away. Stressed or not she could have asked him for help at the time, instead of just … What? Barry tried to steady his thoughts. *Wait till Gillian has left*, he advised himself.

'You don't need to be concerned on that score. You've been most selfless through all of this. It must have been a very difficult journey for you too. So, let's leave it for a week and then get back in touch.'

'Yes. And Mister Kant,' she smiled lovingly.

'What,' he answered apprehensively, a boy momentarily.

'Your daughter too will soon be given the most wonderful gift anyone could desire.' She kissed him on the cheek and descended the stairs to the door.

'One week,' he called after her.

After Gillian had driven away, Barry sagged into his chair and allowed his emotions to swamp him again. Pain and confusion pressed on him until he began to feel he could breathe no more. He had to get out of the apartment. The walls seemed to be moving in on him.

Once outside, he wandered into the docklands, grateful that the planet was still in fact revolving, gravity was working, the warm sea breeze comforting, and the continuum of life was buzzing around him like it had always done before.

Scrambling to make sense of what had just happened, his mind was a beach washed by a high tide depositing fresh flotsam, shells and seaweed that has been floating the ocean for years, waiting to be set down on dry land, new revelations for beachcombers to ponder over, and maybe take home to treasure. But the shine of his discovery had been tainted by a spillage of black tar and would need to be cleaned with great care before it could fully display its worth.

Barry's confusion was absolute. Fury at having his daughter taken from him, albeit by Sarah's naïve misapprehension, fought with supreme joy of being a father again. And his sorrow that Sarah would never know the truth, tussled with regret that he had allowed her to just disappear without being able to convince her that she could rely on him, whoever the father had been.

Then gradually, as gulls circled above, and fishing boats prepared to tie up, into the conflict that was swirling within seeped a warm infusion of anticipation, a growing sensation of jubilation that Melinda and Agalia would meet for the first time as full-blooded sisters. This was not just about him. Both his daughters had been conceived in a time of love that he had shared with their mother.

Chapter Nineteen

In Lutana the following day, not ten minutes' stroll from Luck Avenue, Kant parked the Audi outside his father's house. He tempted fate and left it on the road, the wheels of his car trapping a flurry of glossy junk mail scurrying along the gutter. The air was warm and Mount Wellington glistened, clear in morning sunlight. BKS, with only two contestants to go, had temporarily taken a back seat in Kant's life.

He sat for a few moments before getting out of the car, tussling with his emotions, saying the word quietly to himself, 'Agalia, Agalia.' He couldn't understand why he wasn't feeling utterly elated after the revelation. Until now he'd had an *only* daughter, now he had an elder as well. His aroused sentiments for Gillian aside, he felt saddened that she had been the one to bring him the news. It was irrational he knew. She had been so considerate. She'd certainly had more time to think about the immensity of events and prepare herself. But there was no way he could have prepared himself for what he had been denied all these years. But Gillian had brought Agalia back to her father, to her mother too if Sarah had been alive. It was a courageous act, which amplified his feelings of affection for her even more.

He sighed, looking in the rear-vision mirror. 'So here I am Dad.'

So it was, with his new reality grinding away at his senses, that he was working out in his mind what he was going to say to his father. In the confusion of his thoughts he had perversely decided it would be a good start to tell Desmond before Melinda; at least his father was one step removed and it would not be so emotional. His thoughts were racing. *What did Gillian say? Agalia is thirty-three years old now. All that time I could have been looking after her, nurturing her with Melinda, sisters together, laughing and sharing as a whole family. I could have watched her grow and develop into a beautiful woman, like Mel. I could have …*

A loud thud on his window startled him. He twisted sharply to see a group of young boys, no more than fourteen or fifteen, tatty tight jeans, faces obscured by black hoodies. They were hooligans in the making, no, already made, thumping on his car window and roof. Their ugly facial distortions squeezed together while they frenetically shouted abusive remarks and pressing malice against the glass.

'Ay, y'old bastard, wake up. Whatcha doin' 'ere, ya perve?'

'Lookin' for little boys t' touch up? 'Ere come 'n' get us, ya bastard.'

A glob of phlegm skidded across the windscreen.

'Fuckin' pedo.'

Kant's instinctive reaction was to knock on his window and scowl. The boys sneered and drummed more loudly on the car roof with their hands, yelling more vulgarities, laughing and egging each other on. Kant held the door latch and leaned his shoulder against the door, shoving two of them onto the bitumen. As he tried to extract himself from the car two other boys crashed back against the door crushing his leg. Kant fell backwards onto the seat with a cry of pain.

Adrenaline and a surge of anger kicked in as he heaved against the door and roared at the boys, a warrior with one thing on his mind. The kids could see they had taunted their quarry to a satisfactory tipping point and began to peel off in several different directions, whooping and laughing, stomping through flowerbeds, clambering over fences, shrieking like wild animals after an aborted attack. Innocent blood would flow again somewhere else another day.

There was one boy, Kant noted, younger, who naively entered number twelve across the street, slamming the door as if he would become instantly safe.

Kant extracted his shaking body from the car and leaned against his father's fence to nurse his throbbing ankle. A livid bruise was well on its way. Churning with rage he flicked his remote to lock the car and began a hobbling stride towards number twelve where a side curtain twitched furtively.

'Gotcha, you little bugger,' he sneered, not caring that he had transformed into a hunter-warrior himself. First the crouch, then raise the spear and take aim.

At the front door he rapped hard with white knuckles, shuffling painfully on the spot. Impatiently, he was about to let loose with another round with his fist when he heard shuffling the other side of the door. He took a step back and prepared himself to discharge his barrage of enraged complaint. But before he could summon a single word he was struck dumb, not by the aggressive redneck, nasty-piece-of-work stepfather he was expecting to confront but by the most demure, fragile elderly lady he had encountered for some time.

'Hello dear,' she said curiously, surprised no doubt that someone had come to visit. 'Can I help you?'

Kant was thrown. He even felt uneasy now, holding the hot coal of confrontation he was about to dump on what looked like the most harmless person in the Southern Hemisphere.

'Oh hello, I … er … just had a … a *contretemps* with a group of kids outside,' he blurted out, regretting the use of the word contretemps. Surely a word like that, used in an area like this, would be a red rag to a bull. But the old lady's response baffled him even more.

'I do appreciate your word-use, dear. So much richness in our language is disappearing these days. I blame texting on mobile phones for that. Children have become so passive these days. It burns all their creative possibilities.'

What the…? Kant had been caught off guard and then received an uninvited left jab to his sensibilities.

'Er … yes. I suppose so,' he found himself replying inadequately.

But regrouping swiftly, a skill he used for unpredictable interviews, Kant got straight back to the point. He was furious and needed to be in control for this *particular* assault. The attack on him needed to be dealt with swiftly, no side tracks;

the little shit needed to be taught a lesson. Now! While it's fresh. *I don't care how young he is, he needs to be taught a lesson. How dare he treat people like that? How dare he be so disrespectful to me!*

'A group of kids has just assaulted me as I was endeavouring to get out of my car, and ...'

'I'm so sorry to hear that, my dear. Are you hurt, in any way?'

'I'm bruised but I ...'

The old lady turned her head. 'Here, speak into this ear. I'm a little deaf in this one.' She tapped it as if it was a temperamental transistor radio that had lost its frequency.

'That boy that just came in ...'

'Oh, you mean Jimmy? He's my grandson. He's such a good boy, very helpful.'

'Well, today he wasn't. Is he here so I can speak to him, please?' Despite trying to maintain his wrath Kant's tone was losing its sharpness.

'I'm sorry I didn't catch what you said. You mustn't speak into *this* one,' she replied, tapping her ear again.

No wonder you're deaf in it, Barry thought ungraciously, the momentum of his anger almost entirely diffused.

The old lady's hands were trembling in front of her, the early onset of Parkinson's disease Kant presumed, and the discussion at the door was obviously wearing her out by the way she began gripping the door for support.

'Come and sit down, dear. I have a comfy chair you can use while I make us a cup of tea. I do find it calms the nerves.' She chuckled as if she'd just seen an amusing side to the confrontation, turned and went into the house. Kant followed. 'Go in there while I boil the kettle. Do you like fruit cake? It's just come out of the oven.'

'No, thank you,' Kant said curtly, even though he loved all that was home cooked.

The house was quiet. *The little shit must have run out the back, or is hiding,* he thought, mustering his irritability. *He needs a good bloody hiding. Why in God's name am I here wasting time accepting tea from this barmy old biddy? There's no satisfaction here. And I certainly don't want to be giving her CPR.*

Kant tried settling himself by looking around the sitting room. The throb in his leg had eased. The layout to the house was similar to Melinda and Mungo's place except the kitchen and sitting room had not been opened up. The old lady's place was neat, no excess. Her life's accretion had been pared back to the bare essentials of need; she obviously pursued an orderly life where there was no desire for overindulgence.

Two armchairs, placed at a conversational angle towards each other, had been positioned in front of a three-bar heater mounted on one wall; a convenient coffee table set between them had been pre-prepared with two coasters with the promise of company. He was interested to see several watercolour paintings around the walls. Seasonal views of the Ross Bridge, oast houses amid hop plantations in New Norfolk, and one of a street in Battery Point featuring a colonial cottage in

Hampden Road he recognised, had been hung thoughtfully. Several framed photographs of family members, he assumed, on outings were grouped on a side table. A standard lamp with tassels around the base of the pale pink shade stood by the side of one of the chairs.

But what grabbed his attention most were the ceiling to floor bookshelves on the back wall, crammed with hundreds of books, novels mainly, but two shelves at the bottom held a variety of text books, picture books, photo albums and on the lowest shelf a set of leather-bound Encyclopaedia Britannica.

'I do apologise, dear,' the elderly lady said as she entered the room carrying a tray holding two cup and saucers and a small dimpled glass bowl of Iced Vovo biscuits. 'I didn't introduce myself earlier. You see, I don't get many callers these days and ... well ... I'm Edith Cartwright.'

She placed the tray on the coffee table and held her delicate hand out to Kant. Her skin was so soft it hardly contained her veins that stood out like pale blue worms searching for the darkness in the sleeve of her pastel purple cardigan.

'I'm Barry ... '

'Oh yes, dear, I know who *you* are. Barry Kant,' she grinned as if she had been amusing herself with her little ruse. 'And I have been watching your journey with some interest for some years now.'

'Oh yes?'

'I've seen you on the odd occasion when you've visited your father too. Nice man. He used to grow the most beautiful nectarines, I remember. So distressing when his wife, your mother, died. Dear Pat and I used to cook scones together sometimes. Probably why you've grown to be such a tall man, Barry,' she smiled provocatively.

'So you knew the family.'

'Well, of course I did. I couldn't help but know them. We've both lived in this street most of our lives.' She giggled again. 'I've even had *you* sit on my lap once – when you were a little scrap of a thing and grazed your knees falling off your bike. There were tears, and bits of gravel to pick out of your knee with some tweezers. But I digress. Now drink up while I fetch Jimmy.'

She went to the wall with all the books and pulled a toggle that was attached to a drawstring that disappeared into a hole in the ceiling. Kant could just make out the tinkling of a bell in one of the back rooms.

'I employed a handyman to fix this up so I can get the youngster's attention. His music is often up so loud and my voice isn't what it used to be when I was a lecturer.' Edith tapped the side of the bookshelf proudly. 'You might have gathered already, English was my subject, Barry. I taught at the university for twenty-seven years. And after food and safe shelter I think books are the most important things in life. Ah, here you are, Jimmy.'

The skinny young boy, short hair combed, looked even younger now. His red checked flannelette shirt was tucked into clean denim jeans. He nodded at Kant and then looked remorsefully at the floor.

'I believe you and those other lads were extremely discourteous to Mr Kant just now. What have you got to say? And look at our guest when you are speaking to him.'

'Yes, Gran.'

Kant felt the heat of this retired veteran, a no-nonsense but benevolent matriarch. His memory tugged at the times he had been hauled up in front of similar teachers in his time. They didn't have to say much, they never lost their temper, but when they were finished with you it was as if they had scraped out the shabby shards of mischief from your brain and replaced them with the clean slate they advised you to begin again with.

The boy stood up straight and looked at Kant. 'I shouldn't have done what I did. Them blokes ... '

'Those blokes,' Edith corrected.

'Those blokes are not my friends, but I sometimes do silly things when they come around. Gran reckons I ought to play with kids my own age. I'm sorry if you got hurt, Mr Kant.'

Kant's anger had dissipated long before the boy's arrival in the room; he even felt a little silly for pursuing the matter, and as is the way with so much of humanity's darker side, the real culprits, the organisers, the ones who should have been held responsible, had got safely away.

'Well, thanks Jimmy, for apologising.'

'Now Jimmy, take the bucket with some warm water and a sponge out to Mr Kant's car and wash his windscreen and headlights so that he can see more clearly ahead.'

'Yes, Gran. Sorry, Mr Kant.'

The boy turned and left the room. Kant looked back at Edith, who was munching on another biscuit. Was that a twinkle he noticed in her eye, the canny old bird? Maybe the metaphor *was* meant for him in some way; either way he was grateful to have met the woman.

'His mum was killed about four years ago in a car crash. Head on. His dad was driving, drunk as usual. The poor driver of the other car died too. Terrible business. Jimmy's father won't be out of prison for quite a few years for his negligence, so I have taken the boy in.'

'It must be quite hard for you.'

'Only in so much as I can't really give him what he needs. He has no male role models, except those thugs who cruise around, bored and brainless. My health isn't going to hold out for too much longer, and I fear what will happen to him then. At least for now I can give him a bit of old-fashioned discipline, good tucker and a comfortable bed. They are such obvious necessities, but it is shameful how society is so apathetic about so many unfortunates who endeavour to exist without them.'

'It looks as if it's working for Jimmy though. Thanks to you. Takes maturity to apologise the way he did just then.'

Kant looked out of the window towards his father's house on the other side of the cul-de-sac. He sighed, placed his cup on the tray and stood up. 'It's been nice to meet you, Edith. I'd better continue with what I came for. I have some news for my father.'

'Before you go, Barry, I'd like to say I think you do a marvellous job on your show. That can't be easy either.'

'Thanks. I guess we are both trying to look after the needy in some way.'

'Perhaps. I must say that after I saw the program on the Sudanese fellow I felt supremely thankful for the life I have. We here in Tasmania have so much compared to so many.'

Kant smiled and turned to go. 'No, don't get up. I'll see myself out. And thank you, Edith.'

As Kant crossed the road he felt saddened about two elderly people with no real social contact, existing alone in separate houses across the street from each other. It may as well have been a bottomless chasm.

He put his key into his father's front door and went in. He called out. 'Dad!' But before his father could stir himself Barry had found him napping in the sitting room that looked directly at Edith's house.

'Did you bring the paper?'

'No, didn't know you wanted it. How are you going?'

'Just dozed off. Saw you go into Edith's place. Didn't know you knew her.'

'Apparently she was quite friendly with Mum when I was little.'

'Clever lady. She was a Rhodes Scholar before you were born.'

'How come you don't socialise with her anymore? She'd be good company, wouldn't she?'

'When your kids leave home you don't seem to have so much to talk about, 'cept work. And when your mum died it was a bit hard, like talking to other women. I wouldn't know what to say to them. Zinc production isn't the most interesting subject.'

Barry snorted. 'I reckon she'd keep you in order. You want a coffee?'

'Yeah, thanks. There's biscuits out there too.'

In the kitchen Barry put the jug on. The packet of biscuits, the one he brought two weeks ago, was still open on the kitchen table next to the newspaper. Barry shook his head. While the jug was heating he peered into the fridge, reached for the carton of milk, sniffed it. *Borderline. Powder it is.* And apart from a couple of eggs and an opened tin of sardines the fridge was all but bare.

'There's not much food in the fridge, Dad,' he called from the kitchen.

'Been down the RSL a bit. Caught up with Lenny, leading hand at EZ when I was there. They do a nice mixed seafood, you know, in a basket. On special this week. I like those crumbed crab balls.'

Barry brought the mug of coffee to his father.

'Well, I suppose you are a bit chirpier than the last time I was here. I'm glad you decided that life in sunny Lutana was a better option than going out into the desert to be with the termites.'

'Reckon it must be the sugar I been taking again.'

'For sure.'

'What was you up to with Edith?'

'Nothing really, just some kids being stupid when I arrived. I went to have a go at the kid that went in there. He called her Gran. I'd forgotten who she was.'

'Not her grandson. She never married. It's just everyone calls her Gran since she took up fostering when she retired from the schooling.'

'Really? Anyway, Dad, I came round to tell you some pretty big news. I met someone recently who …'

'You got yourself another lady? 'Bout bloody time. Reckon you could do with a bit of the other. You been looking a bit long in the face.'

'Thanks for your opinion but it's not that. It concerns Sarah and me.'

'Sarah? Isn't she …'

'Dad! How about listening to me? You remember when I went to live in Crete, when I was twenty-four. That's where I met Sarah.'

'Can't remember what I did this morning, but I tell you those days are still a picture postcard. I remember the bloody state you were in when you came home too. Mopin' around 'cos she'd broken your heart, and …'

'Yes, all right, Dad, you don't need to get all melodramatic. It was over thirty years ago,' Barry retorted irritably. 'I'd appreciate it if you could just listen now, please. Sarah became pregnant and believed that it was the result of being assaulted.'

'She … raped? Didn't know that.'

Barry took a breath. 'She took it really badly, and was so confused that she just took off and tried to sort it out by herself. I think she must have felt ashamed because she couldn't even bring herself to tell me. We were both pretty young then, no wisdom to speak of. But what she didn't know, and *never* found out before she died, was that the baby wasn't born as a result of the attack, it was *my* baby. *I've* only just found out from the woman who adopted her thirty years ago.'

'Fair dinkum, Barry?' Desmond stood up and walked to the window. 'Thirty, you say?'

'Thirty-three actually, although her age is relatively unimportant, Dad. What do you think about the fact you now have another granddaughter?'

Desmond scratched the side of his head and turned to look at his son. 'So what you're saying is ... I've got *two* grandkids to buy presents for now?'

'Jesus wept.' Barry grinned with relief. 'I guess so. You're just going to have to get out into those shops and start buying. It's going to be expensive from now on. Look, I haven't even met Agalia yet, so I reckon you've got a bit of breathing space to plan some serious shopping sprees before your upcoming death.'

'I dunno where you get your humour from, 'cos it certainly wasn't from me. What sort of name is *Agalia* anyway?'

'It's Greek. It means bright joy. Sarah gave her that name.'

Desmond smiled to himself, thinking, scheming, fitting himself into the new paradigm. Barry could see he was chuffed. 'What's Mel think? Reckon we should have a bash or something?'

'I haven't told her yet.'

'What! You should 'a told her *first up*. Being her real sister an' all. I tell ya, I give up on you sometimes.'

'I haven't been thinking straight. I just thought I'd let you know first because ... because I guess I knew somehow you would make it all feel so uncomplicated in your inimitability.'

'There you go with them bloody words again. I think I preferred you when you were a nipper, at least I could understand what the hell you were talking about then.'

Barry stood up and embraced his father. 'Thanks, Dad.'

'Steady on, we don't want to get too carried away, eh?'

'No, we don't,' Barry retorted, ruffling his father's hair. 'But I'll grab that necklace now. I'll get it valued at a jeweller's. I think my luck's on the up.'

Chapter Twenty

Rosie was already asleep when Barry arrived just after eight that evening. Mungo had bought pizza and a cask of red. The three of them sat silently, sipping. Barry, who had already eaten a microwave-limp cauliflower cheese pie and an apple Danish from Banjo's on the way, had brought a quality bottle of Pinot to make up for it, to Mungo's delight. Darkness was beginning to soak up the city.

'Nice drop,' Mungo chirped.

'So what's your news, Dad? BKS going international?'

'I can honestly say that wouldn't be good news. No. I went round to visit your grandfather today, and after nearly losing my life to a horde of ruffians I ended up meeting an old lady who said I'd sat on her lap once.' Barry shrugged playfully at his daughter. 'Over half a century ago!'

'She still keen on you and she's finally found the courage to tell you?' Mungo chuckled.

'Something like that. But after, I picked up a pearl necklace from your grandfather. It belonged to your grandmother.'

Barry didn't notice Mungo smirk at Melinda, and she frowning back at him with a slight shake of her head.

'He says it's worth something. I'll get it valued before we get too excited. But he seems to think a mortgage can be paid off with it.'

'Wow. So I wasn't wrong about the wheelbarrow of cash then,' Mungo said, totting up in his head how much a new Korg sound effects unit, three more omnidirectional mics, stands, and, of course, a new car would cost. Not to mention ridding himself of the mortgage.

'Is *that* your good news?' Melinda said impatiently. 'Well, you should hear mine.'

Melinda went on to explain what had happened with Vernon Davidson, and how Rosie had effortlessly disarmed the foe with her innocent charm, and how Vernon wasn't so much a dangerous extortionist as a needy and deprived boy who just wanted some attention and to be trusted with responsibility.

'He even kissed her on the cheek before he left.'

'Probably a first for him … when he wasn't pissed,' Mungo added.

'I hate to agree but you're probably right.'

'Well, I'm very pleased that's sorted out,' Barry said, pouring more red into his glass. He frowned.

'You all right, Dad?'

'Oh yes, I'm fine, really, I'm really fine. It's just that the *real* bit of news I have to give is somewhat enormous. So enormous that it has taken me a while to assimilate it myself. But now I have to tell *you*, my darling daughter.'

'You can be pretty scary sometimes, Barry,' Mungo said.

'I met this woman. I think I might have mentioned her to you, Gillian. I met her at James' place a while back. Used to live in Athens but has moved here for year. She's house sitting.'

'Dad, don't tell me you're getting married!' Melinda burst out. 'Fantastic! It's about time. Oh Dad, I'm so happy for you. I guess it's just a relationship at the moment, well, not *just* a relationship. I mean, you've got to start somewhere, don't you?'

'Yeah, you old dog,' Mungo added as he splished more wine into his glass. 'You gotta grab these fish and pull 'em in.'

Barry coughed. 'Thanks for the counsel, Mungo, and I'm sorry to disappoint you. No, that's *not* it. Look, just let me tell you the full, and I have to say complicated story, before you say anything else. Okay?'

'Sure, Dad. Come on then.'

'Yeah, knock yourself out ... Daddio,' Mungo teased.

'Shut up, Mungy!' Melinda sensed her father's mood was not to be trifled with anymore.

Barry unfolded the full dramatic Greek odyssey from the first day he had set eyes on Melinda's future mother in an obscure town on an island in the Mediterranean Sea over three decades ago. He then told them about falling for and having sex with a woman whom he'd just met. He revealed to them that she, Gillian, had adopted Melinda's full-blooded sister as a newborn baby, and Barry's, as it turned out, full-blooded daughter, over thirty years ago, and that ... 'she is in Hobart, as we speak, preparing to meet up with us all for the first time next weekend. So, there you have it.'

He looked at his daughter, apology etched on his face but with hope endeavouring to burnish some clarity in his eyes. He was still struggling with what he felt was a betrayal, and he still hadn't completely surfaced after drowning in grief at having missed out on sharing the magic of early fatherhood of his first-born with Sarah. No air left in his lungs. But he had begun to feel resolve to accept a situation that could not be changed.

Melinda reached forward for a tissue from a box on the floor and rolled against her father on the old family sofa, putting her head on his chest, dabbing at the silent tears that inundated her eyes and now streamed down her cheeks. Barry held her hand and rested his head on top of hers. The room was silent, except for Mungo, who seemed to find something of great interest in his glass and continued to stare at it, whispering 'fuck' to it.

Eventually Melinda spoke. 'How do *you* feel, Dad?'

'Look, I'm still trying to get my head around it. But I'm starting to feel, well, you know…' But his tears could not restrain themselves. Great glass baubles erupted from within, cascading with a bitter joy onto his daughter's head, dampening her hair. He straightened up and wiped at his eyes with the back of his hands.

Melinda held her father's hand. 'Dad, that's truly wonderful news, daunting but wonderful. But we Kants do love a challenge, remember? When can we meet her? Agalia, my sister.'

'Gillian and I thought this Saturday possibly, if that was all right with you, and of course she wants to make sure it's right for Agalia too. Agalia doesn't know that…her birth mother is no longer alive.'

Barry felt surprised by his easy words *Gillian and I*. It sounded so much like '*us*', almost as if he and she were Agalia's parents, had raised the child together. Was he being disloyal to Melinda by acting as if he had a greater claim on Agalia, whom neither of them had even known about?

Claim? I don't want to claim anything. Agalia's not a trophy to be won. I only provided a miniscule seed. But when a tree grows it becomes part of the forest. Leave me alone, Vashna! Anybody can plant a seed. It's who takes care of the growing, the nurture. That surely is the love aspect that counts.

Gillian's absolutely her mother due to a lifetime of mothering. I am her father, but if I take away that afternoon with Sarah, what have I done to deserve the title? Or was it an evening? Oh Sarah, you deceived so many people and I want to be angry with you but I can't because you were punishing yourself all the time you were with me. Jesus woman, you should have told me!

Melinda, who seemed to have shifted into overdrive, cut into Barry's mind-wrestle.

'Saturday it is. I don't want to wait a minute more. We can go and pick them up and ... God, I haven't even met Gillian yet, let alone her ... my ... oh Dad, this is tremendous ... ly complicated. Mungo, my sweet, go and buy a bottle of champagne this minute. And nothing under ten dollars, d'you hear? Oh Dad. Dad, what's going to happen? What if we don't get on? She might hate this house. What if she's used to a beautiful mansion in Athens and thinks this is ... '

Melinda picked up a cushion and puffed it up.

'Back in fifteen,' Mungo said as he hoisted himself to the

standing position and busied himself out of the house. He seemed glad to have been given permission to leave.

'Dad, does she speak English?'

'Yes. Gillian told me she's fluent in three languages. I guess we're lucky English is one of them.'

When Mungo had left, Barry stood up and went to Rosie's bedroom door and peered in. She was purring peacefully. He turned and came back to sit down next to his daughter.

'And Rosie has an aunt now,' Barry said almost to himself. 'Mel. Look at this.'

Barry handed Melinda the photograph Gillian had given him of when Agalia's first book was published.

'She looks so much like Mum.' Melinda dug her father in the ribs. 'Lucky her! How come I had to have *your* looks?'

Barry beamed. 'She's so like Sarah was when we, you know ... in Crete, when it all began.'

'Oh Dad, I love it that you're so old-fashioned sometimes. I can only feel delight when I think of you and Mum bonking away on that romantic island in the sun.' She laughed, not taking her eyes off her new sister.

Barry smiled sadly. 'Yes, we were so happy. We were completely smitten with each other. I just can't imagine what it must have been like for Sarah then, to do what she did, on her own.'

'Mum was one brave woman. It's a horrific journey for women after rape, Dad. We had a professional development on the subject at school a few weeks ago. And even though Mum was in love with you she would have been filled with humiliation ... and guilt. I think she must have had immense courage and strength. Society doesn't 'see' the damage afterwards because it's all internal. In fact, the public don't even want to admit it even exists. It must have been a very lonely time for her.'

Barry thought of Vince MacLean's *invisibles* around the cold streets of the city.

'But she was blessed to have reconnected with you again, Dad, because the one thing she would have needed for the rest of her life was to be with someone she could feel secure with.'

Melinda paused. She had been staring rather than looking at anything in particular. Now she faced her father with watery eyes.

'Dad, you're the most brilliant father. All those years when we lived down the Huon you gave Mum and me so much. We *all* have secrets, some big some small, and I'm sure Mum did what she did to cope the best she knew how.'

'If only she had known the truth.'

'But *her* truth was that she conceived as a result of the attack. She could have chosen to have an abortion,' Melinda snapped. 'Sorry, Dad, I just ... '

'It's okay. It's all okay. We'll see it through on the weekend, eh?'

'Yes. I can't wait.'

'But look, sorry to leave you in the lurch. I really have to head off now. I have the final contestant tomorrow evening, ironically a similar story. It's going to be a big one and I need to get some sleep. Enjoy the champagne.' Barry raised his eyebrows mischievously at his daughter. 'You never know. It could be your lucky night!'

'Get outa here!'

*

At eight-forty the next morning, on his way to Nerve Two, Kant managed to find a park just outside a city jeweller's in Collins Street. *Lucky park, good omen,* he thought as he pushed a fifty-cent piece into the parking meter and strode into the shop with his mother's necklace wrapped in a handkerchief. A woman, fifty, rounded body all in black, hair so tightly gripped at the back it looked as if it had been painted onto her scalp, glanced up from swishing a feather duster around the glass shelving, redistributing dust. Kant tried to suppress a sneeze. Failed.

'Good morning sir. May I help you?'

'I hope so. I have a necklace I'd like valued, please.'

'I'll just see if Mr Steenburgen is available; he does all our valuations. Very experienced gentleman: he even spent thirty years in Johannesburg in the diamond industry and later with Christie's in London. We are very proud to have him working for us. I'll just be a moment.'

Mm, very proud.

The woman disappeared through a dark-blue velvet curtain at the back of the shop. While she was gone Kant glanced around the shop, then began peering into display cabinets scrutinising the rings and bracelets, necklaces and brooches, none of which he had ever bought Sarah in all their years together. As he began to look out of the window at the cars and pedestrians passing by he felt a pang of remorse that he had not considered that his wife might have wished for him to buy her something to wear around her neck. It had just never occurred to him, and she'd never remarked about it. He couldn't even recall whether she'd worn anything that *she* might have bought herself. Was that, in fact, just one more thing his wonderful wife buried so that their marriage remained on an even keel?

'Mr Steenburgen will see you now.'

Kant was jolted out of his thoughts and swivelled round as if he'd been caught dipping his hands in the till.

He'll see me now? He could have been forgiven for thinking he was being admitted to see a doctor, or worse, a lawyer.

'If you'd like to go through,' she said, pointing to the curtain, which suddenly looked to Kant like a conjurer's disappearing cabinet.

Mr Steenburgen, who was perched on an ancient wooden swivel chair in front of a large table covered with a thousand extraneous and minuscule bits and pieces, was about a hundred and fifty years old, with the bony, hooked fingers of a forest wizard. His scrawny body was so rigidly twisted, no doubt from scrutinising the minutest gems and the innards of wrist watches for one hundred and thirty of his years that he had to lean sideways to view Kant as he entered.

'What have you got there, son?' he asked with his still-broad South African accent.

Kant liked the man already. He felt ten years old again proudly showing his father a flathead he'd caught in the rivulet. Unfolding his handkerchief on the table he held the pearly loop up in the air.

The ancient man took hold of the necklace and put a magnifying glass to his eye, voicing several 'mmms' as he expertly let the pearls slide through his open palm, and several 'yeses' and finally, backed by a lifetime of experience, an 'aah', the old wizard gave Kant his professional response. Their value was 'cleer'. Kant told Mister Steenburgen he would think about what to do with the necklace now and be in touch later.

'And thank you *very* much.'

Steenburgen twisted creakily back to his bench, put a monocle to his eye and withdrew once more into his ancient netherworld of broken timepieces and priceless gems. When Kant left the shop and got back into his car, he was grinning broadly. He turned the CD player up loud and joined, with operatic abandon, Louis Armstrong singing 'What a Wonderful World'.

Chapter Twenty-One

Three … two … one. Action!

Ambient back-lighting silhouetted the figures on the darkened stage. The studio audience, on Single-Note-Farting-Mambo-Dog's cue, began to applaud as the catchy BKS theme music intensified the palpable expectation, inserting a stab of thrill into each hungry grinding jaw.

'Evening John, it's good to have you on the show at last,' Kant spoke loudly over the music, reaching out to shake hands.

It felt strange going through the paces with John now, having already been through his own emotional roller-coaster ride with him weeks ago in the privacy of his office. As the music faded he repeated the words, 'Good to have you on the show, John.' Then, as if he was greeting the latest rising star from Hollywood, 'Ladies and Gentlemen, please welcome John Sturges.'

Kant wasn't sure whether John looked relaxed or if he had become submissive to whatever life had thrown at him.

'John is from sunny Bridgewater and in a moment we'll hear his story. So people, here we are with the last contestant in this fourth series of BKS …' The audience, at the mention of the Pavlovian acronym, cheered and clapped enthusiastically.

'Who will win? Maybe Darlene Sullivan from Collins

Bonnet? What about Derek Turner from Ulverstone? Remember he lost the use of both his hands in that *gruesome* accident at the meat works? Then there was the twins, hah, remember Jack and Jill? Still don't think that was their real names but on this show it's not about your name, it's about ... well ... how cruel life has been to you. I wonder if they still speak.'

More laughter – the callous type of mirth from people who don't give a damn whether the twins do or don't. Jack, who lived next door to his sister, had burned half of Jill's house down. He'd sworn it was an accident. He'd found out that his sister had been having a clandestine lesbian relationship with his wife. Jill had then stormed into her brother's house in a drunken frenzy, wielding a kitchen blowtorch, flambéing the side of his face. Apparently they'd been inseparable before that. Kant continued down the list of contestants, equally distressing occurrences, and all desperate for a quick injection of the magic drug, Money.

'Let's face it, that's why we're all here. To see who deserves the cash prize most. $100,000 goes to whoever you have voted to be the most deserving. Remember Liri Ishmael Mogamba from Sudan? What a great guy. I've already mentioned Darlene, wow! We all know she wasn't *little!*' A shot of vicious laughter spread through the studio like grapeshot. 'Diabetes, dickey heart, no friends ... tragic.'

'So, John, what have *you* got for us tonight?' Kant asked, secretly regretting the trivialising tone of his question, as if John was about to share with the audience a marvellous recipe he'd cooked up for the occasion.

'Er ... well ... I dunno really, like where to start, you know?'

John Sturges peered around at the cameras, folded his arms and then unfolded them. He had the look of someone who was wondering how he'd got there and why. Most of them did. The studio audience thrived on this discomfort. Other people's. John looked down, fiddling with his hands as if he was drying them.

'Perhaps you could start by telling us a little about how you decided to share your story on the show.'

'Er, yeah, right.' John shifted in his chair, settled himself with hands grasping his knees. 'Like ... I sorta met this bloke in a gallery. Started chattin', he did. Real friendly, he was. He come out to me 'ouse, sometime ago too, for a chat.'

'That's right, our researcher Vince MacLean.'

'Er, yeah. That was his name I seem to recall.'

'It was fortunate that Vince is interested in art.'

'Well, I suppose so.'

'I believe you've had a bit of a rough trot, John.'

John Sturges, late sixties, face weathered by harsh storms. Short, stocky build with large strong hands, gnarled finger-nails on nine fingers, the index finger of his left hand, missing in action, was a round calloused bulge.

Timidly, he began. 'Yeah, I dunno, like I'm not sure what you want to know ... like ... '

'Well, I believe you've experienced some form of violence in your life. Where did that come from? When did it start?'

'Guess it was me father what started it when I were little.

Like, ya know, he'd come 'ome of a night 'n' pull us outa bed just to give us a hidin'.'

'For what reason?'

'Oh, ya know, 'cos he was drunk, I s'pose.'

'Did this happen a lot?'

'Oh yes, plenny a times. Me mother git a hidin' too. "Where's that little *bastard*?" he'd shout, then come drag me outa me bed and start beltin' me.'

'What age were you when this happened?'

John paused, looking down at his hands, embarrassed. 'Oh, ya know, two, three,' he said quietly. 'Three years old.'

A rustle of adrenal discomfort drifted amongst the audience.

'That's pretty young, John.'

'Oh well, me mum reckoned I was hard to handle, ya know. I was sorta uncontrollable. I had seven brothers and sisters and guess I musta made it difficult for 'em.'

'You sound as if you're excusing your father for…' Kant puffed out a conscious breath of disbelief, 'for being violent to a three year old! You were virtually a baby! He was an adult who should have been taking care of you.'

Kant began to monitor his own anxiety. He remembered Rosie all those times she had sat on his lap, or tickled him under his chin as he pretended to be sleeping. He scratched his earlobe and presented John with a reassuring smile, one that said we're not going any further with this.

'John, describe to the audience, because as you know, there is possibly some financial gain to be made if your story fulfils certain ... requirements with people watching, what your situation was over the next few years.'

'Okay then. It's a bit hard, ya know, particularly with all these people 'ere.'

Kant hadn't felt on top of his game this week after his meeting with Gillian. And after nearly four seasons now of public blood-letting he was feeling the effects on his own psyche. Of course he knew the more shocking the revelations, the more distressing the pain, the higher the show's ratings rose.

Cash to be won.

Money, the great motivator.

But Kant wasn't sure about John.

John seemed agitated. He rubbed his eye with the back of his hand.

'I wouldn't worry about them, John. Just talk to me.'

'Righteo, well, you know, when you're a child and someone does sommin' to yas ... it's not really the best thing. I just dream when night come, ya know? The thoughts they just come up.'

'What sort of things?'

'Like bein' bashed by the people who are supposed to be lookin' after you.'

'Mister Sturges, John, sorry, eventually your mother and father sent you to the safe care of the Salvation Army. I've got that right, haven't I? They were obviously concerned, even though, as you say, they thought you were uncontrollable. Tell us what that was like.'

John began to talk, his mind rambling from one scant

memory to the next, a litany of agonising mnemonic vignettes that had haunted him for nearly sixty years, of a child abused by parents, and then by the system.

It just kept happening.

'Captain Sullivan, yeah, sadist 'e was. He used to steal our food. Like, me sister visited once, tried to take me out. Couldn't though. Brought Vegemite or somethin', but it ended up on *his* table. We had to sing them sort of religious songs, get a right caning if we didn't do it right. Black and blue marks on me from one end to the other.' He paused. 'You get used to the violence though, like it was a way of life.'

Barry waited.

'I shot through again and again. It didn't make no difference how much they belted me; it didn't make no difference. We had to carry timber up for the saw everyday too, an hour or so. We was only little kids, you know.'

'How little?' Kant asked.

'Seven or eight. They sent me to the boys' home, you know, up North. It was the same there. The head man was in Changi in the War. He was always drunk. They had this room see, the *lock up* they called it. Empty and freezing it was. Concrete floor. They give you a hidin' and put you in; strip you off first. All the other kids'd come round and gawk at ya, ya know, without no clothes on. Real embarrassing it was. But then I was sent to the Dominic catholic school.'

Kant had wanted to talk about the time John had been blamed for the death of the student, but he knew that the events at the catholic school were the real story here, the real tragedy of John's life. They would not go back now.

Kant nodded. 'Yes, I read up on that particular order you told me about, and it seems that their general aim, their testimonial, was to be "the holders of God's love for young people, especially the poor."'

'Was they? Din know that. Anyway, it were a nice place, oh yeah. It was beautiful with lawns and nice flower beds, trees and gardens 'n' that. There was a pond with goldfish too. I used to sit 'n' watch 'em sometimes, like they was real peaceful, little orange things in their silent world. Ha, I tried to kill meself there once, you know, in the gardens.' And with a wry smile that seemed to sum up his life's fortunes, he added, 'and as you see Barry, I wasn't very good at that either.'

The audience was silent, motionless. Hungry for details.

John's remark about his attempted suicide just came out casually, even dismissively. It could just as easily have been a recollection of a small boy swinging across a pond on a rope attached to a branch. Kant scratched at an itch in his armpit. He didn't want to tease out John's aborted attempt at killing himself. It was enough to know that he'd tried.

Kant's breathing became shallow as if the slightest sound would distract John from his train of thought. This was different from all the other childhood cruelty that John had suffered. John knew this too by calling it 'this other time' when he'd first met Kant. And Kant was reminded of all the descriptions of savage acts in war-torn countries, despicable, senseless acts of hatred perpetrated on civilians by fellow human beings. It had certainly shaken the toughness out of Vince MacLean. But this violation of humanity within the confines of the church, this abuse of young children whilst in the care of pious catholic priests was as callously cruel as a human being could be towards a defenseless child.

Kant knew he had to take John back into the darkness. And he hated now that it would make *good television.*

'What happened there, John?'

'It were Father Williams and another one, can't remember 'is name; they were the ones that used to punch youse, like, in the guts, give ya a bloody hidin'. You know, to make you submit,' he added as if he needed to clarify the process of cruelty. 'And then two of us went to the bloke that were in charge, later, but no one would do nothing. I guess they wanted to protect each other ... some of them brothers are dead now anyway. I was only there five or six months though, but it started the first night I was there and never stopped. Not once.' John paused and looked at the ground as if he had just realised again the enormity of what had happened to him so long ago. 'Not one single night,' he murmured.

'Do you mean the beatings?'

John nodded. 'And the other nasty business, after 'n' that.' John's body slumped, as if his spine had crumpled.

'There was five of us in, like, a dormitory. It was always real cold. The priests they come in after dark, my first night there it was. They just pulled us outa bed, see, and give us a hidin' first.

Then they'd just ... rape ya. They didn't care who was watching neither. We were so afraid we learned to pull the blankets up, like, you know, when it wasn't ... our turn. It were real bloody painful, Mr Kant.'

Kant sagged back in his chair. He had gravitated forward and was perched on its edge. He felt as if he had been punched in the stomach. He had preempted this, but when John's words were uttered, an acrid rain falling gently into the studio and thousands of living rooms across the nation, with no crazed explosion of loathing or rage, Kant felt infused by a deep sadness.

There was numbness to John's words as if over time they had been stripped of all the emotional agony. And unlike the river stones of Kant's marriage with Sarah, smoothed pebbles alighting on the ocean's shoreline, John's life had been jagged shards of rock tumbling, turning, churning through treacherous rapids, grinding and splintering themselves until they became lost in the obscurity of dark undercurrents. All the other violence in John Sturges' life was an awful progression of harm accompanying an uneducated, unloved kid at the beginning of his life, bad enough but not uncommon. But rape by a priest! *There* was the ultimate human betrayal, the utter contempt for a child's safety by an adult in a position of power, a so-called religious person in whom society has put their absolute trust.

'And you're saying this happened every night you were there?'

'Yes. Can we get away from that now?' John's chin began to quiver. 'I would rather we talk about something else now.'

John allowed a shudder shake itself free of his body. 'I'm sorry. I didn't think it'd be this hard, ya know. Like, I just wanted it to, you know, go away.'

'I'm really sorry, John.' Kant whispered, having to cough first so his words could find voice.

'Yeah, I'm sorry too. I didn't really want to … you know, tell ya that bit. It's not real good.'

'No John, I'm not sorry *because* you told me.'

'Well, like, most people they don't want to know, see? It's difficult. And like, I'm a grown man and … well … you know what I mean. Some people reckon I should 'a got over it by now.'

'John, you don't need to apologise for anything. I think you're incredibly courageous. There must be many others who could never bring themselves to admit such things, even to their family or close friends. You've survived and maybe this is the beginning of where things can get better for you.'

Suddenly Mackelroy was in Kant's earpiece. 'Bloody hell Barry, it's not a Dorothy therapy session.'

Kant clenched his teeth and scratched his ear, surreptitiously removing his earpiece and placing it in his pocket. He just couldn't leave John perched on a cliff. He continued to face John, who said, 'I dunno. I just dream when night comes, ya know?'

'Talking and sharing, they can often be very healing,' Kant said.

'The thoughts, they just come up every night. Father O'Day, I remember him. Funny, he even had a kindly face. He used to punch ya so hard in the guts. We went to the bloke who was in charge again and again, but no-one would do nothin'.' He paused. 'Probly all dead now anyway. Nobody really wants to know what happened to you so long ago. And these days there's so many worser things happening in the world.'

'That's no reason for putting it under the carpet, John.'

'I s'pose you're right. I just try to keep meself busy. But it's that *thing* inside ya that just destroys your life. You don't really feel like a person no more. You really don't.'

The poor man was long past tears. Kant wondered how many other people in Hobart, or Australia, or even the world had been holding similar terrifying moments of abuse through their lives. How many others constantly woke in the night, next to a sleeping partner, feeling utterly alone, to feel the shame of those actions perpetrated on them as children, unable to explain the void they still floated in as adults, unable to be understood, and here, in one of the safest cities of the world?

Is that what happened to my beloved Sarah?

Kant had broken one of his rules. He had let his own emotions get involved. He certainly had no idea how it would feel to be violated in this manner. And his mind kept flashing back to the lush Piskochefalon valley in Crete, carpeted with grape vines, where Sarah had met the same fate. *But not night after night after night, for months,* he thought, despondent for John and the immensity of the pain he still suffered.

'John, have you sought some form of counselling?'

'I tried, but ... ' He rubbed at his chin again. 'When you're a grown man … you know, it's a bit difficult.' John's eyes began to well up.

Kant was aware of the side camera turning slightly and zooming in. He wanted to yell, 'Keep away!'

'John, we can resume in a few minutes, maybe when you're a bit more …'

But it was John's laugh, a sibilant, primal cackle that stopped Kant mid-sentence and sent a shudder through the audience. He had raised his voice, finally.

'I'm sixty-five years old, Mister Kant. You think a couple a minutes will make any difference? I was savagely attacked by those priest monsters and they hid behind their bloody church and the blind eyes of a worthless God! They were supposed to look after me but they fair buggered up my life!' John sat back, wiping some spittle from the side of his mouth, and said softly, 'I'm sorry for swearing, Mister Kant, but that's the truth of it.'

An oppressive silence gripped the space. Kant was feeling the effects of John's litany of abuses and human breakage even though he had been prepared, unlike the audience. He was beginning to wish he could wrap the show up and head for a slow whisky.

John had been three years old when his own father had vented his madness and violence on his small uncontrollable *little bastard*', five years old when both his parents just dropped out of his life, and seven years old when individuals in the Salvation Army mentally abused him with cruel acts because he frequently absconded to escape their mistreatment. At eight he'd been brutalised and raped by the very people who offered trust and safety within the sanctity of the church, and at twelve, in State Care, he had been subjected to physical assaults and humiliation because he had been indelibly branded as a *bad lot*.

Kant's eyes were washed with sadness as he turned to look out into the audience, then back at John Sturges.

'And your parents. Do you know where they might be now?'

'Dunno. My father just took off when I was little. Dunno if he's dead or alive. Me mother, dunno, she just left. Never seen 'er again.' He shrugged. 'I done some time in Risdon Prison for stealin' a bit back then. They shouldn't a put me there. I was too young. Sixteen, you know. But when I got out I said to meself that it wasn't a good life I was livin', so I made a decision to change meself.'

'What did you decide?'

'I took off to Perth, you know, in Western Australia; done some fishing there for a few years. Made me behave a bit better, you know. Working the sea makes a man strong.'

'John, you've married recently and your wife is from the Philippines?'

'That's right. Sampaguita, she's from a little place called Marikina, near Manila. I was there a few years back and met her at the Shoe Museum. She was a cleaner there. I married her six months ago and her son Joel lives with us too in Bridgewater. He's nineteen, don't speak much English, he's a bit shy 'n' that. Sampaguita's a very kindly lady.' John looked up and smiled widely. A resilient youthfulness shone from his eyes. 'Her name means the national flower of the Philippines. She looks after me real good but I haven't told her what troubles me at night, see. I thought that maybe if I come on your show I might … stop the thoughts. I thought it would be easier if she watched the telly. I'm not real good at being personal like. But you see Sampaguita's got three other kids, big lads, back in the Philippines and can't afford to bring 'em out. I wanna help her.'

'I can see that. And I think you've proved to everyone here tonight that you possess immense strength by coming here, John.'

John pushed his lips together coyly. 'That's kind of you. I did just want to say though, Mister Kant, Barry, it's … ' John paused, unsure.

Kant waited.

'Silly really. I just wanted to tell ya that since I bin with Sampaguita it's the first time in me life anybody said they loved me. So you see, it's not all bad,' John added cheerfully as if he didn't want Kant to get upset about the things he'd been saying.

Kant looked at his guest, and in a split second tried to fathom what that must feel like, for a man in his late sixties, to feel love for the first time.

'That's wonderful, John.'

Kant had been moved by the enormity of John's story. He couldn't even gauge the audience tonight. They had been curiously still. He knew they would have come in wanting to feast perversely on the sensationalism of another's woes, but had they been silenced by something that was far bigger than one man's struggle? Had the collective apathy finally been breached? It was anybody's guess how the public would vote, particularly as their usual attention span was no more than a greedy ten-second grab before indifference set in.

'Is there anything else you'd like to say before we open up for questions?'

'I don't think so really.'

'All right then, let's see if the audience has some questions.'

The questions were slow in coming but as soon as one hand began to wave, a bevy of others followed suit, not all asking questions: 'Why don't you sue the government?' 'What was it like to be done by a priest?' 'I'd cut his cock off.' 'Do you know my dad? He was in Risdon 'bout the time you were in. Only, 'e nicked a few Falcons.' 'Dunno why you're down on ya father; kids need discipline.' 'D'you get your wife offa the internet?'

And so it went on.

Kant began wrapping the show up and as well as having severed connection with Mackelroy by removing his earpiece he did something else he'd never done before on the show. Not getting personally involved with the contestants was almost policy, but as John Sturges got up, Kant went to him, shook his hand and then embraced him warmly. He knew the consolation was as much for himself as for John. But inside he knew the most distressing crime committed now on this man was society's indifference towards him and so many others who had endured the same fate.

'Ladies and gentlemen, put your hands and feet together for Mister John Sturges from Bridgewater. Make sure you fill in your vote cards before you leave here tonight. Next week we will give you the final results of who the deserving winner is of $100,000. Thank you to the studio crew, the producers and Nerve Two. You have been glued to BKS. Goodnight.'

Kant led John Sturges backstage.

'See you here next week, John.'

'Bye then,' John said, looking worn out by the experience. 'And er ... sorry I got a bit muddled, you know, when I was tellin' ya things.'

'You did just fine.'

A firm hand weighed on Kant's shoulder. It was a stony James Mackelroy.

'A word, Barry. Control room. Now.'

Kant didn't turn. He kept his eyes on John Sturges, who trudged as if he was carrying lead weights in his pockets, through the camera crew and stage workers, towards the exit. Nobody, except Kant, took notice of him leaving. He had been the centre of attention for an hour on prime time television, and now that he had exposed his worst fears and humiliation for the vultures to pick over and discard, he had become invisible again.

'Be there in five,' Kant said to Mackelroy, without turning to face him.

'Make that two. I've got a Royal Tennis game booked.'

Kant felt zapped by Mackelroy's intolerance but didn't react, keeping his eyes and attention on John Sturges. John pulled the exit door open, Kant scurried amongst the hectic activity of the studio and followed. It was clouded over outside. The cold grip of autumn had been waiting. At the bottom of the concrete steps Kant found John untying two rather mangy old dogs from the railing. He was patting them, allowing them to lick him lustily, a tender reunion.

'John,' Kant spoke quietly.

'Have I forgotten something, Mister Kant?'

'No. And um, Barry, please.'

Kant wasn't sure what he wanted to say. There was something he would have liked to express to this gentle, dignified man. He felt uncomfortable, as if he wanted to … He didn't know. Help him? How? Why? He didn't want to patronise. But underneath his confusion he wanted to express his sympathy to John for all the hurt that he'd carried through his life, that there really was no excuse, and that from humanity, there should be a *sorry mate*.

'Oh … um … how are you getting home now?'

'I'm gunna walk … Barry,' he replied as if it was the most obvious thing in the world.

'It's a fair way to Bridgewater from here.'

'Oh, that's all right, I don't mind, you know. You sorta get used to things. I like the river too. You can see it most of the way, you know. It's sorta calming. That's what I like about the river.'

Kant could relate to that.

'I *could* give you a lift home if you like. I'm nearly finished here.'

'Oh no, that's all right really, Mister Kant, Barry. I like the time I get with me dogs. Gets me mind off things, you know. The springer gets a bit jumpy if she don't get 'er exercise. An' Donald 'ere, well 'e could walk to Marrawah if ya let 'im,' he said affectionately.

'Take it easy then and I'll see you next week.'

'Okay then. Oh Barry, can I bring my missus?'

'Oh yes, absolutely. We'll reserve the front row seats for wives, partners and family members. Bring Joel too.'

Kant turned and climbed the steps to the studio. John wandered off in the direction of the Brooker Highway.

'What's got into you?' Mackelroy asked as soon as Kant entered the control room.

Kant had witnessed Mackelroy's unscrupulous manner many times. Go for the jugular if it improves the ratings, we are not a soft-centred counselling service, the public don't want pretty, they want blood and guts. But it wasn't that tonight.

'Just seeing if the old fella wanted a lift home,' he replied casually, knowing exactly what his director was angry about.

'Don't get cute, Barry. You bloody well know I'm not referring to that. I thought we discussed every fart on this show before it went to air. What's all this cosy, sorry-you-poor-old-fella stuff you were getting into?' But before Kant could answer, Mackelroy continued, 'The sort of soft treatment the bloody tabloids will turn into a head fucking line. It could ruin our edge. And what's all this hugging the old bastard at the end? We're not doing "This is your Bloody Life".' For a moment, Kant thought this would have been a preferable title for the show.

'Jesus, James, it was the last show of the series. Maybe it should be the last, full stop. I'm tired of feeding these wretched people's lives to the masses. There's no compassion out there. There has to be a better way for these people to find peace. John has more heart than all those audience philistines put together.'

Mackelroy smiled at Kant, looked down at the floor and back up. 'You done? Go home, buddy, you're tired. Go and have a drink with your hippy mate. Find some of that *peace* for yourself. We'll talk Monday. Rest up. And Barry,' Mackelroy tapped Kant's chest with two fingers, 'sort yourself out! Right? I've got to go.'

Mackelroy turned, leaving Kant standing by himself looking out through the control-room window, down towards the stage where he had sat so many times taking frightened and unhappy people through their nightmares.

The place was empty. Only the unvoiced, ghostly vestiges of so much sorrow remained, clinging onto the warmth of the studio. Kant turned out the lights and left.

Chapter Twenty-Two

'Melinda.'

Melinda looked up from the work bench where she was going over the ingredients for bread dough with her class. For many of them 'white death', as Melinda called packeted sliced white bread, was all they had ever tried. It was the last lesson of the day. She was tired and looking forward to being home. Judith Thompson was standing just inside the door. 'Can I have a word?' She was mouthing the words more than saying them out loud.

'Sure.' Melinda turned briefly back to her class. 'Now remember to knead it well; both times, otherwise it won't rise properly.'

The principal had moved to the corridor outside the home economics kitchen. Her expression was grave to say the least. Every possibility that might have upset her crossed Melinda's mind in a flash. She hadn't had time to speak to her about the lesson with Vernon and Rosie so she was puzzled by the interruption.

Simon Mackie, a relief teacher, busied up the corridor, looked at Melinda with a thin-mouthed greeting and went into the classroom to supervise her class.

'Melinda, I've organised for Mr Mackie to look after your class for the rest of the session. I have some difficult news to tell you. Just come down to my office. We can talk there.'

Melinda's heart flicked an alarm-throb into her chest.

'What is it?' she asked, irritated that one of her students had more than likely vandalised something around the school. 'Is it David Such? He was absent again today. I know his dad punched him around again the other night. He showed me the bruises.' Her voice was infused with concern, the sort that accompanies the teacher who takes their duty of care responsibilities very seriously. 'Mr Such is a brute, he should be ... '

Judith put her hand on Melinda's shoulder and started to lead her away from her classroom.

'No, it's not about Sutchy. His mother phoned in to say he was sick. He's gone to stay with his gran for a couple of days. No, it's about your home care. Mrs Gorski?'

'Yes. Yetta. Why, what's happened?' Then came the spill of alarm. 'Oh my God, Rosie! Oh no, has something happened to her?'

In the next moment, that split second where fear aligns itself with the body and the mind's imagination, a searing heat raked through every sinew of Melinda's being. Her heart battered at the inside of her rib cage. It was the feeling that can only be experienced by a mother at the exact point when they realise their young child could be in danger, or worse.

'No, I don't think so. I just had a call from the hospital saying that Mrs Gorski was ... had been ... '

'What? Please, what!'

By this time Judith had shrewdly guided Melinda into her office and closed the door.

Melinda subsided onto the visitors' chair and began to tremble. 'Please tell me Rosie's safe. Has Vernon done something? I couldn't bear it if he … it was all too good to be true.'

'Melinda, I'm afraid I can't say. They just said Mrs Gorski had been taken to hospital by ambulance and that she was on her own.'

'Who? Who! Rosie or Yetta?'

'Mrs Gorski.'

Tears blinded Melinda. 'Oh God, oh God, please let her be all right.'

'Melinda, I've phoned your hus … your partner on the mobile number you gave us for your file. He is going to the hospital as we speak. I'm sure everything will be fine. I'm sure your daughter will …'

'I've got to get home, I'm sorry I've got to go now, can you … my class … oh God please, no …'

Ever in control of every 'situation' that had arisen in her long career as a teacher, Judith Thompson stood up and came round to Melinda's side. 'Maybe you should wait just a little before you drive. You're … distressed,' she said, placing her hand on Melinda's shoulder.

But Melinda didn't hear her, or feel her. She was out of her seat, out of the door, out of her mind with a terrible dread coursing through her body like nitric acid gnawing at every soft tissue in its path. This was no time to be reasonable, sensible. Here, there was no place for Judith's cool control. Her child was in danger, maybe still on her own, frightened.

Melinda could visualise Rosie, hear her. 'Mummy, *Mummy,* where are you?'

What could have happened to Yetta, to just leave Rosie alone in the house? Maybe she's been … Oh please, don't let them be harmed. If Vernon has hurt Rosie I'll kill him.

She tried phoning Mungo but his mobile was engaged. As Melinda sped along the Brooker Highway through the northern suburbs, past scrappy second-hand car yards and litter-coated school yards, past shitting dogs being walked along the river's edge, past battered Utes loaded with firewood for sale, past gardens without trees, kids who should be in school, towards Lutana, her own northern suburb, her mind began to fill with regret. Why hadn't she listened to her father? This sort of thing doesn't happen south of the city.

When are you coming back south of the city? Her father's words bouncing around in her head, as she jammed on the brakes suddenly because the traffic lights at the show grounds had just turned red. The squealing car behind her blasted its horn, screeched rubber and overtook her in the left lane. The violently yelling man in the lowered street-machine swore abusively at her through his closed window as he screeched through the red light.

As Melinda entered the cul-de-sac, heart pounding, the words Four Luck Avenue seemed tainted and bitter. Suddenly the other houses appeared unloved, disdainful of beauty. Only now she noticed the car up the road a bit that must have been parked there for some time, its roadside tyres flat, the back window shattered, obviously stolen and dumped. Melinda remembered the night, the screeching of rubber and the shouting, the empty cans popping along the bitumen like discarded opportunities.

And we've chosen to bring our precious daughter up amongst all of this. Why, in this hell? Why have I been so stubborn?

Melinda did not take a second to settle her churning thoughts before charging towards the house. *What if Rosie is still there?* she suddenly thought. She didn't want to frighten her any more by bursting crazily into her room. *What if she isn't there? Oh my God, what if she's hurt or…?*

Breathe.

The house was graveyard still and tomb silent, except for the pumping thrum of blood in Melinda's ears.

'Rosie? Rosie darling, Mummy's home,' Melinda called out gently, tentatively as the emptiness pressed like a vice around her head.

Rosie's bedroom was empty. In the living area, where only yesterday she had found out that she had an older sister, Melinda froze, mesmerised by a smear of blood on the timber floor, her heart doubling its thump. It looked as if Yetta had had to drag herself towards the kitchen. *Away from her attacker?* The streak of red stopped just in front of the sideboard where it had pooled a little more. Still unable to move, barely able to sustain her lungs with air, to think, Melinda noticed the blood stain on the corner of the coffee table, where Yetta must have hit her head after tripping, maybe. Melinda's heart was now thumping so violently she had to cross her arms across her chest and sit down.

Minutes seemed to disappear in the slow-motion panic of a nightmare as the distraught people who had suffered unimaginable loss she had watched on her father's show flashed into her mind. 'This is what it's like,' they were saying to her. Then visions of recent news footage of bloody reprisals in Libya taunted her: 'You've only lost one child; we have lost so many.' And for a split second she could understand what had driven Gabriel to the top of the Tasman Bridge.

But kidnap doesn't happen here, not in Hobart, not here on this beautiful island. We're so lucky here. That's what people said. 'Hobart, Australia's best kept secret.' She'd heard it said only yesterday in the staff room at recess time.

Dragging herself through a scorching terror, Melinda managed to stand up to gather her thoughts. There had to be a rational explanation. Children don't just disappear here. *It's just my fear, that's all, an illusion, nothing concrete,* she thought, but not believing herself, she stepped over the blood and moved nearer the counter where she could reach the phone. A jet of pungent bile shot up into her throat. She retched and spat into the sink. She took a deep breath and allowed the air to fall from her nose to calm herself.

The phone! Of course, Lotty was trying to get to the phone. She must have called the ambulance; had taken Rosie with her. Got someone to look after her before they arrived and they are both safe now. I must get to the hospital, find Mungo, 'I want to see my little girl,' she quivered helplessly.

Melinda began to sob uncontrollably. *But there's no blood on the handset, surely…*

Trembling, she managed to tap the numbers of Mungo's mobile into the phone. It rang and rang and … rang out. She tried again but it was engaged. *Who the hell's he talking to?* She tapped in her father's mobile number but it had been switched off. Not unusual while they were recording. She waited for thirty interminable seconds then screamed when the phone rang as she was holding it.

'Mel. It's me.'

'Mungo! Thank God. Is Rosie with you?'

'No. I thought she was with you. I can't ask Yetta because she's out to it; they've given her something to make her sleep. She's been stabbed in the stomach. The bastard used her knitting needles. It was that fucking kid, wasn't it? So much for…' But this wasn't the time for blame. 'Do you really think he could have taken Rosie?'

'I don't know. Oh Mungo, I'm so scared. I just want to know where she is.' Her voice, a mere whimper now, was choked with dread. 'I need to find my little girl. I can't stand it anymore. What if she's … ?'

'She's not!' Mungy yelled angrily at the inferred suggestion. 'She'll be fine. People don't just … this isn't a third world country. Just stay calm, I'm coming home now. There's nothing I can do here now until Yetta comes round. The doctor said she'd phone me as soon as there is a change.'

'Mungo, I love you so much, I just want our little girl back.'

'Yeah, me too. The doctor is coming now. Just stay calm. I'll see you soon.'

'I'll phone the police too.'

'Yeah, good ... Mel ... she'll be okay,' Mungo said, attempting to sound composed even though inside he was gripped by the same intolerable fear.

Just talking to Mungo was enough for Melinda. It was a relief, some release of the terror that had wedged itself in her heart over the past hour. And now she fell onto the old sofa and wept loudly. She cried out the pain of her anguish, biting the cushion, clawing at the worn-out fabric as if somehow they had been responsible for the desperate situation she now found herself in.

'Thought I heard summit.'

Melinda straightened up in one frantic movement. There was an intruder in the room with her. She jumped to her feet in defence from this new threat.

'Din know where youse worked, darl.'

Standing in the doorway to the living area, like an apparition from hell, stood the tattooed, the dishevelled, the pierced, the crude, the ignorant Lippy — the bogan bitch from next door.

'What the *fuck* are *you* doing here!' Melinda screamed, shocking herself by the vehemence of her apparent revulsion of her neighbour, as much as her own rudeness towards someone who had done nothing to offend other than the superficiality of her looks and lack of education. Melinda began to sob again. 'Oh look, I'm ... I'm really sorry, it's just that ... '

'She's right, darl. I'm used to it wiv me exes. You should 'ear 'em 'ava go! Water off the old goose's back though. Just popped round to say ya little tacker's wiv me next door. Jeez, she's a character. Guess she gets it from that poofy fella a yours. Nah, only kiddin'.'

Is this a cruel joke? This woman really must be a sicko. But she sounded so matter-of-fact that Melinda, for a moment, wondered whether in fact they had pre-arranged for Lippy to babysit Rosie today and she had simply forgotten about it.

'Rosie's next door? With you? At *your* house?' Melinda, whose voice was edged with unwarranted disgust, was finding the transition from hell into this doubtful bliss difficult to comprehend, and shocked by the disdain that pervaded her sense of this woman.

'Yeah. Hope youse don't mind, darl.'

'How is she?'

'Foin ... '

But before Lippy could utter another word Melinda had sprung towards the door with powerful animal instincts, barged past her neighbour and charged next door. As she entered and scurried along the passage, dodging strewn clothes and upended toys to where she could hear children's voices, the throb of bass guitar seemed to have taken hold of the house; Barnsey was singing, '...life's too short for burning bridges, take it one day at a time, oh oh oh he's a working class man...'

In a room that looked as if it had had a visit from Cyclone

Tracy, her eyes fell on Rosie, who had been plonked in the crater of a sagging beanbag in the middle, festooned with tinsel and other ageing Christmas decorations. She was sucking on a bright red wiener sausage, tomato sauce smeared at the edges of her mouth like an apprentice vampire, swaying instinctively to the music while the other children were wildly rushing around her, chortling and chattering manically as if she were a sacrificial offering to their gods.

'Mummy!' Rosie called out as soon as she spied her mother in the doorway. 'Come and pay with my new friends!'

'Rosie! Oh Rosie.' Tears filled Melinda's eyes again as she stepped forward and leaned over to pick her up. But Rosie wriggled away to remain in the middle of the action which wasn't going to cease just because the adults had arrived to stop all the fun.

'Mummy, I like red sausage. Can we buy some at the shops? Look, they are bight red!' Her eyes suddenly widened with a memory. 'Mummy, Yetta was very sick and went in the ambalence. Can we go and see her and take her a red sausage?'

'Of course, we can go tomorrow evening. She's resting now, my sweet.'

'She's cute, I'll give ya that,' Lippy said, who was now standing by Melinda's side. 'And she's gunna break a few 'earts, you mark my words. Come on then, love, we better crack a coupla tinnies. Hey, what yer cryin' for, gal? She's okay. I ain't done nothin' to 'er, if that's what youse are thinkin'.'

Melinda could not take her eyes off her daughter. She sobbed and clutched at herself, trying to reassure herself that she was not still trapped in a nightmare. Lippy stepped forward and led her into the kitchenette.

'Me exes think I'm a cunt but … hey.'

'No, no I didn't think … it's just that …'

'Come on, darl, she's right.' A smoke-honed chuckle leaped from Lippy's throat, glad to be free.

'What happened this afternoon?'

'Yeah well, nothin' really I s'pose. 'Ere, wrap ya laughin' gear round this,' she said handing Melinda a can of Cascade. 'I 'eard 'er cryin', see? I know youse are a good mum 'n' that, but the cryin' seemed to go on a bit long so I goes round and knocks on ya door, see? Ya little girl sounded pretty upset an' I couldn't hear no one about so I just wen' in. Hope youse don't mind.'

'Mind?'

'Well, anyway, I seen the old lady on the floor, you know, with blood on her 'ead. I reckoned she'd done summit bad to herself. So I calls the ambos. They was 'ere in a jiff and they packed 'er off. Didn't reckon it was worth getting the pigs 'ere, bastards only confuse things. I reckon the old lady 'ad a turn or summit while she was knittin', fell forward and stabbed 'erself right in the guts with them fuckin' needles, and she would a cracked 'er 'ead on the bloody table on the way down. Don't reckon she's the type to top 'erself though.'

'She did have dizzy spells occasionally, but nothing like this.'

'I wouldn't worry, gal. She'll pull through and then she'll be back cookin' all them things that smell so nice.'

'Oh Lippy, I'm so grateful to you. I don't know what I would have done if…'

'Bloody kids, darl, drive ya fuckin' mad, and that ain't no fuckin' lie neither. But youse can't live without 'em, eh?'

'No.'

Lippy swigged at her beer. 'I wanna throttle my little bastards just about every day, don't I, Sean? But they are the only bloody things I love in this whole stinkin' world. And ain't *that* the fuckin' truth.'

Melinda's mobile began to ring.

'Mel, did you call? I've finished now, I can talk. Sounds like you're having a party.'

'Yes, Dad, it's okay now.' Melinda put her hand over her other ear to mute out the children's laughter and the clatter of plastic toys. 'I'll talk to you later, Dad. I'm just picking up Rosie from next door.'

'Next door?' Melinda could hear the surprise in her father's voice.

'I'll tell you later.'

'Okay, but just be careful of that woman.'

Melinda laughed. 'Bye Dad.'

'Mummy.'

'Yes, my little angel?'

'I like red sausages. Can you buy some more at the shops?'

*

The following afternoon Yetta Gorski was propped up in her bed dozing. She looked very peaceful – almost as if it was the first time she'd had a real rest in a long time. *Not a good way of going about it*, Melinda thought. Rosie trotted up to the hospital bed and began tapping the old lady's hand before Melinda could hold her back.

Yetta opened her eyes and found focus on the child. 'Hello little one.' She was still a bit groggy from the sedatives she had been given. She lifted drowsy eyes to Melinda as the muscles in her pale face attempted to form a smile. A drip had been put in her right arm, replacing one tiny drop of blood at a time.

'I'm so very sorry, dear,' Yetta began. 'I don't really know what happened.'

Melinda stepped up to the bed, leaned over and kissed her on the cheek.

'You have absolutely nothing to apologise for. Rosie is safe and the main thing now is for you to get well so you can bake some more of your beautiful food. Mungo will only start complaining that my cooking isn't up to par!'

'You're very kind, my dear. But maybe my days of looking after the little one are over.'

'Well, let's not worry about that now. You're part of the family so we'll just have to work out what to do next.'

Feeling left out of the conversation, Rosie began tapping Yetta's hand again. It looked frail, soft.

'Yetta.'

'Yes dear.'

'You went in a ambalence when you were sick. And now you are better.'

'That's right, little one. And when I'm *really* better I will come to your house and you can help me cook some of those nice biscuits your daddy loves so much. Would you like to do that with me?'

'Yes, pease. And Yetta?'

'Yes, dear.'

'Rosie likes red sausages now. Do you like red sausages?' but before Yetta could give Rosie her honest answer, Rosie continued, 'And Yetta?'

'Yes, dear.'

'You can meet my new friends too who payed with me when you went in the ambalence. They live in the house next door. And they have big bags with *beans* in them!'

Yetta smiled. 'I'd like that very much.'

'Okay sweetheart, Yetta is tired now and we had better let her get some more rest,' Melinda said. She lifted Rosie up to give Yetta a kiss. 'I'll come by tomorrow. Now have the rest you deserve. And don't worry about anything, okay?'

Yetta sank back into her pillows and her eyes began to close. The doctor had told Melinda previously she would probably stay in hospital for a few more days. She had lost a fair amount of blood and the damaged tissue and muscles, although not too bad, would need extra time to heal due to her age. She had been very lucky to have been found so quickly by the neighbour, who had acted wisely and swiftly.

When Melinda and Rosie reached the car, and Rosie had been buckled into her car seat, Rosie said to her mother, 'Mummy is Yetta dead now?'

'No, of course not. But she needs rest though to get better.'

'But I saw her eyes close. I don't want her to die, Mummy. Yetta sings nice songs.'

'She was just going to sleep, sweetheart. She is very tired from the accident. But she'll soon be out of hospital and you can help her do some cooking while she sings.'

'And Mummy, can you buy Yetta some red sausages for a surpise?'

'Sure.'

Rosie scrunched her mouth seriously. 'I think she likes red sausages.'

Chapter Twenty-Three

Saturday morning, Kant stood on his balcony absorbing the eight-thirty rumblings of the harbour beyond. He felt comforted by its affability, spending almost more time on his cantilevered two square metres of balcony than he did in his whole apartment with all its spatial sophistication and comfort. From the nuances of the dock's unspoken language there seemed to be no supposition of failure, no signs of frailty, or warnings of threat. The abstract sounds, emanating from this organic apparatus with a million moving parts, echoed no sarcasm or respect, professed no pleasure or loathing, but washed the city with a sense of impartial resourcefulness and optimism, and no matter what disfigured deeds human beings perpetrated against each other the continuum of life would remain indestructible.

Kant moved inside to boil the kettle.

Vince MacLean was on his way round for a coffee before his weekly amble amongst the bustling stalls of the legendary Salamanca Place market. The spritely magic of Vivaldi's flute concerto resounded around the apartment. Kant didn't know when the music had been composed but it felt as if it could have been conceived in a time in history devoid of ugliness and oppression, and he wondered if there had ever been such a time. On a small scale, compared to the history of humanity,

Kant conceded that both his daughters had been conceived in times of beauty and absolute freedom and he felt grateful for his good fortune.

The bell buzzed. Kant pressed a wall button to unlock the street door for Vince.

'A cheerful wee morning for the market,' Vince called lyrically out as he ascended the stairs, evoking the smell of heather on the moor. Even when the subject was severe he sounded upbeat Kant had observed. There was no morning breeze to sweep away the bustle of the hordes of buyers and sellers, a veritable community melting-pot.

Kant poured two coffees, both black without sugar. They sat in the leather armchairs, leaving the balcony doors open. The two men didn't often socialise outside work time, but Kant enjoyed the informal and world-wise banter he could share with MacLean, their meetings being in passing. Unlike with Mackelroy where he always felt a little guarded, Kant enjoyed MacLean's easy manner and would often pass concerns by him for an opinion.

'I've been buying my veggies from the Hmong people recently. They present their produce as if it's respected. I like that,' Kant said conversationally.

'True. But I canna abide a cauliflower that's *too* respected. They tend to get a big head,' MacLean quipped.

'I know the feeling.'

'So Barry, we're nearly at the end again. And this time I'm sensing a wee change in the weather, if you catch my drift.'

Barry chuckled. 'You're an astute bugger, Vinny. Remind me never to play poker with you.'

'Och, we Scots are too tight to risk our money on a gamble.'

'Yeah right. I've seen you wipe the table with the crew at Nerve.'

MacLean, who regularly cleaned up a few coins at any number of card games in the work canteen, said, 'So, what was it you wanted to confess this morning, my son?'

'Ha! Okay, well to start with I can't stop having lascivious thoughts about a particular lady I've just met.'

'Well, my son, I can assure you that's not a sin. It's merely preliminary preparation for future engagements. But if it helps, drink three Bloody Marys and get on with it.'

'Much obliged to you, Father. Talking of the Catholic Church, it segues nicely into what did you think of John Sturges? I mean, you found him in an art gallery and he doesn't exactly come across as an art aficionado. And then he unleashes his story. Paedophilia and child abuse right across the board is like a rumbling earthquake amongst us, and John's just the tip of the iceberg. I tell you, he's really got under my skin.'

'That's the thing, isn't it? Our outside skin is merely a deception.'

'All that abuse happened so long ago, surely there's an end for recovery.' In Kant's voice was a wish, a plea for the man's suffering to stop.

'Child abuse has been systemic for so long that the public concern has all but evaporated. It's become mere table talk at dinner parties between courses and the victims have become marginalised by silence. Compared to television's nightly tally of bloodshed in a dozen countries around the world, or is that a hundred now, we think it's just one man who's had a raw deal growing up in this idyllic haven we call Tasmania. We're sheltered from the *real* dramas of the world, so get over it, mate.'

'It's coldhearted and is still abhorrent whether it's to one person or a million, even more so because this is supposed to be a paradise and it's *still* bloody well going on.'

'And those bastard priests continue to reoffend, protected by their religious status and worse by the church's cover-up. Those vile holy men who have defiled so many innocent kids in their care don't have a fragment of the dignity and integrity John's shown. I wouldn't be surprised if he wins,' Vince said. 'But there's the rub; no one really wins. Do they?'

Kant sighed. 'I think that's what's been getting me down lately.'

'Aye and it's a big prize now. And *that* can have damaging after-effects.'

'It's not the money with John. He says he just wants enough to help his wife bring the rest of her children out from the Philippines. Money really can't buy what he needs for his peace of mind.'

Kant stood up and went to the balcony. MacLean followed. Below, the bustling market, colourful and prolific, was in full swing.

'*There's* humanity, all those individuals with their unique external appearances, the vibrant, the drab, the vivacious, the pensive, and all concealing their own poignant complexities,' Kant said, as his eyes scanned the activity below.

'Well, I'd better dive in and join them with my own brand of deception, before all the good bargains go,' MacLean added.

As the two men looked out, a sharp, power-dressed woman in her forties trotted alongside the waterfront with a large Doberman dog on a lead, high heels clacking like bullets ricocheting off the pavement. Kant could imagine this formidable CEO workaholic in front of a trembling board of directors, dog at her side drooling high-class saliva. Kant found himself drawn back to the pile of Alistair MacLean novels he'd read in Crete all those years ago where the male protagonists always seemed to own one – the *deadliest fighting dog in the world*, the other MacLean had written. Those dog-eared thrillers, about the only literature available from the wily bookseller in Sitia, were as incongruous in that little seaside port as a reality show in a privileged country where the worst-case scenario was awarded a grand prize.

The woman reached her shiny BMW 4X4, parked a little way along, and lifted the hatch. Kant watched with a moment's awe as the dog glided, propelled by a single effortless leap a couple of metres back, into the back, settling on its personal tartan rug. Its tiny stump of a tail then began twitching, as if saying, 'Thank you so much for giving up that ten minutes of your precious time but can I have five hours next time?'

'I wonder what emotional complexities she's concealing,' Kant mused.

'How about a fifteen-year-old son who's addicted to ice because she's never at home being a mother,' MacLean guessed.

'Maybe. I'd like to think that there are some people who are just fortunate.'

MacLean thanked Kant for the coffee, descended the stairs and evaporated into the crowd. Kant went inside to pour himself another coffee and began to wonder, with all the overseas reporting Vince MacLean had done, what undisclosed turmoil he had managed to bury beneath his personable exterior.

Before MacLean had arrived, Kant had already been awake for several hours when daylight was still just a prophetic pink glow on the horizon. The fishing boats, well-oiled wheel-drums, heavy with miles of netting and floats had already left the docks and were well out past the Derwent's estuary, around the Iron Pot light, heading for the hunting grounds on the continental shelf beyond the sheer cliffs of Tasman Island. Even the early-bird stall-holders hadn't quite arrived to set up.

Unless he made a conscious effort to listen, Kant realised that recently he had become at one with the constancy of the sounds of his surroundings, a kind of symbiotic, perpetual motion. And as he watched the bubbling crowd below he felt like an immigrant who had finally assimilated into his new adopted homeland, a secure home for his heart to expand in again. The Huon Valley had served him well when he was married, and now, this harbour, this city, this apartment even, would sustain him, was sustaining him. He began to feel he could shake off his exploitation of nostalgia as a support mechanism. Max's painting had set something in motion, and now his past life with Sarah, that had shaped him for what he had become now, could safely be placed on the tide to float out to sea.

He looked at his watch. In a couple of hours he would say hello to his other daughter. In a couple of hours his ship would take on new and precious cargo. He tried to put John Sturges out of his mind.

*

As if she and her father were hard-wired, Melinda, restless in bed, had also been up well before the sun had reached the horizon, filling *her* sleepless hours by baking. When Mungo and Rosie awoke the house would be filled with the sweet yeasty aroma of hot bread. She'd even found a good recipe for moussaka hoping it would be a good first step to connecting with her unknown sister. Was she going over the top? *Who cares?* She thought, quivering with anticipation. It wasn't every day you were meeting your older sibling for the first time in your life.

But for now she needed to be active, thinking about the ramifications was unbearable. She felt like a pressure cooker about to blow. Phoning her father would alleviate her tension, but it would be too early to wake him. She looked at the wall clock in the kitchen, five-thirty, and began to sprinkle salt over the sliced aubergine to remove the bitterness.

*

Kant's iPhone rang. He took it out from the pocket of his suit that had been slung over the back of a dining chair.

'I thought you might be up too,' he chuckled.

'Yes, you're right. I couldn't sleep either.'

'Oh it's you! I thought you might be Mel.'

Gillian returned a downy laugh, endeavouring to conceal her weariness. 'Haven't been able to relax; my thoughts keep going round and round till they bump into the back of each other.'

'Ah, the interminable loop. I've been on that merry-go-round too. What time is it?'

'Er … just after seven. Look, Barry, BJ and I, well, we wondered if we could come round a bit earlier. Sounds like none of us can wait till lunch time now.'

'Sure. Well how about you come here for breakfast?'

'I was hoping you'd suggest that. It's taken years to patiently get to this point but the last hours have stretched into eternity.'

'I'll give Mel a call. I'm sure she won't mind. Do you think I should suggest she come by herself for this first meeting? Could it get too confusing if Rosie and Mungo come too? What do you think?'

'Absolutely not! Even though I've never seen BJ so nervous about anything, she's adamant she wants to dive-bomb into the full family swimming pool, to use her words.'

'No fear, eh? Remember the Salamanca market's on this morning so you'll find it hard to park close. Okay, um … ' Barry began to collect his wits, 'I'd better go to the bakery now and … .'

'You don't need to do that. We already shopped yesterday. And Barry…'

'Yes?' There was a young child in the anticipation of his voice.

'Hold on.'

'Hello.'

'Hello,' Barry replied to another female voice on the phone. 'Is that *you*, Agalia?'

'Yes, it is.'

'Agalia.'

'Yes?'

'Oh, I was just trying out your name.' Barry laughed sheepishly.

Hesitantly she replied, 'Well, er… I want to say… I…'

For a few moments Barry listened to the swell of weeping, his own eyes blurred and glistening.

Then, 'Hello,' she repeated.

Barry's chest contracted and his heart pounded timpanically. 'Hello,' he managed to squeeze from his knotted throat. He heaved in a lungful of air and blew it out. He had wanted to say 'my daughter'. *Why is it so hard?* Then an assertive sniff made its way to his ear. He laughed and the tension gave way.

'I will bring a handkerchief,' Agalia said more assertively. 'Maybe the difficult part is over. But still, I will bring one.'

There was just a hint of an accent in her voice. Agalia's English word-use was correct, international and precise as if she had learned the grammar at school and practised it without Australian vernacular.

An energised frisson swept across Barry's chest. *What do I say? The first thing that comes to mind.*

'Agalia, I want you to know that I'm ... so happy you've been a *bright joy* for your mother and father.'

Pull yourself together, man. This isn't a public speaking contest. Just speak normally.

'Your mother, I mean Gillian, is ... certainly a wonderful ... what I'm trying to say is I'm so happy you chose to search for us.'

That wasn't so bad ... For a wooden top.

In a courteous voice Agalia replied, 'I hope you don't mind but I think I would like to call you Pateras. It is what I have grown up with. And it is, after all, who you are, *Father.*'

Barry's relief was immense.

'Ehdahxee! Ola kala,' he blurted out his only memorised Greek words, words that had once answered a million questions and possibilities all those years ago on the island of Crete.

When Agalia laughed this time it was full-bellied, generous and free from restraint, and to Barry's ear, whether it was fanciful of not, was reminiscent of another woman's laugh he had known and adored for over thirty years of his life.

*

Just after her father's call Melinda put the phone down, went back into the bedroom, snuggled in next to Mungo and began tickling him, gently to begin with, then more persuasively as he tried to shrug her off with some drowsy grunts. In about two minutes flat he knew resistance was a lost cause and rolled out of bed to shower.

'Mm, that seemed to work.' Melinda grinned to herself. 'Now for Rosie.'

But Rosie was already awake, sitting up in her bed playing with some colourful fabric scraps, folding them, tying them as a shawl and a skirt for one of her teddies. Melinda had already talked to her about meeting Agalia, mummy's sister, and *her* aunty, who had lived in another country for a long time and now she was coming to visit them all. Rosie had picked up on her mother's excitement.

'I'm ready to see my arty now and I want to wear this,' she demanded, holding up a dress with an embroidered picture of a cat playing with a tangled ball of wool on the bib, not too dissimilar to the tangle of clothes pulled from her chest of drawers and now strewn around the floor.

'Lovely, sweetheart. Aunty Agalia will think you look very pretty.'

Melinda helped her into her clothes, tying her hair back with a purple ribbon. 'We can go as soon as Daddy is dressed because we are having breakfast at Grandpa's.'

'Does Gampa know how to make breakfast, Mummy?'

'Oh yes, he's the best toast maker in town.'

'Does Gampa have apicot jam?'

'Not sure, but whatever he has I'm sure you'll enjoy it.'

As they were all getting into the car Rosie asked, 'Can I bring my new friends, Daddy?' She was pointing to a trio of little faces peering from the front window of the house next door.

'Maybe next time, darling.'

Mungo grinned at Melinda and flicked a surreptitious eyebrow. Rosie waved proudly.

*

Barry had told Gillian to come straight up, that he would leave the street door unlocked. Something inside him told him he didn't want his first interaction with Agalia to be at the front door like a visiting salesman. He had imagined turning around and seeing her standing in the heart of her father's home as if it was the most natural thing in the world. *Hi darling, have a nice trip? Yes, Dad. Good to be home.*

But when he did look up from Max's investment magazine he'd tried to read to distract his thoughts, and saw Gillian and a young woman who had a remarkable likeness to Sarah, standing in the middle of the room, a bolt of electricity shot through his body, momentarily stunning him.

Gillian went straight to the kitchen and deposited a basket filled with delicacies. 'I don't think I even need to introduce you two.'

Barry dropped the magazine and jumped up. He approached Agalia and reached for her hands, then stood back a pace from her. Her hair was fair, like Sarah's the time Barry had first set eyes on her on the dockside in Sitia. She dressed colourfully, playfully, as if the world might end soon and there was no time to be mournful.

'Agalia, welcome.'

'Thank you,' she replied as if mesmerised, not taking her eyes off her father.

'Now that I see you, you are definitely the reflection of *both* your mothers.' He didn't care if his practised words sounded grandiose; he had been certain she would be, and now, seeing his daughter for the first time, he really meant it. And before Agalia could utter another word he added, 'I can see Sarah in your features, and I sense Gillian in the love and care that has so obviously been given you.'

Father and daughter hugged each other for the first time in their lives.

Gillian moved towards Barry and kissed his cheek. She winked at her daughter. 'Told you he was a softy.'

'Pateras, I believe I am fortunate to have had two mothers. I have thought a great deal about what my mother would have gone through. And I'm sorry to speak of this so soon, but I have expressed a lot of varied emotions over time, and now I can honestly say that she did what she did out of love. I believe she had hoped that she and I would meet some day to reconnect. Sadly that was not to be, and she wasn't to know this, but in a sense it *has* happened because it feels as if we are all surrounded by her spirit.'

Barry hugged his daughter again, closed his eyes, and breathed out three decades of lost time.

'I don't think there's any competition here between Nature and Nurture. They have been perfectly synchronised. Agalia, I can't express how good it is that you are here.' And turning to Gillian he said, 'And to you I say, thank you from the bottom of my heart.'

Gillian kissed him, looked at Agalia and smiled cheekily. 'You're very welcome, Mr Kant. Now do you think we can crack open that bottle of champers?'

Clomping footsteps began to ascend from the street, accompanied by Rosie's excited chatter, as she insisted to her father she climb the wooden steps unassisted. As they entered the room the champagne cork popped into the air making Rosie squeal with delight as she ran to clasp at her grandfather's legs for safety.

'Gampa, Gampa, Rosie's got a arty.'

Barry bent down and lifted her up. 'Yes and here she is. Aunty Agalia.'

Rosie made a slight coy compression with her mouth and tilted her head in towards her grandfather's neck, to get a better and safer look at this new person in her life.

Melinda stepped towards her sister and they both grinned at each other as if they were naughty, scheming sisters who were about to plan something outrageous. They had no words, just a huge bear hug, stroking and patting each other's back and finally holding each other at arm's length, turning one way then the other, grinning unreservedly. The observations becoming sways and finally they began to dance around the space like young adolescent girls, chortling and showing off their newfound lack of inhibition to their parents.

Rosie wriggled from her grandfather's arms and grabbed onto her mother's leg, joining in the dance. Melinda picked her up and held her between herself and her sister. Gillian looked on with relief as they were swinging around. Melinda said to Agalia, 'And that gorgeous hunk over there, wondering what to do with himself, is Mungo, my lovely, lovely man.'

Mungo nodded towards the swirling females. 'G'day,' but then decided another quick slug of bubbly was in order.

'Hello Mungo, I'm looking forward to hearing your music,' Agalia sang out.

She turned to Rosie, 'And you, little princess, are my very special niece. I'm *very* pleased to meet you at last.'

'Are you going to be my friend too?'

'Of course, we will be *big* friends!'

Rosie, satisfied with the response, reached for Agalia, who took hold of the child and kissed her on the cheek. Rosie then performed her wriggling act again and went to see what her grandfather and father were doing in the kitchen. Mungo had lined up champagne glasses and was filling them. Barry picked her up and sat her on the counter. Mungo, who had already refilled his glass with champagne, began unpacking the basket, but not before flicking the sides of the glasses with his fingernail in search of a new melody.

Rosie reached out and began tapping her father's arm. 'Daddy, Daddy,' she was whispering coyly.

Mungo leaned down to her. 'What is it?'

She moved in towards her father's ear and whispered, 'Daddy, does Garly have a jyna like Mummy?'

Mungo nearly choked on his champagne. 'Yes, sweet pea. I'm sure she does. Now do you want something to drink?'

'Yes, pease. And Daddy.'

'What?'

She looked proudly at her father and whispered, 'Daddy, you've got a peeni.'

'I know, now let's get that drink.'

As Rosie trotted off, her query clarified, Mungo straightened up and saw Barry smiling. 'Don't say a word!'

Then suddenly it was like Christmas as different packages were pulled from the basket. There was smoked salmon, wheels of soft brie and camembert, some feta, some crackers, smoked eel, another bottle of champagne, dolmades, marinated artichokes and a container of kalamata olives. The assortment was like a honey pot to a family of bears. The sight and smell of the tasty offerings brought everyone to the kitchen. Melinda completed the ingredients for a fine meal with a still-warm loaf of bread and the moussaka which had been placed in the oven to top up its heat.

Barry handed the glasses around, giving Rosie her special fizzy-lemonade champagne.

'A toast to family.'

'To family!'

'Oikogeneia!' Agalia and Gillian said in unison. 'Mia proposi gia tin oikogeneia.'

'Couldn't agree more,' Mungo chimed, downing the rest of his second glass. 'I'll drink to that.'

For several minutes the division of food took precedence. Barry remembered it to be first on Edith Cartwright's inventory of essentials for life, just before home, and then books. He hoped Agalia had brought copies of any stories she'd had published.

Everyone found a space to nestle in and began tasting and eating the variety of offerings. And for a while they remained quietly reflective, as if all mindful of the potency of this intimate family ritual of sharing a meal together for the first time. To Mungo's relief, even Rosie was silent as she methodically and sparrow-like picked out the savoury rice from inside the dolmades' folded vine leaves with her fingers.

Conversation gradually entered the space again as questions arose, about Greece, its language and customs, musical exploits, cooking, art, pruning fruit trees, BKS, and alchemy.

Barry said, 'Agalia, my father is keen to meet you, but he's not exactly the world's best traveller. Anything that takes longer than five minutes in the car is like a mission to Mars. I'll take you to meet him in the next couple of days though.'

'I will look forward to that. Now Pateras, I would like to talk to you about something I believe you will be interested in hearing.'

'Sure, how about we take a short walk in my garden?'

Agalia looked momentarily confused, thinking something must have been lost in translation.

Barry smiled, 'My balcony is my kitchen garden here. I peruse the rest of my estate from there!'

Barry waited for his daughter outside as she fetched her handbag from the kitchen counter. Agalia joined him and shut the doors behind her, but not before she poked her tongue out at the remaining company irreverently, saying, 'Sorry, you're not invited.'

She faced her father and kissed him on the cheek. Her face became serious.

'Pateras, my dream for many years has been to find my birth mother. I always knew I was adopted because Mitera made no secret about it from a very early age. She used to say it was a special gift I possessed, that other children were missing out on – having two mothers was a privilege. When I was at the end of my teens, relieving myself of the usual horrid adolescent behaviours ... '

'I can't believe you had any of those!'

'Just a normal kid I'm afraid. However, at that time I began to have a strong desire to know my origins.'

'I think it's only natural,' Barry said, studying Agalia's face.

'But living in another country made it difficult to make traces. Then I became involved in writing. I had wanted to write a serious novel about a girl who had been adopted, but I found my interests leaned towards writing stories for children. They are, after all, the future custodians of our precious world, and what better way to impart some healthy ideas for ... ' She laughed. 'Sorry, I'm getting awfully sidetracked.'

'Doesn't worry me. I'd like to listen to you for the next thirty years to make up for lost time.'

Agalia shook her head at her father, her face filled with concern for him. 'Pateras, there is no such thing as *lost* time. We have both had our lives *filled* with joy. We are lucky people, and until this week you didn't even know I existed so, and I don't want to sound bossy, but…' she laughed again, 'I just am. And we have the rest of time to get to know each other, for me to know who my other family is; nothing is lost, there is only gain from this moment on.'

Barry wiped at his glassy eyes and leaned on the railing. 'I don't know where you got your wisdom from.' It was his turn to laugh. 'You obviously didn't get it from me.'

'That's not what I ascertain from Gillian. But I don't want to digress again because I have something to give you that I have kept close to my heart all my life. And even though I have to work out how to grieve for my mother who gave me life, it is you that deserves *this*.'

Agalia reached into her bag and took out a white envelope. She handed it to her father. 'Now I will join the rest of the family.'

Agalia opened the balcony doors and returned inside to the others, shutting the doors behind her again.

Barry stared at the envelope. He turned it over to see if there was any writing on it, clues to the contents maybe. There was nothing. Slowly, he lifted the flap and took hold of what was a black and white photograph and placed it flat in the open palm of his other hand.

Barry's lower lip and chin began to tremble, his forehead creased into sharp furrows and his eyes screwed up as he unsuccessfully tried to maintain focus on the image through the tears that were filling his eyes. It was no good; it was like being in a blinding rainstorm trying to read a sign post. He swiped at his eyes frantically with the back of his other hand and peered again. He began sobbing, quietly at first. He didn't care who heard him now, or who saw him, he was so moved and overjoyed by the picture that he even forgot there was a roomful of his family on the other side of a pane of glass, holding their breath while they watched him intently.

After a while he composed himself, looked up at them and smiled. Melinda breathed out. She could not bear to see her father in pain. Or was it pain? She wasn't sure this time.

The grainy black and white photograph was of Sarah at the time of Agalia's birth. A nurse must have taken it for her, more than likely with a cheap Instamatic camera of those times. Sarah was holding her baby, swaddled in a soft white sheet in a hospital bed. The baby's eyes were closed, its tiny round face peaceful in sleep. It was an archetypal image of a young mother gazing at her newborn child with unconditional love in her eyes, a love for *his* daughter.

Despite the age difference, Barry took in the uncanny likeness between Sarah *then* and Agalia *now*. He turned the photograph over. On the back, a little faded but legible, written in Sarah's lyrically looped handwriting, were the words *Bright Joy my love.*

Barry looked out towards the water. The photo was also a poignant reminder of the terrible misapprehension that had ensued; the sense of betrayal still scraped at his insides, something he would have to meet head-on if he was to find peace again. But reuniting with his daughter was a giant step in the right direction.

Barry looked into the apartment, heaved a breath and went back inside.

Chapter Twenty-Four

On the following Monday morning the whole family had scattered across the city. Gillian had taken Agalia to the Department of Immigration to enquire about obtaining an extended visa. She would stay with her mother in Fern Tree for the next few months to work out what she wanted to do from here on. Her life in Athens was well established and she didn't think she could just abandon it just because she'd finally met up with her father and sister. But for now Hobart was exactly where she wanted to be. Tomorrow afternoon Agalia would go with Barry and her mother to meet her grandfather, for her the last link in the family chain.

Barry had shut up shop and gone to meet Max and Vashna in a café on the other side of the docks. He was glad of the down time before the upcoming final episode of BKS at the end of the week. If Max couldn't put some pragmatic numbers together for him then Vashna was sure to have some pseudo-spiritual aphorism that would make his inner turmoil as clear as an old hippy's crystal.

Melinda and Mungo were on their way home after a walk on one of the mountain tracks. They had wanted to be together in clear air after the incident with Yetta. Rosie, tired out, was asleep in the back of the car. Mungo switched the car radio on to catch Lucky Oceans, but Angela Ross still had several minutes of news to read.

'...second wave of killings is said to have happened on Wednesday at the Qasr Ben Ghashir military camp, when guards shot five detainees. As the search for the absent dictator continued, British Tornado jets pounded bunkers in Sirte overnight.

'To local news now, and police have just released the name of a man found dead in the affluent suburb of Sandy Bay. The man has been identified as Gabriel Daniels, the lead oboist with the Tasmanian Symphony Orchestra...'

Mungo reached across and turned the volume up, looked at Melinda and frowned.

'...the tragedy was discovered when neighbours of Mister Daniels went to investigate the high volume and repetition of some classical music. Mister Daniel's wife and children were killed in a car accident two years previously at Mount Field. Police believe this to be the motivation behind what has been described as a clear-cut suicide.

'And now to sport. West Coast Eagles coach...'

Mungo flicked the volume knob off and pulled the car over and parked. He opened his mouth to speak to Melinda but found no words. Starting the engine again he sped off. Melinda placed her hand on his leg. She too looked ahead, shocked into silence.

Eventually, as they drove into Luck Avenue, Mungo spoke. There was an edge to his voice. 'That's how it's done. That's how we remove ourselves from the reality of yet another horrible waste of a life. We call it *clear-cut*, like some bloody editor in the censor's room cutting and pasting so we don't have to deal with anything real that might upset our own comfortable lives. Oh no, *that* wouldn't bloody do. Explained away in one short sentence. I don't know why they don't just put *sport* on first. People have orgasms over the marks of a game of football for years but they won't remember that some gifted musician lost everything that was precious to him and could not continue living with the pain any more. Yes, folks, it was just another clear-cut suicide, so now you can dismiss it instantly from your minds and get on with your own sorry existence.'

There were no tears in Mungo's eyes, just a burning white anger.

Melinda leaned over and placed her hand on his shoulder. 'You did your best, Hun. Maybe he just wanted to follow his family the best way he knew.'

Mungo snapped back. 'Jesus, Mel, that's just as dismissive of the reality!'

'Wow! What do you mean? I'm only trying to ... '

Mungo sighed. 'I'm sorry, I didn't mean to .... But it's like, that's where the rot starts to set in. We say things like that ... like, "He'll be happy now he's with his family", or "He packed a lot into his life", so we can *shove* our feelings to a place of numbness. It's as if we absolve ourselves from caring or feeling.'

'I'm not trying to absolve anything, Mungo! And you're not

the only one who feels things deeply either,' Melinda retorted angrily.

Mungo scratched at his scalp. 'Sorry,' he retorted sullenly. 'I don't even know how I'm supposed to feel. How long will *I* take to forget Gabriel? Or will *I* just end up cynical and self-interested like the rest of the bloody world?'

'There're a lot of good people in the world and you're one of them, Mungy. Everyone has choices, and good choices have to start somewhere, and my choice now is to make sure *our* family stays safe. It's distressing that Gabriel made that particular choice, but I've just met my sister for the first time. *My* precious family is where I choose to put my energy right now. I think you could too.'

'Maybe I could have done more. You should have seen his face, Mel, when he was playing. Maybe I should have asked him to play with us permanently. He told me he was going to try again. I didn't think he meant this. I just watched him wander off.'

'Mungy, you couldn't have done more. At some level Gabriel would have made up his mind,' Melinda answered, endeavouring to keep her frustration at bay. 'You were a temporary anchor for him by offering him kindness; that's *all* you could have done. He was always going to have to face the future on his own terms. Sometimes happiness is just too elusive.'

'Such a bloody waste.'

'A good reason why we mustn't waste what *we* have,' she said. 'We mustn't become apathetic with our lives, Mungy. We *have* to show Rosie how to make the most of every day.'

'You're right.' Mungo took several deep breaths before he spoke again. 'Gabriel *did* have choices.' He looked out of the window, feeling bitterly resigned to Gabriel's fate. 'I bet I know what piece of music he was playing too, poor bugger. And I *do* have that recording of him playing his oboe on that day he came to the studio. You really should have heard him, Mel. For a few minutes he *was* the lark.'

*

The three men sat around a café table in the Atrium, once an outside working courtyard within the sticky confines of the old IXL Jam Factory, now with glassed roof and contemporary internal fittings, new fashionably entwined with the old. The row of colonial warehouse buildings on the east side of the docks with their shy northern hemisphere Georgian windows, fearful of too much sunlight, had metamorphosed over nearly two centuries. They were now home to the School of Art, a furniture outlet selling locally made one-offs, an antique shop, an Aboriginal Art Gallery and the illustrious Henry Jones Art Hotel where patrons pay top price for rooms decked with local art, all swinging a hopeful price tag.

Max sipped at a long black. Vashna, chai latte in hand, was craning his neck around a waitress to see what gateaux the people at another table had ordered. Barry had changed his mind on a cappuccino and was waiting for a lime-flavoured mineral water.

'So tell us, what's she like?' Max asked as soon as they'd pulled their chairs in close and leaned in like plotters before a heist.

'Gillian? Or Agalia? To be honest I haven't really come to terms with falling for a new woman, who turns out to be the adoptive mother of my daughter, who I didn't know I fathered over three decades ago, and have just met for the first time.'

'And there's probably another dozen you'll never know about,' Max added irreverently, placing praying hands under his chin, eyes averting skyward.

'Hilarious.' Barry flicked Max's shoulder with the back of his hand. 'Agalia, my *elder* daughter is ... She reminds me of Sarah, and, yes, she's beautiful.'

'Definitely takes after her mother then,' Max continued in the same vein.

Barry ignored his friend's flippancy. 'She has more of Sarah's characteristics than Mel does. It's hard to grasp she's been alive all these years in a foreign country. She even speaks English with a Greek accent, and when I look at her when she's talking I can't comprehend that I am her real father. She sounds like a foreigner, and it's frightening to think that if I'd passed her in the street a month ago I wouldn't have made any connection, just another tourist. And yet, now that Gillian has brought her here, complete with the full narrative, it feels somehow that I have always known her.'

'The familial taproot goes deep into the psyche's soil,' Vashna said, as if speaking to himself.

Barry looked into an unfocused distance for a moment.

'How was Melinda meeting her sister after all this time?' Max asked.

'Overjoyed. It just seemed to be so easy for her. It was as if they've always been the greatest of friends. Of course, Rosie thinks it's great having an aunt just appear. Seems to sense the significance.'

Vashna put on one of his deep looks. 'And what about you, mate? I mean, Sarah, like she ...'

'Betrayed me? Like, what do I think about my beloved wife, of God knows how many years, not confiding in me that she'd been raped soon after we'd met, she'd had a baby secretly, had it adopted, then married me three years later and never spoke of it?'

'Well ... yes. How *do* you feel about that?'

'It's floored me. My head is still jangling with analysis even though I know it's futile. When Gillian told me I felt so incredibly let-down, deceived. I just can't understand how Sarah could completely bury it all those years we were together. She must have known that Agalia would eventually try to find her. It's as if our whole marriage was a sham. And now I feel guilty for feeling such anger towards her because when she died all I felt was sorrow. Like, I thought she was faultless.'

'I guess it's hard to stay angry with someone who's dead,' Max said, hoping to steer the conversation away from an emotional impasse.

'And I feel wretched for thinking that that was some sort

of karmic punishment put on her. I don't mean dying, but to never meet her daughter, to know the truth and be able to share the joy with me.'

'She was pretty young then, mate,' Vashna said more sympathetically. 'I mean, rape, it doesn't get much worse than that for a woman, particularly when she's young, in love and with everything going for her. Maybe she just wanted to block it out because it was too painful to hold on to. People block all sorts of traumas out, and I'm sure that with some people, after the passing of considerable time, it becomes buried so deep it really doesn't exist in their mind anymore.'

'I hope that's the reason. Maybe that's what I need to do with my feelings now – get a big spade and dig a deep hole for them.'

Vashna gripped his friend's shoulder with a benevolent hand. 'And don't forget, mate, Sarah gave Agalia the most important thing of all. Her life!'

'As always Vash, thanks.' Barry rubbed the back of his neck, chuckled bashfully. 'I came so close to dumping all my frustrations on Gillian too.'

'But you didn't.'

Max looked up from his mobile with an irreverent grin. 'Well, my old friend, there is another way to look at this. Reckon it will clarify a few things for you. This Gillian sounds like she's been a damn good custodian of your daughter for all those years. Sounds like your daughter's pretty together too, in spite of having your genes! Just think about it this way. Gillian saved you a pretty penny on nappies, baby powder, baby clothes, medicines, toys, schooling, wardrobes of clothes with a shelf-life of a week, or is that a day now? Cars, food, jewellery, makeup, not to mention the angst of adolescent pimples, boys, menstruation, enhancements and reductions, you name it, and delivered her to you "job done", and from what I hear a top-line product. Jesus, I know a lot of blokes who dream of child-rearing being like that.'

Barry couldn't help but laugh. They all did. Even the women at the next table were smiling and nodding. If Agalia hadn't been his own flesh and blood Barry could quite easily have agreed with the jest. Or *was* Max joking? With Max never having had children of his own, Barry wasn't so sure. In one breath he'd managed to make his daughter sound like a parcel of shares he'd invested in thirty years ago that had just paid good dividends in an up-swinging market. He loved him for being the keeper of the pragmatic end of the pendulum's swing.

'Gillian's had no ulterior motive other than supporting her daughter to sort out her origins. And Agalia has only just met me and already she's got me to understand that Sarah did what she did out of love. They're a formidable pair.'

Max grunted a long cynical laugh, winking at Vashna. 'It's amazing how men become compliant after sex.'

'And I appreciate your considered diagnosis, *Doctor*,' Kant smiled.

'You're welcome. The first consultation is free.'

And for some reason the two men high-fived each other. Perhaps it was this subconscious undergraduateness, Barry thought – another reason why they had remained friends for so long.

Vashna was shunting his own train of thought.

'You and Sarah were kids really. She could quite easily have had an abortion like so many others did back then. Sarah's decision was about the baby, not about you or her. The demonstration of *real* love often comes with great sacrifice.'

Barry smiled wanly. 'You're a good friend, Vash. And I keep forgetting that throughout the pregnancy Sarah thought it was as a result of the attack. It would have been a completely different story if she'd known the truth.'

It had been only very recently that Barry had felt an easing in his body, reaching a point where subconsciously he had allowed himself to become open to other romantic prospects, to accept the vulnerability of not holding on to the nostalgic memories of his past with Sarah to feel secure, freeing himself to open his heart again.

'Give it time, mate,' Vashna said.

And Max, who was still intermittently on his mobile to his broker, with one ear on the conversation, said, 'Bloody hell, Vash, it's been two bloody years! Give the poor bugger a go. It's time for young Bazza to unlock the bloody box and shag himself silly.'

'Yes, thank you, Max, I *am* here you know,' Barry snapped. Then softening, he added, 'And as always I feel grateful for the offering of your fruitful advice.'

Just quietly, Barry had been gripped by an amused

consternation about the febrile sensations he was experiencing around Gillian, particularly since his recent entry into the halls of eldership. His infatuated desire for Sarah when *they* first met was one thing: when you're young and invincible, pursuing reckless love is effortless. But decades later he could feel the sands had shifted beneath him, the rules of engagement had changed, and now there was a loss of traction on the foundation of all that was familiar. Maybe that was the dark water Vashna had referred to once. In the last few days he had begun to dissect his life, the people of influence, the evocative smells, the disappointments, and great moments. Even in his long and supposedly idyllic marriage to Sarah he could see now that his love had undergone renovations, like the old cottage in which they'd spent so much time together. Hairline cracks had been plastered over before any deeper fissures could be displayed, giving a surface appearance that was satisfactory for two lives to proceed agreeably. And that's just how it had been in the last years, agreeable.

Bugger it. These sorts of feelings aren't reserved for the young. And I can put them to much better use now, he vigorously told himself. Barry suddenly scuffed his chair back. 'Just going for a pee.'

He made his way inside to the foyer of the hotel and then out through the front entrance, squinting in the daylight. He tapped in some numbers on his mobile and went to sit on a bollard on the edge of Fisherman's Dock.

'Hello.'

'Hi Gillian!' was all he could manage at first.

Suddenly he had a flash of when he was thirteen. The girl, who'd just moved in across the road, and proudly displayed larger than average bulges in her jumper, began attending the same high school. Each morning he would wait until she came out of her house to walk to school.

'Hi Cheryl!' he'd call out with neighbourly zeal, and a little stiffy. Then he'd turn his face to the ground, struck dumb by embarrassment and scurry ahead staying on the other side of the road. It was almost the end of first term before he plucked up enough courage to cross the road and walk with her. His pavement was being dug up by the council so he had no option.

'Barry, nice to hear your voice. Everything okay?'

'Oh yes, fine. I'm just having coffee with Max and Vashna.'

Barry heard Gillian chuckle, knowingly. 'And you thought you'd just phone me in the middle of it?'

'Well, I just wanted to say ... you know ... well, like, you and I, we ... '

'Barry.'

'Yes?'

'Look, I'm sorry. I'm not trying to rain on your parade ... *our* parade. I just think it's been such a magical reunion for Agalia, and it has taken so many years to get to this point, and it hasn't all been easy, so how do you feel about you and me putting *us* on hold for a while so we don't confuse the reunion? I'm sensing you need to clear a few things in your mind regarding Sarah and we all need to readjust to who's what to whom.'

Barry felt the throb of guilt. 'I'm being very selfish. Of course, of course we should. We must.'

'Let's just enjoy the moment, shall we? Go on, go back to your friends and pop a bottle of champers or whatever you men like to celebrate with. And Barry, I'm not going to disappear.'

'I feel rather silly carrying on like this.'

'You *carrying on like this* is exactly what I find so appealing about you. Now, BJ and I are sorting out a few things here and we'll see you tomorrow morning when you pick us up to go and see your father.'

Barry grinned inanely, and for the moment he didn't mind feeling silly. A fisherman, who, he suddenly realised, had been watching and listening to his conversation from the stern of his boat winked at him. Barry got up and scurried back towards the café, phone still at his ear. He felt a surge in his chest as he realised he did, in fact, enjoy being organised by a woman.

'Righto, that sounds good. About ten o'clock, do you think? And Gillian.'

'Yes?'

'Thank you for loving Agalia.'

When Barry arrived at the table Max and Vashna looked up quizzically but didn't say anything.

'Righto, who wants champagne?' Barry said jauntily, gripping his friends' necks before settling himself at the table.

'Have a nice pee?' Vashna said with a smirk.

Not taking the bite, Barry replied, 'I'll take that as a yes.' To a scuttling waitress he said, 'Excuse me, could you bring three glasses and a bottle of Janz, please?'

'Certainly, sir.'

So, Mister I'm-just-going-for-a-pee, who do you think's going to win your fourth series?' Max asked.

'Anybody's guess. I know who I'd *like* to win.'

'Who's that?'

'Sorry old mate, if I told you I'd have to shoot you. It's out of my hands now. But I can tell you I *don't* think the Sudanese lad will.'

'How's that?' Max quizzed. 'Pretty grim story.'

'Yes, it was, but I'm afraid he's a product of a disintegrating world that has become over-publicised, and the masses have grown complacent with the evidence.'

'Evidence?' Vashna said before licking at the coffee froth on the edge of his mug.

'Most people here haven't travelled to more than a couple of places in their lives. If they're lucky. Out of Australia I mean. Easy places like Bali, New Zealand, two weeks doing the tourist sights in London. That's their exploration of the world.'

'Nothing wrong with that,' Max added, having only just returned from an art-buying excursion in Auckland.

'Sure. But the rest of the planet they ... we experience through the box. Sun-tanned travel shows, discretely edited one-hour programs of wild animals from countless unheard-of countries that have taken someone else's lifetime to film, and of course the big one ... The Nightly News.'

'Go on,' said Vashna curiously.

'They've become like illusory video games. I wonder how many people could put a pin in the map for Libya, Sudan, Ethiopia, Syria, or even Afghanistan for that matter, where, hey ho, Australia is at war.'

Max looked up from texting. 'I doubt your average bloke in the street could tell the difference between King and Flinders islands.'

'That's a bit harsh,' Vashna said with a surprisingly protective tone in his voice. He could never remember which was which. 'Tasmanians are a very proud race.'

Max snorted. 'That's called parochialism.'

'With respect, Mister Professor of Sociology, so's your superior attitude about how you think everybody is.'

Max shrugged. 'Don't get your caftan in a crinkle. I couldn't give you the right answer either.'

Barry frowned at the sparring schoolboys. 'Shut up, you two. My point is, because the News focuses on reporting a continuum of misfortune it's become no different to updates in the cricket or footy results, except the emotional response gets shorter and shorter until the regular killings of civilians by suicide bombers affects us no more than a cat caught up a tree.'

'I'd say your average Joe's more interested in how Tiger Woods chips out of a sand bunker and who he's screwing than the collapse of civilisation as we know it,' Max said.

'Exactly. In our comfortable homes we're so distanced from the nightly body count from wars, images of bloated, starving, hollow-eyed children dying because of famine, the carnage left after earthquakes and cyclones, you name it. I mean, that's the evidence I'm talking about. It's all there, every night without fail for the taking, for obsessive and inevitably mindless consumption. We can hardly discern fact from fiction anymore.'

'It's enough to make you wonder why we bother to watch the news,' Vashna said.

But Barry wasn't finished. Since meeting Gillian, and then Agalia, his work on the show seemed gratuitous and sensational. He had become riddled with doubt about the validity of the show's rationale.

'It's been troubling me for some time now but recently BKS just tastes like fast food for an aggrieved society which turns a blind eye to the universal malaise. And that leaves a nasty taste in my mouth.' Kant leaned in towards his friends. 'The Earth should be a paradise but it's fucked-up by humanity's apathy. We've become so saturated with horror that one Aussie who happens to be very good at tennis, and wins the US Open, completely swamps all the other shit that's happening in the world. Sport's the antidote and anesthetic in one. It's like a swollen nipple to a hungry baby.'

'Or to a sixty-year-old TV star,' Max smirked, not looking up from the message that had just come through on his mobile.

'Don't be so coarse.' But Barry couldn't help grinning like a teenager being congratulated by his mates for his first pash.

'Am I really that transparent?'

Vashna laughed and mimicked a childlike voice, 'I'm just going for a pee.'

'Apparently I am.'

'Max and I think it's fantastic you've found another soul connection. Don't we, Max? Max!'

Max, whose attention had momentarily drifted towards a group of elegantly dressed women, age-appropriate for a change, who were ensconced in intellectual conversation at another table, said, 'Absolutely old boy, nice bit of skirt; just what you need, the cure-all for a thousand ailments.'

'See how he's got your best interests at heart?'

Barry sipped at his champagne. 'A real trooper. Anyway, the point I'm *still* trying to make here is that the African lad is merely the evidence of yet another television war that's been going on so long, we've tuned out and all our compassion receptors have switched off.'

'Compassion fatigue, it's the most depressing human syndrome of the new millennium,' Vashna mused.

At this point Barry was fascinated by how many thoughts, ideas, opinions, conclusions, proposals, more thoughts could flick through the human head in a nano second. Indeed, making the adage of *your entire life flashing before your eyes* just before you died a distinct possibility.

In the split second after Vashna had spoken Barry had thought about holding Gillian in his arms, feeling her warmth, wondered if she had blatantly tried to snare him. Had felt an apprehensive shiver about how his life would be with an extra daughter, whether she'd stay or go back to Greece, would he like to go there too, give up his job. It was on the cards anyway, maybe only for a short period of time to see where she was brought up and go back to Crete to visit the place of conception. But if he went for too long maybe he would miss Melinda and Rosie, and Mungo too, well, maybe not *miss* him but, well, he was attached to Mel, and what would happen to his father while he was away? He'd hate it if Des died while he was overseas. He couldn't tolerate the thought of his father dying because of his selfishness. What am I if I give up the show, who am I? Am I my own man?

Barry pinched the end of his nose and sniffed. 'Liri Mogamba is caught between two worlds. He's safe here from reprisals but can't be reunited with his family because his sister has gone blind for God's sake. That's not freedom, that's a sentence. It's as if he's hovering in no-man's land.'

'Like all of them,' Vashna said.

'Can you believe, the Australian Government coldly says a fifteen-year-old girl with glaucoma would be too bloody expensive to support here. What sort of compassionate country are we?' Barry's voice had risen. 'I find the whole asylum situation so heartless and arbitrary.'

'Terrorists are winning World War Three because they've filled everyone else's hearts with fear and paranoia,' Vashna said. 'And I can't see it ever ending.'

'Oh, I'm glad we're talking Federal politics now,' Max threw in.

Barry smiled. 'Liri told me if he wins he's going to send his sister to a school for the blind, and pay for all six of his siblings who are still in a refugee camp in Uganda with a hundred thousand others, to complete their schooling in Kampala. He told me, "Education, is our real freedom."'

'That's if he wins,' Vashna said. 'So what are the long term prospects for refugees like Liri?'

'For the ones that are separated from their families it's always a struggle. They just have to cope, and do the best they can on their own. Sure, there are support networks set up here but when they go to bed at night they are still in the dark and isolated from so much that's familiar.'

An image of Agalia as a young girl living in Greece flashed through Barry's mind.

'And family, after all, is the foundation of civilisation,' Vashna said.

'I watched that Sudanese fellow the night he was on,' Max said, seeming more interested in the financial implications of such a win. 'He came across as confident, overconfident even. I'd be concerned about whether he'd be able to manage that much money shrewdly.'

'Sure, but he's a born entertainer, plays and sings and would have been exactly that in the refugee camp or back in his village in Sudan. His music is the one thing he has to keep him afloat,' Barry said. 'But I think it'll work against him on the show. I don't think he'll win because he hides his grief too well.'

*

Gillian and Agalia, who had finished their business in the city, were now sitting on the timber deck of the Ferntree house looking out over the treetops towards the silver waters of the Derwent River in the distance. They spoke in Greek together as if the very essence of their language endorsed their bond.

'Hobart is such a beautiful city, Mitera. There are so many trees, and the houses are all so close to such a craggy mountain.' She chuckled, 'It looks like a giant wave building up to break on the city below.'

'I'm glad you've decided to stay for a while, BJ.'

'What else could I do? Finding that my mother has died I feel like something vital and precious has been ripped out from inside me. And yet at the same time I feel so grateful to have met … my … see, I'm still not confident about what to call him.'

Gillian took hold of her daughter's hand. 'I was proud of you when you met him. You showed great wisdom. Of course he is your father, even though you have only just met him. Cons was your father too; he was always kind and loved you, even though he betrayed me. And there's no hurry to work everything out. God knows I feel confused too, and Barry, like you, feels strained by a bitter and a sweet.'

The two women embraced each other, mother and daughter together in the security of their affection for each other.

Agalia chuckled again to herself. 'Mitera, it sounds like a funny thing to say but … Pateras, he's a very nice man. He very distinguished, don't you think?'

Gillian tilted her head to one side, feigning innocence. 'Do

you think so? I'm just going to have to find out for myself, aren't
I?'

Gillian kissed her daughter's cheek. There was deep tiredness in her eyes. They'd travelled a long and uncertain way,
together and on their own.

Chapter Twenty-Five

Desmond Kant undid a shirt button, lifted his singlet and slid his hand inside, moving bony fingers around on his chest, checking. Barry had phoned half an hour ago to remind him that he'd be bringing Agalia around soon, a new granddaughter, and his heart had begun to beat a little harder, that was all. The last time it did that was when Patricia passed away. Desmond pondered for a moment, pinching up a small wad of slack speckled skin on his forearm, on how, like his daily existence in Lutana, in this street, in this house, in this room, on this chair, the inside of his body seemed to have shrunk too.

After the phone call Old Man Kant had put his newest pair of pyjamas on and got into bed. He'd lain there for several minutes, pillows propped behind him so he could receive the new member of the family in comfort. But it didn't seem quite right having all those women in his bedroom. Besides, despite his diminishing bodily presence he was still the patriarch of this dynasty. So he'd changed into his old dark suit and arranged himself on the wobbly bentwood chair at the head of the table in the kitchen.

The suit felt right, and maybe he should be sitting when they arrived. He wouldn't have to meet them at the door; Barry always let himself in. So for the next fifteen minutes he prowled around the kitchen, up and down from his chair with caged expectancy until he heard the hum of a car outside. He knew every sound, small and smaller that emanated from his compact world. He identified the hum as the Audi. It was the only one in the neighbourhood that purred softly like a Siamese cat dreaming of canaries. Secretly he felt proud whenever it was parked outside his house.

Peeping through the curtain in the front room, which he'd left closed for this purpose, he could see Barry and a woman about his son's age get out of the front doors. He could make out Melinda, still inside yakking with another young'n in the back seat. There was no Rosie or Mungo. He didn't have that much time for the wee one. She talked too much and he found her prattle difficult to keep up with.

As the party approached, Desmond felt flustered, and scurried back to the kitchen and began wiping the table again. He heard the familiar un-oiled creak of the front fly screen. As the chattering group entered the kitchen Desmond began opening the cupboard to reach in for the mugs. He should look busy when they entered.

'Ah, Dad, good to see you up and about,' Barry said, relieved they didn't have to make the meeting in his bedroom.

Desmond placed two mugs on the table and sighed as if he'd just been digging in the garden for an hour. He looked across at the women and nodded. 'Hello there.'

'Dad, I want you to meet Gillian Papadakis and her daughter Agalia.'

Desmond nodded politely again. 'Barry said you were from Greece. Call me Des, eh? I'm sorry I don't have enough chairs.'

Agalia moved around the kitchen table and put her hand out. Desmond took hold of it and, surprising him, she kissed him on the cheek. 'It's an honour to meet you, Des. You must be very proud of your family.'

Desmond looked puzzled by the sentiment but said, 'Oh yes. Barry's a good lad.'

Melinda presented her grandfather with a bunch of flowers, then busied herself searching for a vase to put them in. Agalia, still holding Desmond's hand, hugged his wiry frame. The old man shuffled uncomfortably, stepped back and sniffed. 'I better get them other mugs. Now you lot sit down and I'll put the kettle on.'

'Slow down, Dad, first say hello to Gillian; she's Agalia's mother.'

'I thought you said…' But he stopped, reshuffling in his mind. 'How d'you do.'

Desmond needed time to take control of his escalating anxiety so he reached for more cups, tipped the already boiled water out of the kettle and refilled it with cold. Told everyone to sit down again and rummaged for the sugar and a packet of biscuits. Barry, wishing he'd remembered to bring a packet of Tim Tams or something special, hoped they weren't the ones he'd opened a month ago. He positioned himself against the sideboard, leaving the spare chair for his father, who he thought was looking paler than usual.

The fact that his father had dressed in his suit wasn't lost on him either.

Barry went to the fridge and took out the milk carton, and while his father was busy putting teabags into the mugs he surreptitiously sniffed the milk. He hastily placed it back in the fridge. Gillian and Agalia were watching and smiled knowingly at him.

'Everyone takes their tea black, Dad.'

'Oh, that's good. I like to make a carton last till next pension day.'

'Granddad,' Melinda said. 'Dad told me about Gran's necklace. It sounds beautiful.'

'Your grandmother looked a real treat in it. I bought it for her when we were in Singapore.' He sighed. 'That was some time ago now. Before you were a twinkle in your mother's eye.'

Desmond looked suddenly self-conscious, hoping his remark wasn't offending anyone.

It was Gillian's turn to come to the rescue. 'And maybe before Sarah gave birth to Agalia too.'

'Oh, right,' he replied, still not sure who was what, and to whom.

Sensing this, Gillian deferentially explained the story of the adoption to Desmond, from her point of view. Everyone sipped tentatively at their tar-black tea and nibbled like cautious mice at the rather soft biscuits. Desmond listened attentively, giving fleeting glances every now and then at Agalia, who, he was sure, was the reincarnation of Sarah. But suddenly, as if the whole saga was too much for him, he got up stiffly and began to walk towards the door.

'Sorry, Barry, I gotta lie down a bit now.'

'Sure. You all right, Dad?' Barry asked, looking with concern at Melinda.

'Yeah, don't fuss. I reckon you can wash the mugs while I ... '

But before he could finish Desmond Kant tottered forward and collapsed to the ground. Barry jumped up from his seat and kneeled over his father, who was groaning softly. 'Dad, what's up? Here, let me get you up and get you into bed.'

Gillian helped Barry lift his father and they carried him to the bedroom. Barry was shocked at how light his father was. He could have carried him by himself. In the bedroom he pulled the blankets back with one hand and they laid Desmond carefully down on the bed. This frail man, dressed in a suit, almost devoid of all energy life had given him, lay helpless. Even his voice had weakened.

'Sorry about this, son,' he said as Gillian took his shoes off and Barry pulled the blankets up over him, leaving one arm to lie on the blankets.

'It's okay, Dad, you're just tired. It's been a lot to take in.'

Desmond gripped his son's wrist feebly and pulled him in closer as if he was about to divulge a secret.

'No, son, reckon it's that time. You know what I was tellin' you, 'bout them Aborigines? Well, it's *that* time,' he said. Barry sensed relief in his father's voice, as if he was pleased he was vindicated this time that his silly notion had some foundation.

Desmond's voice had been reduced to a whisper, different to the times he'd tried it on. Barry kneeled on the floor by the bed. He looked up to Gillian and asked if she would call for an ambulance.

'No need, son.'

'But, Dad ... '

'Just you listen. 'Bout time you were the one doing the listening. You've done all right on that show of yours. I've been watching it lately and I reckon you've done some real good for them unfortunates. I just wanna tell you ... like ... that I'm proud of you.'

'Well, that's nice to hear, Dad, and you can continue being proud of me tomorrow when you've had a good rest.'

Melinda and Agalia had come in and were looking on with concern.

'Listen to your old man. You're not doing your bloody show now,' he said, trying to make his whisper sound more authoritative. 'Did you get your mum's necklace valued?'

'Yes, I did, Dad. I was going to tell you the good news this afternoon.'

'See. I always wanted to look after you, but I reckon you stood on your own two feet. A father still likes to provide though.'

Barry's throat was clenched in a woody knot.

'Dad, you *have* provided, all of us have benefited. I wouldn't be where I am now if it weren't for you and Mum. And Dad ... Dad!' Desmond had momentarily closed his eyes, but woke with a small shudder. Barry breathed out. 'Dad, you were spot on, the necklace was worth a lot.'

'What did I tell you, son? Now you can pay your mortgage off. A father likes to help.'

'And you did. The money will be a great help. I *really* appreciate what you've done. Now you need to get some rest.'

Agalia, who had been watching quietly next to her pateras and sister, knelt down too and held Desmond's hand. 'Papous, I am so happy that I have finally met you.'

'What's that you call me, gal?'

'Papous. In Greece it is the name we use for grandfather.'

'It suits you, Granddad.' Melinda said, putting her hand on Agalia's shoulder.

Desmond peered strangely at Agalia as if he recognised her from somewhere. He lifted his hand and patted the back of her hand. 'It's a good thing you turning up again. Young Barry's been such a mopey old bugger. Now he's like a bloody kid with twenty bucks in a lolly shop. You look after him now. He can get a bit silly in the head sometimes.'

'I will, Papous,' Agalia whispered as she kissed her grandfather on the forehead, who, she suspected, thought he was talking to Sarah thirty years ago.

Desmond's lips trembled slightly as he looked up at Barry, who was still holding his father's hand. His loose skin, alabaster white with ginger specks, was ready for its final shedding. 'Remember what I said about the box, nothin' fancy, you hear me?' he managed before his body gave the slightest shudder and Desmond Kant closed his eyes for the last time. As the residue of his life fell serenely from his body, he passed in spirit and the warmth of his hand the patriarch's baton on to his son.

*

Edith Cartwright sat reposed, tranquil, the newspaper on her lap. She had been thinking about death, and such was her love of words, their resonance and their usage, the word necropolis with its Greek origins came to mind. She'd imagined an exotic, futuristically styled transit lounge for the spirits of the dead to enter before they embarked on their final journey to infinite grace, from Lutana which, poetically in the Aboriginal language, meant moon.

The nervy buzz of the Flymo in young Jimmy's hands filled the otherwise quiet of the cul-de-sac. A closely trimmed nature strip, Edith had often said, was a fairly accurate barometer of a healthy life. Unfortunately for young Jimmy, he was about the only recipient of that counsel these days. But he was surprisingly patient with the old lady. Most of her friends had already left for *their* final journey. She looked across the street towards old Mr Kant's house.

'So many things diminish with age,' she whispered.

Jimmy sensed the old lady's gaze from within the house and looked up. The boy smiled. With Edith he felt safe for the first time in his life. They waved to each other, a moment of joyful connection for Edith in an otherwise prolonged existence of her own solitude.

She glanced down at the paper again. *Celebrity's Father Dies.* She would have cheered out loud, jigged around her neat living room if it had read *Gentle old man in Lutana passes away peacefully.*

Under the headline was a photograph of – *Star television personality Barry Kant.* Not Desmond Kant Senior.

Barry Kant was accompanied to the Cornelian Bay Cemetery by family members. His daughter Melinda, left, a teacher at the Claremont Polytechnic, is seen holding her father's arm.

Holding his other arm is a mysterious, equally young woman. Rumours abound with fans of BKS of a budding new romance for the sixty-year-old host of the Barry Kant Show, screening live on Thursday to millions of viewers nationwide when the final winner of the fourth series will be announced. Prize money has been increased to $100,000.

In a closed ceremony, Barry Kant's eighty-two-year-old father, Desmond Kant, who had resided in Lutana all his life, a stalwart worker at the EZ Company for forty-eight years, was buried next to his wife Patricia, the article stated blandly.

Chapter Twenty-Six

Kant sat at his desk, fingers drumming, the tightly screwed-up newspaper dumped in the bin next to him. Mackelroy, preoccupied by his thoughts, was endeavouring to prepare two coffees without spillage. He was, if nothing else, tense.

Traditionally the final night of each series went out live, prime time at seven-thirty. It was the only way to keep the result secret till the last minute. TV stations were notoriously leaky. But there was something else, something far more catastrophic than a pre-disclosed winner that had made Mackelroy silent. Silence was never his thing, but for these few moments, in his lead-man's office, on the threshold of the winner's episode, Mackelroy, director of the most popular reality show on Australian television, was at bursting point.

Mackelroy turned and placed one cup on Kant's desk, then sat down in one of the armchairs. Eventually, after another ear-crushing silence of some sixty seconds he stood up again, folded his arms before flopping back into the chair.

'Jesus Christ man, I just don't understand you!'

'You won't be the first on that score, James.'

'What's changed? I can see it…No, I can't. Something's happened. It's that bloody woman, isn't it?'

Kant looked up at Mackelroy and raised his eyebrows.

'Sorry. Bit harsh.'

'I was going to ask which one! It doesn't always have to be about women, James.' Kant smiled, 'It often is, but in this case ... '

Just the day before, Melinda had told her father about Mungo's interaction with Gabriel Daniels on the Tasman Bridge, their playing music together and the recording they'd done. She had even managed to explain Mungo's rationale about his music, which her father had finally conceded, seemed to have some merit. She had also told her father not to blame himself for the man's subsequent suicide, that he shouldn't forget that the spirit of the show's aim was to help, and in many cases it did turn people's lives around. Ultimately people were responsible for their own lives.

But the weight of the news had collapsed around Kant like a dark canopy, already being tormented by doubt about the show's value since his initial meeting and subsequent broad-casted interview with John Sturges. After John had disclosed his torment with such humility Kant quite simply had begun to feel like a fraud. It felt as if the show had given him, the great Barry Kant, somewhere to hide, somewhere he could exercise *his* public masquerade that, like a fire barrier to his own pain, could fool everyone, including himself, keeping the heat off his own limitations as a human being.

But then the wiry knot of deception within him had begun to unravel. Something in him had softened, and he felt, for the first time since he'd accepted the job, his own vulnerability.

Not the dreadful debilitating weakness that had descended on him that first night he'd slept in the cottage without Sarah, but a rawness like a snake that has just shed its skin in preparation for a new shiny covering. He was finally healing within and was opening up to acceptance of a new direction in his life.

'I'm really sorry, James, but what's to understand? I've given it enormous consideration. There's so much about the show's ideology that just seems to rankle now, and the poor people I have to deal with week after week, they're even in my dreams. That can't be healthy. I'm not their saviour. And I'm beginning to despise the audience for their lazy lack of concern and their ignorant prejudice. It feels as if they are contemptuous of the very people that courageously put themselves through the public wringer, in effect, for *their* pleasure.'

Mackelroy thumped the arm of the chair. 'Yes, and you *know* that's what makes good TV! Isn't that why we're here, Barry? Jesus Christ, I can't believe what I'm hearing. You can't just resign now. The whole thing's gone ballistic. We can call the shots now; it'll go worldwide next season, you'll see. The Yanks have got swimming pools of cash just waiting to invest ... In *you! You're* the one who's created this phenomenon. Fuck, man, you can't just chuck it all in now.'

Kant, for the first time in years, felt that he had made a decision without the pressure of other people's agendas. He had seen himself for who he really was when he was at his dying father's bedside. He had simple roots and he'd shunned them for so long, denied them to himself even, keeping on at his daughter to move away. And after his brief encounter with Edith Cartwright he felt prickled by his own prejudice. Her house wasn't an oasis in some desert or an eccentric microcosm in a cultural wasteland. Her home, her example, her presence in Lutana, her very being, were all part of a whole, and not just in a disadvantaged suburb but in a beautiful city, in a tourist State, in a hugely diverse Nation.

Now it was time for the real Barry Kant to stand up.

It was a waste of precious energy beating himself up anymore over what Sarah had kept from him. He'd felt furious about the deception and yet humbled by what Agalia had implied was her mother's selfless courage. Now the signs were right for him to steer into the traffic again and navigate a path through the hubbub of congestion, away from the screaming bedlam of universal needs, towards genuine fulfilment and peace. *Of course* he felt nervous about his decision to resign, and he felt the heaviness of Mackelroy's disappointment, but he was convinced, despite the risk, it was the best thing he could do with *his* life at *this* moment.

'James,' he said patiently. 'Don't forget BKS was *your* brainchild. It's had an incredible rise to popularity. You can't get better than best. Think about it; you're a creative being and this is just one inspiration you've engineered. I've been happy being in front of the camera for the duration. But, you know the old saying, leave the audience wanting more.'

Mackelroy's frustration was smudged with desperation even though deep inside, he knew this was it. His tireless colleague had never looked so self-assured before, and there was something about the clarity in his eyes, and the composure in the shape of his mouth that seemed to push his cheeks up fractionally as if he was about to smile. Even so, Mackelroy couldn't quite let go.

'Jesus, Barry, look at bloody Springer, and Oprah, and even Michael Parkinson. They didn't give up after four bloody seasons. They're *still* going!'

'Who?' Kant said with a grin. 'Maybe that's what they'll be remembered for ... going on for so long.'

'Four measly series? We've only just begun.'

Kant couldn't help himself, 'The Carpenters! God that was a *terrible* song.'

'Before my time, old man.'

'There you go. I'm just a dinosaur. But seriously, sometimes *less* really is *more*.'

Then looking at his colleague, as only a person who has a clear conscience can, Kant said, 'I'm not *giving up*, as you say. It's been a fantastic time. You and I have created a sensation that will be talked about for years. But you know as well as I do, people get quickly bored with sensations. That's the whole point of them. Constant renewal, that's what the public thrives on. It's like sugar and MSG in junk food — as soon as it wears off we crave it more. I'm not *bored* with the show, but I do feel saturated with all the grief that's been pouring out of this island of ours. I feel stained by it and now I need to hose myself down, dry off and walk in the sunshine again.'

Kant looked down and scratched at the corner of his eye. *Mm, liberating!*

'And *you*, James, my friend and sparring partner, will have blank cheques thrust in your face from now on. You'll be offered carte-blanche for whatever you dream up next. Really, it's just the beginning of another aspect of your TV career. And don't forget I've got twenty-odd years on you. I need something different now. I can't remember the last time I walked along a beach.'

'All that effort I ... '

But Kant didn't want to hear another *grooming* account. 'James, for whatever you devise next there'll be other personalities, and much younger than me, whom you can knock into shape, just like you did with me for this little escapade. And they'll be a lot easier to manipulate because you'll be the old fart next time. Yeah, it happens.'

Mackelroy sighed. He knew that was the truth of the small screen. The public had the attention span of goldfish. And TV personalities were indeed like fashion merchandise, as transient as the stuff that came out of their mouths, and could be quickly formed by some skilful sculpting by a shrewd artistic director. And if Mackelroy had been sufficiently perceptive he would have realised his difficulty was as much about letting go of Barry Kant as of his personal father figure.

'Maybe introducing you to *Gillian* was the thin edge of the wedge,' Mackelroy said, the fight in him almost extinguished.

'Don't be so daft. Gillian and her daughter were on a mission to find Sarah, and got me instead. You just sped things along, for which, I have to say, I'm eternally grateful. But that has no bearing on my decision.'

Mackelroy shifted in his chair and folded his arms defensively. He looked down-trodden. 'You know, I envy you.'

'Envy? Huh, I wouldn't wish your life away. In twenty years you'll be envying young buggers like you are now, with everything in front of them.'

Mackelroy laughed. 'Sorry mate, it's not your senior citizen status I covet.' It was reassuring to see him laugh. 'No, old man, it's your family.'

'My family?' Kant, puzzled, wasn't sure where this was going.

'I see you with them. I hear you talk about them. This thing about finding your other daughter after all this time ... it's the stuff of ... ' He chuckled, 'Movies! No, I envy the affection you all seem to have for each other. It's really quite heartening, you prick.'

'We have our moments,' Kant replied fatuously to offset some discomfort.

'Sure, but it's fundamental to you all. Seems to come easy. And it isn't always that easy for some of us.'

Kant stood up and began to stroll around the room, cautious of Mackelroy's sudden display of frankness. He was unsure if Mackelroy was reaching out, or simply confessing to his own self-centred style of existence.

'Other people's families always look better than your own: happier, more holidays, always seeming to finish the cryptic crossword, effortlessly. Besides, I'm a sixty-year-old father who's only just been told he's got two daughters not one. That revelation has not all been easy, I can tell you.'

Kant sipped at his coffee, cold now, and sat down next to his director. 'James, we've still got one more show to put out, and I'd like to have a musical segment to get things going. This group I'm thinking of has a pretty unconventional sound to say the least but it might fit right in with what might happen. What do you think?'

'Might happen?'

'Yes. But you're just going to have to trust in the power of improvisation … again. It's been the nature of the BKS beast after all. I've got some things I want to say, might not go down too well with the punters but we may as well go out with some controversy. Best publicity you'll get for your next project.'

'I feel I ought to stay angry at you a bit longer, you prick. And of course you're not going to give me any more information than that, are you?'

'How could I? It wouldn't be improvised if I did.'

'I admire the smart old bastard that you are. Maybe that extra twenty years you've got on me helps, not to mention the fact that you're a fucking legend out there in the burbs. So, okay, BK, work your magic one more time. Let's go out with a bang and not with a pissy little whimper.'

*

The sun had just disappeared behind the mountain. Melinda and Agalia strolled along the footpath at the edge of the river. On its low-tide gravelly edge, plovers strutted, screeching intermittent warnings over the distant hum of the highway. As they looked out over the rippled waters of the river Agalia's pent-up emotions finally spilled over. The relief that her quest had finally found resolution was enormous. And despite the sorrow of not meeting her birth mother it had been compensated to some degree by the unexpected joy of meeting her father and sister.

'Melinda, to be with you after all this time, and now knowing we actually came from the same womb, is profoundly wonderful for me.'

'Me too. And I promise I will tell you everything I know about and have learned from our mother.'

After their walk, back in Luck Avenue, the two sisters had opened a bottle of champagne. The television was on in the living room. Rosie was in her bedroom chattering to her teddies and assorted dolls, surrounded by every saucepan and cooking utensil she'd found in the kitchen cupboards. She was in the throes of cooking a gourmet meal for her 'family'. It was just as well they all loved spaghetti. It was all they were fed these days.

Melinda and Agalia giggled like naughty children as the champagne cork exploded into the air.

The six o'clock News was filled with Barry Kant's shock intention to quit after the final live broadcast of BKS on Thursday night. The sensational news had even leaped ahead of soldiers wounded by a roadside bomb in Afghanistan, ahead of the imploding European economies, the crisis of American debt and an impending world economic catastrophe. It even took precedence over a homegrown Tassie boxer who'd just won a second world title fight at the Derwent Entertainment Centre.

The final BKS, screening at 7.30 on Nerve Two, would be watched by millions around the country. In the United Kingdom, where a television counter-culture of desperate people searching for monetary redemption was expected to spring up in recognition of the BKS popularity, an outbreak of look-alike reality shows had already become an easier alternative to online fraud for the disenfranchised.

The newsreader began solemnly: 'First on the news tonight is the shock resignation of Barry Kant, the host and star of BKS...'

The sisters huddled together on the couch like kids watching the cartoons.

'... The director of the show, James Mackelroy, stated categorically that Thursday night's finale would be the last. He said that Barry Kant, the charismatic and highly acclaimed host, rivalling such greats as Oprah Winfrey in America and Michael Parkinson in the United Kingdom, would be pursuing other creative avenues. He did not discount the possibility of an alternate television production for his lead man. Barry Kant has remained tight-lipped about his future but has said that the Thursday night show will delight audiences with some fascinating viewing surprises.'

Agalia and Melinda, holding hands, nestled in the comfort of the sofa, each one buoyed by their own unique affection for this man, whose name seemed to be on everyone's lips.

After the news, on a local current affairs program that was following up on the story, a reporter, in her late twenties, wearing a black business suit and holding a large, black, phallic microphone close to her mouth, was standing in front of the Nerve Two building. She began to pace stealthily around in front of the entrance as if she had just been parachuted into a battle frontline amid Al Qaida insurgents. The young woman talked in urgently subdued undertones, stooping slightly to avoid being hit by crossfire in this highly volatile locality behind enemy lines in Moonah, just north of Hobart city.

'... It is believed that Barry Kant who has recently quit his position as host on his now world-famous show gave in his notice due to fierce differences with his director James Mackelroy, who moved to Hobart from Sydney three years ago. It is not clear what the dispute was over but undisclosed sources have hinted that the show could have overspent on its budget and that both men, more than likely, have been declared bankrupt. Speculation around James Mackelroy's possible connections with the Sydney-based underworld has given rise to fears of a more sinister intrigue at work here.

'Behind me here is the place where the dramatic events are believed to have unfolded, where a brief statement was released by the Nerve Two TV Station, an appropriate name for a place where everybody's nerves must be at breaking point.'

There was a two-second panning infill of the Cornelian Bay Cemetery taken from a helicopter.

'Rumours still abound that Mister Kant, whose reclusive father died recently, has been going through some sort of nervous breakdown due to the stress of the show. It is believed that one of the contestants from a previous show, a Gabriel Daniels of Sandy Bay, killed himself recently in a bizarre suicide ritual. Unconfirmed sources reported that he took an overdose of sleeping tablets before accompanying, on his oboe, his favourite piece of music, *The Lark*, which he had on high volume. It has been speculated that the show's producers could possibly be in the courts soon, after being sued by the man's family.'

Suddenly the reporter had been teleported to outside Kant's apartment by the docks. She was wearing a new set of clothes – smarter, tighter, more revealing, looking as if she was ready for a couple of vodka chasers with the girls at the nearest wine bar, a two-minute walk from where she was now standing.

'I'm standing outside Barry Kant's exclusive multi-million-dollar bachelor apartment. A few days ago, to add to the drama, he was seen arm-in-arm with a striking young woman, some thirty years his junior, which also suggests that he might be going through some sort of life crisis. Fans of the TV host have described this place as his love nest where the famous presenter throws wildly decadent parties. It has also been speculated by unconfirmed sources that Barry Kant's flamboyant lifestyle has made him a target for blackmail, a ... '

Melinda reached for the remote and switched the television off, and turning to Agalia with a smirk said, 'That's my dad.'

'Excuse me, *our* dad!' Agalia added with glee. 'At least she says I'm striking.'

'I'm surprised she didn't tell us what you were wearing on that secret tryst at the cemetery.'

The two women laughed, chinking their half-full glasses together.

Chapter Twenty-Seven

On the Wednesday, the day before the final live broadcast of BKS, just after midday, Kant punched some numbers into his phone, opened his car door and got in. He held the phone with one hand as he looped the seatbelt over his shoulder.

'Where are you, mate?'

'Flipper's fish punt at Constitution Dock. Crumbed prawns going down nicely, thank you. What's up?'

'Stay put, I'll meet you there. You're going to take me visiting. Just leaving the station; see you in fourteen – twenty if I get booked for speeding.'

He hung up and fired up.

Fifteen minutes later Kant pulled in near the fish-and-chip punt. Vince looked at his watch as Kant got out of the car and took a couple of chips from MacLean's packet.

'You're late, but not long enough to be pulled over by the cops. Where we going?'

'John Sturges' place. I'd like to have a chat with him.' Kant got in the passenger's seat, and asked Vince if he would drive, which he did willingly, aiming the car back out into the traffic. 'More than that though, I want to see his place, see him at home while I tell him he's won a hundred grand.'

'Lucky man.'

'I really hope so.'

'You been out there before, BK? The suburb's a bit of an eye opener.'

'That's why I want to see him, and as you've already been to his house I thought you could drive me there. I feel knackered. You can also fulfil my fantasy of having a chauffeur – could be my last chance.'

'Well, I'm a wee bit sorry I did'na bring my cap, gov'na.'

'I'll let it pass this time, Vincent.'

The two men sat silently as the northern suburbs passed in a grubby peripheral smear. Eventually the car tyres doop doop dooped a disco beat as they crossed the expansion joints on the long approach to the Bridgewater Bridge crossing of the Derwent River.

Turning right into the suburb the Audi immediately stood out, its shiny burgundy line too new and too stylish as it entered streets of rusted and dented Utes and old fuel guzzlers with spoilers and raucous baritone exhausts. An abandoned blue Datsun sedan with four flat tyres and smashed windscreen sat amongst weeds and parched grass outside a scruffy corner shop. Two young boys sitting on its roof were sharing a can of Fanta, endeavouring to dent the roof more with their shoe heels. The shop's windows were completely obliterated by fluro signs advertising the latest reduction in the price of Weetbix, white sliced bread, Fanta and a number of even more special offers for cheap two-in-one hair products. MacLean had subconsciously slowed down as if he were entering a foreign land and was intrigued by its differences, and watchful for potential threats.

'Just as well I *have* been here before,' MacLean said, pointing to a signpost that had been graffitied into illegibility.

'God, shouldn't these little blighters be in school?' Kant said, as they approached a gaggle of scruffy ten year olds pushing and shoving each other along the edge of the road, the pavement smacking of too much authority for them to walk along.

Vince began to sing the Pink Floyd song, 'We don't need no eju ... cation, we don't need no thought ... control ... ' He stopped, and said, 'Watch this.' He waved at the group, which instigated a flurry of fingers being stuck up at him, and a stream of juvenile swearing followed by more shoving and laughter. 'Works every time.'

Kant sighed. 'That's exactly why I've wanted Mel to move.'

'It's harmless enough. It's their territory, and primitive as it seems, it's just their way of letting you know. There was a burnt-out car over there when I first came,' MacLean said as he pulled the car in towards the kerb and parked just behind a dumpster. 'Must have heard you were coming and decided to spruce up the neighbourhood.'

John Sturges' house was a small weatherboard dwelling, on a slight angle to the road, well painted with a turquoise gloss, the window trims white. There was no fence and the whole front garden and nature strip were bare except for closely cropped grass. Tethered to a steel star picket a goat was straining to stretch a few more centimetres out of a thick nylon rope.

Kant noticed the venetian blind tweak in the middle. 'He's expecting us. I phoned yesterday.'

They were greeted at the front door by a slim, shiny-skinned lad wearing heavy black-rimmed glasses. Sampaguita's son Joel nodded shyly and beckoned them into the sitting room, the layout not too dissimilar to Melinda's place in Lutana.

'Please come this way. Thank you,' the boy said with polite, newly learned English.

The house was dim inside, heavy curtains partially closed over the windows in the sitting room. Sunlight, segmented by the blinds behind them, striped everything it fell on. The room was congested with heavy wooden furniture. Gaudy Philippine pictures of oxen pulling carts in rural settings, peacocks, and workers in the field hung in glossy varnished frames around the walls. Small wooden carvings of the Virgin Mary and an assortment of leaping frogs were placed around the mantelpiece above an electric bar heater. An absence of books allowed for the shelving in the room to be crammed with a veritable souvenir shop of tokens of a culture left behind. Tie-dyed fabrics, embroidered with more frogs in oranges, purple and reds had been draped over the furniture. There seemed to be very little of John Sturges in the space.

Several parols, traditional Philippino Christmas star decorations covered with silver beads and other shiny attachments, hung around the walls, optimistically devout displays of a respected heritage in this cosy oasis amidst a bleaker desert outside.

John, forehead still glistening with sweat from his morning's mowing, smiled at the men as they were shown into the kitch-en, which was open to the living area. The boy then silently loped off into the house.

'Mister Kant,' John acknowledged, before nodding know-ingly at Vince.

'Thanks for letting us come to your home, John. Vince had to drive me because I have a terrible sense of direction,' Kant said in return.

John seemed nervous, as if he wasn't sure how to conduct the next two minutes of social etiquette. His only other visitor to the house was the landlord on his six-monthly house inspec-tions, so he was bemused that the famous man was now stand-ing in his kitchen.

'You have a nice home, John. It looks as if it's had a woman's touch,' Kant said, glancing around.

John, chuffed by the compliment, grinned coyly as if having a woman in his house to create a well-loved space for them to cohabit in was on the risqué side of things.

'Sampaguita has a good way. She brought some of 'er stuff out when she first come 'ere. She should be 'ere in a minute. 'Er shift finished a while ago and the bus drops 'er off just down the road a bit.'

'I'm looking forward to meeting her,' Kant said.

'How's Joel going with his English at TAFE?' Vince asked.

'Yeah, real good. 'E done lots a work on it. 'E's been 'elpin' me with some chores. Good worker,' John replied proudly. 'Mister Kant, and er ... Vince, do youse want a cup of tea?'

'Aye, that would be grand,' Vince said.

'Yes, I'd love one too. And John, please call me Barry.'

'Yeah, righto. Look, er ... would you like to sit in there while I do it? There's a bit more room for youse.'

Barry and Vince sat on the two armchairs so the remaining two-seater couch could be used by John and his wife so they wouldn't have to look backwards and forwards to talk to them.

'Ah, 'ere she is now,' John suddenly said, as if the minutest sound of her footsteps from outside was hardwired to his senses.

The door opened and Sampaguita entered. She was barely five feet tall, slim as a clothes peg and wore a pale-blue dust coat hiding her street clothes. Her thick black hair, with prominent stands of grey appearing, was tied back in a ponytail. But most conspicuous was her broad and generous smile.

'Hello Mister Kant. I am honoured that you come to visit our home. I hope John has offered you some refreshments.'

Kant shook her hand and Vince followed. 'Hi, I'm Vince.'

'Oh, I remember you from when you came first to speak with John. You are from Scotland. That is correct?'

'Aye, lassie,' Vince smiled, putting on a show of his finest Highland brogue.

'I got the tea on, darl. Did youse bring them biscuits?'

'Yes. I purchased those chocolate ones you like so much.' Then turning to the two men she said, 'I'm beginning to like the Australian food very much,' and then proceeded to take a packet of chocolate-coated Teddy Bear biscuits from her bag.

'If you will excuse me I will remove my work clothes and we can share some tea together.'

When Sampaguita returned she was wearing a shiny lime-green silk shirt and black slacks, with gold slip-ons on her dainty feet.

When they were all seated and the tea was distributed Kant clapped his hands together. 'Now, John and Sampaguita, Vince and I have come here today to give you both some good news.'

Sampaguita, who was sitting upright on the edge of the couch, looked excitedly as a child might before opening a birthday present; her dark brown eyes wide open with anticipation.

'That's nice Mister … er Barry,' John said, still conducting himself formally.

'John, you have been selected by the public as the winner of this season's show.'

'Well, that's real kind of them,' he replied, not quite at the point of registering the implication that he had won one hundred thousand dollars.

MacLean and Kant looked at each other; they had seen this delay in realisation before and waited, but not for long. Suddenly John's eyes opened, his mouth dropped and he turned to his wife. 'I think we just won a bit 'a money, darl.'

'Yes. But it is you. *You* have won the money, John.' She looked at Kant and said, 'Thank you, you are very kind.'

'Oh, it's not me who's kind. It's the people out there that think you deserve it. We don't normally inform the winner prior to the show but in your case I wanted to because ... well, I just wanted too. You must keep it close to your chest though.'

John stood up and went into the kitchen. He put his hands on the edge of the aluminium sink and lowered his head. It looked as if he was about to do the dishes. He clenched his arms in front of his chest and began swaying gently. Then he grabbed onto the side of the sink again as his chest began to shudder. The sobbing began softly to begin with. Gradually, unable to suppress his torment anymore, great heaving waves surged up from deep inside him before crashing into the sink to slurry down the drainage system to join all the other emotional sewage and toxic accumulations to be washed out into the river.

Sampaguita rose and went to her husband. So petite, her skin was as smooth and dark as treacle next to her rough-hewn man of weathered lumber. She placed her hand on his shoulder, her man of humble strength and courage. She did not hurry him, for she too had experienced the discharge of long-suppressed anguish, and waited for the expression of his pent-up secrets and agony to free themselves. She knew there would be more to come, later, and then again, until the body and soul were ready to accept the past and open itself to the promise of a peaceful future.

Eventually, John turned and straightened himself up. Sampaguita held his elbow and led him back to the sitting room.

'John is a strong man, Mister Kant. Really,' Sampaguita said lovingly.

'Yeah, sorry about that,' John said.

Yet somehow he seemed more self-assured, clearer, as if granite boulders had been lifted from his shoulders. It was as if the win had given him a safety net, allowing him to finally express his feelings publicly, in front of relative strangers and indeed his new wife, no more having to bear the shame alone.

'Barry, youse've been good to me. You too, Vince. I remember when youse first come up to me in the gallery when we met. Treated me good, you did. I remember that. Sebastian too, and I know he can turn a few 'eads. A lotta people just pass ya by.'

'Well, John, you can certainly afford to buy one of those big abstract paintings now,' Vince chuckled. 'Maybe even two!'

John wiped his cheek with the back of his hand, and then said something Kant wasn't expecting.

'Thing is Barry, I don't actually want no money. What I want, what I've always wanted is ... well ... just peace really. And that's what I reckon you've brought me today. Of course, I won't tell no-one.'

The room fell silent as everyone absorbed his declaration.

'I hear you, John, and I think I know where you're coming from but surely you can use the money to, I don't know, maybe pay to bring Sampaguita's other children out here. That's not going to be cheap.'

John looked at his wife. There was a small child in his expression, one who'd realised he'd forgotten to buy his mother a birthday present.

'Well, yes. I did forget.' And turning back to his wife, who had become an integral part of his new awakening, and had by all accounts supported him through the unfolding ordeal in recent weeks, he said, 'Sorry, darl, of course that's what we can do. And we'll need a couple more beds and some blankets. I reckon I can get 'em some mowin' work and ... '

Sampaguita placed two fingers to his mouth. 'We will do that, John, and my children will work hard to earn a living when they arrive here, to repay the kindness we have all been shown. Now Mister Kant, I will talk with my husband and we will tell you what we need to do. And Mister Kant,' she added with an assertive grin, 'I'm not *asking* you.'

'I understand perfectly, Sampaguita. And I have to say, I'm not surprised.'

'I will telephone you a little later if that is satisfactory to you. Now, just before you go, would you like another of these rather amusing biscuits?'

'I would indeed.'

Kant thanked her, and before he and Vince left he explained to John and Sampaguita about coming to the station at seven tomorrow, half an hour earlier than the on-air time. He reminded John about Dorothy and how she would prepare them all for being in front of the camera. That all the contestants would be seated on stage and their partners and families would be seated in the front rows of the audience stand. And Sampaguita should be prepared to come up onto the stage when John was finally announced as the winner.

As Kant shook John's hand he said, 'You're a very fortunate man, John.'

John beamed. 'I am that. Sampaguita's a very good woman.'

*

At the same time, one suburb away, the continuum of life was in progress.

Blackened, charred scraps of paper floated, weightless in the updraft from the fire that was burning in a rubbish bin. A triumphant Vernon Davidson was tipping the remains of his coke over the flaming article about Kant's resignation on the front page of the newspaper he'd stolen from the corner shop. Steam gushed up from the hissing remains of the other residual uncollected garbage. Vernon lit up another pilfered cigarette, flicked the match defiantly into the tinder-dry grass on the edge of the dusty roadside. He slunk back into the bus shelter, ritual complete, and sat down again next to his mates Ponga and Joe. Cigarette smoke clung to their heads like the Bridgewater Jerry fog of a morning.

'I fuckin' showed him. Faggot,' Vernon bragged to his mates as he shoved himself between his mates to sit down.

'How come 'e believed ya?' Ponga asked incredulously.

'Cos 'e's a fag. And I told him I'd bash the crap out'a 'is little granddaughter if 'e didn't get 'iself off the fuckin' telly. Thinks 'e's so fuckin' great on that show.'

'BKS,' Joe cooed with a tinge of appreciation for the show. He always felt better about his own shitty life after watching it.

'Shut up, ya fag.'

'*You're* the fag,' Joe replied, squaring up the flattery.

Ponga, who'd just dropped one of his infamous puffs of flatulence, nudged Joe and smirked and turned back to Vernon. 'Yeah Verny, and 'ow come youse ended up lookin' after the little girl then? And we reckon you had a soft spot for 'er. Or is it Miss Kant?'

'Yeah, reckon you'd like to root 'er, wouldn't ya?'

'Fuck off,' Vernon replied. 'She's just a fag.'

'Sure, Verny.'

'Yeah, suuuure, Verny,' Joe echoed, stretching out his mocking words. It wasn't often they got one over Vernon.

'Youse two can get fucked. It was me what got the bastard to resign. Not youse fuckin' dickheads. 'E was real scared when I phoned 'im, you shoulda heard him whine when I said I was going to kill the kid.'

'Yeah, sure you did. Give us another ciggy,' Ponga said, his voice half-edged with disbelief and half with awe that his mate's audacious antics could possibly be true.

'Go fuck ya'self faggot. Come on, I'm not waitin' for the bus no more. Let's fuck off. Don't wanna go nowhere, anyway.'

The three boys slunk off, kicking at the gravel, breathing the dust of neglect on the edge of the roaring traffic, and headed off to nowhere in particular.

'Carn, Verny, giv's another ciggy,' Ponga could still be heard bleating as they left the highway and climbed up a verge by a used-car yard.

'Get fucked.'

'Ah, come on.'

'Jesus, Ponga!'

*

As Kant walked up the path to 4 Luck Avenue later that day, his heart was full, shiny and buoyant like a newly filled red balloon after his meeting with John and Sampaguita.

Inside the house there was an audible bump on Rosie's bedroom floor. Melinda, who was chatting with Agalia and Gillian, momentarily looked up. She quickly realised Rosie had slid off her bed and was now scurrying to the front door to greet her grandfather who had just stepped into the hallway.

'Gampa, Gampa, have you come to have dinner with my dolls?'

'Yep. What have you cooked?'

'We are having sketty and pink ice cream and it will be ready in five minutes.'

'That just happens to be my favourite.'

Rosie reached up and took him by the hand and began pulling him towards the living room. Excited and flustered at the same time she said, 'Gampa, Gampa, my new *arty* is here and ... and ... that lady too.'

'You mean Gillian?'

'Yes,' she giggled, putting her hand to her mouth, giving her grandfather a bashful smile. 'Rosie forgot.'

'That's okay, sweetheart, because there are lots of new people around at the moment.'

'And they're all going to have sketty too.'

Rosie stood proudly with her grandfather in front of the women to present her find. 'Look, Mummy, I got Gampa!'

'Hi Dad,' Melinda said.

'Hi Dad,' Agalia echoed with a huge grin to match her pleasure.

Gillian hoisted herself up from the couch using her daughter's shoulders for support and gave Barry a hug.

'Are you going to kiss Gampa now?' Rosie chirped, thrilled by this new prospect. She wasn't exactly clear what that was but it felt kind of exciting.

'Oh yes,' Gillian replied as she kissed Barry on the lips. Then she bent down and picked Rosie up and kissed her on both cheeks.

As they all began to resettle, find a drink and somewhere to sit, and begin an uproarious post mortem of the ludicrous reporting on the box, Mungo walked in with a six-pack. He too was upbeat and bubbly.

'What are you looking so pleased with yourself for?' Melinda, who knew his every trait, asked immediately. 'You've got that obscenely smug look on your face. I haven't seen that since I told you I was pregnant with Rosie.'

'Oh, it's nothing really. Just that GST is going on BKS tomorrow, as a front-line act on National TV. That's all.'

He grinned at Barry, who winked back.

Melinda shrieked with glee. 'Wonderful, wonderful! What's happened? How come you…' And turning to her beaming father she asked, 'Dad, what's going on?'

Mungo leaned down and kissed her, then Agalia. 'Hi Sis.'

'Hello Mungo.'

He straightened up and unscrewed a stubby. 'The rest is top secret. You'll just have to stay tuned to the box tomorrow. I'm sorry but my lips are sealed.'

'Don't know how you're going to drink that beer then!' Melinda said, itching to have more details.

Mungo swiped his index finger across his mouth indicating the zip of silence. So Melinda gave up and turned her attention to her father, suddenly remembering something. 'Hey Dad, you told Grandpa the necklace was worth a lot. So you got it valued?'

'I sure did. It's astonishing.'

'Wow!' Mungo said, suddenly having visions of his extravagant shopping list.

Barry looked around at the expectant faces enjoying every second he held them in suspense. 'Mr Steenburgen, the South African wizard oracle from the jeweller's, said we could probably get between sixty and seventy for it.'

'Wow, that's amazing, Dad. Good old Grandpa,' Melinda whistled.

'Jeez, he was a dark horse. Seventy grand! Who'd have thought? The canny old bugger,' Mungo snorted, rubbing Shylock hands together.

Barry smiled enigmatically as he eyed Gillian and Agalia,

'He certainly was. But that's *exactly* what he said – sixty to seventy… er, full stop. And who'd have thought I'd use this word in connection with my dear old father – Steenburgen said they were *cultured!* I think I might just buy myself a nice new pair of sandals with the proceeds. And I can feel a seaside holiday coming on.'

After a minute's silence, in memory of fallen prospects, the evening began to wrap itself around the Kant family. Pizzas were ordered, delivered and devoured, and two bottles of quality Tasmanian Pinot that Barry had brought were opened.

And later, as everyone was indulging in the Marcel Marceau meal of sketty, set out on Rosie's bed, Barry looked around the room at the feasting, joyous company, and, for the first time in years, felt utterly happy.

My family, all these people. Yes, it is easy, James Mackelroy. You were right, he thought.

And Kant hoped his director would discover something similar eventually. And for John Sturges, after a lifetime of being haunted by the abusive experiences of his youth, and unable to find release or tranquility, there was now a very real prospect of discovering peace at last.

Chapter Twenty-Eight

With one hour to go till **BKS** went to air, Nerve Two was a disturbed hornet's nest. The studio crew, usually punctilious with their preparation of lighting, cameras, tripods, booms, consoles and monitors, and seating arrangements for the contestants, was in a flap. Little things were going wrong, bent plugs that didn't quite fit, intercom ear-pieces that had mysteriously gone missing, until they were located inexplicably in a make-up box in one of the dressing rooms. There was a frenzied buzz that this was to be the biggest finale, perhaps because it was the final episode, ever.

A veritable forest of indoor palms and other large-leafed plants had been deposited on one side of the stage for arrangement. Mackelroy was in his viewing box with the console technician setting up the TV monitors, sequencers and sound CDs. They had gone through this preparation many times before but tonight there was a definite turbulence to the proceedings.

On the other side of the stage, Mungo, Paul and Sammy had spent most of the day constructing scaffolding that would house them all with their keyboards, computer samplers and percussion instruments on platforms at different heights. Their set resembled an urban building site. From various steel bars in the mid-section hung odd pieces of curved metal, different lengths of PVC piping, an African djembe, a drum kit, bells, Indonesian gongs and other percussive instruments all placed where they could quickly be reached by Paul, who was excited about performing his musical monkey antics around the bars. Lights, sequenced to flash and change colour, had been housed around the scaffolding, activating as his feet touched on each new platform.

For Sammy and Paul, the night before it had been pure elation mixed with sheer terror when Mungo had told them they were to appear as a guest act on BKS, going National.

'Bullshit, ya bastard,' was Sammy's immediate reaction.

And, 'No way man!' was all Paul could manage, until Mungo, maintaining his composure, said, 'I'll just have to do it on my own then. More money for me.'

'We're being paid too?' Paul jabbered.

'Oh, all right, if you insist,' Sammy added. 'How much?'

'Four hundred bucks.'

'Holey moley!' Sammy burst out.

'Jeez,' Paul added, transposing a third of four hundred dollars into beer and pizza.

'Each,' Mungo added casually, taking pleasure from the array of expressions on his impoverished muso friends' faces.

'Jesus, mate, there you go again taking the piss.'

Mungo had just smiled at his mates and raised his hands.

In Dorothy's dressing room the contestants were nervously hanging about waiting for powder touch-ups to hide facial blemishes and shiny foreheads, and in one case clever make-up camouflage for an 'unfortunate' last minute black eye received during a domestic difference of opinion.

Mackelroy, now very jittery, kept looking at his watch, his voice barking orders through the intercom into the studio at regular intervals.

'Come on, people, we've got thirty minutes till zero and the place is a shambles. Somebody get those God-awful plants off the stage; this isn't bloody Jungle Boy.'

Kant had closed the door to his office, having put his 'Do Not Disturb' sign on the outside handle. Not that anyone ever obeyed. Gillian was expertly preparing two long blacks from the coffee machine as Kant, attempting to centre himself, endeavoured not to sink too far into the armchair.

'When I first saw your apartment I thought you might be practising to become a monk. It's a relief to see all your well-loved collections here,' Gillian said.

'For a while I used to sneak back here at night to feel and smell my old life.'

'Our junk's our history,' Gillian said. 'It's all we've got, I guess, until we create new stuff. Then we start blending the old with the new.'

'Gillian,' he said, looking up at her. She was cutting up some small squares of French nougat she had brought.

'Mm,'

'I've got something I want to ... '

'Mmm,' she interrupted, teasing. 'Give me? What now? I thought we'd agreed to be a bit, er ... circumspect.'

'I don't even know what that means,' Kant said as he reached over and felt her bottom. He was about to feel more but the office intercom buzzed. It was Mackelroy. 'Fifteen minutes, boyo.'

'I'm hot to trot,' Kant replied, reaching for Gillian's hand and guiding her onto his lap.

'What I want to give you will have to wait now, but ... well ... I'm fairly sure I've fallen in love with you. I didn't think I'd ever ...'

But Gillian kissed him before he could finish. 'And let me tell *you* something, you sweet man, the feeling's mutual.'

Kant sighed, Gillian smiled, then Kant smiled and Gillian sighed.

'Could you help me with my tie, please?' he asked, as if it was a most regular question in their lives. 'I can never seem to get the top bit right.'

'Sure.'

'For once I might get on stage without Dorothy telling me off.'

*

'ACTION!'

Theme music, applause, One-Note-Mambo-Man going crazy, two seated arcs of nervous-looking contestants either side of Kant, who was lounging back, looking remarkably relaxed, belying the cold lines of sweat trickling from his armpits. His fingers were still tingling from the feel of Gillian's body. The main lights dimmed as a single, soft spotlight fell on the host, Camera Two zooming in on Kant's face. He was wearing a grey suit, lime-green shirt, light-mauve tie, legs crossed, and holding an envelope up like Moses on the mount, except the contents were not the Ten Commandments, but nevertheless life-altering prospects if used wisely. Maybe they were the same. In reality, the envelope was empty.

The music faded and Kant continued to sit without speaking. He acknowledged the five contestants on either side of him with a nod, he peered out into the audience, the front rows filled with expectant family members, and replaced the envelope into his inside coat pocket like a conjuror performing a sleight of hand. At the point when he thought the audience would burst with impatience he turned to face Camera One, 'Welcome to BKS, live, nationwide. I'm Barry Kant.'

While the audience roared, loudly primitive, and allowing them a few more moments of bellicose rapture, Kant looked at Arjuna De Silva, who had been seated next to him, and asked how he was keeping. The hit-and-run driver, an intoxicated financial adviser, who had maimed Arjuna's wife three years ago into a life of paralysis from the waist down, and had bought himself a sharp lawyer, ended up getting a three-year suspended prison sentence and a one-thousand-dollar rap on the knuckles for careless driving. Mister De Silva, whose wife bore the real sentence, smiled weakly and nodded, 'Well, thank you.'

The cacophony of applause had subsided and Kant stood up

and walked to the edge of the stage, forming a face of repentance and gravity.

'Good evening everyone. Before we start I would like to come clean with the Australian public about certain rumours and allegations that have recently been reported in the media, namely my midlife crisis, my resignation, my *liaison* with a much younger female, the show's financial difficulties, and the impending legal battle with my director. Well, I'd just like to set the record straight … it's all true.'

The audience, who had not seen his tongue firmly embedded in his cheek, was left speechless. The only sound, if anyone had exceptional hearing, was Mackelroy chuckling in Kant's earpiece. He was looking down on the audience from above like a mischievous God shaking his head with glee.

Kant took in the paralysed looks in front of him.

'You can hardly wait, can you, vampires? To bathe in the bloody carnage of yet another wrecked life. But not just some ordinary man or woman in the street you can forget in two minutes. Oh, Mrs De Silva can't be here tonight because she's battling pneumonia.' He looked around towards the contestants, who were looking around, puzzled. 'But *my* life! Yes, the flawless and sainted Barry Kant, your TV messiah who stands before you now.'

He hadn't expected this gullibility. Was this the silence of guilt? Or was this the quiet before the gigantic, orgasmic storm of the starved voyeur?

'My young lady wanted to come tonight but she … my

two-year-old granddaughter, that is, is tucked up in bed as we speak. And gladly, is oblivious to all of this. And the other rather gorgeous woman happens to be my daughter. That's all I'm saying. You're just going have to make up the rest for yourselves. Why not, the media does. Who cares about the truth?'

Kant sat back down and drank some water from a glass. He hadn't meant to sound *so* aggressive. Gillian's coffee had been strong enough to lift his hair.

'And I'll tell you another thing, *vampires*,' he said getting up again and launching himself to the edge of the stage. 'I want you all to get up and go home now.' Kant thrust his pointing hand towards the fearful faces. 'I'm exhausted by your perpetual lust for other people's misfortune.' And to Camera One, 'And you lot at home, turn your tellies off because tonight we only have *good* news to report, so you'll only be disappointed. And that man in the back row, close your mouth! Yes sir, you!'

Several men in the vicinity of Kant's gaze looked around awkwardly.

Indignant gasps rose out of the shocked babble as if they had all been condemned to an eternal reality show in purgatory. A few people stood up and looked around uncomfortably. Even Single-Note-Farting-Mambo-Dog-Man, who had not been prepped on purpose, was at a loss as to what to do. Kant remained staring at the gathering, waiting for humiliation to sink its teeth in deeper.

But then in a softened but clear voice he said, 'Come on, sit down, I'm only kidding. If only you could see your faces.'

He looked around at the contestants, all laughing loudly as one and pointing at the ship of fools as requested to do earlier by Kant himself. The tables had been turned as the entire studio audience had for a short while lost their dignity on National Television.

'Oh, and by the way, did you hear, they removed the word *gullible* from the dictionary?' Kant was enjoying himself so much he'd reverted to a school boy gag. *An oldie, but a goody.*

One or two people began to clap uncertainly, then came the outpouring of relief, expressed by cheers and whistles and applause for their hero. *Of course* this wasn't the last show. They'd just been 'had' by the great Barry Kant, that's all. What an amazing man!

A quiet short-memoried anticipation descended on the audience once more as a spotlight flooded Liri Mogamba, who had settled himself on the front of the stage ready with his adungu, his personally carved African harp.

'Ladies and gentlemen, all the way from Sudan, now a proud Tasmanian, Mister Liri Mogamba.'

Liri grinned confidently and began playing and singing, rocking to the rhythm and verbalising his heartfelt message to his country's folk in the front rows and indeed the world. The members of the Sudanese Dinka community, who had come to support him, began to clap whilst joining in with the chorus, with wholehearted harmonies.

'She was born on the wrong side of the fence ...

Wearing scars from a culture of violence

An eye for an eye will make the whole world blind.

He was born on the other side

Full of fear and full of pride

Fighting somebody else's fight in time

Where today's reason becomes tomorrow's crime.

An eye for an eye will make the whole world blind ...'

By the end of the song, repeating the chorus several times, the whole audience was clapping and swaying evangelically. Liri stood up and bowed and returned to his seat next to Darlene Sullivan, from Collins Bonnet, who leaned over and kissed him on the cheek.

Kant waited for the audience to settle before he spoke.

'So, next time you're about to vilify a refugee who's trying to make a life for themselves here, give a thought to how you'd feel if your parents were taken away to Risdon Prison and murdered, and you were sent to live in the heart of Sudan to make a life for yourself, on your own.'

The audience fell silent again after their unexpected moment of free expression.

'Oh, come on, don't look so serious. Now, I have the greatest pleasure in introducing another act. Yes, quite the Variety Show tonight! They call themselves the Global Synthesis Trio: they are young, they are talented and they have a vital sound constructed with recordings made in and around the city of Hobart, combined with conventional instrumentation.

'The piece they are going to perform is a world premiere suite called *The Urban Lark*. The recorded oboe that you'll hear was played by Gabriel Daniels, who appeared on an earlier series of BKS. His wife and children had been killed in an appalling car accident, and he had struggled with his profound loss ever since, sadly taking his own life recently. But he has left a legacy in the form of his music with the Tasmanian Symphony Orchestra, and now tonight, posthumously, with the Global Synthesis Trio!'

Alternating silver and red lights began to flicker around the scaffolding as a heavy drone, courtesy of an inner-city air-conditioning unit, filled the studio. It was soon joined by a steady beat, originally drummed with fingertips onto Mungo's phonebook's Yellow Pages opened at Tree felling and Travel agents, and cleverly augmented.

The sampled sounds grew more complex. Synthesised iPhone rings, pneumatic drills, blind crossing beeps, and car horns sounded at random as short keyboard riffs wove in and out with just a few bars, emulating various styles of music. Just as a particular genre became recognisable it would change like the incessant moving of a radio dial from one station to another. There was a reprieve in the confusion as some bars of simulated Plain Song stilled the raging city just before a minor key shift signified a descent into a darker, brooding clamour, both Paul and Sammy clanging and rattling dangling pieces of metal, shaking tubes filled with gravel, creating the sense of mayhem and disorder from a disturbed world.

Gradually the jarring sounds began to dissipate as the synthesiser poured out harmonic waves that pulsed into the belly of the studio like the voice of a gigantic choir at full tilt in a Gothic cathedral, resonant, rich, before rising heavenward. Then Gabriel's improvised notes on the oboe could be heard, recorded not three weeks ago in Mungo's studio. They called plaintively through the endless noise of urban discord, but then, as if the oboe's call for pastoral harmony and peace had been acknowledged, the sounds softened more until there was only the accompaniment of synthesised strings and the oboe now playing parts of Vaughan William's *The Lark Ascending*.

It was a masterful fusion of sounds, the jarring, amplified chaos of noise that is second nature in our city lives gradually finding stillness. Gabriel's oboe had transcended the gravity of a leaden life on earth into the weightlessness of grace beyond.

In the living room at 4 Luck Avenue, Melinda, jittery with excitement, watched the performance with Gillian and her sister. She was filled with pride for her man's ability to splice together such a profound musical piece in which he had managed to incorporate the intensity of Gabriel's struggle and eventual glorious release. If she'd believed in a skyward heaven then she would have been sure that *that* was where the final notes from Gabriel's oboe now rested.

She wiped at her eyes.

When the last sounds died away the audience remained stupefied, mesmerised, transported by the musical journey that had engaged their thoughts and hearts, turning their sense of truth inside out. When it finally came, the applause was thunderous. The three young men, chuffed and grinning at each other like Wonderland Cheshire Cats climbed down from the scaffolding, put arms on each other's shoulders and bowed low as one.

'Well, I don't know about you but I could quite easily end the show there,' Kant said, holding an arm out as the audience cheered the musicians once more.

'But, we have other important business to deal with now. So I want you all to look at these fine characters on either side of me now and pretend you haven't heard their stories. Pretend you don't know of the terrible things that have happened to them. Now I want you to look around at each other. Go on, don't be shy.'

Kant gave pause.

'No difference, eh? We heard Liri's story. It was so awful. And, you know, there are millions of refugees with just the same sort of story as his. Our world is home to a veritable plague of human tragedy. How do we fix it, this condition we humans suffer from, most of which is perpetrated on the weak and the vulnerable by other human beings that look just like you and me?'

Kant stopped and looked at Liri and smiled. 'Nice playing, son.'

'Thanks, man.'

Kant stood up and produced the envelope again, holding it high like an auctioneer's hammer about to descend.

'So, what do I hear? One hundred thousand bucks for this studio filled with gorgeous apathy. Going once … twice. Let's start a little lower then. Fifty cents for this bag of greedy, self-indulgent me-lollies. Sold to the man with five bathrooms, children he hardly knows and a TV so big he can't even get it into the house.'

Kant emulated a hammer-bang with his arm. The audience, already bewildered by his previous antics, did not dare clap.

'Okay, moving on. Let's get onto the piece-de-resistance, ABUSE! Are we feeling uncomfortable again?' Kant asked as he walked up the audience dividing aisle. 'There's a lot of it around. It reminds me of that song, you know, men and women do it, goldfish do it, such and such do it, let's fall in love … You know the one I'm talking about? Except *we* have …' Kant waved his arms as if he was conducting, 'fathers do it, mothers even do it, those other priest-fathers do it, teachers do it, footballers can't stop doing it, even doctors do it, maybe we all do it. ABUSE! That's not love.'

Kant walked back to the stage and sat down. He waved with exaggerated hand movements to Camera One. 'Come on lad, come in close. I want to say something to the nation. My last chance before I have that nervous breakdown I'm supposed to be having. You've voted this man here, John Sturges, to be the winner! For suffering physical violence from his own father, of *all* people! From carers at the Salvation Army, *yes, the Salvos!* From supervisors and guardians in State Government institutions, and for being endlessly tormented by the memory of beatings and *rape* perpetrated on him by the so-called holy brothers within the sanctity of the Catholic Church. This man, this humble, courageous and dignified man, has won one hundred thousand dollars.'

The audience had been numbed, as if they had been injected with an anesthetic cocktail of self-disgust and guilt for their own apathy. Dog-Fart made a vain attempt to whip up some sort of reaction, anything.

But there was nothing, just an itching silence.

'But wait, there's more!' Kant cried out. 'John told me that he doesn't want it. What do you think about that, vampires? He doesn't...want...the money; he just wants peace of mind! Imagine that! Imagine if that was all the world leaders wanted. Of course, I told John he could probably make good use of it. I know *I* certainly could. Particularly after tonight.'

Mackelroy chuckled to himself.

Kant looked across at John, who was looking surprisingly calm, as if the process of the last week had imbued him with a healthy dose of serenity.

'John, could you come and join me over here, please?'

A spare chair had sat empty all night ready to receive the winner. The two men confided closely as the audience waited.

'Now John, would you like to tell the audience what you told me just before the show?'

'Well, see, when I learned I won the money I was sorta ... well, like embarrassed really. It's a lotta money and I reckon these other folk 'ere deserve something too. You know, like, my wife wants to bring 'er kids out from the Philippines to live with us but I don't reckon it'll be that much. I could do with a new lawn mower and I guess a Whipper Snipper would come in 'andy. They'd certainly make my work much easier, and see, when Sampaguita's boys come out from the Philippines they can do a bit of work with me ... '

'John,' Kant said, aiming to get him back on track.

'Oh yes, Barry, sorry. Well I talked with me wife and we reckon we'd like to give the other contestants ten thousand dollars each and we'll keep ten too.'

The studio filled with gasps and cheers from the audience, and looks of disbelief from the other contestants, who had not been prepped.

John wiped his chin, suddenly nervous. 'I 'ope that's all right, Barry? I mean, I don't want to sound ungrateful or nothin'.'

'John, why don't we ask the audience if that's all right? It's about time they said something useful.'

'Well, okay.'

John looked around at the other contestants who were going through their own transition of hesitation, and in a couple of cases outright disbelief, through hopeful anticipation to incredulous jubilation.

John smiled coyly back at the nine now-beaming faces on either side of him.

And there was no doubt in the audience's mind, who erupted, standing as one in wild ovation for this quiet man who had unassumingly challenged all the detractors and the self-satisfied, and had given hope to the down-trodden and the voiceless. And in Mackelroy's eyes it was the faultless finale to a series of programs that had dared to go out on a limb.

John Sturges stood up to shake Kant's hand and was swamped by a rush of contestants and dozens of cheering family members and friends, and a beaming Sampaguita, who had been washed onto the stage in the surge.

Mackelroy looked on from his box, marvelling at the sight. He turned to his technician, who had already cracked open his usual end-of-program can of beer, and said, 'Soak it up, mate. *That's* what this wretched world needs.'

Another Beginning

The BKS sensation eventually died down, its finale firmly set in the musty book of legendary Tasmanian sagas. A month had slipped by and there was now only the odd paragraph, written by uninspired tabloid journos trying to reignite interest with yet another angle that would appear no further forward in the papers than page four. The tide of public attention had well and truly gone out, leaving behind the old bevy of tired programs, dawdling fish cut off from the sea now wallowing around in shallow and tepid rock pools, some even stranded like drying starfish on the gravelly shores of ennui.

Mackelroy had been visited by some Sydney film makers with an offer of directing a...well, he wasn't saying yet. And humanity at large, in its endless cycle of death and rebirth, continued to dismember itself in conflicts of greed and hatred; there had been rumblings of discontent in Syria, while a restless viewing public retuned its TVs for the next sensation.

And although summer had blown into autumn the perverse nature of the Tasmanian climate had put on one of its hottest days of the year so far. Even though the mercury had pushed through a thirty-two degree barrier, just a few degrees short of schools having to close, almost every Tasmanian had something to complain about, particularly the thousands of school kids.

*

Barry and Gillian stood at the water's edge on the Bellerive beach, a suburban stretch of sand on the eastern shore of the city. Barry was holding a new pair of leather sandals and wearing an old, comfortable pair of shorts he'd dug out from a cardboard box in the depths of his garage. The tips of his shoulders were going pink in the sunshine, the cool sand and salty water making sweet vibrations between his toes. Gillian, whose colourful floral shirt was shaded by a large straw hat, had rolled her cream slacks up to her calves.

Before them, windsurfers swished by, yachts tacked, the waters shimmered, and further down the river a large tanker sat moored waiting for a berth upstream.

'Barry, I'm going back to Melbourne.'

Barry turned and frowned.

Gillian kissed him on the cheek. 'Don't look so alarmed. I need to go back for a while to see my mother. Her condition is still deteriorating, and the last time I saw her she barely recognised me and ... well it could be the last chance I get to say some things to her.'

Gillian took hold of his arm and they began to stroll along the beach. 'There have been big changes for all of us and it's made me think of completing things with Mum. I also think that Agalia and you, and Melinda, would benefit from having some time together without…any distractions. BJ's still in a daze and will need some time to adjust. She told me last night that she hoped you'd take her down to the old cottage where you lived with Sarah, to see where she might have been brought up had things been different.'

'I haven't even considered my next move. And you're right; it might be a good place to begin.'

'Don't worry, I'll be back in a few days, because, Barry Kant, you and I have some unfinished business, I believe. At least I hope we have!'

'Mm, let me see…yes, Gillian Papadakis, it's quite possible.'

*

'I want to make it quite clear to you both. I'm your father…not your chauffeur!' Barry said, looking in the rear-vision mirror of his car as he drove along next to the Huon River with Melinda and Agalia sitting together on the back seat, having not stopped nattering from the moment they got in the car at their father's apartment forty minutes ago.

'Take the next right here, will you, James?' Melinda said, mimicking an aristocratic madam.

Barry indeed did turn right, driving away from the broad river and into a lush valley, collared by cherry and apple orchards. Roadside stalls advertised bags of apples, fresh apple juice, and cherries by the bucket. Barry slowed as the road began to narrow, its old potholes still in need of some fresh bitumen. The road curved down through a copse of English elm trees, then crossed a one-lane wooden bridge spanning a small creek. As the car approached the cottage his heartbeat quickened. It was the first time he'd returned since selling up.

The day before, Barry had managed to contact the new owners, whom he'd not met. A young couple from Sydney in search of a rural paradise to bring up their children they hoped would be born there. The agent had assured him they would love the place too. *Of course* Barry could visit and look around, they'd said on the phone. They'd have the kettle on the stove, ready.

'Here we are,' Barry said as he drove into the space where he'd parked a thousand times before.

Melinda jumped out and Agalia stepped out tentatively, looking around, breathing in the scented air, absorbing every small detail.

The place seemed smaller, trees had grown taller, thicker, the hedges wider. The pine front door was now a glossy red, the driveway had been levelled with fine gravel and the herbaceous borders were still a chorus of colour. Barry knocked and waited. His chest contracted as a surge of anticipation surfaced.

'Hello there, welcome,' spoke a curly-haired woman in her mid-twenties. She wore jeans and a loose black tee-shirt, which was struggling to cover her protruding pregnant belly. 'You must be Mister Kant. I'm Geraldine. Gerry.'

'Yes. I'm Barry. These are my daughters Melinda and Agalia.'

'Hello there. Come in. Matt sends his apologies. He couldn't get away from work. But he tells me you'd like to look around the place. You might notice one or two changes but the essence of the place we've kept. It's what sold it to us in the beginning. We just love all the fruit trees. I've become quite the country bottler,' she said proudly.

'When are you due?' Melinda asked as they settled with cups of tea around a wooden table on the lawn.

'Still have a month to go. I'm so excited. This is such a beautiful and abundant place to bring up a child. I'm having a home birth too.'

Agalia, who had sat next to Gerry, placed her hand on the young woman's stomach and said, 'You are right, this place has been filled with love. And my mother, Sarah, set up a crèche in Huonville many years ago. It's still going, I believe, so who knows, maybe your child will attend one day.'

Gerry stroked her stomach; she was beaming. 'Now just make yourselves at home and walk around wherever you like.'

Barry looked at Agalia and smiled. *How can I begin to know what she is thinking?*

He stood up and led his daughters, one on each arm, around the property, pointing out every twig and petal. It was as if time had stood still. At the pond he said, 'Mel, why don't you take BJ to the house and show her inside? I'd like a moment to myself here.'

'Sure, Dad.'

As he watched them stroll back towards the house, a deep sadness began to rise in his being. He turned and walked around to the far side where the pond wasn't visible from the house. On the little jetty he'd built twenty years ago to tie up a raft he'd also built, he sat down and allowed his tears to drip into the still water. Tiny rings began to spread on the smooth dark surface before gradually dissipating into the body of the pond.

'Oh Sarah, my Sarah, I just want to let you know I really am flowing on now, in our river. I feel so grateful for everything you have given me ... and all those times we shared. I want you know that *both* our daughters are wonderful. Goodbye my love.'

As Barry got up, a small flurry of breeze, appearing from nowhere, ruffled the surface of the pond. He gazed at the water for a few moments, smiled, then wandered back to the cottage to find his daughters.

In memory of Loro Emmanuel Mogga, born in Kitane Village, South Sudan

25-12-1980 – 4-9-2013

He came to Hobart as a refugee in 2003: a vivacious and creative young man, who was a leading light in Hobart's Sudanese community, and who made musical instruments, as well as playing and singing with several bands around Hobart. He struggled with his isolation from his siblings, who were unable to come to Australia because his sister had juvenile glaucoma. We had raised $12,000 to do this but after exhaustive legal attempts to bring them here we chose to use the money to put all his siblings, still in a Ugandan refugee camp, through schools to finish their education. I had spoken on the phone to his brother Joseph, who told me that education would be their freedom. Joseph is currently completing an engineering degree in China. Loro died having not seen any of his siblings since he'd arrived in Tasmania. He leaves behind a daughter Holly, and her mother Pria, who, along with many people in Hobart, miss him greatly.

Loro was the inspiration for my character Liri — Nick Glade-Wright